THE RED HORSE

THE RED HORSE

A Billy Boyle World War II Mystery

James R. Benn

Published by Soho Press, Inc.
227 W 17th Street
New York, NY 10011

Library of Congress Cataloging-in-Publication Data

Names: Benn, James R., author.
Title: The red horse : a Billy Boyle World War II mystery / James R. Benn.
Series: The Billy Boyle mysteries ; 15

ISBN 978-1-64129-100-2
eISBN 978-1-64129-101-9

Subjects: GSAFD: Mystery fiction.
LCC PS3602.E6644 R43 2020 | 813'.6—dc23
LC record available at https://lccn.loc.gov/2020015482

Printed in the United States of America

10 9 8 7 6 5 4 3 2 1

For my wife, Deborah Mandel

Hear my soul speak.
Of the very instant that I saw you,
Did my heart fly at your service
—William Shakespeare, *The Tempest*

'Tis a fearful thing
to love what death can touch.

—YEHUDA HALEVI, 12TH CENTURY
JEWISH PHYSICIAN, POET, AND PHILOSOPHER.

THE RED
HORSE

CHAPTER ONE

SOMETHING WAS WRONG.

The wind bit at the back of my neck, and I hunched my shoulders as gray clouds scudded across the sky, outpacing me as I trudged along the gravel path. I stuffed my hands into my pockets, thankful for the warmth.

Thankful I could hide the tremor in my right hand.

Because they were watching.

I couldn't let them see how bad it had gotten.

My boots scrunched on crushed stone, the wide walkway stretching out before me. It looked like a straightaway, but the low wrought iron fence on either side curved slightly to the left. It was a circle. A long circle, but all the same, circles lead nowhere.

Which was where I was, evidently.

I don't know why. I haven't figured it out yet. All I know is that beyond the ornate fence, painted a gleaming jet black and hardly higher than my hip, there is another fence. In the woods, about ten yards in. A serious fence. Ten feet high and topped with coils of barbed wire. Patrolled by British soldiers who watched from the other side, silently staring me down.

I pushed on, trying not to attract their attention as they moved through the shadows beyond the wire. Two days ago, they'd let me outside. Not the soldiers, but the doctors, or nurses, or orderlies, or whatever they were. They said I could walk, that it might help me sleep.

But I can't sleep a wink. Maybe that's why I'm a little confused. Sometimes it feels like I can't stay awake, either. Or move, for that matter. I didn't want to go outside, but they insisted, so I started walking.

Two days I've been walking this circuit. My eyes are gritty with fatigue, but every time I stop to sit on a bench, my lids stay open. There's a haze over everything—the woods, the guards, the massive stone structure constantly off to my left, its towers and turrets visible above the treetops and across the lush green lawns. My memory is hazy too. I don't remember how I got here, although I recall waking up in an ambulance.

Before that, all I remember is France. Paris, to be exact. But everything is jumbled up, like in a dream, where things look familiar but nothing makes sense. I know this place isn't a dream, because nothing looks familiar and nothing makes the slightest bit of sense.

It isn't a dream or a nightmare. No, it's worse.

Why?

The answer to that one was coming up ahead. The gravel walkway sloped downhill as it curved around the rear of the scattered buildings. I hadn't even counted them all. There was the main building, four stories of sandstone set down in front of a green lawn, with a tall clock tower at the center. Wings extended off either end at right angles, like giant arms, encompassing a smattering of smaller buildings, all covered in the same sooty stone, soiled by the chimneys spouting coal smoke into the gray skies.

A service road cut across the path ahead. The gate was set in the woods, part of the security fence guarded by soldiers. I'd caught a glimpse of them a few times as they opened the gate to let in trucks bringing supplies. Their forest-green berets marked them as elite Commandos. I didn't look in their direction anymore. They might think I was planning an escape.

Which might not be a bad idea if I knew where to go.

I quickened my pace as I passed the stone pillars that once had marked the entrance to the grounds. I could see the old metal sign that had greeted visitors; it was rusted and pitted by age, but still clear enough to announce what this place was.

Saint Albans Pauper Lunatic Asylum.

I was sure I'd been here before. I hadn't seen the sign back then, but I'd driven through a back entrance to visit a British major. I hadn't stayed long, but I knew this was the same joint. Except everything was different. Maybe because they'd let me leave that last time.

So, I know I'm at Saint Albans. About an hour outside London, if I remember correctly, not that my memory's all that good right now. I do know I'm not a pauper. But there are some strange people here, and the place is surrounded by barbed wire and guards, so I guess it is some sort of asylum.

Lunatic? As I walked the path, I eyed the other residents. Or patients, probably. I tried not to make eye contact, not being up for a friendly chat. I saw the whistling man, an American who strolled the circuit regularly as he whistled a tune. The same tune. All the time. We passed each other, his eyes focused straight ahead and a little toward the sky, as if he were waiting for angels to swoop down and take him away.

I came to a Brit sitting on a bench. His wool cap was pulled down, covering his eyes. His arms were crossed and his legs jittered, boot heels keeping time. I'd seen him around. He was one of the mutes. Never spoke. There were a few of them here, all wearing the British battle dress uniform.

But that was all I could tell about them. Everyone was in uniform, but the rule at Saint Albans was no rank or unit patches. No identification, except for the color of your uniform. Last names only. It made sense, in a way. If the place was full of lunatics, it wouldn't do for a crazy colonel to start issuing orders to loony lieutenants.

I picked up the pace as the path took me closer to the south wing. That was the medical area where people wore pajamas, bandages, and casts. They spent their time in bed, rolling around in wheelchairs, or limping about on crutches. I hadn't run into any mutes or whistlers among them.

But I hadn't been in the south wing in a couple of days.

I couldn't handle seeing Kaz.

Lieutenant Piotr Augustus Kazimierz, that is. Kaz and I work together. We had some trouble in Paris and ended up here. I'm walking around and he's not.

Bad heart. Really bad. My brain is sort of scrambled, but his ticker is shaky. He always had some sort of problem with it, which is why he ended up as a translator working in General Eisenhower's headquarters. Kaz had been given a commission in the Polish Armed Forces based on his brains, not his brawn. But he'd built himself up, strengthening his body and using his brilliant mind as part of Ike's Office of Special Investigations.

Until Paris.

Everything had fallen apart in Paris. Kaz's heart, my mind, and, well, something else.

I can't think about that now.

I pressed on, head down, not looking at the medical ward windows for fear I'd see Kaz looking at me. Wondering. Worried about his future and my sanity. I didn't want to think about that either. Or that other thing clawing at the edges of my mind.

I walked faster, staring at the façade of the main hall now that I'd turned the corner. A few faces gazed out at me from the offices at the front of the massive building. Bored typists, doctors in their white coats, a few uniformed honchos, Yanks and Brits who gave the orders around here.

I made for the entrance, glancing up at the tall clock tower dead center. Ten minutes of five, but that time was only right twice a day. The thing was busted.

I stopped, uncertain if I wanted to go inside or take another tour of the estate. I stood there, rooted to the spot, paralyzed by the simple task of deciding if I wanted to go indoors. This sort of thing was happening all the time, and I didn't like it much. Like I said, something was wrong.

I stood still, unable decide which way to go.

Which is why I saw the two men up in the clock tower. The door to the tower was usually locked and off-limits. They were nothing but blurs of brown uniform, heads and shoulders barely visible above the crenellated stonework as they scurried around, circling the white flag-pole with the British Union Jack flapping at the top.

Then there was only one man, and he was flying.

CHAPTER TWO

HE MUST HAVE been a mute, because he made no sound.

Until he hit the ground.

The sound of boots pounding gravel snapped me out of my stupor. I ran toward the body as the front door slammed open and people tumbled out. White coats, uniforms, and suits. Behind me, a couple of guards were making a beeline for the body.

I got there first. I pushed aside a Yank in his unadorned khakis and a Brit major in his service dress uniform.

"Don't touch anything," I said. "I'm a police officer."

Why the hell did I say that?

I knelt by the body, my mind a jumble of thoughts as I studied the dead man. Sure, I'd been a cop before the war. I'd even made homicide detective before I traded blue for khaki. But why did I announce myself like that?

Maybe it was the situation. People had a habit of rushing into a crime scene and obscuring what evidence there might be.

"Sure, you're a policeman," one of the guards said, his hand grasping my shoulder. "Now come along."

"Wait a minute," I said, shaking his arm off and raising my hand. He stepped back, and I could see his palm resting on the butt of his holstered pistol. It was a typical pose, putting enough space between us so he could draw his weapon without me grabbing it. I took my time, studying the corpse, committing everything I saw to memory. I may have had a few screws loose, but I knew what was what when it came to murder. Or suicide, maybe.

"Okay," I said, rising and taking a few steps back, my hands raised slightly, apologetically. I didn't want to risk being pistol-whipped.

"Get these patients away," the major snapped, sparing a moment to frown in my direction. He was a thick-faced guy with a brown mustache and a stiff gait that seemed to pain him. Or he didn't like his mornings ruined by patients falling from great heights, I couldn't really say.

I gave the guard a friendly nod to let him know I wasn't going to cause any trouble. I let him pull me back a few steps as his partner gathered the other Yank and an older Englishman in his darker khaki wool serge. As the major stood over the body, one of the white coats knelt and felt for a pulse. Purely for the record.

One other white coat stood aside, watching me. Maybe I was paranoid, or a lunatic, or both, but it was odd that he spent more time looking at me than at the guy who'd taken a swan dive onto packed gravel. Beneath his white jacket he wore captain's bars on one collar and the caduceus of the medical corps on the other. He wasn't a stranger. Captain Theodore Robinson, US Army psychiatrist. Blond hair, glasses, and an athletic build. Track star in college back in Wisconsin, he'd told me. We'd had a few chats, which consisted mainly of him yakking because I didn't have much to contribute. But the army paid him anyway, he said, so I sat and listened. I'd been bored, but the army paid me too.

Robinson's gaze finally wandered to the body. Mine went up to the clock tower. Nobody was leaning over, distraught at not being able to stop this guy from falling. I looked at the main entrance, where by now, the second man would have burst through, telling his story of trying to talk the jumper out of his fatal leap.

Nothing.

"What do you think?" I heard the major say.

"We've been worried about Holland for a while, haven't we, Dr. Robinson?" This from the British white coat. Older than Robinson,

gray showing at his carefully trimmed temples, dark bags under his
eyes, and a thin, sharp nose that made him look like a sparrow hawk.

I didn't hear Robinson's response as the guards ushered us inside. I
thought about saying something about the other person I'd seen up in
the tower, but I was low man on the totem pole around here, and I
could end up in a padded cell if I spouted off to the wrong person.
Like the guy who'd tossed poor Holland to his death.

Or, I was imagining things, and then they'd put me in a straitjacket
for sure. My best bet was to clam up and keep my head down. I let the
guard shove me inside, resisting the impulse to unleash a smart-aleck
wisecrack and give him a chance to kidney punch me when no one
was looking. He wore sergeant's stripes and a mean grimace splashed
across a face in need of a shave. A private trailed us, Sten gun at the
ready, looking angry enough to squeeze off a few rounds for the hell
of it.

"You guys been at it long?" I asked, once we were inside and the
door slammed shut behind us.

"At what, Yank?" the sergeant said as his companion stood by the
door.

"Guarding this place. Patrolling the perimeter, that sort of thing."
I was going for polite conversation to learn anything about their routine, but the grizzled non-com wasn't going for it. "Have you been on
duty all night?"

"Yes, while you've been dreaming of Betty Grable, we've been
tramping through the woods to keep you safe, lad. Now go on, leave
the business outside to the major. He knows how to handle these
things."

"Okay, Sergeant," I said. "I didn't catch your name."

"Didn't give it, but since I know who you are, Boyle, seems only fair
you should have it. Sergeant Owen Jenkins," he said.

"Well, Sergeant Jenkins, I'm flattered. What do you know about
me besides my name?" I asked, wondering if it might be something
that was news to me.

"You like to walk," he said, taking one step forward and fixing his
dark eyes on me. "And you're not friendly, not the way a lot of Yanks

are. Most of you lot talk too much and too soon, if you don't mind my saying so. Not you, though."

"The conversation in here isn't to my liking," I said. "Maybe if we met in a pub we'd get along better. What's the best watering hole around here? Or are you new to the area?"

"New?" Jenkins said. "Why'd you say that?"

"With all the fighting in Normandy, this must be like a rest area for you fellows," I said. "What do they do, rotate you in for a few weeks of easy duty before you head back to the front? You can't be stuck here permanently, can you?"

"Next time I see you, Boyle, best walk the other way," Jenkins said, his finger stabbing my chest. So much for making polite conversation. I didn't think a tough British sergeant would be so sensitive. "Or you'll be here, permanent-like."

"Come on, Sarge," his private said, walking to a window and glancing out front. "He's tetched in the head, remember? Pay him no mind. They're taking the stiff away, so let's go have a smoke."

"Bastards," Jenkins said, apparently taking in me and everyone else in residence at Saint Albans. "Living easy while our lads are fighting and dying. Leastways you and the others without any wounds. It's one thing to be shot up, but where's your wound? You're nothing but a coward in my book."

He turned on his heel and marched out the door, slamming it against the wall.

"Don't say anything, sir, willya?" asked the private, glancing at the open door as he whispered. "Sarge is a bit on edge, is all."

"Don't worry, kid," I said, looking more closely at him. His wool field service cap was pulled low over his eyes, but it didn't disguise the fact that he had no worries about a five o'clock shadow. "Who would believe a nutcase like me anyway? What's your name?"

"Fulton, sir. Private Martin Fulton."

"Okay, Fulton. Now tell me something and I'll keep this all under my hat. How did your sergeant know my name? Are you watching me during the day? Keeping tabs on me?"

"No, that's not our job. Sarge asked that big fella who was here the other day, the Yank sergeant. He said you were a captain and that we should watch out for you, that's all."

"So you are watching me. Thanks, Fulton, now get back to your bully boy pal and stay away from me. Get it?"

Private Fulton's face worked itself into a twist, as if he couldn't understand plain English. He shook his head and walked away, muttering. Watch out for me, he'd said. Spy on me, more like. Jenkins, Fulton, and others, I bet. I'd have to watch them.

And have a talk with Big Mike. There was no reason for him to go around spreading rumors. He was supposed to be my friend. Some pal.

I heard a flurry of voices from outside. It sounded like Robinson and the others were at the door, about to enter the foyer. I darted into a hallway, not wanting to draw attention to myself or answer any questions. My bootheels were loud on the tiled floor, and I scurried as quietly as I could to a small alcove in the center of the hallway. On a stairway, the walnut banisters gleamed brightly, polished by countless hands over the decades. Next to the stairs was a door, an engraved sign proclaiming it to be the entrance to the clock tower. NO ADMITTANCE.

The door was wide open.

It was as good as an invitation.

I shut it behind me and walked up the narrow staircase. The stone steps were worn, and my footsteps echoed as I made my way, wondering what was going through Holland's mind as he took his final steps. How had he gotten in? I knew the door was kept locked or was supposed to be.

Perhaps someone had been working on the clock, or doing some other repair job, and left the door open. I stopped to catch my breath, took a gulp of air, and kept going. I could picture a workman panicking as he saw Holland at the top of the tower. Maybe he tried to bring him back down and Holland fought back. Maybe it was an accident. If so, the workman might have hightailed it, trying to avoid any blame.

Or, was Holland murdered? Was that what Jenkins meant when he said I might find myself here *permanent-like*?

I came to the top of the stairs. I opened the access door and stepped out. The Union Jack snapped loudly in the breeze above my head, startling me. The space was smaller than I'd imagined, taken up by beams that held the flagpole in place and the thick stonework of the battlements. I walked around, looking for a trace of evidence as the wind whipped at my face. Up here, the breeze would carry away any loose bit of fabric or paper.

Had Holland left a note? Probably in his pocket. That's where jumpers stashed them sometimes. I leaned over the edge, looking down at the spot where he'd landed. A small darkening stain and scuffed stones were the only vestige of Holland's final act upon this earth. Who was he anyway? What demons delivered him here? And down there?

From this vantage point, I could see the attraction. Vault over the wall and in seconds you'd have not a care in the world.

I could also sense the fear. The trembling fear of being pursued, unable to speak, his voice tamped down into the darkest corner of his mind, cornered and pushed against the hard, cold stone.

Hands grabbing him and hoisting him over.

The scream silent inside his head.

"Boyle."

I jumped. Not like Holland, but I jumped, my heart thumping at the surprise.

"Step away from the wall, Boyle," Robinson said. "Let's go to my office and have a chat."

"Sure," I said, walking around the flagpole, keeping my distance. I'd learned one thing, anyway. Dr. Robinson was light on his feet.

CHAPTER THREE

"HAVE A SEAT, Boyle," Robinson said. There was a couch in his office, but that seemed too melodramatic, so I took my usual spot in a worn leather armchair. Robinson had changed out of his lab coat and wore a nicely tailored Ike jacket. It fit his trim body well, which I guess was one of the benefits of having been a track star. As for the tailoring, that told me he had good taste and cared that people noticed. It occurred to me that I might already know more about him than he knew of me.

Robinson picked up a pen and pad from his desk, sat himself in a straight-back chair, crossed his legs, adjusted his glasses, then looked at me. The man took his time getting settled, but maybe it was part of a psychiatrist's routine. It gave him time to observe me, even while he fiddled with his pen.

"Why are we here?" I asked. "Couldn't it wait until two o'clock?" That's when we had a session scheduled.

"The army calls that 1400 hours, Boyle. You're an officer. A captain with Supreme Headquarters, Allied Expeditionary Force."

"Yeah. I work at SHAEF. So?"

"Oh, I don't know," he said, flipping through his notes. "I guess I find it odd that after more than two years in the army, you haven't picked up on the standard issue lingo. Now, I do see guys who count on their fingers to figure out the twenty-four-hour clock, but they do it. You, on the other hand, are one smart guy. It must take more mental effort to *not* say 1400 hours than to simply give in to it."

"It takes five syllables to say it the army way. Three to say it the normal way."

"See what I mean, Boyle?" Robinson said, tapping his pen on his pad. "You're a sharp fellow. Intelligent enough to try to distract me with a wisecrack and not answer the question."

"Listen, Doc, if I'm calling in an artillery barrage, I'll say 1400 hours to be sure they don't deliver twelve hours too late. But around here, two o'clock will do just fine, see?" I felt myself on the edge of my seat and eased back into it. "So, make your point or let's call this quits."

"Take it easy, Boyle. Only making conversation," Robinson said, sounding like me when I talked to Sergeant Jenkins. We were both fishing for something useful. "It must have been a shock to see a person leap to their death."

I shrugged.

"You must have seen worse in combat," Robinson continued.

"It was different," I said. True enough. People wearing the same uniform usually refrained from killing each other. Not all the time, though, which was one reason I was in my line of work. I crossed my legs, matching Robinson sitting across from me. I tapped my fingers on my thigh, as he was doing with his pen and paper. It was a trick my dad taught me to use in interrogations. Match your posture and movement with the suspect, and he might open up more easily under questioning.

"Why do you think Holland jumped?" I said, scratching my jaw as he rubbed his.

"No idea," he said. "What I'm more interested in is why you're mirroring me."

"Is that what you call it?" I said, laughing despite myself. "All I know is that it's an old detective's trick. My old man swore by it, but I never knew if it really worked."

"It can create the impression you and the person you are conversing with have things in common. And it's a two-way street, since by adopting the other's pose, you may begin to feel empathy for them. I can see it would be useful in getting a suspect to cooperate. But does that mean you feel I'm a suspect?"

"You're keeping me locked up," I said, trying hard not to avoid his eyes. That would be a dead giveaway that I was lying. It could have been him up there. Not in the white doctor's coat, of course, but he could have discarded it.

"You have the run of the place," he said, spreading his arms wide. "That's hardly locked up."

"What if I wanted to go into town? Those Brit Commandos would drill me dead, no questions asked, if I ever made it over that barbed-wire fence. I can't leave, and that's locked up in my book."

"Commandos? Drill you? You're overreacting, Boyle."

"Hey, there must be a town around here somewhere. Want to go for a beer, Doc?"

"No. I don't," he said, scribbling in his notebook. "Tell me, why did you say you were a policeman? Outside, when you approached the body."

"Holland," I said. "That was his name, right?"

"Yes. Thomas Holland. Now, why did you announce yourself as a policeman?"

"Force of habit," I said. Robinson waited, so I took a breath and gave him the basics. How my dad and uncle were homicide detectives with the Boston Police Department. How I'd followed in their foot-steps. I left out the part about getting my promotion to detective mainly because a copy of the exam had found its way to me the night before I took it. And how Uncle Dan was on the Promotions Board. People who weren't part of how things worked for the Irish in Boston had a hard time understanding that sort of thing. It was our depart-ment, our city. Back when an Irishman couldn't get an honest day's work, being on the cops meant a steady job for you and your own. It meant something, something this blond track-and-field star from somewhere in the Midwest would never understand. Maybe his grand-daddy from the old country might, but not this corn-fed all-American.

Uncle Ike? I didn't go anywhere near that story. Then they'd really think I was bonkers.

"You came upon a sudden death and your police training took over, is that it?" Robinson asked. I think he'd been talking for some time before that, but I'd been lost somewhere else. Back home.

"Yeah, yeah. Are we done yet?"

"One more thing. Why did you go up in the tower?"

"Scene of the crime," I said. "I was still thinking like a cop."

"Crime?" Robinson said.

"A head doctor ought to know suicide's illegal," I said. "Or were you thinking of something else?"

"I had a shock when I saw you at the edge," Robinson said, ignoring my question.

"Is that why you followed me up there?" I asked. "You were worried about my state of mind?"

"That's my job," he said. "But I didn't know it was you. I saw the door was open and wanted to be sure no one else had wandered up there. It's kept locked for a reason. It's a hazard in a place like this."

"The door was open when I came to it," I said. "But I shut it behind me. So, how'd you know anyone was up there? Or were you following me?"

"By open, I meant unlocked," Robinson said. "Do you think people are following you, watching your every move?"

"You said one more thing. That's two. See you later," I said, as I rose and made for the door.

"What happened in Paris?" Robinson said, his words like a dagger at my back. I froze, my hand on the doorknob. I couldn't turn it. My body went rigid as sweat trickled down the small of my back, the wood grain of the door swirling before my eyes.

I felt Robinson place his hand on mine, and together we turned the knob. With his other hand on my shoulder, he gently pushed me along into the corridor.

"I'll see you at two o'clock," he said, and shut the door behind me.

"Fourteen hundred hours," I whispered. I laughed, even though I couldn't figure why it was funny.

I headed for the south wing. Time to see Kaz, like it or not.

I crossed the foyer and spotted the English gent I'd seen earlier, the older fellow who'd been shooed away along with me and the other Yank. He was cracking open the door carefully, as if afraid of what he might find.

"Hello," I said, tapping him on the shoulder.

"What? Oh, you gave me a fright, young man," he said, turning his face toward mine. His unkempt hair was black and flecked with gray, his shoulders slumped, his eyes downcast over a pair of spectacles perched on the tip of his nose. He looked more like a professor than a soldier, and I wondered how he'd ended up in this joint.

"Is the coast clear?" I said, giving him a conspiratorial wink.

"You mean our minders, do you? Yes, they've cleared off," he said. "Along with poor Holland."

I pushed the door open, holding it for him as a stiff breeze blew over us. "I'm Boyle," I said, keeping to the local custom of last names only.

"Sinclair," he said, taking the steps carefully, like a man twice his age.

"Did you know Holland?" I asked, as we stopped by the spot where he'd fallen.

"Know him?" Sinclair said, as if the question startled him. "Of course not. No one knows anyone here. Secrets, that's all there is here. And when there's nothing but secrets, no one knows a damned thing!"

Without another word, Sinclair turned away from the small pool of drying blood and walked to the pathway, taking small, careful steps. He sounded nuts, until I thought about it. Whatever this place was, he'd figured it out. It was a house of secrets, and odds were, with Holland in the morgue, at least one secret was safe.

For now.

CHAPTER FOUR

I STOOD IN the hallway outside Kaz's room for a while. Not because I couldn't move, but because I didn't know what to say when I went in. Kaz was my best friend, and I'd let him down. We looked out for each other, but right now there wasn't a damn thing he could do for me, and the kind of help he needed was beyond my ability to give.

He needed a heart that wasn't ready to give out.

And not just to stay alive. Kaz had lost his entire family to the Nazis. When the Germans invaded Poland, he was studying at Oxford. He was a student of languages, about half a dozen of them. Kaz's father had been readying the family for a move to England, where they'd join Kaz and start up the family business again. Everything was set, the family fortune transferred to Swiss banks, property sold off, and then the Germans had invaded. Kaz's father had been smart enough to see what was coming, but he couldn't see how soon it would arrive.

His family had been wiped out when the Krauts eliminated the Polish intelligentsia, along with anyone else who might oppose them.

Until a few months ago, Kaz thought everyone in his family was dead. Which explained a lot of the risks he'd enjoyed taking to get his revenge on as many Fritzes as possible. But then he'd received word about his kid sister, Angelika. She was alive. Somehow she'd survived and was part of the Polish Home Army, the underground organization of the Polish government-in-exile.

Which was among the most dangerous things to be doing in occupied Europe right now, especially after the heroic but failed Warsaw Uprising. Kaz was desperate to hear news of Angelika and to help get her out if possible.

He'd made me promise to see to it that he stayed on active service, in uniform and part of the fight, so he could act whenever the opportunity presented itself. But the only uniform he was wearing now was hospital pajamas, and I didn't see any way I could change that.

But maybe I could be a better friend. So, I knocked on the door and pushed it open.

"Kaz?"

"Yes. Billy?" he said, from a chair by the side of his bed. He was wearing his hospital pajamas, but under a silk and velvet dressing gown. His family's Swiss bank accounts were all in Kaz's hands now. He had more money than he knew what to do with, but he didn't let it go to his head. Well, maybe a little bit when it came to his tailor.

"How are you?" I said, standing in the doorway, uncertain of his reaction.

"Reading the newspaper," he said, folding a copy of the *Times* and tossing it on the side table, as if he'd answered my question. ALLIES ENTER HOLLAND it declared at the top. That much closer to Poland. "Have a seat. What have you been up to?"

"Walking," I said, pulling up a metal chair that scraped on the linoleum. "Sorry I haven't dropped by."

"I know, I've watched you. I was glad to see you up and about. Fresh air is just the thing to clear one's mind."

"Yeah," I said. "I'm still a little foggy, but better. Definitely better." Which wasn't a lie, given the shape I'd been in when I'd first arrived, strapped down on a cot in that ambulance. "Anything new from the doctors?"

"No. Continued monitoring and bed rest for now. Which means they have nothing to offer. I've asked for a consultation with my specialist, but they won't allow an outsider entrance. So, I shall have to wait to be released to visit Harley Street. Although I have little hope of any assistance there. Every doctor here says there is no remedy."

"Do they all agree with what that French doctor said? Mitral something-or-other?" A doctor in Paris had seen Kaz when he had his heart attack. It was under trying conditions, with street fighting raging all around, and I'd hoped the doc had been off the mark.

"Mitral valve stenosis, yes. One of my four heart valves cannot do its job and pump blood properly. Physical stress makes it worse, resulting in rather severe fatigue and irregular heart rhythms. Dr. Hughes confirmed it often results from having rheumatic fever in childhood, from which I did suffer."

"Who's this Hughes guy? Does he know what's up?"

"Major Cuthbert Hughes, Surgeon and Medical Superintendent of Saint Albans. He does seem knowledgeable."

"Nose like a hawk? Dark bags under his eyes?"

"Yes. Has he talked with you?"

"No, not exactly. Did he say when they'd spring you?"

"He was evasive on that point," Kaz said. "But I do have hope. I know of three patients who have been released in the last two days. What about you?"

"I have another session with Robinson today. I'll ask him," I said.

"No, Billy. I mean, how are you? Are you still having difficulties?"

"With what?" I asked, glad that for the moment my hand wasn't trembling.

"With understanding why you're here. I'm here because of my heart. Do you know why you're here?"

"Listen, Kaz, I took some pep pills. Too many, I know. But I was looking for you most of that time. I need to work it out of my system, that's all. Don't worry about it."

"I do worry, Billy. I worry because you promised you'd help me stay in uniform. I doubt I can ever work on an active case again, but I need to stay in the service. I can't get information about Angelika as a civilian. All doors would be closed to me. But as an officer serving with General Eisenhower, I have a chance, even if I am at a desk. You must speak to the general. I don't think I have ever asked you for a favor, Billy. But I do need one now. Speak to your uncle."

Kaz was right. The general could guarantee him a spot on his staff, an office job that would keep him at the heart of things at SHAEF. And I was the guy who had General Eisenhower's ear. When we were alone, I called him Uncle Ike, although he was really a distant cousin. We were related through my mother's family and his wife's people, one of those situations tailor-made for special favors. Dad and Uncle Dan called in a few markers at the start of the war and got me assigned to Uncle Ike, who was an unknown colonel in Washington DC at the time. The idea was I'd spend the war years there, safe from another war to save the British Empire, which was how the Boyle family viewed this whole affair. Dad and his brother had gone off to the last world war with their older brother, Frank, and came back without him. Being good Irish patriots, they balked at the idea of losing me this time around, especially since the English still had their bootheel on a good part of Ireland.

Uncle Ike welcomed the idea. He said he liked having a trained detective on his staff, but neglected to mention he was headed to Great Britain to head up US Army forces. I went along, surprised to find myself investigating low crimes in high places and generally in danger of getting shot or blown up instead of enjoying the nightlife in our nation's capital.

All of which brings us back to General Eisenhower. Uncle Ike.

"Sure, Kaz," I said. "I'll speak to him as soon as I get out of here."

"I need you to come to your senses now, Billy. I don't have the luxury of time. They could discharge me from the service tomorrow and I would have no recourse. Pull yourself together. I know it's difficult, but you must. For your own sake, as well as mine and Angelika's, please."

"Okay, okay, I'll get my head screwed on straight, I promise." I got up and stood by the window, staring out at the forest beyond the grounds. I couldn't look Kaz in the eye. He never asked for favors and he never pleaded for anything, and here he was doing both. But it wasn't that. It was my own uncertainty. I didn't even know how to begin. I needed to feel normal. Like before. Before Paris.

"You have to come to grips with reality, Billy. About this place and about what happened—"

"No," I said, cutting him off as I turned and held out my hand, as if the words might bounce off my palm. I didn't want to hear them, couldn't hear them, wouldn't let myself hear or speak them. "Shut up, Kaz. Not another goddamn word. Or else I swear . . ."

All I felt was pure rage pouring out from my gut, filling the room, and driving away the thoughts that clawed at the edges of my mind. I saw that my open hand had become a fist. Kaz sighed, a look of pity rather than fear on his face.

"Lunch," an orderly announced, barging into the room without bothering to look at either of us. He set a tray down next to Kaz and left behind the aroma of a sausage roll and boiled carrots. I felt myself gagging as the smell filled the small room.

I bolted, slamming open the door and pushing the orderly aside as I made for the nearest bathroom.

I retched, giving up what little I'd eaten as the bile at the back of my throat helped tamp down the memories from that damned City of Light.

It's a helluva thing when you're thankful for the distraction of threatening your best friend and then puking into a toilet bowl.

I got off my knees, splashed cold water on my face, and almost laughed. I had just enough time for lunch before my appointment with Robinson.

CHAPTER FIVE

I WAS A fool. I cursed myself as I made for the mess. Us loonies in the north wing didn't rate room service, so we ate in a cramped dining hall. I liked sitting next to the mutes, since it cut down on small talk.

I'd gone to see Kaz for a couple of reasons. One was to be a buddy, and I blew that one to hell and gone. The other was to tell him about Holland and what I saw up in the tower, which would have to wait until I apologized. If he'd listen.

To kill some time, I got a cup of joe and a doughnut. Just the thing to calm my nerves and my gut. I scanned the tables for an empty spot and then saw a fellow Yank, the same guy who'd been at the scene with Sinclair.

"I'm Boyle," I said, taking a seat across from him. "I saw you this morning, out front."

"Miller," he said, pushing aside a bowl of congealed brown mush strewn with lima beans. Mutton stew, they called it. Good a name as any. "You're talkative all of a sudden."

"What do you mean?" I asked, studying his face. Black hair, prominent cheekbones, and a thin mouth would have made him good-looking, except for his brown eyes, set deep in their sockets and squeezed close together.

"I've tipped my hat in your direction a few times," Miller said, leaning back and shaking a smoke from a pack of Luckies. He fired it up and took a long drag, like it was life itself. "Out there, on the path. But you kept on walking, like you were too good to be bothered. I thought maybe the cat got your tongue, like some of these silent types." He shot a glance to one of the Brits who was alternating between his mutton and long looks out the window.

"No, sorry, I had a lot on my mind, I guess. No offense meant," I said. "So, this morning. Did you see Holland?"

"Holland? That the guy who jumped? No, I heard him hit the ground, though. Once you've heard that sound, it's hard to forget. Hard to mistake it for anything else but flesh and bone. Did you see him go over?"

"Yeah," I said, nibbling at my doughnut. I raised the cup and managed to take a sip without spilling. As I set it down it rattled in the saucer.

"Nerves, huh?" Miller said, his gaze lingering on my right hand.

I laid it flat on the table. "So they tell me," I said. "What about Sinclair? He see what happened?"

"I doubt it. Guy's got his head in the clouds. He doesn't let on much, but I think he's some sort of scientist or professor. Said he came here for a rest cure," Miller said, twirling his finger in circles around his temple. "Nervous breakdown, maybe."

"What about you?" I asked. "You nervous in the service?"

"Nah," Miller said, taking a long drag on his cigarette. "They think I enjoyed it too much."

"Enjoyed what?" I dunked my doughnut. Easier not to spill the java all over me that way.

"Killing people," he said. "That's what we're here to do, right?"

"That's the general idea. Although the brass does seem to prefer we kill Germans, for the most part." I worked on the soggy doughnut, taking small bites and managing to keep them down. I waited for Miller to fill in the silence. Always better than peppering a guy with questions.

"Things aren't so simple, not out where I've been," Miller said, crushing out his cigarette with nicotine-stained fingers.

"Where's that?"

"Southern France. The OSS sent me in to organize a Resistance group in the mountains. You heard of the OSS, Boyle?"

"Sure. You're some sort of secret outfit," I said. I knew the Office of Strategic Services well. One of their agents had smuggled Kaz and me into occupied Italy a while back. I even knew the joke that their initials stood for "Oh So Social" since so many of them were drawn from the top layer of society, from the Harvard Club to Wall Street, which was the world of their boss, Wild Bill Donovan. But the less Miller knew that I knew, the better.

"Secret enough that they decided to lock me up in here until they figure out if I'm more Baby Face Nelson than Sergeant York," he said, giving a sharp laugh with bitter overtones.

"What happened?"

"There was an informer in the group. A woman. Young girl, really," he said, lighting up another Lucky.

"You knew that for certain?" I asked.

"Smoked her out with the oldest trick in the book," Miller said. "I had her deliver a message to another Resistance group asking for more plastic explosive to blow up a railway bridge. She came back with the *plastique*. Only problem was I knew that cell had already been betrayed. Everyone was killed or arrested."

"She got the *plastique* from the Germans?"

"Yes," Miller said. "I had no intention of blowing that bridge, but she didn't know that. I got into position about a half mile away with my binoculars and settled in to see if my suspicions were correct. The plan was to plant the charges at midnight. A little before dusk the Germans showed up, along with those *Milice* bastards. I watched them set up their ambush. They had a long night, waiting for nothing." The *Milice* were the Vichy French militia. Pro-Nazi thugs who hunted their own people.

"What'd you do?"

"I slit her throat," Miller said, cocking his head to blow smoke at the ceiling. He grinned, as if reveling in a fond memory. "It was quick, best way to do these things. She had no idea what was about to happen. Merciful, I say."

"Did you have any other proof?" I asked.

"Proof? What more would you need? The girl was a menace to everyone. No telling how much death and torture she'd been responsible for. It had to be done, and she had to be made an example," Miller said, going quiet and drumming his fingers on the table, his gaze lingering on something beyond the window glass. Something in France, perhaps.

"I guess your OSS bosses didn't care for the example you set," I said, finishing my coffee left-handed.

"My own partner ratted me out," Miller said. "Claimed I was out of control. He was too scared to act and jealous that I wasn't. A couple of the *maquisards* complained as well. Bastards. I probably saved their lives." The *maquisards* were hard men who took to the mountains and fought both the Germans and the elements. If *they* didn't like Miller's rough justice, he'd gone too far.

"I guess they didn't appreciate the execution of one of their own," I said.

"Or that I sprang it on them," Miller said, spitting out a bitter laugh. "I did it in front of twenty of them in their encampment as we were planning out a raid. I thought it would be instructive."

"I bet it was," I said. In regard to his mental state, at least. "Was that the only thing that landed you here?"

"Jealously and small minds, Boyle. That was enough. They didn't like the way I handled prisoners, either. As if you can take prisoners while the Krauts are chasing you all over kingdom come. Right?"

"Right," I said, getting up. "Gotta go. Time to see Sigmund Freud." I had no need to listen to Miller brag about what he'd done to his prisoners. I was more concerned about what he may have done here.

"Don't fall for Robinson's line. He wants you to think he's a nice guy. But he works for the brass. All he wants is to get in here," Miller said, tapping his head. "And I ain't lettin' him in."

"Good advice, thanks," I said, happy to get away from the guy. He gave me the creeps.

Then I thought about it. How different was I? I wasn't letting Robinson help either. It was like I'd put a big DO NOT DISTURB sign on my forehead. Listening to Miller rant had chilled me. He clearly did enjoy killing, as well as talking about it. As unsettling as that was, the worst part was seeing myself in how closed off he was. He didn't want help, maybe because he liked the way he was. I'm no medico, but I knew I didn't like what was going on inside my brain. I could see myself sitting in that dining hall weeks from now, telling anyone who had the misfortune to sit near me how the odds were stacked against me, all the while keeping my nightmarish thoughts under mental lock and key. I didn't much like what the future seemed to have in store.

I knocked on Robinson's door.

I was nervous.

No, I was scared as hell.

"How are you doing, Boyle?" Robinson asked as soon as we were settled into the worn leather armchairs by the window. Usually he sat at his desk with a notepad, but now he was empty-handed. "After all the excitement this morning."

"Fine," I said, resisting the temptation to tell him I'd seen someone in the clock tower with Holland. I couldn't have him wondering if I was seeing things. "I just had lunch with Miller. He was there too."

"Uh-huh." Robinson's face was impassive.

"He's a strange one. Enthusiastic about the war, I hear. Too enthusiastic, even for the OSS."

"Boyle, I'm not going to comment on another patient. These sessions are strictly confidential. Anything said in here goes no further," Robinson said, even as he picked up a pad to scribble a quick note.

"But you report on us to your superior officer, don't you? Isn't that what this place is all about? Deciding who's fit enough to keep serving, and who's going to be weeded out?"

"No, Boyle, that's not what we're doing here. I'm here to help get you back on your feet," Robinson said.

"Or give me a Section Eight," I said.

"There are specific criteria for a Section Eight discharge," Robinson said. "I don't think you're a psychopath, alcoholic, or bed-wetter, so don't worry about that. You've been through a lot, and I want to help you regain a sense of your own emotional balance and mental health. You can't say you're feeling yourself lately, can you?"

"Not exactly," I said, looking out the window. I could make out the fence through the trees, about thirty yards out. Movement flickered between branches as the guards patrolled along the path. How many of them were out there?

"Boyle?" Robinson prompted. "I asked you a question. Do you consider yourself a well-adjusted person, under normal circumstances?"

"Sorry, I was watching the guards. Why do you need so many of them? Worried about a mass escape?"

"Never mind the guards," Robinson said, with a quick glance out the window. "We're talking about you. Before you came here, before Paris, did you consider yourself well-adjusted?"

"I don't think I'll ever adjust well to the army," I said.

"A remarkably rational statement," Robinson said. "A wisecrack masking a deeper truth. But you don't feel well-adjusted now, do you?"

"No," I said, gasping out that single word and burying my face in my hands. I listened to the seconds tick away on the clock. I heard the scribble of Robinson's pencil on paper, like a claw on flesh. "Everything's wrong. Shattered. I don't know how to get back. It feels like it's going to be like this forever."

"When you were brought here, you were severely exhausted, in a state of profound confusion," Robinson said. "It takes a while to come back from that. You were physically and emotionally spent. Add to that the effect of the drugs you'd taken, and anyone would have a hard time."

"It was only a few pep pills, Doc, come on."

"You continue to minimize the seriousness of the drugs you took. It was methamphetamine, and from what you said, you took enough to win the Kentucky Derby without a horse. Just because the Germans give them to their troops doesn't mean they're safe. We're talking about Nazis, remember."

"Pervitin," I said. "That's what it said on the container."

"Right. You took enough of it to scramble your brains for a while."

"But I didn't get hooked," I said. "I'll be happy to never see the stuff again."

"No, you weren't taking it long enough. But the quantity you ingested over a short period of time did some temporary damage. That's why you're feeling disoriented and depressed. Is that an accurate description of what's going on?"

"Okay, okay, I'm not feeling on top of the world, if that's what you mean."

"Irritable too," Robinson said. "Did you sleep much last night? Honestly."

I shook my head. "I can't sleep. I'm tired all the time, but once I shut my eyes it all starts up again."

"What does?" Robinson said, his pencil poised in midair.

"Paris. You asked me what happened in Paris."

"I did. Several times," Robinson said. He sat back, crossed his legs, and waited.

So did I.

"Will it stop, if I tell you? Will I be able to sleep? And I need to get out of here, so I can help Kaz. He's depending on me. If I tell you everything, will you let me go?" Panic was rising in my gut, a thousand questions and a cavernous fear filling my mind. My hand trembled and I stuck it under my arm, desperate to quiet it, to hide what it meant about me.

"Don't worry about anyone else right now. Tell me what happened, and we'll take it from there. Sit back, relax, close your eyes, and tell me the story. About Paris."

Robinson was talking in soothing tones, almost a whisper. I let my head rest against the back of the chair and took a deep breath. I let him talk some more. I listened, hearing the easy cadence of his words, the rhythm of relaxation.

I started to talk. This is what I told him.

I'd been on a mission in occupied Paris. Kaz and me, to be specific.

But first, I need to explain about Diana. Lady Diana Seaton, the woman I love. She's an upper-class Brit, and I'm from a Boston family of working-class stiffs not that long off the boat from Ireland. We're as different as can be, but sparks flew from the first moment we met. That was back in '42, and since then we've only had brief snatches of time together. You see, Diana works for the Special Operations Executive, SOE. She's worked undercover in Italy and France, maybe other places for all I know. Up until recently, she was in Paris, operating under the code name Malou.

So Kaz and I got into Paris dressed as civilians. Malou was our contact, and things were meant to go like clockwork. We looked her up and began to do our job. It was supposed to be easy.

Yeah, right.

We weren't more than a couple of days ahead of the advancing Allies, and all we had to do was complete our mission then find a safe place to hide until the cavalry arrived. Easy.

We hadn't counted on the Parisians launching a fight against the occupying Germans. After four years of brutal occupation, they didn't want to wait to be liberated, they wanted to do it themselves.

There was a lot of shooting. People died. Kaz had a heart attack.

I got ahold of a supply of Pervitin and used it to keep going, day and night. It worked. Like gangbusters.

We were betrayed.

"Boyle," Robinson's voice was sharp, his forehead wrinkled in concern.

"What?" I shook my head, trying to think straight, uncertain as to where I was.

"You stopped talking a couple of minutes ago. Are you okay? You drifted off on me."

"Sorry," I mumbled, rubbing my eyes and looking down at my shoes. This was the hard part.

We were betrayed.

And I was there to see it happen. I'd been powerless to stop it. Unarmed, alone, pumped up on Pervitin, jittery as all hell, and facing a city full of retreating Krauts shooting anything that looked like a threat.

I watched Diana being taken.

By the Gestapo.

It was all my fault.

"It's my fault, all my fault. I trusted the guy who betrayed us. I should have seen it coming. I should have." The words echoed inside my head as I tried to open my eyes. I couldn't. I felt a hand on my shoulder, shaking me. Then I felt a hard surface against my ribs. I was on the floor, and Robinson was helping me up.

"I couldn't stop them," I said, as I sat back down on the chair. How the hell had I ended up on the floor? "I followed her to Gestapo head-quarters, but they loaded up a truck with prisoners and took off for Germany. She's either dead or in a concentration camp."

"It's not your fault," Robinson said. "But it's certainly normal to feel like it is."

"Well, I don't feel normal. How the hell did I get on the floor?"

"Boyle, you were telling me about a painful emotional event. You fell to your knees, curled up into a ball, and spoke about the greatest losses you've ever felt. The woman you love arrested by the Gestapo, your best friend nearly dying. You're letting yourself experience the toll it's taken on you. Of course it doesn't feel normal. But believe me, talking about it is better than letting it fester inside your mind."

"Do I have any chance of getting out of here?" I asked. "Of feeling like I'm not going nuts?"

"You know what the frontline prescription is for dealing with combat fatigue?"

"Yeah. A doctor once told me the quick fix for a lot of guys was three hots and a cot," I said. That meant being pulled off the line for some hot chow and a good night's sleep. Maybe it was only a few hundred yards to the rear, but the brief respite helped a lot of GIs. If they didn't buy the farm when they went back into combat the next day.

"Well, you've had your hot meals. Time for the cot. With something to help you sleep."

"Why didn't you suggest this before, Doc?" I asked. "I really need the shut-eye."

"Because we needed to get at the root cause of your problem. Some of it is the aftereffects of the drugs. You've been in the thick of things, so there's the stress of combat as well. But I recognized there was something else haunting you. Until that was out in the open, there was no use giving you the rest cure. We'd just be back where we started."

"Okay, but can I go see Kaz first? I kinda lost my temper with him and said a few things I shouldn't have. I need to patch things up."

"No. My primary concern is your well-being. Mend your fences with your friend later. Right now, you've got a date with a syringe."

CHAPTER SIX

I DIDN'T LIKE it at all. Robinson escorted me to my room and ordered me to change into those scratchy hospital pajamas. An orderly stood by, arms folded across his chest, daring me not to comply.

I wasn't in the mood for a fight. Besides, my right hand was shaking so much I probably couldn't land a decent punch. I traded my khakis for the blue pajamas as I stared out the window. A favorite pastime in my not-well-adjusted state. Maybe this forced rest cure would work, but if it didn't, I needed to keep close tabs on the guards and their patrol patterns. It might come in handy.

"Ready?" Robinson asked, pulling a needle out from a leather case.

I was, except for the fact that I didn't like needles much. I lay down and rolled up my sleeve. "You sure I can't take a sleeping pill, Doc?"

"This is much more effective than the pill form," he said, drawing a solution into the syringe. "It's a barbiturate and will put you into a deep, restful sleep. Somehow this treatment has earned the nickname Blue Eighty-Eight. Maybe because it packs a punch, like the German eighty-eight. Quite safe, given that we're only using it once. Now, you'll feel a little pinch."

I looked away. I felt a big pinch, then he held the needle in my arm for what felt like a long time. "How long before this stuff kicks in?"

"You'll be asleep in a couple of minutes," Robinson said. "I'll check in on you later, and the orderlies know to watch you as well."

I bet. I watched him leave as the big orderly closed the door halfway. Clattering noise echoed in the hallway, the usual hospital hustle-bustle. If I couldn't sleep at night when it was quiet, how the hell was I supposed to saw logs in the middle of the day?

I got up on my elbows and took another look out the window. Bad angle, I couldn't see a thing. So instead, I thought about what I needed to say to Kaz. About my plan to escape and get to Uncle Ike, to beg him to keep Kaz at SHAEF. Then I'd try to find out where the Gestapo had taken Diana. Someone in Intelligence had to have a line on which prison or camp the Krauts took women to. My best hope was that they didn't know she was SOE. If she was Malou to them, a French girl caught up in a Resistance group, she had a chance. Not a good chance, but better odds than if she'd been identified as a British agent.

Memories of Paris flooded my mind. Barricades, gunfights, dead Germans. Kaz looking pale and weak. And Diana. Always Diana.

I BLINKED MY eyes open. Still daylight. Robinson sat in a chair, a newspaper folded on his lap. I felt strange. The first thing I noticed was how stiff I was. I stretched my legs, my muscles protesting the movement.

"Awake, Boyle?" Robinson asked, setting his newspaper aside.

"Yeah," I croaked, pushing myself up on the pillows. My mouth was dry as a summer's day in hell. Robinson handed me a glass of water and I gulped it down. I looked at him, trying to put my finger on what else was niggling at me. "It's not even dark yet," I said.

"It's been dark," he said. "Twice. You've been out for nearly forty hours."

"Jesus," I said, my head falling back to the pillows. I stared at the ceiling, the sudden awareness of what I was feeling striking me like a mortar shell.

I didn't feel crazy.

I looked at Robinson again, and the orderly standing behind him. I wasn't seeing them through a distorted haze of suspicion. It was only a doctor and a guy bringing me a cup of coffee.

I sat up, cradling the ceramic mug in my hands. I thanked the orderly, who smiled. He looked like a normal joe.

I was confused.

And I was hungry. That hadn't happened in a while.

"You must have given me a helluva dose of that stuff," I said. "Forty hours?"

"It was a fairly low dose, actually," Robinson said. "I wanted to knock you out, so you could sleep. But the sleep cure isn't all about drugged sleep. You need the real thing, and your body let you have it once your brain calmed down."

"I am a little groggy," I said, as I sipped the steaming black java. "But I feel different. Better."

"Tell me what better means," Robinson said.

"I don't know if I can," I said. "Before, it was like having jolts of electricity snapping through my mind. Everything was vivid and blurry at the same time."

"And now?"

"I'm still worried about Kaz. I still wish I could have done something, anything, to help Diana. I still feel that pain in my heart. But my brain isn't buzzing with it like a thousand hornets. Hell, I'm even talking to you about it. That's a switch."

"Good," Robinson said. "This is a good first step."

"First step?" I asked. "How about you call it the last step and cut me loose?"

"Sorry, Boyle, it isn't that easy. I need to observe you for a while to confirm you're fit for duty. This is the army, remember? They have rules and regulations for everything."

"Sure," I said, returning to the coffee. I drank some more, studying Robinson as I did. He seemed like a decent guy. But as I worked to clear my head, I kept returning to one insistent, crystal-clear thought.

I *had* seen a man with Holland up in the clock tower. I couldn't write it off as a hallucination or the influence of the drugs that had raged through my body.

Holland had been murdered, and Robinson was one of the first on the scene.

Robinson was a suspect, along with everyone else who'd been near the clock tower. I had to be careful. Part of my brain was telling me not to be paranoid, while the other half knew that the worst thing I could do would be to start openly investigating this killing. If it turned out Robinson was involved, he could send me off to a real loony bin with the stroke of a pen. And if he wasn't, I ran the risk of him thinking I was delusional and keeping me here longer.

I had to play it safe and watch myself at the same time. How would I know if I was delusional? The deluded delude themselves first, right?

"Hey, Doc, are there any side effects from the barbiturates you gave me? Or from this sleep cure in general? I'm not going to get the DTs or anything, am I?" I grinned to show I was half-joking, trying to sound rational and only a bit concerned.

"No, not at all. The drugs were a one-time dose, and sleep is nothing but restorative. Don't worry, Boyle, you're doing fine."

"Holland hadn't just come off the sleep cure, had he?" I asked. Robinson gave me a sharp look, and I wondered if maybe I'd spooked him with the question. Or perhaps I'd dreamed the whole thing, who knew?

"Why do you ask about Holland?"

"Well, the guy took a nosedive from the highest point around. I thought maybe he'd woken up after a two-day nightmare and couldn't take it. So put my mind at ease, Doc, and tell me he wasn't part of the shut-eye brigade."

"I told you, Boyle, I won't talk about other patients. It's unethical. Now if you're ready to get up, let's go get you some food," Robinson said.

"I should see Kaz first," I said.

"I've told the baron you'd be by to see him as soon as you woke up. I figured he'd be concerned about you after all you two have been through together. You can drop by and visit him as soon as you get some nourishment in you. You've been without food too long."

I had to agree, especially after I tried to stand up. Second time, it was easier.

An orderly led me to the showers and left me with a clean set of khakis. I stood under the water, hoping the craziness I'd been experiencing would swirl away down the drain.

Then it hit me. Robinson had been adamant that he wouldn't reveal anything about another patient, including whether he'd had the sleep cure. But he'd told Kaz that I'd been dead to the world.

So, which was it? Did my friendship with Kaz outweigh his ethical concerns? Strange.

As I shaved, I took a long look at myself. My face was thinner, and I had bags under my eyes despite my forty-hour slumber. I had a long way to go before Mrs. Boyle's bright-eyed boy made an appearance in the bathroom mirror.

Robinson escorted me to the dining hall like an overprotective mother hen. He nursed a coffee as I wolfed down scrambled eggs, bacon, and toast slathered with butter and jam. The cop side of my brain considered how much this kind of food would net on the black market, and how the kitchen staff might sneak butter and bacon home with them. The other side of my brain focused on feeding my body. When I finally pushed my plate away, Robinson cracked a smile.

"Okay, I don't think you'll faint from hunger anytime soon. Come on, let's take a stroll and then you can visit your pal."

"Whatever you say, Doc. You haven't steered me wrong yet," I said. But maybe he'd helped Holland take a wrong turn off the tower. I kept my suspicions to myself and followed him to the path where I'd made so many circuits around the great house.

"Let's walk, and you tell me if anything looks different to you, okay?"

"Sure," I said. "Is this some sort of test?"

"Why do you always think there's a dark motive for everything, Boyle?"

"Probably for the same reason you never give a straight answer. It's in your nature as a head doctor. Me, I see everything from a cop's viewpoint. Suspicion comes with the territory."

"Point taken," Robinson said with a quick laugh as he picked up his pace to stick with me. "I find straight answers usually don't lead to the truth. It's best to let people arrive at it by their own route, no matter how circuitous."

"We're on a circuitous route right now, Doc, but I don't know what I'm supposed to look for. How about dropping a hint?"

"You've been concerned about the guards, haven't you? You've alluded to escaping, but said the fence was too high and the patrols too frequent," Robinson said.

"Hey, I was just blowing off steam, Doc. I didn't much like finding myself in a prison."

"Who would?" Robinson asked, stopping at the side of the path and staring into the woods. I did the same.

There was something different. I squinted, trying to focus on what was beyond the veil of green leafy branches.

The fence. It wasn't ten feet high. And it wasn't topped by coils of barbed wire.

I stepped over the low iron fence at the edge of the path and walked closer, searching for the guards I was sure would chase me away. There weren't any.

The fence? It was the same kind of iron fencing as along the walkway, but about six feet high. Where the low fence by the walkway was painted a glossy black, this one was rusted and flaking, left untended for too long. I reached through the dense undergrowth and grasped one of the railings, my hand coming away stained with rusty grit. Where I'd seen coils of barbed wire, there was a single strand of the stuff. I could have climbed up and over this thing with no more to show for it than a tear in my trousers.

"I don't understand," I said. "I saw it with my own eyes. It was much higher, with bright coils of barbed wire."

"Like you saw the Commandos patrolling the perimeter," Robinson said.

"That much is true," I said, pointing to the far side of the fence. "I can see the path, it's well worn." A few yards away, the bare earth showed where a footpath ran the length of the fence.

"Of course we have guards," Robinson said, taking my arm and leading me back to the walkway. "But why do you think they're Commandos?"

"Those dark green berets they wear," I said. "I've seen them before."

"I'm sure you have," Robinson said. We walked for a while and I couldn't help but stare at the fence. It was nothing like I remembered. I stumbled along in confusion until we met up with two guards crossing the path by the gate.

"Captain," one of them said in greeting as he saluted Robinson.

"You fellows off duty?" Robinson asked, putting a hand on my arm as he stopped to chat.

"We are, sir," one of the men answered. "And after twelve hours, I'm ready to put my feet up." He looked too old for the Commandos. The guards I'd seen were tough, young, and fit. This fellow was on the pudgy side and wore spectacles. There were flecks of gray at his temples, and his uniform was baggy and ill-fitting.

No green beret.

"You're Home Guard?" I asked. The Home Guard was made up of volunteers, those too young, old, or unfit to serve in the regular army. It was England's second line of defense, originally created to slow down a German invasion and buy time for the regular forces. Today, they were often given jobs that could free up other troops for front line service.

Like guarding this joint.

"That we are," he said, clapping his companion on the back. It was the same young kid who'd been with Sergeant Jenkins.

"Private Fulton, right?" I said to him.

"Aye, sir. You're looking better, if you don't mind my saying it."

"Not at all, Private. Your Sergeant Jenkins, he's Home Guard too?"

"Of course, sir. We all are," Fulton said, and went on his way. Home to his mother, most likely.

"They're here to keep people away, for the most part," Robinson said. "They are guarding you, but from prying eyes. There are a lot of secrets in this place, and we can't have any unauthorized folks getting too close."

"Now I know why you took me on this walk," I said. "If you'd told me, I wouldn't have believed you."

"I needed to know if you were seeing and thinking clearly," Robinson said as we continued.

"I made all that up? The fence, the Commando guards? How could it seem so real?"

"Well, you didn't make it up. I'm sure you've seen fences topped with barbed wire in a prison or POW camp. And you said yourself you've seen the Commando berets before."

"But why? I don't get it." I almost said I wondered if this was a dream and I was still deep in the sleep cure, but I kept that one to myself.

"The human mind is a wondrous thing," Robinson said. "It does what it must to keep us safe. In your case, you simply weren't ready to face what happened to Diana Seaton, and you needed a distraction. So your vivid imagination went to work. It used the reality of this place and combined it with other images in your subconscious. Combine that with the aftereffects of the drugs you took, and you've got a story that made sense to you."

"That I was being kept prisoner, that escape was impossible," I said.

"Exactly. Which is precisely the predicament Miss Seaton finds herself in. As long as you thought it was you yourself in such danger, you didn't have to think about her. But it was always there, beneath the surface. You can't escape the subconscious."

"Oh, my God," I said, blurting out the words before I could stop them.

"What?" Robinson said, halting and standing in front of me. "Are you all right?"

"Yes, yes," I said. "What you said hit me hard, that's all. That I was worried about me when I should have been worrying about Diana."

"It's okay, Boyle. It was nothing but your mind protecting you. Now you're ready to face facts, so we can work on getting you out of here."

"I know. It was a shock to realize it, that's all," I said. "What next?"

"For the rest of the day, take it easy. Visit your friend and relax. I'll see you tomorrow at ten." I told him I'd be there, and we went our separate ways.

He hadn't noticed the lie. I wasn't almost knocked over by the revelation that I'd substituted Diana's predicament for my own. I was almost knocked over by the unbidden memory of a single word.

Sweden.

Go to the Swedes, a dying man in Paris had told me. As with much of what happened when Diana was taken, that moment had been tamped down deep in my brain. But it had bubbled to the surface and now offered the slightest bit of hope.

Why Sweden? I had no idea. Probably nothing I should mention to Robinson. Maybe I wasn't really a prisoner here, but the Brits and the army called the shots, and when a guy who knew too many secrets started talking about a neutral country, the prison bars might get real all too quickly.

CHAPTER SEVEN

I FINALLY MADE it to Kaz's floor in the medical wing. I'd walked around the grounds once, trying to work up my courage. It took a second circuit, but that got me to the south wing's rear entrance, which opened onto a solarium where patients sat in comfortable chairs amid plants and sunlight. Not very prison-like, I had to admit. Two women sat in a corner, one of them in a wheelchair. She was in her early twenties, with brown wavy hair, a hint of freckles dashed across her cheeks, and a vacant stare. Her companion, blond-haired and about the same age, sat close to her, hands clasped around her friend's and tears brimming as she tried to blink them away. One of her legs was heavily bandaged, and crutches lay on the floor next to her.

I looked away as I passed them, not wishing to intrude. SOE agents, perhaps, plucked back from occupied Europe after being wounded. In body, if not spirit. If Diana survived the Gestapo, which one would she look like? I sent up a quick prayer to Saint Anthony, the patron saint of the missing, to grant her strength and luck and to bring her back safely.

I tried to put the image of the woman with the blank stare out of my mind. Then I remembered how that didn't work so well before, so I let that picture stay with me and tried to imagine the freckled young woman rising from her chair one day. Maybe with a smile on her lips. A daydream, yes. Maybe a fantasy, but it gave me hope.

"Billy!" Kaz said, greeting me with more enthusiasm than I deserved. He stood, tossing the book he'd been reading on the bed. "Come, sit and tell me how you are. Rested?"

"I am, Kaz," I said, as I pulled up a chair next to his. He sat, turning up the collar of his dressing gown. He looked thin and pale, and I wondered if I'd been too off my head to notice it before. "Forty hours of sleep is plenty restful."

"Dr. Robinson came yesterday to tell me about the sleep cure. He had high hopes for it," Kaz said. He cocked his head a bit, as if he were studying me for any clues as to my mental health.

"Listen, Kaz, about the other day. I'm sorry. I was off my rocker, more than I realized. I didn't mean it," I said.

"I know, Billy," he said. "I knew you were having difficulties and still I pressured you about seeing General Eisenhower. I am the one who should apologize. It was too much of a burden to place on your shoulders at this time."

"Well, let's split the difference. Half an apology each?"

"An admirable compromise," Kaz said with a lopsided grin. A scar stopped his smile on one side of his face, the puckered skin too hardened to allow for a totally joyful expression. The scar, which ran from eye to chin thanks to an explosion that had killed the woman he loved, was a constant reminder of his loss and the memories that bound us together. Daphne Seaton had been Kaz's one true and great love, and she'd been taken from him by this war. Diana was Daphne's sister, and now the grim tide of treachery had taken her as well. But not with the same finality as it had taken Daphne. At least as far as I knew.

We shook on our deal, his hand feeling slight and bony in mine. Kaz was spindly and fragile in a way he had never been, even when he was a lightweight academic translating documents in Uncle Ike's headquarters. After Daphne's death, he had built himself up, working out with dumbbells in his suite at the Dorchester and taking impossibly fast walks through Hyde Park. He'd managed to shed the image of the weakling with a troubled heart, but in Paris it had all caught up with him.

"Kaz, have you heard about the fellow who went off the clock tower the other day?"

"Of course," he said. "Such news travels quickly in a small, closed society. Holland, correct?"

"Yes. That's what I was coming to see you about the other day," I said. "I witnessed the whole thing."

"It must have been gruesome," he said.

"It wasn't pretty, but that's not what I mean," I said, lowering my voice. "Someone was up in the tower with Holland. I think he was murdered."

"Billy," Kaz said, with a quick glance at the door. "Are you sure you really saw that? You were mixed up at the time, you know. Are you certain?"

"Yes," I said. "I know I wasn't thinking straight, but I'm as sure as I can be." I filled Kaz in on my hallucinations about the fence and the guards. "But this memory didn't fade after I woke up. It's still as real as it was that day."

"All right. Let's accept that you did see a murder," Kaz said. "Perhaps you should investigate. That might allow you to confirm what you saw."

"I don't know. I should focus on getting out of here. That's the only way I get to speak to Ike about you and find out about Diana."

"That is the first time you have mentioned her name," Kaz said. "Here, in any case."

"That's been most of my problem, according to Robinson," I said. "But never mind the Sigmund Freud routine. I've got to appear perfectly rational to Robinson to get him to release me. I can't go around squawking about a mystery man in the tower."

"Billy, I certainly endorse the notion of you reaching General Eisenhower, even if he is likely in France at present. But consider the implications of a murder in this establishment." Again, he glanced toward the open door, but there was so much hustle and bustle going on in the hallway, no one could hear us.

"Listen, I'm just starting to get used to the idea that we aren't in an insane asylum guarded by bloodthirsty British Commandos. Do you know what this place is, exactly?"

"Saint Albans Special Hospital," Kaz said. "Formerly an asylum for paupers and lunatics, so you were partly correct. It opened in the 1870s and was shuttered in the last decade due to the high cost of maintenance. Fairly progressive in its day, but I digress. It was reopened in 1940 by our friends at the Special Operations Executive to provide care for agents who needed time to recuperate in a secluded setting, closed off from the outside world. And to allow secrets that might be inadvertently revealed to remain within these grounds. Over time, the patients have grown to include anyone within the military or government who suffers an episode, mental or physical, that qualifies for high-security care."

"You have been busy," I said.

"On the contrary, I have nothing to do," Kaz said. "Nothing but engaging in idle chitchat with those who find the company of a Polish baron amusing."

"Playing the baron card again, huh?"

"Exactly. Everyone from surgeons to orderlies has been helpful regarding Saint Albans as an institution. But no one will volunteer a thing about the patients. They are well drilled on the importance of security."

"Robinson is a Yank, and there are American patients as well," I said.

"Yes. Your Army Medical Corps is providing support, the idea being that it was more efficient to combine resources than to start a separate unit for Americans. There are only a few, from the OSS and other hush-hush groups. The English have been at the game much longer, as you know, so there has been more time for the burden of underground operations to wear people down."

"Okay, I get the setup. You think it's important to look into Holland's death?"

"At least to determine if it was murder, and if so, if it is a danger to security. Was it an unbalanced patient who threw him off, or someone with a vendetta, perhaps?"

"You know that I can't tell anyone else? Robinson was there at the scene, along with Hughes, the fellow you told me about, the chief medical officer. There was also a thickset British officer, a guy with a heavy mustache and a bit of a limp."

"That must be Snow. Major Basil Snow. Head of security. Although Hughes is nominally in charge of the hospital, the word is Snow has the final word. He's SOE."

"A bit suspicious that they were all at the scene within seconds," I said.

"What's the layout here?" Kaz asked, spreading out his hands. "I have not been far from this room." He got up and looked out the window. It was a fine view of the green lawn and dark woods, but it gave little sense of how large this building was.

"This is the south wing. I'm in the north wing, with the other lunatics. Between us is the main building with the clock tower. That's where all the administrative offices are."

"So they could have been in a meeting and heard or seen the fall," Kaz said. "I think the key would be to find out more about Holland. Why was he here? Did he have enemies?"

"Easier said than done. And are you sure about this? It might delay my release."

"Only if you get caught."

"Doing what exactly?"

"Breaking into the administrative offices and reviewing the file on Holland, as well as anyone connected to him, of course," Kaz said. "There is a great concern about security here, but it is mainly focused on keeping people from the outside from entering, and secondarily containing patients until they are recovered. But there is a weak spot."

"They're not worried about security within the hospital," I offered.

"Right. No more than the normal hospital would be, in any case. I sense a certain laxity within these walls. It seems that the presence of guards and the overall emphasis on secrecy creates a false sense of security. After all, why be suspicious about the very people you are protecting?"

"There may be an excellent reason, if I'm right that there was another person in the tower. Okay, I'll give it shot. Any idea where they keep the files?"

"Billy, I can't do everything, can I? I am sure you can handle it. Simply a matter of casing the joint and opening the can," Kaz said. He enjoyed American slang, especially the gangster stuff.

"A can opener specializes in cheap safes, Kaz. I'm counting on file cabinets with simple locks."

"Ah. I must pay closer attention," Kaz said, pointing to the book on his bed. "*The High Window*, by this Raymond Chandler fellow. Very American. Funny, there's a man who fell to his death, and Marlowe— the detective, not the playwright—suspects foul play. Is that always the case with detectives, I wonder? Are you so jaded by experience that you see murder instead of suicide?"

"I got a good look at Holland's body, Kaz. I've seen a lot of jumpers, and I know what a fall can do to the human body. From that height, the internal injuries are horrible, but usually contained. From higher up, the torso might rupture, but he was relatively intact. There was bleeding from the scalp, but that's to be expected hitting gravel at a fair downward speed."

"What aroused your suspicion, then? Other than seeing another person with him," Kaz said.

"His shirt was untucked. Pulled clear out of his trousers on one side. I've seen shoes flung off feet, but this was different. Someone grabbed Holland, lifted him up, and threw him over."

"In the process, pulling his shirt free," Kaz said. "It must have been a fairly strong man."

"Maybe. But Holland was a slight guy, average height. Wouldn't have been hard to lift him up and over."

"But you heard nothing, no scream?" Kaz said, his brow wrinkled as he rubbed his chin, trying to piece things together.

"Holland was one of the mutes," I said. "For the life of me I can't see why anyone wanted him dead."

"Interesting," Kaz said. "That is something to think about."

"Excuse me, gentlemen," Dr. Hughes said from the doorway, another white coated doctor and a nurse behind him. "Baron, it is time for your examination."

"My daily torture," Kaz said, returning to his bed.

"Let me know how the book turns out," I said, as I walked past Hughes and gave him a friendly nod of greeting.

He ignored me, as if we hadn't both viewed a dead man a couple of days ago.

Doctors can get jaded, I guess, just like cops. Maybe he didn't want to think about Holland's death.

Or what I might have seen.

CHAPTER EIGHT

I HADN'T BEEN able to ask Kaz about Sweden before Dr. Hughes had come in. In Paris I'd told him what the German officer had said before he died.

"Geh zu den Schweden."

Go to the Swedes, Kaz had translated. But now I couldn't remember what had happened next. Those last moments in Paris were a blur of exhaustion and violence. The next thing I remember was waking up in an ambulance on my way to this place.

Big Mike had been there, I suddenly recalled. Where was he now? Where was Colonel Harding?

I had no idea. Maybe Kaz had told me when I was out of it. I'd ask him later.

I went out the side door. I needed fresh air. And a plan to get to the Saint Albans patient files.

Back to the pathway. It was a crisp, blue-sky day with an edge of autumn chill in the air. Just what I needed. I turned up the collar on my field jacket, took a couple of deep lungfuls, and trudged on, going through a mental list of the problems I needed to solve.

Where were Big Mike and Sam Harding? Staff Sergeant Mike Miecznikowski was part of the SHAEF Office of Special Investigations. The biggest part, if you went by size. A good six feet of Detroit cop, with the broadest shoulders in the US Army. If Kaz was the brains of our small outfit, Big Mike was the brawn. And heart, now that I thought about it. I knew he'd been here, at least when the ambulance brought me. And he talked with Sergeant Jenkins. Might be worth checking with him, although he hadn't been exactly friendly.

Colonel Samuel Harding was our boss. West Pointer, regular army, but still not a bad sort. He had several jobs at SHAEF in addition to riding herd on us. He was an intelligence liaison with Resistance groups and governments in exile, which meant that he and Big Mike were as likely to be at the front in France as they were to be in London.

I had no way to contact them. Unless I could get to a telephone. Maybe tonight, if I could locate which office held the patient files. If I could get an open line to SHAEF, I might be able to get a message to them.

Now all I had to do was figure out how to break into a secure office. The good news was that I was already inside the facility. The Home Guard patrolled the fence, but I'd only seen them inside the building on rare occasions. There had to be a mess area for them in one of the smaller buildings, since I never saw them at meals.

It made sense. The less contact they had with patients, the better.

All right. I turned around. Time to reconnoiter. I hadn't paid a lot of attention to the layout inside the building. I'd been more interested in scouting out escape routes through the woods. My north wing digs were on the second floor. I'd taken the staircase down and went direct to Robinson, not paying any attention to the other offices. The third floor was locked. I didn't even want to think about the poor souls up there. There was a fourth floor, but that was terra incognita.

Time to focus. I walked in the main entrance, not even glancing at where Holland had hit the ground. No distracting thoughts. Inside, I crossed the foyer and headed straight down the hall to Robinson's office. The door was shut, which I knew meant he was out or in a session. A shuffling gait took me closer, my boots quiet on the polished floor. I didn't hear voices. I laid my hand on the knob and tested it. Shut tight. It didn't look like a tough lock to pick, but I didn't have anything in the way of tools, penknives not being encouraged in the north wing.

"Are you looking for Dr. Robinson?" A woman's voice shocked me, and I whipped my hand off the doorknob like it was red hot. I turned to face her, hoping not to look too guilty. She clutched a stack of files and looked at me with a combination of helpfulness and pity, in the right proportions given my status here.

"Yes. I didn't have an appointment, but I wanted to speak with him for a minute," I said, moving away from the door. "I didn't know if it was all right to knock."

"It doesn't matter, he's up on the third floor. Do you want to leave a message?"

"Sure, that'd be great, thank you," I said.

"Come along then," she said, heading toward the foyer. She was in her thirties, with pulled-back dark hair, a pencil stuck behind her ear, and an expression of intense curiosity.

"My name's Boyle," I said.

"I know. I've seen you going to your appointments. We don't have that many Yanks here, so you stand out. Sorry, but I can't tell you my name. I don't mean to be rude, but it's not encouraged."

"I understand," I said, as I followed her into a large office. There were two desks and a wall filled with file cabinets. Beautiful four-drawer filing cabinets. "Security."

"Always," she said, plopping the stack of folders down on her desk, right next to a telephone. She handed me a pad and pencil.

"I hear that Major Snow is strict about rules and regulations," I said, while I wrote out a brief note to Robinson, telling him how much better I felt and thanking him for his help.

"Do you now?"

"Sorry," I said, folding the note and handing it to her. "Just making conversation."

"It's not encouraged," she said, the hint of a smile playing across her face. British humor and understatement, all rolled into one.

"Sorry I'm late, Clarissa," another woman said, scurrying into the room and throwing herself into a chair behind the other desk. "The line in the dining hall was beastly long."

"Security breach," I whispered. I gave Clarissa a wink and walked out, chancing a sideways glance at the two tall windows filling the room with light. The latches would be within reach, barely. The window frames were ancient, decorated with peeling paint and spiderwebs. They looked like they hadn't been opened in decades. But they did look out on the entrance. Did Clarissa and her office mate hear the body hit? Look up and scream in horror? Maybe see someone running away? I'd have to come back and poke around. Right now, I had to find an easier way in.

I stood in the foyer, looking down the hallways that radiated in three directions. I was about to explore, preparing a cover story about forgetting where Robinson's office was. A lost, harebrained patient wouldn't seem out of place. Then I spotted the figure of a limping man through the glass window in the main door. Major Basil Snow himself, coming up the front walk. I moved quickly, making it to the door before he did. I opened the door and held it for him, standing aside on the front step.

"Major Snow," I said, giving him a salute.

He returned it, then halted, an irritated look on his face. "We don't bother with that here. Not with patients. No rank, only last names. Surely you understand that by now?" He hesitated, and I could tell he was searching for my name.

"Boyle, sir. Sorry, force of habit. It's not easy setting aside what the army drummed into my head."

"Quite all right," Snow said. He had dark eyes set above pudgy cheeks, his face finished off with a heavy mustache that hid his upper lip and seemed to have designs on the lower. "Boyle? You were the fellow here the other day, busying yourself with the poor chap who ended it all."

"Yes. Again, force of habit. I was a policeman back in the States."

"You seem to be a man of steady habits, Boyle. How are you getting on here?"

"I'm feeling much better, Major. I did the Sleeping Beauty routine with Dr. Robinson."

"Sleeping Beauty? Oh, his sleep cure, you mean," Snow said, offering up a chuckle to show he took my Yank patter in stride. "It seems to work well. Usually. What kind of police work did you do, Boyle?"

"Detective. Homicide, mostly." I didn't bother mentioning I'd made the grade right after Pearl Harbor, which didn't leave much time to actually work the job. And that I'd passed the written test with a bit of assistance. Well, a lot, maybe. Details. He wasn't from Boston, so he wouldn't understand.

"Really? Do you have a few minutes to spare, Boyle? I'd like to hear your opinion of what you saw," Snow said.

"Sure," I said. "Glad to help." Plus, my arm was getting sore holding that door for him. I followed Snow to his office. He took the right hallway off the foyer and got out his keys to open a door kitty-corner from the entrance to the clock tower. No wonder he was Johnny-on-the-spot.

"I shouldn't be doing this, Boyle," Snow said as he gestured toward a chair, then took his seat behind the desk. It was a long, narrow room. Bookshelves filled with medical texts that hadn't been dusted in decades took up one wall. Behind him, French doors led to a garden thick with weeds and a few brave flowers that arched their stems toward the sunlight. "I don't want to tax you during your recovery, even though you seem a damn sight better than you did a few days ago."

"I understand, Major. I won't tell Dr. Robinson."

"Very good, Boyle. You obviously have a sharp mind. Wouldn't do for me to interfere with the medical treatment here. I'm the security man, that's all. But you can see how Holland's death would be a concern."

"I can, Major. If you had any reason to think it was not suicide or an accident. Do you?"

"I have a reputation for following regulations and being rather strict about it," Snow said. "Probably deservedly so. It's my job to enforce the rules and keep everyone here safe from the outside world until they are ready to leave. Not a job for the kindhearted, I must say. But here I am, bending, if not outright breaking, my own rules by asking you, a patient, for help. Does that answer your question?"

"Yes and no," I said. "Which leaves you a lot of room for maneuver and me very little." I watched his eyes as he held me steady in his gaze. Narrow and pinched, they were the last thing you noticed about his face after taking in the almost comical mustache.

"See, I knew you were a smart chap. That's it exactly. I can't have word get out that I'm playing favorites with the patients. But perhaps I can help move things along once Robinson decides you are fit enough. You do seem well, Boyle. Are you? Or are you about to go stark raving mad on me?"

"I feel surprisingly better, Major. But tell me, what exactly do you want me to do?"

"Oh, nothing drastic. And certainly nothing in an official capacity, mind you," Snow said, wagging his finger at me. "Ask around, see what people think. You can start with Sinclair. I don't know if he and Holland were close, but I did see them walking together on occasion. Use your investigative skills and let me know if you think anything warrants opening up an official case."

"You must have some reason to think it wasn't suicide," I said.

"Let's say I appreciate caution and skepticism," Snow said, his fingers steepled as he leaned back and studied me. "Did you notice anything untoward when you inspected the body?"

"Not that I recall," I said. "I wasn't exactly firing on all cylinders that day." No reason to let on to my suspicions so soon. We were just getting to know each other.

"Certainly," Snow said, sitting up straight and slapping his hands on the desk. Interview concluded.

"Okay. But answer one question," I said as I stood. Snow nodded his assent. "How many keys are there to the clock tower door?"

"I have one, and there's another in the clerk's office in the foyer. They have a whole collection of keys," Snow said. "But there could be others. We had a devil of a time sorting things out when we moved in here. We found keys hidden away in drawers and filing cabinets. No telling how many are still floating around. Some doors were never unlocked, but there are more rooms than we'll ever need. God willing."

"Thanks. Anything else you can tell me?"

"You said one question, Boyle. That is all."

I got the message and beat feet. I walked past the clerk's office and saw Clarissa and her pal working away, the furious clack of typewriter keys following me as I turned and headed for the door to the clock tower. It was locked. But now I knew that Clarissa's office was unattended on occasion and a key was stashed in there. Locked in a drawer, or out in the open? I'd have to find out.

Right now, I needed another walk. I needed to think about Snow and why he'd recruited me. And if he'd grease the skids if I came up with anything.

But what if it was murder, or even an accident? That might not put the head of security in the best light. Which might put me in a dark hole somewhere with no light at all.

CHAPTER NINE

KAZ WANTED ME to investigate this murder. Now Snow did too. By the end of my walk, I had to admit Holland's death bothered me. If he did jump, what demons led him to take that leap? If he was pushed, what did the killer have to gain? Why was a dead Holland necessary to the murderer? The guy was a mute, but perhaps that had been about to change? Who would be privy to that knowledge, and who would be frightened by it?

I needed more information, and that's why I engaged in a little reconnaissance on my way back inside. There was plenty of dope in the clerical office files, but the door would most likely be locked at night. I moved down the central hallway, checking doorknobs. Locked, locked, locked.

Until I got to the door opposite Dr. Robinson's office. As I closed my hand on the knob and turned it slightly, I felt it move. The door looked like it once had a window, maybe frosted glass by the small pieces still embedded in the frame. Bare wood covered the opening. I thought about knocking, but blundering in seemed the better choice.

I opened the door. It was a wide room, with two sets of French doors overlooking a patio with weeds growing between the paving stones. At a desk between them sat Major Cuthbert Hughes, the head medical honcho, scribbling away.

"Oh, sorry," I said, doing a good imitation of a double take. "I thought this was Dr. Robinson's office. Guess I got turned around."

"Across the hall," he snapped, his pen poised on paper and his eyes riveted on me.

"Right," I said. "I don't mean to bother you, Dr. Hughes—"

"Then don't," he said, making a twirling motion with his finger, like I should do-si-do my way out pronto.

"I wanted to ask him about my pal, Baron Kazimierz," I added quickly, counting on the British affinity for titles to distract him from calling the guards.

"Ah, yes. The baron. Charming fellow. Unusual for a Pole."

"The charm or the title?" I asked, taking a tentative step into the room, leaving the door open for a quick exit.

"The title, of course," Hughes said. "You're Boyle, aren't you? The fellow who thought he was a policeman when Holland tumbled from the tower?" He gave a sharp laugh as he tossed his pen onto the papers. I figured he'd indulge me for a minute or so.

"Force of habit," I said. "I was a police detective before the war. When I saw all of you tromping over the crime scene, it just came out."

"Crime? Well, yes, suicide is a crime," Hughes said, his eyes narrowing as he studied me. "It was suicide, don't you think?"

Suddenly everyone wanted my opinion on the subject.

"I wouldn't know," I said. "I never met Holland, so I don't know why anyone would want him dead. What do you think? I do have a cop's curiosity, I have to admit."

"I thought you wanted to know about the baron?" Hughes said, picking up his pen and smiling. The guy was enjoying this.

"Listen, Doc, there's not a lot to occupy my mind here, now that I've had a good stretch of sleep and I'm not hallucinating. It wasn't fun, but it did tend to keep my mind—what there was of it—occupied. So, forgive the intrusion," I said, finally executing that do-si-do.

"Come back, Boyle," Hughes said, waving in the general direction of a chair. "Have a seat. You do seem to have taken to Robinson's sleep cure. Myself, I prefer to cut into a problem, fix it, and then stitch it up.

The mind is an enigma, and I don't pretend to believe in all that Freudian mumbo jumbo. Still, in your case, Robinson has done well."

"Not so much with Holland?" I asked, settling into the visitor's seat.

"I imagine it's difficult to work with a patient who cannot communicate," Hughes said. "Or will not. Some of the mutes may simply be hiding something. Cowardice, perhaps."

"It would be a way of dealing with a secret too terrible to tell," I said. "What brought Holland here? I assume there's no confidentiality when it comes to dead patients."

"That is not the issue, Boyle. It's the Official Secrets Act. Hush-hush from on high. But I can say that some cases are simply presented to us with little background, other than that the poor soul was recently brought back from an experience in occupied Europe."

"A poor soul such as Holland?"

Hughes shrugged and spread out his hands. Yes, then.

"As for the baron," Hughes said, "I understand you were with him when the French doctor rendered his diagnosis."

"Yes. Mitral stenosis, I think it was."

"Correct. Baron Kazimierz listed you as next of kin in the absence of any living family. Were you aware of that, Boyle?" Hughes leaned back, hands folded across his chest. He seemed to enjoy dangling bits of information, just enough to keep my attention focused on him. But he was the chief surgeon in this joint, and that meant he probably thought the world revolved around him. I didn't mind playing along, especially if there might be a payoff.

"No, but I'm not surprised. His family didn't survive the Nazi occupation, and we've grown close," I said. Kaz probably saw no reason to list Angelika as a contact, especially while he was a guest at Saint Albans. The SOE might be suspicious of anyone who had a relative in Nazi-occupied Europe. Or possibly held by the Germans, as Diana was. It would be a tempting double-agent setup. Feed the Krauts information in exchange for leniency or even freedom.

Hmmm.

"Well, I suppose he would allow this much to be said," Hughes went on. I realized he'd been talking while I mulled over the need to keep silent about Angelika and Diana. Especially Diana, who I knew was already in Gestapo custody.

"Yes, I'm sure," I said, trying to stay focused. All I could do was think about Diana and worry if I'd already said too much when I was off the deep end.

"There is little to be done, I'm afraid," Hughes said. "With the narrowing of the mitral valve, blood cannot flow properly into the main chamber of the heart. This abnormality produces the symptoms the baron exhibited in Paris, no doubt brought on by the strenuous nature of whatever it was you were doing there." He waved one hand leisurely, as if encompassing the enormity of the fighting and death we had witnessed. Casually, as if it was of little interest.

I decided I didn't like this guy. But I needed his good graces.

"Is it going to kill him?" I asked.

"Mitral stenosis can have serious complications," Hughes said. "If he avoids stress on his system, further damage to his heart may not occur. He will most likely continue to have fatigue and shortness of breath, but there is a chance he could live a long life. However, not one filled with exertion and excitement."

"There's nothing you can do? I thought a chief surgeon would have a few ideas. You can't fix it?" I tried to look incredulous, like I thought he was a god. Which is how a lot of surgeons thought of themselves. But a bit of sarcasm might have crept in, since he pursed his lips in silence before he finally answered.

"We do not operate on the heart. It is far too delicate to be handled. It would do more harm than good, of that I am certain," Hughes said.

"Kaz—the baron—can still be of use in the war effort," I said. "When I first met him, he was working at headquarters translating documents. He could manage that, couldn't he? It's his field of study."

"Perhaps so, but that is not for us to decide. Fit for service or unfit for service, that is what we are mandated to decide. I have no interest in telling the government how to employ our patients. I have paperwork enough," Hughes said.

I rose.

"When it comes to Baron Kazimierz, the British government

should be glad to have his services, even if it's at a desk. Please give that some thought, Dr. Hughes. A recommendation from you would carry a lot of weight. Kaz would be in your debt," I said, my eyes straying to the latches on the French doors behind Hughes.

"I appreciate your concern, Boyle, but I have no need for indebtedness from a Pole, even one of slight nobility. England is full of displaced and penniless foreigners," he said, picking up his pen and signaling we were done. "Please ask Miss Williamson to come in, will you?"

"Sure," I said, taking in the rods locking the French doors tight. "Well, if you want to follow up on the baron after he's released, drop by the Dorchester the next time you're in London. He keeps a suite there. Permanently."

"Really?" The pen never made it to paper.

"Yeah. Has since I met him in '42. Nice place. Ask any of the staff when you visit, they'll bring you right up to Kaz. They're tremendously loyal. The baron's a generous guy, you know. Who's Miss Williamson, anyway?"

"Perhaps I will, Boyle, perhaps I will," Hughes said, the wheels of greed turning. A quick scribbled line in exchange for the largess of a titled noble? Why not? I saw his eyes wander as he did his calculations, then focus as he remembered my question. "Oh, the young lady in the clerical office, by the main entrance. I need her for dictation."

"Okay, I'll tell her," I said, mustering a smile Hughes didn't deserve.

"And Boyle, if you hear anything untoward about Holland's death, do tell me. We can't have any improprieties here, you understand?"

I nodded my understanding. As if a dead agent wasn't impropriety enough.

CHAPTER TEN

I KNOCKED ON the open door to the clerical office. Clarissa was at the rear of the room, a stack of folders in one hand and file drawers open to receive them.

"If you're Miss Williamson, Dr. Hughes would like you in his office for dictation," I said, taking a step into the room.

"Does he now?" Clarissa said, finishing her filing and carefully locking the drawers. She was a stickler for security, but she also had a subtle streak of sarcasm, which I liked. She took her time walking to her desk and gathering up a notepad and pencil. The keys to the filing cabinet went into her top drawer, which she locked with a key tied around her wrist. "And what were you talking to the chief surgeon about?"

"We have a lot in common," I said, holding the door open for her and glancing at the window looking out over the front lawn. "We both saw Holland fall from the tower the other day. You must have seen it too. You've got a perfect view."

"I was getting tea, thank goodness," Clarissa said. "Poor man."

"Did you know him at all?" I asked, blocking her way enough to slow her down.

"It's not encouraged," she said, smiling at what now had become our private joke. "He seemed sad. Some of the mutes are simply quiet. Holland was deeply depressed, I think. Which may explain what happened. Now, please move aside. Dr. Hughes doesn't like to be kept waiting."

"Sorry," I said, moving out of the way and closing the door behind her. "People tell me I talk too much."

"I'm surprised you let them get a word in edgewise," Clarissa said, hustling off down the hall. She looked back and smiled, perhaps to let me know she was joking. Or to make sure she saw me exit the main doors.

Which I did, then turned around after a few steps. I listened for the echo of a door shutting and hoped Hughes hadn't changed his mind, or that Clarissa's office mate wouldn't show up in the next minute or two.

I opened the office door and then jumped up on the windowsill set deep into the foot-thick wall. I tried to turn the latch, which was caked with rust and dried flaking paint. It didn't move. I tried again.

Nothing.

I hit the latch with the heel of my palm, and the whole window shuddered under the impact. This was making more of a racket than I'd counted on, and I listened for the sound of hurried footsteps. But the hallway was silent. I pushed against the latch again, trying to think how I could talk my way out of this one if somebody walked in or spotted me from outside. I was basically spread-eagled against the tall window, perfectly framed, an obvious candidate for a padded cell.

The latch gave way. Grit and grainy rust rained down on the sill, covering my shoes. I wanted to test the window, but it was so worn and warped I couldn't chance it getting stuck partway open. I hopped down, wiped away the debris, and left quickly on light feet, closing the door quietly behind me.

I had my way in.

And once in, it was a simple matter to pop the lock on Clarissa's desk. It was a typical security error. Lock the files, then store the key in an easy-to-pick locked drawer. To be fair, she'd probably never considered anyone gaining access through the window.

I hustled back outside. I stood on the steps and took a deep breath, the cool mid-afternoon air sharp at the back of my throat.

I needed one more thing before I could relax and wait for midnight darkness. I strolled around the back of the north wing, leaving the walkway and weaving between the smaller buildings, most of them locked tight. Storehouses and work sheds, to judge by the tire tracks in the soft earth and lines of sawdust outside a carpenter's shack.

Then I found it. A low stone building, a single story with light glowing through the windows. Just the place where I might find what I needed, the canteen for the Home Guard guys. Two soldiers stood by the door, smoking cigarettes and eyeing me with suspicion.

"Hey fellas," I said, trying to sound upbeat and completely sane at the same time. "Is Sergeant Jenkins around?"

"Yeah, he's inside," one of them said. "But the patients don't usually come around here. Never, really. You better head back, mate." He sounded almost friendly, but the kind of friendly that could turn to mean if he didn't get his way. Which was to have me gone.

"I know," I said. "But they're cutting me loose tomorrow, and I wanted to apologize to Sarge. We had a misunderstanding. Mostly due to me being bonkers at the time."

"Going home? Good for you, then." He still didn't move away from the door.

"Well, not home. Back to the war. I'm not supposed to say anything else about it. You know how it goes," I said. I figured they'd take me seriously if they thought I'd been given a clean bill of health, and I was about to have a return engagement with the shooting war.

"Best behavior, mind you," he said, stepping aside and opening the door. "Sarge'll give me what for if there's anything less."

I stepped inside and a half dozen heads turned in my direction. It was like walking into a neighborhood tavern in a strange town. A banked coal fire in a small stove gave off a warm glow, perfect for the Home Guards taking a break from making their rounds in all sorts of weather. A few rough wooden tables and a counter with a tea kettle, some mugs, and various items of gear were about it as far as furniture went. But it was cozy, even with the rifles stacked near the door.

"Boyle," Sergeant Jenkins said. He had the seat of honor, close to the stove. But his greeting was nowhere near as warm as his feet must have been, stretched out to within inches of the coals. "What do you want?"

"I wanted to say I'm sorry, Sergeant. When we last spoke, my head wasn't screwed on straight. I said some crazy stuff, and I wanted to set the record straight before I get released."

"Well, I suppose I've heard worse apologies," Jenkins said. He rose and extended his hand. "You feeling yourself then?"

"More every day," I said as we shook. He invited me to sit. I joined him, the rest of the men relaxing as their sergeant did. I let the warmth wash over me as the murmurs of conversation rose once again.

"I haven't seen you about," Jenkins said. "You've been mad for walking. What happened?"

"The sleep cure," I said. "Doc Robinson's specialty. Forty hours solid."

"Now that's a nap," Jenkins said, with a friendly laugh. "Did the trick, did it?"

"Snapped me out of it," I said. "It was well-timed, too. Seeing Holland go off that tower was a shock. I thought I was seeing things, you know?"

"I wasn't much surprised," Jenkins said, nodding his head at the memory. "He was a lonely man. Some like being silent, it suits them. Holland wore his silence like a curse."

"He never spoke?"

"Not that any of us ever heard," Jenkins said. "Didn't much go for company either. Some of them mutes sit together, like they know there'll be no conversation demanded of them. But Holland steered clear of most everyone. He did sit with a young lass now and then. A mute like himself. As I said, not surprised. But a terrible thing, still."

"He kept mostly to himself, but did anyone else approach him? Give him any trouble?" I asked, rubbing my hands in front of the warm stove, trying not to sound too nosy.

"Why?" Jenkins asked, cocking an eye at me. Friendly as we were, I was still a patient and he was a guard.

"I wondered what led him to make that decision," I said. "I was a policeman before the war. I saw plenty of jumpers back in Boston, and even talked a guy down once."

"How'd you manage that?" Jenkins said.

"I told him I couldn't imagine the kind of pain that got him out on that bridge. I asked him to tell me about it. We got to talking, and finally he decided he didn't want to die. At least not right then. I guess I've been curious ever since. What can make a guy take that leap?"

"For me, I'm glad I have no idea," Jenkins said. "I won't ask why you're here, Boyle, but I'd wager some of these people have seen things beyond imagining. The Nazis are a cruel breed, but you know that much, I'm sure."

"He may have seen horrors, you're right," I said, pausing for a moment in silent testimony. "You didn't notice anyone having an argument with him, or following him around?"

"Can't say as I did. You lads ever see anyone pestering poor Holland?" Jenkins shrugged as the younger men shook their heads and confirmed Holland was usually alone. "Sorry, Boyle, but you'll just have to wonder. Now, we need to get back out on patrol."

Jenkins stood and pushed his chair back. The other men gathered their gear and made for the door. Each one grabbed a flashlight from the counter. Torch, the Brits called it.

"Thanks for your time, Sergeant," I said, moving slowly between the chairs as I followed the crowd, Jenkins on my heels. I eyed the torches being scooped up, while the smaller blackout lanterns were left behind. Small rectangular cases with a metal handle, they projected light in the red spectrum downward, enough to see where you were going but not enough to be visible from the air.

"What's with the torches, Sarge?" I asked as we passed the counter. "You don't use them in the blackout, do you?"

"You *have* been away," Jenkins said as he reached in front of me to grab a torch. "New regulations now that Jerry's not sending many bombers our way. Buzz bombs, yes, but we haven't seen bombers in weeks. It's a dimout nowadays. Light the brightness of a full moon is allowed."

"Must make life easier," I said, following him out as I surreptitiously stuffed a blackout lantern into the pocket of my field jacket.

"That it does, Boyle. Good luck to you, lad."

I waved as we went off in different directions. Things had definitely gotten easier for me. The files would be simple to read in the faint red light. No bright lights for someone to spot from outside the building, and nothing to ruin my night vision. Life was as good as it got in the loony bin.

I felt the early evening chill as I made my way to the dining room, shivering as I stuffed my hands into my pockets, grasping the metal lantern. I had a decent plan to get in and read the files. But still, nothing felt right. So far, there was not a thing anyone had said about Holland that hinted at a motive. Or even a relationship with a single person at Saint Albans.

Except for Doc Robinson, and he wasn't talking. From what I'd learned, Holland was likely to have been as uncommunicative with him in his sessions as he was the rest of the time. Maybe the files would tell the real story.

Maybe not. After all, the SOE and the OSS were not known for their fidelity to the truth.

CHAPTER ELEVEN

I STASHED THE blackout light in my room and headed to the dining hall for some chow. The place was emptying out, but I spotted a few familiar faces. Miller, the OSS guy, sat with two silent young women who ignored him as best they could. One of them, a painfully thin waif with her dark hair hacked short, looked like she was ready to ignore the whole world. Her friend, fuller of face with dark unkempt curls shading her eyes, tugged at her sleeves, trying to hide the bandages at her wrists.

Miller cackled and drew his finger across his throat, the punchline to whatever macabre story he was telling. Neither of the women laughed. The thin woman stood, her chair kicked back, brandishing a knife in her hand. A butter knife, but her grip was so intense I was sure she could plunge it into the soft skin of Miller's neck, right where he'd traced the deadly line, her own bandaged wrist revealed in the swift movement.

Instead, she threw it onto Miller's plate, splattering the remains of his meal across his chest. I thought about going over. I caught her eye, half-hidden behind the curls, and gave a nod. She didn't need my approval, but I wanted her to know—what? That I'd back her up? Cheer if she took a fork to his eyeball?

No. I wanted her to know that I knew what it was like where she'd been. And that Miller was an idiot.

She nodded back and she guided her friend away from the table while Miller sputtered, dabbing at his khaki shirt. I got a plate of sausages and potatoes, a cup of tea, and took a seat by myself. Miller saw me and made his way over.

"Turn around," I said, giving him nothing but a glance as I worked at the sausage, wondering what the hell it contained. "I'm in no mood for your bullshit. I'd tell you to leave those women alone, but you wouldn't listen, and Shirley Temple will probably kill you in your sleep anyway."

"Her? She's crazy. Couldn't even manage to kill herself. Slit her wrists in the wrong direction. You have to cut along the veins, not across them," Miller said, flashing a smile straight out of the funhouse.

I pushed back from the table and walked toward him. I moved a couple of chairs, which scraped across the floor, the harsh noise echoing against the wood-paneled walls. I felt the rage build from my gut and coil in my clenched fists.

I stopped a foot short of Miller. He backed away.

"I told you to turn around," I whispered, my hands trembling. He backed away, grasping at chairs as he scuttled off, finally turning around as he muttered to himself.

"Watch out for that one, young man. He is clearly insane." It was Sinclair, his hands cupped around a mug of tea, a couple of tables away.

"He's in the right place for it," I said, heading back to my seat.

"Some of us are confused. And tired, very tired. But he has the eye of a maniac. You look half-mad yourself. But then all Yanks are mad, so it's hard for me to sort them properly."

"Mind if I join you, Sinclair?" I wasn't in the mood, but he seemed semi-coherent, and I didn't want to be rude to an older gent.

"I do. Don't like company. But pay me no mind, lad, I'm an old wheezer and dodger, not worth listening to. Might get you and me in more trouble, see?"

I didn't, but I simply nodded and went back to my table. I rubbed my eyes, feeling my temples throb and my heart pound like a bass drum in a marching band. My fork clattered against the plate as I tried to spear a bit of sausage.

The shakes. They were back. I switched the fork to my left hand and kept my right in my lap. I managed a few bites, but I'd lost what appetite I'd come in with. My hand trembled even as my heart rate eased up. I took a deep breath and tried to calm myself.

It didn't work. I guess forty hours of shut-eye wasn't enough to fix whatever was wrong with me. I'd been hit with a sudden flash of anger, and although Miller deserved a punch or two, my guess was it wasn't all about him.

I'd lost control, and if I wanted to get out of here, I needed Robinson and the other honchos to think I was ready to be cut loose. So I ate, because that's what normal people do. I drank the tea, with a lot of sugar, because that's what completely sane Yanks do in England.

Then I took the stairs to my room to rest before breaking into the hospital file room. Because that's not crazy at all.

I STRETCHED OUT on my bed to wait for nightfall. I thought about who might have been on that roof with Holland. Going by pure meanness, Miller was a good choice. He'd likely take a life out of sheer boredom. Even Sinclair, as slow-moving as he was, could tip a body over that wall easily enough. But there were too many possibilities to consider. It could have been a guard or an orderly, angered by Holland over some disobedience. Another patient who held a grudge, perhaps someone who knew him in the field. I knew I needed to find a clue in those files if I wanted to report back to Snow and prove I was compos mentis.

I awoke with a start. It was pitch black. I blinked my eyes until the luminous dial of my watch came into focus. Three in the morning.

Damn. I was lucky I hadn't slept until dawn. After yesterday's deep sleep, I didn't think I'd be tired. I'd been wrong. I had to stop myself from falling back onto my pillow as I rolled out of bed and checked the view outside my window.

I waited for my eyes to adjust to the darkness. The main building was to my left. I could see faint glimmers of light on the third floor.

Two rooms where the blackout curtains weren't pulled down fully. Dimout curtains, I guess they were now called. Across the way, I made out a few subdued lights in the south wing, one on each floor, probably nurses and orderlies on duty.

Here in the north wing, it wasn't exactly a prison, but the rear stairwell was locked at night. At the end of the corridor, at the top of the staircase that led down to the administrative wing, a guard sat at a small desk. Depending on who had the duty, he read, did a crossword puzzle, or leaned back and took a nap. It wasn't exactly tight security, but anyone would have had a hard time sneaking by him even if he was dozing.

Which was why I wasn't going out by the staircase. I knotted my two sheets together and tied one end to the iron bedstead. I dragged the bed to the window, wincing as the metal scraped across the floor. I pulled hard on the knot, testing it before I tossed the sheets out the window. It held. Good news.

The bad news came as I looked down. The sheets didn't reach the ground. Not even close. I didn't mind a bit of a drop, but I couldn't risk the noise I'd make hitting the ground. I hauled in my makeshift rope and added my spare wool trousers. That gave me the length I needed.

Out went the sheets again. Telling myself that the second story wasn't all that high, I grasped the white sheet and went out the window, digging my boots into the crevices between the sandstone blocks where I could.

I heard the bed shift and felt a sudden drop of a few inches. Which seemed like ten yards as I hung on in the darkness, working not to send my boot flying into the first-floor window below me. I prayed that my weight wouldn't flip the bed and send it crashing against the wall. Even if the guard was sawing some serious logs, that would get his attention.

I took a deep breath and pushed off from the wall, going down hand over hand. I dropped past the window, felt the wool of my trousers, and then my feet hit solid ground. I let go and rolled away, searching the shadows for any sign of movement.

Nothing. No running guards, no shouts of alarm. First part of the plan accomplished, no sweat.

Then I turned around.

Not that I'd had much choice, but using white sheets for my escape hadn't been the best idea. Even with only a faint glimmer of moonlight, they stood out like bright beacons against the sooty sandstone, an arrow pointing right at my window.

Okay, so maybe my brain wasn't working perfectly yet. I still had a good chance at this if I hustled. It was too early for anyone to be awake and gazing out their window, and late enough that the guards on duty were simply going through the motions, not conducting a full-scale search of the grounds.

I hoped.

I ran low, keeping an even pace to avoid any sudden moves that might draw the eye of a semi-alert sentry. As I rounded the rear of the north wing, I spotted another room with a thin line of light showing from the bottom of a blackout curtain. It hadn't been lowered all the way, leaving an inch or so for the light to seep out. Someone on duty, or had they forgotten to turn off the lamp?

I crawled under the window, resisting the temptation to peek inside. It would be good to know who was up, but not at the cost of someone spotting the whites of my eyes and sounding the alarm.

I made it to the corner of the north wing, flattening myself against the stonework as I watched and listened for any sign of movement. I stuck my head out and scanned the front of the main building. Quiet.

What were the chances of a guard being posted at the main entrance? Fine time to think about that possibility. I kept my eyes on the woods and the path on the other side of the fence. A patrol could come along at any time, but I ought to be able to catch a glimpse of their flashlights, even if they kept them dimmed.

Nothing. No light, no sound, no telltale whiff of tobacco from a guard sneaking a smoke. Time to move.

I made my way to the main entrance. No lights were on along the front, so my luck was holding. No guard stood by the door. I darted to the file-room window and crouched beneath it, doing one last check, which was made more difficult by the sound of my heart pounding loudly in my chest.

I hoisted myself onto the narrow ledge, balancing on my toes as I grasped either side of the window frame. I had maybe three inches of stonework to stand on and less than that around the edges to hang on to. If I had a third arm to push up and open the window, it'd be a cinch.

Clinging to the gritty sandstone with my left hand, I used my right to push on the window. It didn't budge. One foot slipped, and I had to grab hold with both hands again as I regained my toehold. I tried again once I'd steadied myself. This time I was ready to apply more pressure, and I grunted as I worked to force the window open.

I heard voices. How loud had I been? I stopped forcing the window and clung to the sides of the frame, waiting to get a sense of where the chatter was coming from. The door at the main entrance opened. Flashlight beams played across the walkway behind me as the voices hit the night air and became distinct.

"No sign of Sarge."

"Unless he's already been by looking for us."

"Don't worry so much. That's one less circuit to make. And cut your torch, no reason to let him spot us."

The two Home Guards walked behind me, still chatting about their non-com and oblivious to the GI clutching the wall for dear life not five yards away. God bless goldbricks everywhere. If they stayed on the walkway, there was a good chance they wouldn't spot the hanging sheets. They'd have to get closer for that, and these guys didn't seem the type to go the extra mile.

I gave the window another shove. It moved this time, the warped wooden frame groaning. If those two guards had been in the foyer doing their Sad Sack routine for a few minutes longer, they would've heard the racket.

One more push and I had enough clearance to slither in, push aside the blackout curtain, and close the window behind me. I dropped to the floor and let my breathing calm down as the silence settled in around me.

Silence in a big old building is noisy. Odd and faint sounds came to my ears. The creak of wood expanding. The metallic ping of heating ducts contracting. The scritch-scratch of mice making themselves at home in the walls.

A single harsh sound. Something being dropped? Someone was awake, perhaps in one of the lighted rooms, or on patrol. It was time to move. I pulled the blackout lantern from my jacket and went to Clarissa's desk. Using a letter opener, I jimmied her desk drawer and grabbed the filing-cabinet keys.

In the gloomy night, the wall of files was even more daunting. I held up the lantern and looked for the *H* section. Then I saw the cabinets were divided by years. Good, that made it easier. I moved down to 1944 and found the *G-L* cabinet, then the right key, and there it was.

Holland, Thomas. I sat on the floor and opened the thick folder, letting the blackout light cast its reddish glow across the page. Admitted 21 May 1944. They hadn't updated his file. According to the SOE bureaucrats, he was still alive.

A photograph was clipped to the inside of the file. Thomas Holland as I'd never seen him. Youthful. Smiling and staring at someone off camera, a drink in one hand, outdoors on a bright spring day. On the back *Sorbonne 1938* was scrawled in a flowing hand. Another photo showed him posed with a friend, their arms around each other's shoulders and broad grins lighting their faces. *Georg, Paris*. A lifetime ago.

Flipping through his personnel file, I saw that he'd studied music at the Sorbonne in Paris. That probably meant his French was excellent. He was brought into SOE in 1941 and underwent the usual rounds of training. Wireless, explosives, weapons, and hand-to-hand combat. High scores all around, including languages. He was graded as fluent in French and German. A selection board had passed on approving him for operational status. Their report was four typewritten pages and I didn't bother with much of it. I found Holland's personal history much more interesting.

His father, William, was a chemist who'd served in the trenches during the Great War. His mother was a German Jew who'd emigrated with her family in the twenties. She'd converted to the Church of

England before marriage. Greta Mosinger became Gretchen Holland, imparting to Thomas an affinity for the German language and perhaps a personal reason for striking back at the Nazis.

The next photograph was more somber. His false identity photo. Longer hair, a suit jacket much the worse for wear, and a scowl on his face. The perfect Frenchman under the Occupation.

He'd been on one mission in 1943, serving as a courier with the Jockey circuit in the Rhône Valley. His false identity had been that of a teacher recovering from jaundice, which had helped protect him from being picked up by the Germans for slave labor. He'd been called back to England to be part of a new mission earlier this year.

This assignment was with the Stationer circuit west of Paris. Holland's job was to coordinate weapon drops and distribute arms to the Resistance for use in support of D-Day. A big job. So far, everything about Holland was exemplary. I turned the page.

He'd been betrayed. A member of one of the Resistance groups he'd worked with had been turned and revealed the location of an upcoming drop. The debriefing report in the official file was brief, noting that Holland was noncommunicative upon his eventual return to England. Docile, but unresponsive, the report concluded.

Attached to the short report was a longer account by fellow agent Peter Rowden who had been an eyewitness to it all. His debrief was more extensive and gave a full account of what had happened. He also had been part of the Stationer circuit and had been picked up by the Gestapo the day after Holland's capture as he'd tried to board a train and escape. The entire circuit had been blown.

Both men had been imprisoned at 84 Avenue Foch, the most terrifying address in Paris. It was the headquarters of the counterintelligence branch of the SS, used for interrogation and torture prior to execution. The Gestapo had known that Holland possessed important information about arms caches and Resistance groups. Rowden had occupied a cell next to Holland and witnessed him being brought back every day from interrogation. Holland told him that the first sessions began with cigarettes, coffee, and conversation as the Germans tried to convince him to see the wisdom of cooperation.

Holland refused. The interrogations moved on to torture as soon as the sympathetic routine produced no results.

They beat Holland, and each day he came back bloodied and bruised. He told Rowden he would never talk.

Then they moved on to the magneto torture. Two wires, one attached to a finger and the other to the genitals. He came back from those sessions writhing in pain from the burns, telling Rowden he still hadn't talked.

Until the day came when he was brought back and said nothing.

Then the Germans focused on Rowden. What did he know? Where were the arms caches? He could tell they hadn't learned anything from Holland. They finally gave up on Rowden, guessing that he was telling the truth when he claimed not to have the information they wanted. It was true enough, but in his own report he said he would have given away anything to stop the pain.

One day a dozen prisoners were taken from their cells and loaded aboard trucks headed to the train yard for transport to concentration camps. Which meant death. As the small convoy neared the station, the Resistance ambushed the vehicles. Several prisoners were killed, some escaped only to be captured later, but Rowden and Holland made it out alive.

A Lysander flew them to England a week later.

A sigh escaped my lips as I finished the report. Docile, but unresponsive. Now I knew why. Holland never uttered a word. He kept his promise not to talk and somehow found himself marooned in his own silence, unmoored from speech and the possibility of betrayal.

CHAPTER TWELVE

I CLOSED THE file on Thomas Holland, lingering for a moment over that photograph of him from a happier time. A man of tremendous courage, he kept his secrets until the end. Dr. Robinson's notes had been sparse, describing Holland as compliant but nonresponsive and having little chance of a full recovery. An updated notation from two weeks ago mentioned a small improvement, but nothing else before he died.

And there was hardly anyone to mourn him. According to a note appended to the file, Rowden, the other survivor of the Stationer circuit, had died in a V1 rocket attack on London in June. Holland's parents were both dead, his father of a heart attack right before the war and his mother in a bombing raid on Portsmouth during the 1940 Blitz. His only living relative was an uncle, a British Army captain serving overseas on active duty, meaning don't ask where.

Who would remember Thomas Holland? And more to the point, who had a grudge against him? He betrayed no one, went above and beyond what was expected, and seemingly had no enemies except maniacs wearing swastika armbands. Who at Saint Albans wanted him dead?

I'd have time to think about that later. Right now, I needed to check some more files. After I returned Holland's, I glanced at my watch. Twenty after four. I had a solid hour before I had to think about sunrise and folks rubbing the sleep from their eyes.

Next up was Miller.

Frederick Miller. Admitted 22 July 1944.

As with Holland's file, the first photograph was from another place and time. Miller in uniform standing in front of what looked like a barracks, his arms akimbo and a grin lighting his face. The kind of snapshot you'd send home to your folks to show them how great life in the army was.

Miller had volunteered for the OSS and ended up in southern France, as he'd said. More weapon drops to the Resistance. There had been plenty of *Maquis* waiting for arms, and this small army had had a big role in disrupting German reinforcements headed to the D-Day beaches.

It was a dangerous job, according to the OSS officer who evaluated his performance. After D-Day Miller and his group fought with the *Maquis*, ambushing columns on the road and blowing up train tracks.

There was a traitor in their midst, a woman, just as Miller claimed. But it wasn't Miller who uncovered her. According to a fellow OSS agent, it was the leader of the Resistance group, Valentin, who came up with the ruse concerning the explosives.

Miller volunteered to execute her, to forestall any bad blood among the local *Maquis*. Her family was well-known in the area and killing her might fester for years, long after the war was over. So Miller took her into the woods.

He let her go. He fired a shot, then another, into the ground. He'd fired his weapon in battle, but face-to-face with this Frenchwoman, he couldn't do it.

The *Maquis* moved out. Two days later, in a village three kilometers from where Miller had been so merciful, Valentin's entire family was shot in the village square. His wife, two children, an uncle, and his bedridden mother all dead because of the traitor whose life Miller had spared, never imagining she would repay his kindness with retribution.

Miller insisted he had killed her, but the other OSS agents didn't believe him. Neither did Valentin. The mission was abandoned and the team returned to England. Miller began to talk of other killings, fanciful encounters with Germans and Vichy fascists, in which he dispatched them cheerfully and with a great deal of blood.

Delusional, Robinson had written. Paranoid grandiose delusion. Irritable, angry, but capable of nonimpaired functioning at times. Delusions rooted in the guilt he feels at not eliminating the subject. Further treatment required. Convulsive therapy recommended, whatever that was.

Eliminating the subject. So easy to write in a report while safe in a warm office in the heart of England. Shooting a woman in the head while she looks you in the eye, pleading for her life—much more descriptive but frowned upon in army medical reports.

I couldn't look at his photograph as I put away the file. Miller was a good man, trapped within his own fairy tale of ruthlessness and violence. Maybe that made him a potential murderer, but I doubted it. Precisely the opposite. His killings were all in his head.

Angus Sinclair was next on my list. I had to go back to the 1943 files to find him.

Admitted 2 December 1943. Nervous breakdown.

His picture looked like Sinclair now. Maybe a little chubbier around the cheeks, but that was it. He'd been a professor at University of Cambridge with a bunch of degrees and letters after his name, most of which made no sense to me. Kaz would know.

He'd gone to work for the British Admiralty in 1939, employed by the Directorate of Miscellaneous Weapon Development, which was a mouthful of nothing. His file was thin, with lots of stamps proclaiming access denied, restricted, and most secret. Not much to go on.

Robinson's notes indicated nervous exhaustion from overwork and severe stress. He'd given Sinclair the sleep cure when he'd first arrived, which had helped. Sinclair was better able to communicate and function, but he had lost all desire to keep secrets. He'd mention top-secret projects and wonder aloud at the progress his colleagues were making. Complete loss of inhibitions regarding security, Robinson had written, recommending continued incarceration until the end of the war.

Loss of inhibition, I thought as I returned the file. In someone else, that might lead to a violent physical reaction. With Sinclair, it seemed like he used his words rather than his fists.

Tough call for Robinson to keep him locked up here for the duration, not that it was the worst jail I'd ever seen.

Call? The word rattled around in my brain for a moment. Then it hit me.

Jesus, why hadn't I thought of that before?

I could make a call. A telephone sat on Clarissa's desk and I'd passed it by without a thought. My brain really was jumbled up. I'd planned on checking Kaz's file to see what Dr. Hughes had to say, but that could wait. I flicked off the light and made for Clarissa's swivel chair, wincing as the seat creaked under my weight.

I lifted the receiver. No dial tone. Then a click and a tinny voice.

"Operator."

"Connect me with the London exchange, please," I said, keeping my voice as low as possible without whispering. I didn't know where Colonel Harding was right now, but someone at SHAEF headquarters would be able to get a message to him.

"Please repeat?"

"The London exchange," I said loudly as I cupped my hand around the receiver.

"Very well. Security code, please."

Oh no.

Now I knew what was going on in that room with the lights on. They had an internal switchboard. Of course.

"Sorry, I can't hear you," I said. "We have a bad connection. Say again?"

Then I hung up.

I hurried to the door but stopped in my tracks. If the guards were called out, they'd be coming down the hall. The only way out was the window. I chanced a flicker of red light, scanning the file drawers to be sure they were all closed up tight. I opened the window and slid out, making sure the blackout curtain fell in place before I closed the window. There was no way to lock it.

I hit the ground and darted away from the building, reaching the edge of the woods on the other side of the walkway. If anyone was watching, they'd spot me, but I didn't think they'd react that quickly. This gave me some cover and a view of the building. I melted back farther into the shadows and watched as lights flicked on in first one room then another, the curtains leaking pale yellow around the edges.

I moved along the edge of the tree line, staying low and hitting the dirt when beams of light broke through the undergrowth. Guards coming in from the outer path. Then two more, perhaps the goldbrick twins, circling around from the rear of the building. Good, they were all converging on the front door. They yammered and flashed their torches everywhere as one of them finally produced a key and opened the door. There was a brief argument about who should stay outside. I took advantage by running in the opposite direction and crossing the path, heading for the guards' mess behind the main building. Where better to hide than the place everyone is leaving?

I drew closer, darting behind a tree as I watched a line of men head out of the guardhouse, splitting into search teams. I didn't have much time. Either they'd pick me up out here or find my room empty. Either way was big trouble.

I took a chance. Instead of skulking around, I stood tall, straightened my shoulders, and took long steps, heading to the rear of the north wing and my waiting sheets. Best thing to do in a search when you can't hide is to look like you belong. I swung my arms, swiveled my head as if I was on the lookout for escaped lunatics, and tried to ignore the growing crescendo of shouts and orders rising from every direction. I dropped the blackout lantern in the grass, where any careless guard might have left it.

Two hospital orderlies jogged across my path twenty yards ahead, their voices a murmur of aggravation and resignation. No one likes getting rousted for a night search, and they weren't exactly giving it their all.

I passed by one of the smaller outer buildings, and then I saw them. A bit of a wind had kicked up, and now the damn white sheets were swaying in the breeze. Fairly calling out for attention.

I ran the last few yards, figuring if anyone spotted me now, they'd see the sheets for sure, so what did it matter? I grabbed the dark trousers first and went up hand over hand, shinnying up the fabric rope until I was on the windowsill, tipping over into my room, the mattress cushioning my headfirst fall.

I heard voices in the hallway. They were doing a head count.

I pulled off my boots at the foot of my bed. I whipped off my jacket and untied the trousers from the sheets, throwing the clothing into a corner. Then I began to work on the sheets. The knots had been pulled tight, and I tried to dig my fingers in to pull them apart.

The door flew open.

Sergeant Jenkins stepped in and took one look at me, his face softening.

"Oh, lad. So that's what you meant when you said you were going to leave this place. Come on, there's no need for drastic measures. That's the coward's way out."

He beckoned for an orderly, who appeared at his side, shaking his head sadly.

I looked at the knotted sheets and the open window.

I laughed. First a quick *ha ha* as I realized what he meant. I tried to put on a solemn face of contrition, but another round of laughter burst out as the absurdity of it all hit me square between the eyes.

I laughed like crazy.

CHAPTER THIRTEEN

THE ONLY THING worse than waking up in a padded cell was waking up in a padded cell that hadn't been fumigated since the turn of the century. With nothing else to do but bang my head against the fetid, stinking cushions, I shut my eyes and tried to come up with a good story.

I couldn't come up with a damn thing, so I fell asleep.

I awoke to an orderly standing over me and saying Dr. Robinson wanted to see me. I might have slept ten minutes or two hours. It was hard to say. Especially since they'd confiscated my watch. I understood why they'd taken my belt and shoelaces, but what did they think I was going to do with a wristwatch? Stab myself with the minute hand?

The orderly took me by the arm and hustled me down the corridor. We went into a vestibule that led to another locked door and finally the stairwell. He held me by the arm the entire way down from the third floor. It was nice that he didn't want me to throw myself down the staircase, but it was irritating at the same time.

"Not what I expected from you, Boyle," Dr. Robinson said as we took our usual seats. That statement was a reminder of the principal's office, so it was easy to come back with a tried-and-true answer.

"It wasn't what it looked like."

"Sergeant Jenkins said it looked like a suicide attempt," Robinson said, narrowing his eyes as he studied me.

"I'm sure it did, Doc, but it was all a misunderstanding. Hey, I can see how he thought that, so I don't blame the guy."

"Explain, Boyle. And make it snappy, I've got a busy day ahead of me."

"I've been curious about Holland's death," I said, trying to spin this story so it held together. "We've talked about it, right? Well, I couldn't sleep, and I got to wondering how many ways Holland could've killed himself. Easier ways."

"Easier than the fall from that tower?" Robinson asked.

"The fall is easy. Taking the leap is the hard part. I've pulled back jumpers who were scared out of their wits, too scared to move much less jump," I said. True enough.

"Okay, I can see that," Robinson said, granting me a brief nod.

"So, I got to thinking about hanging," I said. "Holland didn't have a belt, since his trousers had a pair of suspenders. Not good at all for making a noose. And shoelaces don't seem all that reliable, or quick."

"You'd be surprised," Robinson said. "It all depends on how desperate you are to leave this earth."

"Well, you'd know if Holland was desperate or not," I said, watching Robinson for any reaction. His stone face revealed nothing. "He sounded even-keeled to me, even with his mute routine."

"You were saying?" Robinson glanced at his watch. He was impatient, and that impatience might get me thrown back into the soft-sided hoosegow.

"I wanted to see if a guy could hang himself with those sheets. First, I tried twisting them like a rope, but there wasn't enough length after that. Then I got the idea to tie them together and toss them out the window."

"And you weren't going to actually test that out?"

"Hell no, Doc. I could see it'd work. One length of sheet tied to the bedstead and then out the window, using the second sheet as a noose. That way you have a chance for a snap of the neck as well as strangulation."

"You want me to believe you were up before dawn testing out suicide methods?"

"What else would I be doing with those sheets?" I asked, summoning all the virtuous innocence I could muster.

"You didn't leave your room?" Robinson said, drumming his fingers on the arm of his chair.

"Not until they took me to that padded cell. Listen, Doc, that place needs to be fumigated."

"You didn't try to make a telephone call?"

"Doc, this ain't the Ritz. I don't have a telephone in my suite."

"Tell me again about your interest in Holland's death," Robinson said, leaning back in his chair. Something had shifted. Maybe he'd bought my story. Or maybe he figured Holland wasn't the type to kill himself and had his own suspicions. If so, that made three after Snow and Hughes. Three guys who had their doubts about suicide, but none worried enough to put anyone on the case except for me, their own local head case.

I filled him in on my brief career as a detective with the Boston PD, and how when I was a patrolman my dad brought me along when homicide got the call to investigate a stiff. I'd been brought up on murder, which was an odd thing to admit to a psychiatrist. But it was true enough in my family and not so unusual for the Boston Irish. We'd made the police our own territory and controlled it like a fiefdom in the old country. Detection of crime was our stock-in-trade, and I'd been trained to sniff it out at an early age.

"You're Dick Tracy in khaki, then," Robinson said with a quick snort of laughter, when I'd finished the tale of my time in blue.

"Glad you find it funny, Doc."

"Not at all. I'm a big fan of Dick Tracy. Don't you read the funny papers?"

"Sure. I just didn't think an educated guy like you would," I said. "So, it's a compliment?"

"The highest. But watch out. If someone murdered Holland, you could end up more like Fearless Fosdick." *Fearless* was a parody comic strip, poking fun at straightlaced Dick Tracy with the square-jawed detective Fearless Fosdick, who routinely got shot through with cannonball-sized bullet holes. Funny stuff, a laugh riot of mayhem and murder.

"If?" I asked. I got the sense Robinson knew more than he was saying and was using the funny-papers routine to warn me of something real and dangerous.

He didn't reply. Which said a lot. Instead, he got up and went to his desk, opening a drawer and taking out my belt and shoelaces.

"Here, Boyle," he said, tossing them to me. "In my professional opinion, you're not the sort to kill yourself. Certainly not with a couple of bedsheets, anyway. Sheer stubbornness, maybe. Go get yourself some breakfast."

"Thanks, Doc. For that first part, anyway," I said, lacing up my boots. "How can you tell?"

"About suicide? There are a lot of warning signs. Like when someone doesn't seem to be on an even keel. Know what I mean?"

"Yeah, I do," I said, standing as I put on my belt. I'd just described Holland as being on an even keel, even though he was a mute. "You don't have my watch, do you?"

"No. Check with Jenkins, he brought these to me. One more thing before you go," Robinson said, walking me to the door. "Who do you know in London?"

"General Eisenhower, of course," I said, leaving before I let loose with *Uncle Ike*.

That had been the most instructive therapy session I'd ever had. Robinson had told me that I wasn't about to kill myself—always nice to hear—and that Holland hadn't been the type either. He knew I'd been the one who tried to make the phone call to London, but he'd let that slide. Plus, he warned me about an unknown person who might fill me with holes at any time.

All without saying anything directly, except for some chatter about the comics. I wondered how much trouble he could get into for even spilling that much. Or if Major Snow might be risking his neck by asking a patient to investigate a possible crime. Also, was Dr. Hughes going to do Kaz the favor I asked in return for the future payoff I'd hinted at?

An odd bunch, all around. Now I wished I'd taken the time last night to read their files. There was always tonight. The window was still unlocked, far as I knew, and Robinson, at least, had no objection to my nighttime rambles.

The window. Unlocked.

Damn.

I stopped in my tracks and patted my pockets.

There it was. The key set from Clarissa's desk. I'd put it in my shirt pocket when I went for the telephone. When I had to skedaddle, I'd forgotten all about the small keys tied with a piece of faded blue ribbon.

I had to get them back to her. If she discovered the keys missing, there would be a full-scale search and shakedown. A patient getting to a telephone was bad enough. A patient getting into the files was a catastrophe.

By the growl in my stomach and the scurry of staff through the corridor, I knew the workday had started. I put the keys in my left trouser pocket. No reason to risk a shaky right hand fouling things up, even though it was steady enough right now.

I strolled into the file room, trying for cheery and nonchalant. The place was crowded, Clarissa and her office mate moving chairs while several of the Home Guards shoved desks to the side of the room.

"Cleaning day, Clarissa?" I asked, stepping aside as two of the Home Guards dragged a desk across the floor, narrowly missing my toes.

"I don't have time to chat, Mr. Boyle, not today," she said, sorting through a pile of file folders laid out on a table. "I've lost something and must find it."

"We'll be in a world of trouble, Clarissa," her friend whispered, worry lines wrinkling her forehead.

"Can I help?" I asked, approaching the table.

"No, you may not," Clarissa said. "You shouldn't even be here. Sorry to be rude, but you must leave."

"We'll come back later and move these desks back, Miss," one of the guards said. "Sarge'll miss us if we're gone too long."

"Yes, thank you," Clarissa said, brushing an errant lock of hair back from her eyes.

"Are you sure I can't help?" I asked, leaning on the table. "I know how to keep my mouth shut. I can see you haven't reported it yet."

"Not officially, no. Those boys offered to help," Clarissa said.

"Just like me. Now, what did you lose?"

"Really, I can't say, and you can't stay. I can tell you're a decent sort, but you'll only get me in more trouble. You must leave."

"I'm sorry," I said, shoving off from the table, raising my hands in mock surrender. "I didn't mean to upset you. Good luck."

"We need it," her friend said as they returned to flipping through files.

They got it. Not a minute down the corridor, I heard the shriek of relieved surprise.

Now they were left to wonder how those keys ever got dropped into that file folder.

CHAPTER FOURTEEN

I SHOWERED AND shaved, washing away the lingering moldy odor of the rubber room. A fresh set of olive drabs and I felt like a new man, although I would have preferred the feel of freedom. I hit the dining hall and got my fill of coffee, fried Spam, and powdered eggs.

I sat back and surveyed the room. No Miller, which was good. He'd been irritating, but now that I knew his secrets, I felt guilty about how angry I'd gotten with him. Since I couldn't let on I knew what had really happened, I'd have to act like I still despised him. Tough to remember when you know the guy is crushed by guilt himself.

I got up as Sinclair entered, in the company of the two young ladies from yesterday's confrontation with Miller.

"Ah, Boyle," Sinclair said as we drew closer. "Have you met these two lovelies? Faith and Iris, this is Boyle." Sinclair chuckled like an older uncle at a family gathering.

"I'm afraid Faith is the silent type," Iris said, shaking my hand. Iris was the one with curly hair who'd taken a butter knife to Miller. The one I called Shirley Temple.

"First names for women, is it?" I said, returning the briefest of nods from Faith. She sat at a table, fidgeting and glancing about as she pulled the worn sleeves of her sweater.

"Of course," Iris said. "We're sent to face torture and death, but the doctors here seem to think we shall swoon if called by our last names. Treating us as mere *girls* makes it easier for them, perhaps."

"Guilt?" I said, returning to that familiar theme.

"Likely," Iris said. "Especially those here who have never been in the field. It upsets their vision of how the sexes should behave. Or maybe they can't abide the notion of a woman who could kill them seven different ways. I don't care; I simply want to get out of this place."

"I know the feeling," I said, as Iris crossed her arms and shivered. Although she bore no obvious marks, I figured she'd been imprisoned, or perhaps been in hiding for so long she lost what weight she'd had. But I knew enough not to ask questions.

"Apparently someone tried an escape last night," Iris said. "Lots of noise and lights in the early morning hours. I hope they got away."

"I for one enjoy myself here," Sinclair said. "Fine accommodations and no pressure. No problems with magnetic fields here, you know. And the food is better than at the Weston installation, although that is not saying much. Excuse me, Boyle."

"Magnetic fields?" I said, as Sinclair toddled off to fill his plate. I was glad to leave the subject of last night's escapades behind. "He must really be off his rocker."

"Rumor is Sinclair literally cannot keep a secret," Iris said. "He's a scientist of some sort, so perhaps it's not so strange to be working with magnetic fields at a naval base. That's what Weston is, up in Somerset."

"We all have our stories, don't we?" I said. Iris seemed to know things, so I decided to press her with a few questions. I laid my hand on her arm as she turned to go. She flinched, turning with a start.

"Sorry," I said. "I only wanted to ask a question. A minute ago, you said something about people here who hadn't been out in the field. You meant the staff, right? Have any of them seen action?"

"Basil, for one. Major Snow. He was wounded on a mission in Italy. Common knowledge within SOE," she said.

"His limp?"

"Yes, I think so. That's why he's behind a desk now. I don't know about any of the others," she said, turning away.

"Any idea what was behind Holland's death?" I asked, keeping my hands to myself this time. Iris stopped.

"They claim he jumped," she whispered. "Faith isn't certain he did."

"She told you that?"

"She shook her head when she heard. In the negative," Iris added. "Faith and Holland would sit at the same table, never saying a word. No apparent communication, but there they'd be the next day. Going through the motions of eating or drinking tea, seemingly oblivious to each other. Certainly, to the world around them."

"What do you think? About Holland?" I asked.

"I think it's awfully odd that you have so many questions. Sinclair's your man for that. As I said, there's no secret he hasn't told, if the gossip is to be believed. Good day, Boyle."

With that, Iris left, patting Faith's shoulder and whispering to her before heading to the growing line for breakfast.

I'd overplayed my hand. Now Iris was suspicious. Or maybe she thought asking questions was my particular brand of crazy. Sinclair and his answers, me and my questions, what was the difference? At least mine made some sort of sense. To me anyway.

I made my way through the foyer, waving to Clarissa at her desk, everything back to normal in the filing room. Outside, I stopped to button my collar against the wind. One circuit around the place to clear my head, then I'd pop in on Kaz.

I had to wait by the main gate as they opened it for a staff car to enter. A British Austin 10 with two men in the back seat, one an army officer, the other a gray-haired civilian. As the vehicle drove slowly by, its tires crunching on gravel, the officer looked at me, his eyes narrow beneath the brim of his service cap.

He didn't look happy. But who would be, entering this place?

Well, Angus Sinclair was happy here. No magnetic waves and plenty of grub. The doctors were doing the same jobs they'd have in a regular military hospital, so they were hard to judge. Dr. Robinson had plenty of interesting cases, so this place had to be heaven for a psychiatrist.

Maybe the Home Guards liked it. It gave Sergeant Jenkins and his men something to do, a way to contribute to the war effort. Now that fears of a German invasion were gone, the Home Guard wasn't needed as much as it had been. It was a volunteer outfit, so these fellows were here of their own accord. It was in addition to their regular occupations, but they got to wear the uniform, carry a weapon, and have a night out now and then. Yeah, they probably saw this place as a plus.

Me, not so much. I circled around back and saw Jenkins and two of his men hustle out from their small building and head for the entrance. A reception committee for the visiting brass? And why were they here? Looking into the death of Holland? Perhaps Snow was in trouble with his bosses. If he'd been an SOE agent behind the lines in Italy, and wounded in action to boot, this assignment had to be a bit of a letdown. Where would he go from here? Discharged from duty?

No use trying to put the pieces of the puzzle together when most of them were missing. There were dozens of reasons for a high-ranking visit. Each patient here held secrets others had died to protect, and any one of Saint Albans's prisoners might bring the brass running for good cause.

I trudged along, the wind snapping at my neck, my hands in my pockets. Holland's companion in silence, Faith, was the only new factor. She appeared too delicate, mentally and physically, to do him any harm. And from what Iris said, they were simpatico. What about Iris, though? She was in a weakened condition, thin as a scarecrow. Would she have had the strength to push Holland over the parapet? Or perhaps Holland had come out of his stupor and made unwelcome advances on Faith.

Trained in seven ways to kill people, Iris had said.

Did Holland know or do something that threatened someone's status here at Saint Albans? I couldn't see how, but decided I needed to speak with Faith. Whether she would—or could—answer, I had no idea.

I turned the corner on the south wing of the building. An ambulance and a jeep were parked out front. Orderlies were unloading a stretcher case from the ambulance, hurrying inside as the patient lay silent, face swathed in bandages.

Then I noticed the two guys getting out of the jeep. Big Mike and Lieutenant Feliks Kanski.

"Geez, Big Mike, am I glad to see you," I said, rushing over to the jeep and slapping him on the arm. I wanted to hug him, but the guy was so big I couldn't get my arms around those shoulders. "Feliks, good to see you too. Are you here to visit Kaz?"

I was all smiles at seeing them, but the look on their faces said nothing but bad news.

"I must attend to Skory," Feliks said, his eyes following the stretcher. "Excuse me, Billy. Sergeant Miecznikowski will explain."

Feliks took off before I could ask what the hell he was doing in England. The last time Kaz and I had seen him, he was fighting with the Polish 1st Armoured Division in France. That was right before the trip to Paris that ended with me and Kaz in this joint.

"First of all, when are you getting me out of here?" I said to Big Mike. "And secondly, what the hell is going on? Who's Skory?"

"Good to see you, too, Billy," he said. "The last question is easy. Skory is a code name. He was important enough to rate a pickup at an abandoned airfield in Poland. He got shot up when a Kraut patrol stopped him on his way there. As for the first, sorry, but I can't spring you. That's up to the doctors. You okay? You do look a lot better than the last time I saw you."

"The last time you saw me you had me strapped down in an ambulance bringing me here," I said. "I sure as hell hope I look better."

That had been right after Paris. Big Mike was a good guy, the kind of guy who you want in your corner. But I did feel left behind. It was bad enough he dumped me here, but then not to see hide nor hair of him, that was a bit much.

"Hey, slow down, Billy. Sam and I were both here, a couple of times. You don't remember?" Big Mike looked at me like I was crazy. Okay, he had every right to, I guess.

"No," I said. "I don't. When?"

"The day after we brought you here. You were out of it, that's for sure. Kaz was in bad shape, too, but he came around faster than you. You still got the shakes?"

"How do you know about that?" I asked. "And no. Not often."

"You told me. Showed me. When we came the second time, a few days later."

"Jesus. Sorry, Big Mike. I was somewhere the hell else. The doc gave me something to sleep, a Blue Eighty-Eight, and that finally snapped me out of it. Slept for more than two days. Woke up with my head almost screwed on straight."

"That'll be a pleasant change! Come on, let's get inside," he said.

"Okay, what's going on?" I asked, as we settled into a couple of chairs in the dayroom. We sat by the window, which had a nice view of the fence. We were far enough away from the pajamaed patients leafing through books and magazines that we could talk without being over- heard.

"It's bad news. About Angelika."

"Is she—"

"No, she's not dead," Big Mike said, holding up a hand to put the brakes on the nightmare I was seeing in my mind. "But she was taken by the Gestapo. Captured outside of Warsaw."

"As good as, then," I said.

"We don't know. We do know that she was alive last week. She was put on a transport to a camp in northern Germany. Ravensbrück. It's for women prisoners." Big Mike sat back, his hands on his knees and his eyes avoiding mine. Neither of us said a word.

There's something else he's not telling me.

"It's Diana? That's where she is too, right?" I said, filling in the blanks left by his silence.

"Yes. We heard from the French Red Cross that they'd gotten a list of names, all French nationals, who'd been arrested and sent to the camp. Diana's name was included. Her false identity, I mean. The Krauts don't know she's SOE," he said.

"Thank God she's alive," I said. Her cover story was that she was a high-class hostess in a Paris brothel. When things had gone south in Paris, she'd been picked up as a member of the Resistance, but the Gestapo only knew her as Malou, a Parisian. Her French was flawless, her identity papers were the best SOE could print, so her story held. Now all she had to do was survive a Nazi concentration camp.

"It's good, Billy. Best we can hope for, under the circumstances. Listen, I know this is a shock for you, but now we have to think about Kaz."

"Jesus," I said, my head falling into my hands. I'd already known Diana was in the hands of the Gestapo, so hearing she was alive, no matter where, was its own silver lining. But Angelika had been free, if on the run. News that she'd been arrested and deported to a concentration camp inside Germany couldn't be dressed up as anything but a disaster. "Can he take it?"

"I'm worried too," Big Mike said. "But we have to tell him. Feliks said he'd do it but wanted some help."

"Is that why you're here?"

"That's a long story. For now, let's just say I had a reason to come along for the ride."

"But wait, what is Feliks doing here?"

"He was transferred to the Polish Army Second Department," Big Mike said, standing and motioning for us to go.

"Intelligence," I said. "And that's why he's here with Skory. Which is why you're here with him."

"Yeah. A few days ago, Skory was in occupied Poland. He's important. Feliks was active with the Polish Home Army before he escaped the country, so they pulled him out of France to work on this. More on that later, okay? Let's go see Kaz."

I took Big Mike upstairs and we found Feliks. Skory was out cold, with orderlies finishing getting him comfortable in bed. Big Mike had told me he'd been drugged for the ride, and Feliks didn't expect him to wake for a few hours.

"Lead the way, Billy," Feliks said, when he was satisfied with the arrangements. Then I remembered Kaz had thought Feliks and Angelika might have been involved romantically back in Poland. War throws people together and rips them apart. Feliks looked gutted, his young face ravaged by worry, his eyes heavy with darkened bags.

I couldn't imagine what it would be like for Kaz.

CHAPTER FIFTEEN

KAZ'S FACE BRIGHTENED at the sight of Feliks, like mine had. It lasted a second, and then his expression went numb, his eyes darkening as if a cloud had passed over them.

"Angelika is alive," Feliks said, moving to the side of the bed and stooping to embrace Kaz. Feliks's statement belied his somber mood.

"What is wrong? Why are you here?" Kaz said, his voice trembling with dread.

"I have news," Feliks said, stepping back and pulling a chair close to the bed. Big Mike and I stood behind him, feeling the tension in the air. Feliks looked around, unable to meet Kaz's eyes. "It could be worse."

"Angelika has been arrested," I said, unable to stand the hemming and hawing. "She's been sent to Ravensbrück."

There. Done. Feliks glared at me, as if I should've softened the blow, but I knew Kaz had been in agony since we walked into the room. Now it was out there.

"You are certain?" Kaz asked, his steely eyes focused on his Polish friend. Feliks was the one with the intelligence contacts. He was the one who knew of Angelika's work with the Home Army. "Tell me everything."

"The message came through only yesterday. Angelika had been travelling to Poznań to deliver a message about an operation to the units there. She never arrived," Feliks said, his hands pressed to his temples. He looked exhausted. He was fresh from the battlefield, and delivering horrible news to Kaz, never mind reliving it himself. "The units scattered, fearing she would be forced to talk."

Feliks took a deep breath. Kaz betrayed no emotion. Both men were fighting off visions of what the Gestapo did to people to extract information.

"We have people at the rail yard there," Feliks continued. "They reported seeing Angelika in a crowd of a hundred or so young girls being loaded into cattle cars. Among many other people."

"She was with other girls of the same age?" Kaz said, his eyes widening at the slightest sliver of positive news. "That suggests she was part of a roundup, does it not?"

"Yes," Feliks agreed, placing his hand on Kaz's arm. "There was less than a day between her disappearance and the sighting at the rail yard as well."

"Not enough time for an interrogation," Kaz said. He looked to me, his expression begging for me to agree. It was the thinnest of threads on which to pin his hopes for Angelika's survival, but it was all he had.

"Right," I said. "Sounds like she was picked up off the street in a sweep. But why?"

"Angelika plays the piano," Feliks said. "Beautifully."

"Okay," Big Mike said. "But what does that have to do with Ravensbrück?"

"Perhaps a great deal," Kaz said, twisting the hospital sheet with his hands. "She has lovely, delicate hands. The hands of a child when I last saw her, but swift and sleek when she played." He looked to Feliks, who nodded his agreement.

"The Germans have developed a new weapon. A rocket. One that may pose a great danger," Feliks said. "They have factories for building parts in many locations. One is close to Ravensbrück."

"They employ slave labor," Kaz said. "I don't know about this latest weapon, but for the V1 flying bomb, they used young girls for constructing the most delicate mechanisms. Those with the slenderest of fingers."

"At least she was not sent to a death camp," Feliks said. "A train left for Auschwitz later the same day."

We'd heard about Auschwitz. A place where Jews, Poles, and many others were put to death. A camp built for the extermination of an entire race, along with anyone else who didn't fit in with the Nazi order. I would have found it hard to believe if I hadn't read the report. A Polish spy who'd escaped from Auschwitz brought out the truth about what went on in that pit of horror. Women and children gassed upon arrival. Those with strength enough to work put through labors that killed them. Yes, any place was better than Auschwitz.

Even Ravensbrück.

"How sure are you about this?" Big Mike asked. "It seems like you're jumping to a conclusion without much to go on. Sorry, Kaz, I want Angelika to be as safe as possible, but there could be any number of reasons the Krauts sent her to Ravensbrück."

"There is more," Feliks said, jumping in before Kaz could agree with Big Mike's logic. "Our spy in the rail yard reported that Angelika's group was unusual. Mostly city girls. Well-dressed, or as well-dressed as possible for a Pole in any city occupied by the Nazis. No country girls, no peasants."

"No callused, thick fingers," I said.

"Correct. Our man didn't know what was behind the selection, but he thought the group unique enough to mention," Feliks said.

"Did he know Angelika by sight?" Kaz asked. "Are you certain she was on that train?"

"Yes," Feliks said. "She'd been acting as a courier in Poznań for several weeks. She'd been to the railroad yard before, to pick up information on German troop movements from that very fellow. We are certain it was her."

"Very well," Kaz said, slamming his hand on the mattress. "Then we must trust she can keep her head and survive. She has done well since the occupation, hasn't she Feliks?"

"Yes, yes, she has," Feliks said eagerly, grasping at this small hint of hope. "She means everything to me, you know. My family is gone. She is all I have. I am sorry, I should have protected her." He looked ready to break.

"The best way to protect Angelika is to do your job," Kaz said, granting Feliks no sympathy. "Let us finish this war, that is our job. Hers is to live until we do. Do you understand?"

"I do. Thank you, Piotr. Now, we must return to Skory. Hopefully he will regain consciousness soon. There is someone from London coming to see him. We will return when we can," Feliks said. He left, Big Mike stopping to take Kaz's hand before he followed him out.

"Big Mike, I have a favor to ask," Kaz whispered.

"Sure, buddy. Name it."

"Will you deliver a letter for me? To Walter, the concierge at the Dorchester Hotel? It must be delivered to him in person. It's important."

"Yeah, no problem. We're headed back to London tomorrow morning," Big Mike said.

"I will have it for you within the hour," Kaz said, holding Big Mike's hand tightly in his. "Give it to Walter. You will have to wait for him to retrieve something for me. Then bring it back here, as soon as possible. Will you do that?"

"Sure. No questions asked. I'll get here as soon as I can. Colonel Harding is working on this project with Skory, so I'll have good reason to come back. Listen, both of you. There's more to this Kraut weapons project. I'll tell you later, on the q.t. But it's linked to Ravensbrück. It might help us keep tabs on Angelika and Diana."

Big Mike dashed out of the room, following Feliks.

"That'd be great, Kaz," I said, sitting down and pulling the chair closer to his bed. "Right?" He looked away, letting his head drop into the pillow. His eyes squeezed shut and he passed a long minute like that.

"She was only a little girl when I last saw her. She'd grown tall, but was still awkwardly coming of age, all pigtails and freckles," he finally said, sitting up and staring at the wall. No tears, nothing to betray the enormity of his feelings but the utter simplicity of his words.

CHAPTER SIXTEEN

I SAT WITH Kaz for a long time. He hadn't said anything else, and there was nothing I could say to offer comfort. Between the two of us, I think we understood that everything we had called good news was wishful thinking at best. Maybe there was a chance for Diana and Angelika, but whatever hope of survival they had rested with them, not us. We couldn't even help ourselves.

"I am sorry, Billy," Kaz said, coming out of his silence.

"For what?"

"This news was a shock, of course, but I should have thought about Diana. She is in the same camp, as Big Mike informed me. I should have acknowledged that. You have your own worries, don't you?"

"Yeah. And getting you out of here is one of them," I said. I checked to be sure no one was listening and leaned closer. "I dropped a heavy hint on Dr. Hughes. I told him you'd be grateful if he supported your release and approved you for staff duty. Extremely grateful."

"What did he say?" Kaz asked in a whisper.

"Nothing. But when I described your lodgings at the Dorchester, he was impressed. Impressed enough not to throw me out for suggesting such a thing."

"Excellent," he said. "Good thinking Billy. I was planning an approach myself, but now you have broken the ice. I will proceed as soon as Big Mike returns from London."

"Yeah, I meant to ask. What's he bringing back for you?"

"One thousand pounds from the safe at the Dorchester. Walter holds a considerable amount of funds for me," Kaz said.

"That's over four thousand bucks, Kaz," I said. "You sure you need to lay out that much dough?"

"I will present it as the down payment," he said. "The remainder, twice that amount, will be given upon my release. I wish the offer too tempting to be rejected."

"It'd sure as hell tempt me," I said. "I bet Hughes will bite."

"I hope you are right, Billy."

"Yeah, he's an odd one. I can't figure why he's so eager for me to investigate Holland's death. Snow I can understand, security is his job. But what angle is Hughes playing?"

"Did you learn anything last night?" Kaz asked. I glanced at the open door and the mix of orderlies and patients in the hallway.

"Sure, like a padded cell isn't as comfortable as it sounds. Hey, can you take a walk? Too easy to be overheard in here."

"I am supposed to be on bed rest, but I've managed to take a few strolls. If Dr. Hughes doesn't catch me, no one else seems to take notice," he said, donning his silk robe and stuffing his feet into leather slippers. "Come, we'll find a secluded corner. It may do both of us good to talk of things other than concentration camps."

Down the hall, away from the nurses' desk and the flurry of activity around it, we passed an open ward, with a half dozen beds filled with patients in casts of various sizes. One guy with his leg raised by a pulley and his arm in a cast from shoulder to wrist stared at Kaz, perhaps jealous of his mobility and snappy sleeping duds. Kaz looked right back at him, and I wondered if he dreamed of injuries that would knit themselves back together.

At the end of the corridor, a wide room with a broad expanse of windows displayed a motley collection of chairs, an afterthought of furnishings from the attic. Well used, like Saint Albans itself. The room had been given a fresh coat of paint, but it had been hastily applied, slapped on over peeling and chipping layers from the last century.

We sat on a couch overlooking the grounds. Two Home Guards

walked across the lawn, rifles slung over their shoulders, a reminder that despite the bright paint, this was still a prison.

"I cannot get used to the idea that our time together is over," Kaz said. "The best I can hope for is to sit at a desk, it seems."

"That's right where you were when I first met you," I said. "You never know what's in store, so don't count yourself out." It was not much of a straw to grasp at, but it was all I could come up with. I didn't want to think about the end of our partnership either.

"True enough," Kaz said. "I certainly never could have guessed we'd end up in an insane asylum. But I think my heart condition will decide matters, no matter how much I wish otherwise. Now, tell me how you ended up in a padded cell."

"I'll get to that. But first, I want to ask you about something you said the last time we talked. When I said there was no reason for anyone to kill Holland, you said that was an important clue. What did you mean?"

"I said that when you told me he was a mute," Kaz said. "Unless you learned something new last night, my thought is that he was killed either as a message to someone else—a warning perhaps—or because he was ready to speak once again."

"Couldn't he still communicate by writing?"

"Not if his silence was psychological, based on something he experienced. Perhaps his silence extended beyond the simple spoken word? Think of going mute as a mechanism for cutting himself off from the outside world," Kaz said.

"Now you sound like Doc Robinson. When he's making sense," I said. "I've thought about that, but I keep coming up against the question of what Holland might have learned that posed a danger to anyone. If you're right, he'd cut himself off from human contact; that argues against anyone confiding in him, much less having a conversation."

"Is it not Dr. Robinson's job to attempt to communicate with patients in your ward?"

"Good point," I said. "But there was nothing in Holland's file to indicate he'd been spilling the beans about anything. Or could if he'd wanted to," I said.

"But what did you do to land yourself in a padded cell?"

"I can tell you that," a voice said from behind us. "But I am more interested in how you got out so quickly." It was Dr. Hughes. He'd come up behind us and surprised the hell out of me. I watched him for any sign he'd heard more than the remark about my accommodations but saw nothing except a stern stare focused on Kaz. "Baron, you should be in bed. No strenuous activity, remember?"

"If a walk down that hallway is considered strenuous, I am in for a life of indolence," Kaz said.

"It could be worse," Hughes said. "A wealthy man can hire someone to push him about in a rolling chair. It would add years to your lifespan."

"Such a cheery notion," Kaz said. Hughes was swimming right toward the bait.

"Please excuse us, Boyle," Hughes said. "I need to examine the baron in his room. But do drop by my office later today, would you?"

Without waiting for an answer, Hughes took Kaz by the arm as if he were an old lady and led him down the hallway.

Neither of us had said it out loud before, but this was it. We were pulling out all the stops to keep Kaz in uniform at some desk job, but it meant the end of our partnership. We'd spent most of our time together over the last couple of years. Risked our lives together, saw the horrors of war together, faced death and sorrow together.

How do you leave all that behind?

I had no idea.

I stood and gazed out the window, hoping for inspiration from the clearing sky and leafy branches swaying in the wind. Mother Nature kept things to herself, so I went to find Big Mike. Walking along the corridor, I thought about what Kaz had said. Robinson did spend time with Holland, but I had my doubts about how much communication went on during those sessions. Faith also spent time with him, but in total silence by all reports. I needed to speak with Iris and get her help. Faith was a bit too jumpy to approach directly.

Which brought me back to Kaz's other notion. That Holland's killing was a message. A signal to someone. Meaning what?

I asked at the nurse's station where the new patient had been taken. I was told to move on. I didn't want to use his code name, since throwing that around might get me tossed back into the padded suite. Instead, I wandered off, glancing into rooms on either side of the main corridor. Five rooms were occupied, all by patients in a lot better shape than Skory. I kept going, finding the next rooms darkened and unfurnished. Beyond those, the hallway was unlit. It went the length of the building and hooked left, sunlight barely illuminating it.

No fresh coat of paint here. Falling plaster littered the floor, and rooms were stacked with discarded furniture and heaps of rotting mattresses. On one wall the word *help* had been written in large letters, the substance used for the scrawl best left unconsidered.

Several doors were nothing but bars, holding cells for the poor souls of Saint Albans. Here was the essential truth of this place, the true function that brooms, mops, and paint couldn't disguise. It was all for our own good, as it had been for the original inmates. And for the good of the war effort, as it had been for the greater good of society. Saint Albans was an asylum, a prison to keep what was in our minds locked up tight.

If these walls could speak, they would scream.

CHAPTER SEVENTEEN

I WAS ABOUT to give up when I made out echoing voices at the other end of the corridor. There was no one in sight, but as I approached the far end, the sound grew louder. I glanced up the stairwell but was stopped cold by a Home Guard standing at the third-floor landing.

"Turn around, mate," he said. "No one allowed without authorization."

"Ask Lieutenant Feliks Kanski," I said. "He'll vouch for me."

"You're not authorized. Can't make it any simpler. If you don't want trouble, move on. Now."

I held up my hands and backed off. This must be where they had Skory stashed. He had to be hot stuff to deserve his own special security within Saint Albans. Trouble, I had enough of, so I walked back through the ruined halls and waited outside Kaz's room, far enough away for Hughes not to spot me. I hadn't figured out how much, if anything, to tell Kaz, and I needed more time to work that out.

Hughes left a minute later, headed in the opposite direction.

"How'd it go?" I asked Kaz, soon as I got through the door.

"We had to do a bit of a dance," Kaz said. "A distinguished medical man such as Dr. Hughes would not stoop to accept a bribe. But a consulting fee, that is another matter."

"Nicely done," I said. "You look happy with yourself." His face was lit with a joy I hadn't seen in a while.

"Well, I upped the stakes," he said, smiling. "The good doctor will release me for desk duty, given that I suffer no further setbacks. An understandable precaution on his part."

"Okay, but what else?"

"I insisted on being allowed a second opinion about my mitral stenosis, with a significant finder's fee for him, of course," Kaz said.

"But you don't need him to find anyone. You have your own doctors in London," I said.

"Yes, the best Harley Street has to offer," Kaz said. "The stumbling block was security, as usual. Hughes refuses to release me too soon since he wishes to keep an eye on my condition. It wouldn't do for me to drop dead before he collects the last payment."

"Got it. He won't allow your guy on the premises."

"Correct," Kaz said, "without a background check, which would take weeks. But Dr. Hughes did come up with an alternative. A US Army surgeon will be visiting Saint Albans tomorrow."

"Your second opinion is going to be some unknown army doctor? You sure that's smart?"

"Our esteemed Dr. Hughes thinks very little of his ideas, which gives me great hope," Kaz said. "Hughes adheres to the opinion of most doctors that the heart is too delicate an organ to operate on or to even handle. Such a viewpoint veers toward superstition, but I have encountered it before. My own physician told me the medical profession shuns those who dare question that long-standing belief."

"I'm guessing this Yank doctor thinks otherwise?"

"Exactly," Kaz said. "He is touring British military hospitals to lecture on removing shrapnel from the heart. Demonstrating the operation, when possible. Hughes reluctantly admits this procedure may have some value but doubts it can be applied to other maladies."

"Such as mitral stenosis," I said.

"Quite so. But by granting me a consultation with an American doctor with a security clearance, Hughes fulfills his side of the bargain and earns his fee," Kaz said. "I do hope Big Mike hurries back with the funds. I sense that Hughes shares the common English distrust of foreigners and will not wholly commit himself until his pockets are stuffed with fifty-pound banknotes."

"Funny that the guy taking the bribe doesn't trust people," I said. "I'm not sure how much longer Big Mike will have to stay here. I looked for him, but they seem to have Skory hidden away upstairs with a guard stopping anyone who gets close. By the sound of them yakking, there's a bunch of people up there."

"Skory must be important to rate such special treatment," Kaz said. "Big Mike did promise to tell us more about the Nazi weapons program. I assume Skory is connected somehow."

"And to the girls the Krauts picked up. And perhaps Ravensbrück, if I understood what he was saying."

"We shall have to wait. For now, amuse me with the story of how you ended up in that padded cell," Kaz said, grinning at the prospect. For the moment, our situation and common fears faded into the background as I went over what I'd found.

I started with Miller, who played at the violent daredevil, but who, in reality, couldn't pull the trigger on a traitor. His decision caused suffering, pain, and death. Much of the pain was in his own mind, apparently. I didn't see him as the killer. Robinson thought he needed more therapy. Convulsive therapy, according to the notes.

"I've never heard of that," Kaz said. "It must be a new treatment, perhaps for war neurosis. I agree, Miller has shown himself to be incapable of cold-blooded execution. But consider the possibility that he now feels he must show he can do it. To prove himself."

I admitted it was possible, but not probable. Then on to Holland himself. He'd withstood terrible torture and withdrew into himself. He'd held out against the Gestapo, but not against his own mind. No friends here, except for Faith. But you couldn't call them friends, really. Silent companions, at best. Robinson's notes were of no help.

"You should talk to Faith," Kaz said. "Through Iris, of course. There is always a chance she noticed something."

I agreed and went on to Sinclair. An egghead who worked at the Admiralty. Not a field agent, but some sort of technical specialist who'd had a nervous breakdown and lost all inhibitions against keeping secrets. Apparently he knew a few, even though he referred to himself as nothing but a wheezer and a dodger.

"Wait," Kaz said, holding up a hand. "Wheezer and dodger, you say?"

"Yeah. He described himself that way to me. Does it mean anything?"

"It means Sinclair is more than a specialist. Wheezers and dodgers is a nickname given to the Admiralty's Directorate of Miscellaneous Weapon Development. From the last two initials, you see," Kaz said. "And because many of the personnel were older and drawn from academia. Churchill himself takes an active interest in their work."

"Which is what, exactly?"

"Advanced weapons development," Kaz said. "All manner of things, most of which are top secret. Some reports indicate they've had success degaussing ship hulls to protect against magnetic mines, although nothing has been confirmed. They have several projects with rockets as well as improved anti-submarine weapons."

"If it's all so top secret, how do you know about it?"

"Billy, reports come across our desks at SHAEF all the time. I merely caught up on my reading the last time we were there. Seems like ages ago, does it not?"

I had to admit it did. Kaz pressed me on what else I'd found in the files, and I was forced to tell him I stopped searching as soon as I'd gotten my bright idea to use the telephone to contact Colonel Harding in London. I told him about all hell breaking loose and Jenkins finding me in my room with the knotted sheets.

At least it gave Kaz a good laugh.

"It's a good thing Dr. Robinson took pity on you," he said. "Too stubborn to kill yourself?"

"Something like that," I said. "But let's get back to our suspects. Or lack of them."

"You must watch for anything unusual," Kaz said. "Any action that Holland's death would have triggered. In the absence of any clear motive, be alert for when one does appear."

"Feliks and Big Mike showing up with an agent smuggled out of Poland is unusual, but that can't have anything to do with it."

"Right. It is doubtful, since that journey began long before Holland was killed. Still, keep your eyes open for any connections. And try to speak with Faith. She was close to him."

"I will," I said as I rose to leave. "Get the lowdown from Big Mike in case I miss him. I'll check back later."

"Billy?"

"Yeah?" I stopped in the doorway, the busy rush of people in the hallway at my back. I turned to Kaz in his small room thick with memories and despair. His eyes welled with tears that did not fall, his mouth quivered with words that could not escape his lips. The world carried on around us in the corridors of Saint Albans, in the fields and forests beyond, but between us there was nothing but suffering leavened by the thinnest vein of hope.

"Yeah," I said. I slapped my hand on the door and left.

CHAPTER EIGHTEEN

WONDERING HOW BEST to approach Faith, I hoofed it over to the north wing, cutting across the wide lawn. Iris was the key, but since she was so protective, I'd need a damn good plan to convince her to help. Not that I had much hope Holland had said anything to Faith.

I hunched my shoulders against the growing winds as I walked along the gravel path on my way to the main entrance. Off to my left, something moved behind the shrubs under the windows. I spotted a flash of khaki battle dress hidden behind greenery except for a flash of brown and the whites of eyes peering at me between branches.

"Who the hell are you?" I asked, equal parts angry and amused at whatever game this guy was playing.

"Classified," he said, standing and pushing his way through the bushes. "I have to stay in practice. No lolling about for me. They call this a rest camp, but I know there's no time to rest."

"I'm Boyle," I said, extending my hand.

"No, no names," he said, taking a quick step back. His eyes darted around, as if deadly threats loomed everywhere. He looked up to the clock tower, finally returning his gaze to me. He was broad faced, on the short side, but with plenty of muscle and tense energy. Tiny beads of sweat gathered under locks of brown hair falling across his forehead.

"Smart," I said. "You can't reveal what you don't know."

"Yes. They're clever with their interrogations. Watch yourself," he said. Judging by his accent he was what the Brits called a toff, a rich upper-class type. But his eyes shone with a crazed wariness that hinted at something coiled and prepared to strike.

"I do," I told him. "Have time for a cup of tea?"

"You don't drink tea," he said, pulling a notebook from his tunic pocket. He slapped it against one palm. "Coffee, all day long. I've been watching. Taking notes. You walked a lot when you first came here. Then they put you to sleep. No telling what they did to you then, my good chap. Now you don't walk as much, but you ask a lot of questions. Of everyone."

"Still, I don't get many answers," I said, eyeing his notebook. "I bet you do, though."

"They're all in here," he said, tapping his head. "My notes are in code. It's unbreakable. Once I write things down, they go directly into my brain. Never forget a thing."

"Why'd you look up to the tower?" I asked, watching as he wrote a few lines in his notebook, his pencil stub racing across the lined paper. As good as I was at reading upside down, I couldn't make anything out.

"Wanted to know what time it was, of course. You've lost your watch, by the way."

"Somebody swiped it while I was sleeping. You don't have their identity in your notebook by any chance?" I smiled as I said it, so he'd know I was kidding.

"No, I don't. I'm sorry. You're not a spy, are you? Here to test me? I can't be everywhere, you know."

"Hey, pal, I was only joking. Don't worry about it. I'll get another one when I'm released."

"You haven't been here long enough," he said. "Not nearly." I thought it best not to ask how long he'd been a guest at Saint Albans.

"Hey, I need to call you something. What's your given name?"

"No name," he said, his head bowed. "No name."

"Okay, No-name, you want to grab a cup of whatever?"

"No, no thank you. I have work to do. Must stay sharp, we could be called up again anytime," he said, starting to move off. "And that's all right. You may call me No-name. Because it's no name at all, don't you see?"

"Wait," I said, resisting the temptation to reach out and hold him by the arm. "How do you know so much about me? I've never seen you before."

"Ah. Put in a good word for me, will you? Reconnaissance and observation, two of the most important skills for a field agent. Must go. See you around, old boy," he said.

I was sure he would.

I couldn't resist looking up again at the clock tower. It hadn't been keeping time since I'd first seen it, being permanently stuck at ten minutes before five. A skilled observer would know that.

He'd seen something up there. Maybe now, maybe a few days ago when Holland came down the hard way. I went inside, nodding to Clarissa in her office. She didn't nod back, probably because of the sentry standing by the door. A new addition to her office décor. I hoped they hadn't decided to guard the place at night as well. I might need to make another visit.

I stopped at the door to the tower staircase. It was unlocked. I pushed it open and listened. No footsteps, no voices. I made my way up the stone stairway, taking careful, quiet steps. I could feel a presence above me, like a cold breeze at my backbone.

I opened the door to the top of the tower.

It was Faith. Alone. Standing at the edge of the parapet, resting her elbows on the stonework, her gaze cast downward to where Holland had fallen.

I let the door close quietly, so as not to startle her, but loudly enough so she'd hear. I took a couple of steps, so she'd know where I was.

"Why?" she whispered, the word nearly lost in the wind as she drew her sweater tight across her chest.

"I don't know," I said, surprised at the sound of her voice. I leaned on the parapet a few feet away from her. "I'd like to find out."

"Does it matter? He could have died over there," she said, waving her hand in the general direction of the war, somewhere over the southern horizon. "Or he could have spent the rest of his life in a place like this."

"When you put it like that, it doesn't seem like it matters. But it does to me."

"Why?" This time she faced me, looking me hard in the eye.

"Because someone got away with murder, and they might do it again. There's enough death to go around. You don't think he jumped, do you?"

"No. He wouldn't. He was putting his soul back together, bit by bit," Faith said, the sound of her voice fading into a whisper.

"Did he tell you that?"

She smiled, as if I had asked a silly question. "He was a mute, remember?"

"I thought you were too," I said.

"When I want to be, which is often. He'd begun to speak a few words at a time, yes. But only to me, as far as I know. It was difficult for him," she said. "Oh, look, the lords of the manor."

Below us, Major Snow led a group of men along the walkway, their heads bent close and their hands moving madly as they engaged in an energetic conversation. Too far away to hear, sadly. Doctors Hughes and Robinson were with another white coat I hadn't seen before. The other two men might have been the guys I'd seen earlier pulling in, a civilian and an officer, both British, both with a few years on Snow.

"What are they saying, do you think?" Faith asked.

"I don't know, but if they look up, they'll call the guards on us. What brought you up here, anyway? And how did you get in? Isn't that door kept locked?"

"You forget we're trained in the fine art of lockpicking. SOE agents, anyway, I don't know what you Yanks get up to. As for what brings me here, it is Holland. He was so comforting to sit with. He's gone, but I can pretend he's right here. Or maybe he is . . ." She broke off, catching me looking at the bandages on her wrists. "Oh no, Boyle, I haven't come up here to jump. I had my chance at self-slaughter. I couldn't cut deep enough. But I did cut, give me that much."

"You and Iris both?" I asked.

"Yes. It's what brought us together here. The shared desperation and stupidity of failed suicide," she said, a bitter laugh escaping her lips. We stood in silence, feeling the wind against our faces.

"Do you want to go back?" I asked, thinking about my own time behind enemy lines as I tossed a glance to that distant horizon.

"Yes. So I might feel alive again. Feel anything. Even terror would be welcome. Now, Boyle, one more question. Then I will descend the stairway into silence. It's much better than putting up with inane conversation, don't you think?"

"I do. I just couldn't keep my own mouth shut long enough to pull it off," I said. "Here's my question. Who would have wanted Holland dead?"

"I truly do not know. But I wonder, did he make anyone here look to be a failure? Perhaps he was an embarrassment, a testament to faulty treatment. Or a botched mission."

I studied Snow and his group below as they took the walkway to the front entrance. It was a good question. "Maybe Robinson?" I said. But my only answer was the tower door slamming shut behind Faith.

The noise caused Snow to look up, then quickly away. I studied the unknown officer, barely able to make out the crown and two stars on his shoulder boards. A colonel. Snow's boss? Come to check up on him? Maybe that was standard after a patient death. Or maybe it was simply a routine inspection. The civilian had seen Snow's upward glance and did the same. There was something about him, something familiar I couldn't place. He tipped back his black homburg hat as he looked up, allowing me a good look at his face. Neatly trimmed gray mustache, round cheeks, finished off with bags under his eyes. An overworked bureaucrat, maybe a retread from the last war. Perhaps I'd seen him at SHAEF or in London.

Before they'd gotten through the door, I was down the stairs, unwilling to sit through questions about what I was doing in the tower, and how I'd gotten through the locks. I knew a bit about lockpicking but there was no reason to let them know that, and I had no desire to rat out Faith. I eased the staircase door shut and darted out, as I heard the murmur of voices echoing in the foyer. No need to run into a gaggle of brass and high hats if I didn't need to.

I took a swing around the asylum to stretch my legs and think. My legs got more out of it than my brain, so I decided to treat my stomach to an early supper and see if that helped. Mutton stew was the evening's dish, made tolerable by not much mutton and an abundance of carrots and potatoes. The food helped, and I began to think about my pal No-name. If he was writing anything other than jumbled scribbles in that notebook of his, he could be in real trouble. I needed to find him, if he wasn't hiding out in the shrubbery.

Upstairs, I checked in with the guard at the entrance to my floor and was about to ask if he knew where No-name bunked. He had a clipboard and a checklist in front of him, but instead of writing down my name and the time, he looked down the hallway and nodded.

The crash of bootheels sounded, harsh echoes advancing down the hall as the guard stepped behind me, blocking my escape.

I was trapped.

CHAPTER NINETEEN

A COUPLE OF burly orderlies grabbed my arms and manhandled me upstairs to the third floor. One was muscle-bound, the other thinner and in need of a bath. The guard darted ahead to unlock the door. He didn't meet my eyes as he held it open, staring down at the linoleum as if the cracked and warped patterns were of intense personal interest.

"Hey, what gives?" I asked, twisting my arms as I tried to figure out what the hell was happening. "Where are you taking me?"

"You have an appointment," the smelly one said. "Take it easy, mate."

"Okay, okay, so I missed my session with Dr. Robinson," I said, remembering where I should have been hours ago. Not that we were headed for Robinson's office. "No need for the rough stuff."

"Calm down, it'll be easier that way," the other orderly said, tightening his muscular grip on my arm. A third orderly approached us, leading Miller, who shuffled along, his eyes glassy and dazed, his haughtiness and bravado gone. He stared at me, his forehead wrinkled, as if he were trying to figure out how he knew me or what century it was.

I didn't like this.

This hallway was as grimy as the third floor in the north wing, but when they steered me into a room everything changed. It was sparkling white, the windows spotless and clean. An exam table stood in the middle of the room, draped in a white sheet. A nurse stood next to a device in a polished wooden case, its protruding dials and knobs looking like something from a Frankenstein movie.

"Boyle, is it?" This from a doctor in a white smock, the same fellow I'd seen walking with Hughes and Robinson. He was ruddy-faced and dark-haired, with a thin pencil mustache, the kind that looked good on Ronald Colman and in this guy's imagination. He busied himself leafing through a file, glancing up to check my face against a photograph. "I'm Dr. Fielding. Dr. Robinson has scheduled you for a round of electric convulsion treatments. He's explained it to you, I'm sure. Now hop on the table and we'll get started. And don't worry, it sounds worse than it is."

"No, he hasn't mentioned anything about this," I said, backing up a step. "What is that contraption anyway?"

"Come, come, don't be nervous, lad," Fielding said. "Nothing to worry about." With that, he signaled the orderlies who lifted me onto the table. The nurse cooed soothing words I couldn't make out as a rising terror filled my mind. This was wrong. Robinson wouldn't spring this on me with no warning.

"I want to talk with Dr. Robinson," I said. "Now."

"Sorry, not possible. I have his signed order here for a series of electric convulsive therapies. You've had ample time to discuss this with him. Now lie back on the table. It can be done the easy way or the hard way."

The orderlies decided on the hard way before I had a chance to respond. They shoved me flat, one of them then grasping my ankles and the other positioning himself at my shoulders in a smooth and well-practiced move. The nurse lifted the sheets on either side to cover me, revealing leather straps, which the orderlies cinched tight, immobilizing me.

"What the hell is this?" I searched their eyes for even the slightest of sympathetic glances, but they were strictly business. "Please tell me what you're doing, for God's sake!" I could hear the fear in my voice, which had nothing on the panic flashing red in my brain.

"Standard practice, Boyle," Fielding said. He held a *U*-shaped instrument, which was attached to the box with the dials. The electric part of the therapy was obvious, since the box was plugged into an outlet with a heavy-duty cord. "We pass a current of electric energy through your brain. It simulates a seizure, which oddly enough helps to curb certain instances of mental illness. Robinson should have covered all this." He shook his head at the failure of his colleague to follow the established procedure.

Before I could protest, the nurse put a wad of gauze into my mouth and tied off the ends around my head.

"That will stop you from biting your tongue," Fielding said, setting electrodes at my temples. "The restraints are to keep you from injuring yourself, don't worry about them. Now, the first few shocks will be at the lower end of the spectrum. We shall begin with one hundred and eighty volts for a few seconds. Ready?"

I shook my head no.

Everyone else said yes.

I didn't know what hit me. A sharp burning pain flashed through my head as my body arched against the restraints, muscles clenching and limbs writhing, my jaw trying to saw through the mouth guard.

Then it stopped, and it felt like I dropped back onto the table from one hundred feet up. I tried to breathe, but I couldn't get enough oxygen. I gasped as my chest heaved but no one was paying any attention. The orderlies looked bored, the nurse looked anywhere but at me, and Fielding studied his chart.

"Good. Now two hundred, please." The nurse worked a dial as I tried to ready myself. But I had no idea how to prepare, no defense against the shock of pain that seemed to have been everywhere, in every cell of my body and in the deepest recesses of my mind.

"Stop this now! Immediately!"

The voice boomed with authority. I recognized it, but not the man himself.

"Turn that infernal contraption off and release this man!"

"You can't interrupt a medical procedure! Get out of here," Dr. Fielding said. "Who do you think you are?"

"Charles Cosgrove of His Majesty's Foreign Office. And if you do not comply immediately, each one of you, you shall find yourselves posted to the most miserable, flea-infested field hospital in North Africa within twenty-four hours, I promise you."

It was a specific threat, delivered with authority, by a man I barely recognized. But the attitude, bluster, and tone were genuine Major Charles Cosgrove of the British Army, whom I'd last seen six months ago, not far from this spot, recovering from a heart attack.

"What gives you the authority to make such threats?" Dr. Fielding asked, taking a step back as he did, putting some distance between him and Cosgrove's indignation.

"My authority comes from the highest levels of the British government and this American sergeant," Cosgrove said, stepping out of the way as the clomp of boots heralded the arrival of Big Mike. It was an unbeatable one-two punch.

Fielding gave in, removing the electrodes as the orderlies unstrapped me, and I spat out the mouth guard.

"Tell me, Dr. Fielding," I said as I sat up, fighting off a wave of dizziness and struggling to comprehend Cosgrove's surprise appearance. "Did Miller just come from one of these sessions? He was in bad shape. Is he going to be okay?"

"There is often a period of confusion after a full session. Some temporary memory loss is possible as well. But you had only one dose at the lowest setting. Nothing to worry about, I assure you," Fielding said, his gaze darting nervously between Cosgrove and Big Mike.

"But if you'd given me the whole nine yards, I might have ended up like Miller? He didn't seem to know what the score was." Which is how I figured somebody wanted me.

"Yes. It's a side effect that can last for several days. Longer, in some cases. But what's this about?" Fielding asked, looking to Cosgrove for answers and getting none.

Welcome to the club, Doc.

"Good to see you, Major," I said, easing myself off the table and ignoring Fielding. "You too, Big Mike. Let's get the hell out of here."

"That would be a pleasure," Cosgrove said.

"Like old times," Big Mike said with a grin, grabbing my arm and leading me out of that room.

"Yeah, always in trouble," I said, with a glance back at Fielding's open mouth.

I'd met Major Charles Cosgrove back in 1942. He'd been in uniform then, part of MI-5, the British security service. Colonel Harding and Cosgrove had worked together, which meant that I'd had to take orders from both of them. That was a trial with Cosgrove, since he was a British officer of the old school who looked down on Yank interlopers and their smart-aleck remarks. Which only led me to make as many smart-aleck remarks as possible. But we found a way to work together effectively. Until a heart attack laid him low and he ended up at Saint Albans.

He was the officer I'd visited here, months ago. A lifetime ago. I hadn't paid much attention to the other patients, since he was strictly a short-timer, housed in one of the smaller buildings out back reserved for VIPs visiting on a temporary basis.

"I hardly recognized you, Major," I said as we descended the staircase. He looked to be about fifty pounds lighter. The gray mustache he'd worn in the old-fashioned walrus style was nicely trimmed up, and with his well-tailored gray suit and neatly combed hair, he looked younger. A dapper gent.

"Strictly civilian these days, Boyle. But I don't mind the title. Wore the uniform so many years I rather think I still have it on. Come, we'll catch up in Snow's office and see if we can determine who's bungled things."

"I still can't believe you're here, especially since this is where I saw you last," I said, as I noticed another change. "And you're not using a cane anymore."

"That heart attack was a godsend," Cosgrove said. He didn't explain, but his tone was fervent.

We marched into Snow's office. He was conferring with Robinson, and we seemed to have caught them in the middle of a hushed argument. They both rose, which I took as a mark of respect to Cosgrove. I wondered what he did at the Foreign Office, and how high up he was.

"Boyle, thank God you're all right," Robinson said, setting down the telephone. "Fielding just called."

"I'm sure in the grand scheme of things God played a part, but it was Major Cosgrove who came to my rescue," I said, taking a seat in front of Snow's desk. Cosgrove walked briskly to Snow's seat behind his desk and sat himself down, leaving no doubt as to the pecking order.

Big Mike stood by the door with his arms folded, creating a pleasant sense of coiled menace. Snow and Robinson took the other chairs, and Cosgrove barely waited until their rear ends were settled in to go at them.

"What level of cock-up are we dealing with here, gentlemen? Medical incompetence? A breach of security?" Cosgrove eyed both men. Robinson's jaw dropped and Snow rolled his eyes.

"Come, come, Charles, it's obviously a mix-up in the paperwork," Snow said. "You've known me long enough to realize I run a tight ship. No one's gotten through my security."

"Wait a minute," Robinson said. "Just because you two are old chums, don't plan on laying the blame on me. I never ordered convulsive therapy for Boyle."

"Electric convulsive therapy," I said. "Don't leave out the most shocking part."

"Is this your signature?" Cosgrove asked, sliding a paper across the desk. "I removed this from Fielding's torture chamber."

"Firstly, *electric* convulsive therapy is not torture. It's an accepted procedure to calm patients with suicidal and depressive thoughts. Secondly, I did not sign this order for Boyle to receive it, although this is a reasonable forgery," Robinson said, shoving the form back to Cosgrove. "And thirdly, Boyle is in no need of such treatment, although others here have benefited from it."

"Who has access to these forms?" Cosgrove demanded.

"Medical personnel, of course," Snow said. "Any time a physician orders treatment of any sort, it's recorded. There's plenty of blank copies floating around, anyone could have filled it in and forged Robinson's signature. Doctors have notoriously bad penmanship, to which I can attest."

"Are these forms delivered to Fielding in person?" Cosgrove asked.

"No, not unless it's an emergency. They're left in the clerical office, where the professional staff check for messages," Snow said.

"Often several times a day," Robinson said. "Anybody could have left that in Fielding's message box without arousing notice."

"I might think of one," I said. "My sanity. I saw what Miller looked like after his go with the electrodes. I doubt he could put two full sentences together."

"Miller is one of yours, Dr. Robinson?" Cosgrove asked. Snow gave Robinson a nod of permission to spill.

"Yes. An American officer. He came back from occupied France in a bad way. Delusional and guilt-ridden, without going into excessive detail. He had his first session today, and there will be two or three more after he's rested. Memory loss and confusion are typical, but they both pass with time. What we hope for is to interrupt the delusions and allow his brain to function more normally."

"How does nearly electrocuting someone do that?" I asked. "All I know is that it hurt like the devil."

"As does the dentist, Boyle," Robinson said. "But you go for your own good. It's the same thing with convulsive therapy. It was developed in Italy during the 1930s, supposedly after a doctor noticed a butcher shocking his pigs before slaughtering them. It had a calming effect, he claimed."

"If you're comparing me to an animal being led to slaughter, I think you might be onto something," I said.

"It's a matter of creating a seizure in the brain," Robinson explained, ignoring my comment even as Snow managed a grin. "We know that mental patients who experience natural seizures report a period of relative calm afterwards. That's what the electrodes simulate, and why you must be secured, so you don't injure yourself thrashing about."

"Enough with the medical explanations," Cosgrove said, waving his hand for Robinson to stop. "I think Boyle's remark is more to the point. Being led to the slaughter is an overstatement, but this has to have been done for a reason."

"If that's true, and I'm not suggesting it is," Snow said, with a guilty look in my direction, "then it may have something to do with Boyle volunteering to look into Holland's death." He drummed fingers on his knee, glancing nervously between Cosgrove and Robinson.

"Major Snow has told me of your assistance, Boyle," Cosgrove said, cocking an inquisitive eyebrow in my direction. I hadn't volunteered, but I had agreed to look into it, so I gave Snow the benefit of the doubt and let the comment slide. SOE agent or not, he was still a bureaucrat with egg on his face.

"I can't say I found anything out," I said. "Nothing worth this setup."

"Wait a minute, what are you talking about?" Robinson said, rising from his seat. "You can't use a patient of mine for something like that. I said he wasn't in need of shock therapy, but I didn't say he was ready to be your stooge."

"Hey, I resemble that remark," I said in a nasally voice. Big Mike laughed. The Brits didn't get it. "All I did was ask around about Holland. I was curious about what happened, so it wasn't an act. I just talked with people. Not much else to do around here."

"Did you learn anything of value?" Cosgrove said.

"All I picked up was that Holland didn't antagonize or speak to anyone. No previous attempts to take his own life and no apparent reason to take up the habit. There are only two possibilities in my book. One is that he knew something, and if he ever broke his silence it would come out. But you'd know more about that, Doc," I said, looking to Robinson. Again, Snow gave him the nod.

"I saw no sign of Holland ending his silence. He'd retreated so far into it I'm doubtful he'd ever have come out. He was tortured by the Gestapo and didn't break. But whatever iron will he exercised has shut down his mind and taken over completely."

"Good God," Cosgrove said, closing his eyes for a moment. "Boyle, what's the other possibility?"

"That Holland was killed to produce a reaction," I said, looking around for one. Nothing. "Is he what brought you here, Major Cosgrove?"

"Only partially. I came with Colonel John Blackford. He's director of the German Section of SOE. He has a staff member here recovering from nervous exhaustion who he needed to consult with. With your permission, I believe, Dr. Robinson."

"Yes," Robinson said. "The sleep cure worked wonders for Lieutenant Densmore, as it did with Boyle. It was more physical exhaustion, as it turned out. He's here as a guest. A voluntary stay, at the urging of Colonel Blackford, but he's free to leave whenever he wishes."

"Colonel Blackford said he knew Holland," Snow offered. "He mentioned it in passing, but I didn't think much of it. The colonel has held several posts in intelligence, from Monty's 21st Army Group to various SOE training stations. Stands to reason he'd know a number of active agents."

"Blackford and I were both curious about Holland," Cosgrove said. "We'd served on a selection board together and approved Holland for his first mission. Solid marks as I recall. I'd planned to ask about the matter, but it was not my primary reason for coming."

"You both know Colonel Blackford?" I asked.

"Yes. It was a small army between wars," Cosgrove said. "The three of us have served together at one time or another, as we all gravitated to intelligence work. I did liaison duty with the colonel in his German Section over the winter, right before our last collaboration."

"Have you two worked together recently?" I asked, wondering what Cosgrove's connection might be.

"Yes," Cosgrove said, with a knowing glance at Snow, who sat stonefaced. "SOE business in Italy. Classified stuff, I'm afraid. Anyway, Blackford and I ran into each other at SOE headquarters and discovered we had the same destination. We drove together from London, and that's when I saw you on the pathway."

"Are you in hot water, Major Snow?" I asked. Cosgrove's explanation made sense, but he was only one half of the equation. "Is Blackford here to investigate you?"

"No, I don't think so," Snow said, absentmindedly rubbing his leg, perhaps remembering the wound that had put him here on desk duty. "If he was, there'd be no secret about it. If SOE took the Holland matter seriously, I'd be relieved in an instant. Suicide in a place like this is not totally unexpected, or preventable, as far as that goes. Wouldn't you say, Robinson?"

"True enough, sadly. I can't say I see that Holland's death was a lure for anyone, Boyle, but it does stand to reason you may have angered someone with your questions. Have you thought of that?"

"Another patient, you mean?"

"Certainly. Who else have you questioned?"

"I doubt anybody thought they were being questioned," I said, leaving out my chats with Clarissa, Jenkins, and Dr. Hughes. No reason to invite them into any hot water about to brew up. "Tell me about the guy with the notebook. One of your SOE boys, I'd guess. Wouldn't tell me his name."

"Griffin," Robinson said, not bothering to wait for the okay from Snow. "He was pulled from an SOE team right before they were dropped. Had a severe anxiety attack. He's convinced himself he's here for further training."

"The real reason?" I asked.

"He knows too much about the mission, and his nerves can't be trusted. We need to keep him secure until the entire operation is over," Snow said. "Which could be months."

"He's harmless enough," Robinson said. "But very observant. And intelligent, even with his mind a bit jumbled."

"I'd say he bears further scrutiny," Cosgrove said, with a quick look at Snow. "Dr. Robinson, is Captain Boyle recovered sufficiently to be released?"

"I think he could use more of a rest and to come to grips with his emotions," Robinson said. "But if he's needed, I'd say he's fit for duty. Perhaps not one hundred percent, but close enough."

"I'm glad to concur with the doctor's recommendation," Snow said, with a curt nod in Cosgrove's direction.

"Thanks for the vote of confidence, Doc," I said. "But maybe you shouldn't cut me loose right away."

"I can't believe you enjoy being locked up, Boyle," Cosgrove said.

"Not one damn bit. But someone's tried to have my brains fried so I'd forget what I've learned. I wouldn't mind finding out what it is they're afraid of, and what I'm supposed to know. Just hold off for a day so I can dig around."

"They may have another go at you," Snow said. "Perhaps more directly."

"I'll watch my back," I said. "You still want to be sure about Holland, don't you?"

"Certainly," Snow said. "Very well, I'll prepare the release orders and hold them until you're ready. What about the baron?"

"I spoke with Dr. Hughes," Cosgrove said. "He's agreed to allow an American army physician to examine Baron Kazimierz. We shall wait upon his recommendation, if that's satisfactory."

"Hughes mentioned that to me," Robinson said. "I'm surprised he concurred. He has strong feelings about operations involving the heart. He believes it could be fatal."

"Perhaps he saw the profit in it," I said. "For Kaz."

Big Mike coughed and shuffled his feet.

"It seems we have covered all the points," Cosgrove said, leaning back in his chair. "Major, perhaps you could allow us to borrow your office for a while longer. Boyle and I need to catch up. Would you mind?"

"Make yourself at home, Charles," Snow said. "Refreshments are in the usual place."

"Thank you, Basil," Cosgrove said, standing as Snow and Robinson left. "And it is good to see you again, even under these circumstances. Check on Blackie, will you? He was getting settled in."

"I shall. And I'll have a guard posted outside the guest quarters, for both your sakes," Snow said. "Same thing with your room, Boyle."

"Don't make it too obvious, Major," I said. "We don't want anyone thinking we're in cahoots."

"Be careful, Boyle," Robinson said, stopping by the door. "You've been through a lot lately. There might not be smooth sailing ahead."

"When is there ever, Doc?"

Big Mike opened the door and ushered them out, shutting it with a loud thud.

"This place is nuts," he said.

"Pithy," Cosgrove said.

Maybe he'd gotten my Three Stooges joke after all.

CHAPTER TWENTY

COSGROVE PULLED A bottle from the file cabinet behind him and poured three glasses of brandy. We toasted and the fiery liquid hit the back of my throat like a flamethrower. The booze warmed my gut as I fell into the chair and took another slug. A smaller one this time.

"Take it easy," Big Mike said. "You haven't had a belt in a while. No telling if your brain is still scrambled."

"Yeah," I agreed, setting down the glass. "First, thanks for getting me out of there. Second, how the hell did you find me?"

"I was taking the major over to see you," Big Mike said. "The guard on your floor didn't seem to know where you were, but he looked worried. Maybe a little guilty. So, I explained things to him."

"And well explained, I'll add," Cosgrove said, smiling as he shook a fist in the air. "He directed us to Fielding's lab on the third floor. Just in time. What was it like, Boyle?"

"Like having electric eels in my head, topped off with uncontrollable spasms," I said, suddenly moved to finish my drink.

"You must have gotten close to something, Billy," Big Mike said.

"I wish I knew what," I said. "The only thing I didn't mention was that Dr. Hughes had asked me to sniff around as well. More casually than Snow, but he was definitely interested in whatever had happened with Holland."

"Basil told me he and Hughes were together when Holland went over. Close, as you were," Cosgrove said. "It could be natural curiosity."

"Maybe, but I do wonder about the good doctor," I said. Then, lowering my voice, "Did Big Mike fill you in on Kaz bribing Hughes?"

"He can save his money," Cosgrove said, with a dismissive wave of his hand. "It was I who arranged for Dr. Harken to make a stop here on his tour of British military hospitals. I fully intended that he examine Baron Kazimierz. If anyone can help him, it will be Dwight Harken."

"You place a lot of faith in this guy, Major," I said, sliding my glass across the desk.

"I should. I trusted him with my life," Cosgrove said. He refilled our glasses, took a healthy swig, leaned back, and told his story.

After his heart attack in March, Cosgrove had been sent to recuperate at Saint Albans. In the guest quarters, not the heavily supervised hospital. He'd been examined by doctors who'd prescribed bed rest, sedatives, and a lot of luck. He received his medical discharge from the service, went home, and consulted his own MD. The doctor told him to avoid excitement and gave him a supply of digitalis pills to take in case of chest pain.

Cosgrove took the pills but not the advice. He still desired to serve, even if in a civilian capacity, and was determined to find a way. For an old warhorse like him, it was unthinkable not to stay in the fight until Germany was defeated. He began to make the rounds of heart specialists.

The fourth doctor he consulted offered some hope. Dr. Brendan Powell asked questions about Cosgrove's symptoms and his history of chest pain. About the attack itself and previous medical conditions. Finally, about the wounds he'd suffered in the Great War. Dr. Powell was a maverick within the British medical community. He believed surgery on the heart was possible, going against the overwhelming opinion that it was dangerous and the long-standing belief that the heart itself could not stand manipulation, much less cutting.

Powell had recently met the American surgeon Major Dwight Harken, who scoffed at the conventional wisdom as well. Harken had been removed from the Mediterranean Theater of Operations by the head of US Army Medical Service, who had forbidden the removal of foreign objects in the area of the heart.

Harken now worked under a more enlightened command at the US Army's 160th General Hospital near Oxford. Powell had observed Harken operating on wounded GIs, removing shrapnel from within the human heart.

POWELL LEARNED ABOUT tiny shrapnel fragments migrating to the intracardial region and embedding themselves in the heart's inner chamber, where they were capable of doing great damage.

All of which led Dr. Powell to ask Cosgrove about his own wartime injuries that day in his London office, a question that took Cosgrove by surprise. The major had been wounded in an artillery barrage back in 1917. Army surgeons had told him they'd gotten most of the fragments out, but that he'd carry small splinters of metal within him for the rest of his life. And not to worry about it.

Powell took X-rays and found several one-centimeter fragments sitting within the cardiac shadow on the image. The shrapnel had taken a twenty-seven-year journey through Cosgrove's bloodstream and ended up deep within his beating heart. That's what had felled him and could kill him at any moment, courtesy of a blood clot forming around the metal, breaking off, and traveling to another organ. All thanks to some German artilleryman from the last war.

Dr. Powell was eager to try Harken's technique. The British medical corps had not approved this new procedure, and he hoped to push for its adoption. Harken agreed to observe the operation, but it was Powell's show. Harken didn't like Cosgrove's chances. He was not in the best physical shape and considerably older than the GIs who were being brought back from battle. He feared the loss of a patient would give the medical naysayers a reason to outlaw this radical new procedure.

But Cosgrove consented, willing to take the chance. Powell would be operating in a well-equipped, modern London hospital, not a

Quonset hut in the Oxfordshire countryside. So, with Harken at his side in an unofficial capacity, Powell opened Cosgrove's chest.

"The fellow plucked the blighters out between beats of my heart," Cosgrove said, draining the last of the brandy in his glass. "Powell explained the details, but I preferred to blur the vision in my mind. No use thinking about it, eh?"

"I'm amazed you're looking so fit, Major. That must have knocked the stuffing out of you," I said. I figured that having his rib cage cracked open would have laid up a gray-haired gent like Cosgrove for months.

"All part of Harken's regimen," Cosgrove said. "They demanded I get out of bed the next day and walk the corridors. I wasn't in the mood for it, I don't mind saying, but I wanted to prove him wrong about my being too decrepit for the operation. In a few days I was feeling limber. Up and out, that's his motto, and, by God, it worked. So much so that I kept up the walking regime to keep myself fit."

"So, when you heard about Kaz and me getting put in here, you decided to have Dr. Harken in for a second opinion," I said, thinking about the threads that had pulled Cosgrove back to Saint Albans.

"I did," Cosgrove said, busying himself with another refill. The liquor had hit me hard, but I still knew there was a missing piece to this puzzle.

"I didn't know the Foreign Office kept tabs on Saint Albans," Big Mike said. He shot me a quick glance, and I knew his cop's instinct was at work. It was like a friendly interrogation, but it was still an interrogation. Cosgrove was obviously keeping something back, and the best way to find out what was to tug gently until he had no choice but to give it up.

"Well, I knew Skory would be brought here, and when I contacted Basil to make arrangements, he mentioned you and Baron Kazimierz. He knew of our work together and thought I'd be concerned," Cosgrove said. "Which I was."

"Fast work," Big Mike said. "Especially since you had no way of knowing Skory would need a hospital. He was shot right before the aircraft picked him up."

"What are you getting at?" Cosgrove demanded, slamming one

hand flat on the desk. That was more like the old Cosgrove. "The RAF Dakota that picked him up was in radio contact the entire time. I knew every detail of his injuries."

"Listen, Major," I said, "we appreciate what you're doing for Kaz. I hope Dr. Harken can help him as much as he helped you, even if shrapnel isn't Kaz's problem. But I know you well enough to know there's some other angle you're working. Why exactly are you here? Holland isn't really your main concern, and you could have arranged for Harken's visit from London. Skory is unconscious. Maybe he'll be awake tomorrow, who knows? But it all begs the question, what are you doing here now?" I knew I should be grateful; after all, he'd rescued me from the high-voltage treatment. But that didn't mean I liked wondering what his next move was.

"Come on, Major," Big Mike said. "You're a good man. How bad can it be?" Cosgrove didn't answer for a long minute. I began to think it might be damn bad at that.

"Nearly dying, then being granted life, is a strange experience," Cosgrove said, rising and walking to the window behind Snow's desk. He pulled the curtain and stared into the darkness. "I wanted to do something good. To balance things out."

"What's out of balance?" I asked, wondering if there were things he'd done in the name of God and country that he was now ashamed of.

"I am aware that the baron's sister, Angelika, is in Ravensbrück. And I am aware as well of the reason she was picked up," Cosgrove said.

"Her small hands," I said.

"Indeed. Otherwise, she might have been left alone. Or killed. No telling with these Nazi swine," he said, pulling the curtain tightly shut in an angry gesture. "I'm also aware of Diana Seaton's incarceration there." With that, he turned to face me.

"Okay," I said, waiting for the bad news.

"She is an SOE agent in Ravensbrück under a false identity. That is a tremendous advantage to us," he said.

"To us? What about her?"

"And to her, yes," Cosgrove said. "The Germans are holding other

SOE agents in Ravensbrück, but they were known to them when taken. Miss Seaton, however, is simply a French girl involved with the Resistance as far as the Gestapo knows. Hundreds like her are in that camp."

"Major, please tell me what this means," I said, walking to the window and facing him. "What's going on?

"I have a plan. A plan that may result in Miss Seaton being freed soon. Very soon." It should have been good news, but the way he said it I knew bad news was not far behind.

"But not Angelika," Big Mike said.

"No. Not Angelika Kazimierz," he said. "As a matter of fact, it may well result in her death."

CHAPTER TWENTY-ONE

"I NEED SOME air," Cosgrove said. He stashed the brandy and strode out of Snow's office, Big Mike and me trailing him into the night, neither of us able to form a coherent sentence or ask a decent question.

Diana, alive and free. It was too good to be true. But at too terrible a price.

Or was it? So asked the small, selfish voice in my brain.

I never knew Angelika. Kaz had already thought her dead once. What was the difference a second time around?

I immediately felt ashamed.

After that, I realized that if Diana ever found out her freedom was at the cost of Angelika's life, she'd never recover.

When I first met Diana, she was racked with guilt from her experience at Dunkirk. She'd been with a First Aid Nursing Yeomanry detachment, working the headquarters switchboard for the British Expeditionary Force. Until the rear area was overrun with panzers and everything fell apart. She'd been evacuated on a destroyer crowded with the wounded; the decks were covered in stretcher cases. The ship was hit by Stuka dive-bombers. As it capsized, she watched the men strapped to their stretchers slide into the cold Channel waters.

She survived. And always wondered why. It had nearly crippled her, but she'd come through, like the tough British lady she was. But if this plan came to pass as Cosgrove had laid it out, nothing could ever make it right.

"Wait up, Major," I said, double-timing to keep up with him. For all his gray hair, he could move at a damn brisk pace. "What's the plan? And what's Angelika got to do with it?"

"It's the bloody V2s," he shouted, then looked about guiltily, discomfiture flooding his face over the unseemly outburst. "We have to stop them, at all cost."

"Okay, I've heard about the V1 rocket," I said, glancing at Big Mike. He was more in the know than I was, but he simply raised his eyebrows. Cosgrove was spilling top-grade stuff.

"A child's toy in comparison," Cosgrove replied, his arms pumping. "The V2 is a guided missile. A supersonic weapon that is impossible to shoot down and carries a twenty-two-hundred-pound warhead. The first have just hit Paris. There will be more."

"I don't get it," I said, trying to keep up physically and mentally. This sounded like Buck Rogers stuff. "What the hell does this have to do with Diana?"

"It's the Swedes, Boyle," Cosgrove said, stopping on a dime and facing me, his eyes narrowed with anger and frustration. "That is the main reason I am here. To make certain you and the baron never speak of Sweden again."

"How do you even know about that?" I asked, as he resumed his pace.

"I wrote up a report for Harding," Big Mike said. "Kaz filled me in as soon as he was well enough."

"It was the mention of the Swedes that caused it to be flagged and brought to my attention," Cosgrove said. "You haven't told anyone else, have you?"

"No. I couldn't make any sense of it, so I thought the smart move was not to tell anyone here. They already thought I was crazy," I said. "And I still don't understand any more than I did when that German officer told me to go to the Swedes about Diana."

"Keep your voice down, man!" Cosgrove said. "Come, we'll go to my quarters. I don't want to chance anyone overhearing you. That would result in an extended stay at Saint Albans. Big Mike, tell Boyle about Skory's connection to this." With that, he bent his head and tramped on, stones crunching under his determined steps. He wasn't ready to explain everything, which I could understand, since the plan probably included trading lives for the greater good or some similar rationalization for betraying people who needed your help. I wanted Diana safe, but I didn't want to end this war with innocent blood on my hands. So I listened as Big Mike put a few of the puzzle pieces together.

"The Krauts have a weapons research center on the Baltic coast," he began. "They've been testing a new rocket, this V2. The Polish Underground has been keeping tabs on them and snatching parts from the rockets that crash along the Polish coastline."

"Stands to reason they would have a few crashes, if they're working out the kinks," I said.

"Yeah. The Poles had their scientists study the collected parts. Then about three weeks ago a V2 rocket, mostly intact, landed in a marsh. The Krauts couldn't find it, but a local farmer had seen it hit. He contacted the Polish Underground, and they got some scientists and professors to take a look at it. They took photographs and disassembled the most important components."

"Let me guess. One of those scientists was Skory."

"Right. He was the lead guy. The underground contacted the SOE who devised a plan to get Skory and the V2 parts out. He had the photographs and about a hundred pounds of components. The Brits stripped down a Dakota and loaded it with enough fuel to make the round-trip flight. They picked up Skory, but not before he'd been shot up at a roadblock on his way to the airstrip. The hardware and photos got here safely, and the doctors say he'll be okay."

Big Mike clammed up as two men walked toward the three of us, their white coats marking them as doctors even in the darkness. Dr. Hughes and Dr. Fielding, in an animated conversation. They didn't look up until we were a few yards apart, and I saw the surprise register on Fielding's face. He probably didn't like being reminded of the one who got away. Hughes frowned, and I realized it was after curfew for patients. But he didn't say anything. Maybe word had gotten around that I had influential friends. Or maybe Big Mike looked scary in the dark.

"Like I was saying," Big Mike picked up when they were out of hearing, "the doctors say Skory will be awake tomorrow and ought to be up and about in a couple of days."

"And we know Angelika was picked up for the purpose of working on delicate machinery. I can guess what machinery we're talking about, given Feliks's involvement with Skory."

"It's a guess, but a good guess," Cosgrove said. "We know Jerry has farmed out production of different components for the V2. We've bombed their facility at Peenemünde enough that they can't make all the parts there. And we know there's a V2 factory right outside the Ravensbrück camp, run by Siemens and Halske, an electrical firm."

We took a path off the main walkway, and I saw the dim outline of the guest quarters ahead. It was a long single-story building with a wide front porch and four entrances. This was where I'd visited Cosgrove months ago. Funny how at the time I hadn't paid much attention to the place. It was just another secret SOE outpost with a lot of security. Now I knew why.

"Blackie," Cosgrove shouted to a figure on the porch.

"What ho, Charles!" The pungent odor of tobacco floated on the night air as the rosy glow of his pipe lit the face of Colonel Blackford. He sat in a wicker chair, legs crossed, collar undone, and looking thoroughly at ease. High cheekbones sat on an angular face, a shock of black hair trimmed close on the sides accenting the narrowness of his features.

"Very glad to meet you," Blackford said, after Cosgrove had done the introductions. "I've heard a great deal about you, Boyle. I must say the first reports were colorful and occasionally dicey. Lately they've been rather laudable." He grinned and saluted me with his pipe.

"Always glad to be on the major's good side, Colonel," I said.

"Care for a drink, gentlemen? I have a decent bottle of Scotch inside," Blackford said, eyeing the three of us.

"Not now, Blackie," Cosgrove said. "We still have a bit of work to do. Did things go well with your man Densmore?"

"Well enough. I didn't want to push him too hard. Dr. Robinson just came by to tell me to expect my chap to be released in four days, which is none too soon. I'll finish my work with him tomorrow and then toddle off. Let me know if you'll need a ride, Charles," he said, with another briar-pipe salute.

"Wait, where's the sentry?" I asked. "Snow was going to have a guard posted."

"Basil went off to attend to that a few minutes ago," Blackford said, puffing his pipe back to life. "Told him it was silly, but he insisted. Can't take chances in a madhouse, eh?"

"I could tell you some electrifying stories, Colonel, but we don't have time." I tossed off a salute as Blackford stood and stretched his long arms, returning the salute with a vague, distracted movement and a grunted good night.

The three of us filed into Cosgrove's room. A couch and two easy chairs faced a fireplace in the small sitting room. We arranged ourselves as Cosgrove looked everywhere but at me.

"Okay, Major," I said. "Connect the dots for me. How does all this V2 stuff get Diana out and Angelika killed? And what the hell do the Swedes have to do with it?"

"Sweden first," he said. "But I must caution both of you. What I am going to tell you is highly sensitive information. If word of this got out it would be disastrous for all concerned."

"Understood," Big Mike said.

"We've learned that some high-ranking Nazis have seen the writing on the wall and are interested in saving their own hides," Cosgrove said, settling into his chair and the story. "Heinrich Himmler, head of the SS, among them. He's been persuaded by Walter Schellenberg, one of his most trusted deputies, to release some concentration camp prisoners as a sign of goodwill."

"He can't believe that will make any difference at this point," I said, knowing Himmler was responsible for uncountable deaths.

"It will not," Cosgrove said with a growl. "In his mind, the timing may seem fortuitous. The Swedish government has been after the Germans to release Scandinavian prisoners into their custody. The Danes as well have been demanding the return of four hundred Jews who were rounded up in 1943."

"But the Germans occupy Denmark," Big Mike said. "What clout can the Danes have?"

"Even though Denmark is occupied, they've been allowed a functioning government, and it has been demanding the release of its citizens. Probably one reason why those Danish Jews are still alive. A bit of a miracle, since most of the four hundred are those who were too old or infirm to take part in the escape to Sweden engineered by the Danish resistance."

"This is good news, right? That offer is tailor-made for Himmler's purposes. Has he agreed?" I asked.

"Not yet. But Count Folke Bernadotte, head of the Swedish Red Cross, is working on a proposal. Our contacts in Sweden tell us Himmler is petrified Hitler will find out and keeps getting cold feet. Schellenberg, on the other hand, is all for it and has suggested a trial release of one hundred prisoners."

"And if Adolf doesn't tumble to it, then they can go on to bigger and better things," Big Mike said. "Having proved to Himmler that it can be done secretly."

"Exactly," Cosgrove said. "Himmler hopes the Swedes will help him to broker a peace deal. The German officer in Paris who mentioned the Swedes to you must have known of the plan. I take it he was acquainted with Miss Seaton?"

"Yes. We'd had dealings with him before. He was Abwehr. Anti-Nazi, as far as I could tell," I said. The Abwehr was the German Army's intelligence service. It had recently been taken over by the SS following the July 20 bomb plot against Hitler. The Abwehr officer in Paris was under suspicion as well and had been happy to tip me off about the Swedes. He'd died before he could tell me what his cryptic comment meant.

"The Abwehr spends as much time spying on the SS as on us, so I'm not surprised," Cosgrove said. "I was astonished to see reference to the Swedes in your report, especially linked to Miss Seaton's transport to Ravensbrück. I came as soon as I found out."

Cosgrove took a deep breath and sat back. This was like pulling teeth.

"You've got an in with the Swedes," I said, thinking it through. Otherwise, why all the hubbub? He had to have a spy in the Swedish government. As I tried to work it out, I was distracted by the scuff of boots on the porch. I looked toward the window.

"Gotta be the guard," Big Mike said, standing up and pushing aside the curtain. "Can't see anybody, but he might be walking the perimeter."

"As you say, Boyle, I do have contact with the Swedes," Cosgrove said once Big Mike returned to his seat. "Enough so that I've arranged for her cover name, Malou something-or-other, to be on the list of one hundred people to be released."

"You can't get Angelika's name on there?" Big Mike asked. Cosgrove hung his head, slowly shaking it, his lips a thin line of reproach.

"No. They were adamant. One name only, in case everything falls apart. If this doesn't go beyond the trial run, they want to get as many of their own people out as possible," he said. "Even though Sweden is neutral, there were Swedish citizens residing elsewhere in Europe who were picked up for various offenses, or simply because they were married to the wrong person. They go first. One was the best I could do." He raised his hands in a helpless gesture.

I stood and paced the small room. Three steps, then I turned around, then three more. I got to the second turnaround and everything fell into place.

"You want Diana back because she's a trained agent and will keep her eyes and ears open. If there's anything to learn about the V2 facility at Ravensbrück, she'll pick it up. The Gestapo doesn't know she's SOE. They think she's a small-fry Resistance fighter, so they won't worry about cutting her loose. And Angelika will be dead because as soon as Diana is in your hands, you'll bomb the V2 factory outside the camp."

"This is war, Boyle. Trust me, it would be far easier on me if I didn't know the people involved. Far easier," Cosgrove said, his voice trailing off into a faint murmur.

"So Kaz gets a second chance," I said. "That's his consolation prize. He gets an American miracle worker in exchange for a dead sister. Too bad it will break his heart all over again."

"I would have done that anyway, damn you!" Cosgrove said, jumping up to face me, his voice raging through clenched teeth. "How do you think it makes me feel to have cheated death? It should have found me by now and taken me for all the things I did in the last war and this one. But it hasn't. It's left me here to make choices that chill my soul. But by God, I will make them, if only to prevent that burden from falling on another man's shoulders. If I can stop these vile missiles from raining down on us, thousands of lives will be saved. And if I find some small recompense in doing this favor for the baron, what of it?"

His hands were clenched at his side, his entire body vibrating with righteousness and guilt, a deadly cocktail of repressed emotions.

"I'll never mention Sweden again," I whispered, my jaw clenched tightly as I held his stare. "Make sure Kaz never knows you left Angelika there to die and bought him off with Dr. Harken."

"Billy, come on," Big Mike said, grabbing my arm and pulling me back, putting a couple feet of distance between me and Cosgrove. "What's he supposed to do?"

"The right thing. Something human, I don't know. But not this," I said, wrenching my arm away. "I'm going back to the madhouse. It'll be a welcome change."

I slammed the door on the way out. It felt good, the way silly gestures do, for about a second.

"You! I thought they still had you locked up, Boyle." It was Sergeant Jenkins, sitting in Blackford's wicker chair, his rifle across his knees.

"It was all a misunderstanding," I said.

"There's a lot of misunderstandings you're in the middle of," Jenkins said, drumming his fingers on the rifle stock. "Like with that electrical therapy, or so I hear."

"Yeah. You could call it that. Or maybe someone wanted me confused and forgetful for a while. You see Miller around today?"

"That Yank? I did. Not himself, he was. I'd be careful, Boyle. And speaking of not being careful, you're out after curfew. I ought to bring you back at the point of my bayonet."

"Hard to do sitting down, Sarge."

"If I thought it made sense to get up out of this comfortable chair and bother with a bloke like you who hobnobs with the high and mighty, like this lot," he said, crooking a thumb toward the guest quarters behind him, "I would. I might even think about it for the next minute or two. If you're thick enough to still be here, I'll tell you my conclusion."

"Got it," I said, stepping off the porch. "How'd you draw the short straw tonight anyway?"

"Too few men on duty. It's getting harder to convince the lads to give up a night or two when they've been at work all day. It's nothing like when we were ready for Jerry to drop out of the skies and land on the beaches. Everybody was eager, believe me. Now there's talk of standing down the Home Guard. I had to send for someone to come in from the village. I'll be here an hour or so till he shows up. What's this all about, anyway?"

"Brass, Sarge. Who knows what they're thinking?"

"God only," he said. "Same in every army."

CHAPTER TWENTY-TWO

I HIT THE sack thinking about Cosgrove. About how mad I was at him and his insidious conniving. His plan had laid bare the duplicity and double-dealing of this lousy war. He'd shown how men manipulate the lives of others from the comfort of London offices, dealing out death and survival like chips at a roulette table. On the front lines, behind the lines, or even behind barbed wire, people thought they played a role and had a choice in their own destiny. Maybe they did. But men like Cosgrove also made them dance like puppets, and no matter how glorious the cause, how high the stakes, it still belittled them and cheapened their suffering.

Cosgrove knew it. The stink of guilt trailed him like a dead fish.

Trouble was, I'd made those trade-offs, played God here and there, gave life and dealt death a hundred times over. In a place so far down in my heart and soul that I might never find my way back from it, I could sacrifice hundreds of people, maybe thousands, to get Diana back. Especially if they were strangers to me. A nameless company of GIs, families living in a row of London townhouses, sailors on a sub-marine, prisoners in a wooden barracks, they all could vanish in a flash if it would bring Diana home safely out of the hell of Ravensbrück. I could close my eyes and never see their faces. But I knew Diana's face.

She haunted my dreams.

I tried to sleep. I didn't think I'd be able to, but it had been a helluva long night and day, beginning with a bit of B and E, evading guards, a sojourn in the padded cell, and having my brain zapped. I tried to stay awake and think everything through.

But mostly I didn't want to see the vision of Diana again. Not until I'd sorted this craziness out in my own mind. At least I was in the perfect place to work on crazy.

"BILLY, WAKE UP." The words floated above me, faint and far-away. "Wake up!" I felt a hand on my shoulder, shaking me like a rag doll. It was Big Mike, towering above my bed.

"Jeez, what time is it?" I said, prying open one eye. It was light, I could tell that much. I'd slept like I was drugged and felt like I still was. "Whaddaya want?"

"You gotta get up, Billy," he said, his face flushed with urgency. "It's Cosgrove. He's dead."

"Oh God," I said, swinging my legs off the bed and rubbing my eyes. "His heart?"

"You might say that. There's a knife in his chest."

I looked up at Big Mike. I couldn't take it in. Major Charles Cosgrove had been part of my life in Europe since I'd first arrived in '42. Not always the most pleasant part, but an important one. But I had to put that aside and figure out what this meant. Who'd wanted Cosgrove dead? I couldn't see a connection between Holland and his arrival, other than a secondary interest in what had happened. I was missing something. Big time.

"Hang on," I said, grabbing a towel and heading to the washroom. "I'll just be a minute."

I cleaned up and used the time to try not to think about how Cosgrove and I had parted company. I'd taken out my own frustrations on him. He'd delivered the news about his plan and that made him an easy target for all my guilt about abandoning Diana in Paris and my worries about Kaz. I guess I figured we'd work things out in the morning. Trouble was, the clear light of day would never dawn for Charles Cosgrove.

I grabbed a clean set of olive drabs, got dressed, and found Big Mike pacing in the narrow hallway. He was shaken.

"This is strange, Billy," he said. "Really strange."

"Okay, first tell me who's at the scene," I said as we clambered down the stairs.

"Colonel Blackford. I told him not to let anyone in. His dander was up."

"You found Cosgrove?" I said as we left the building.

"Yeah. He wanted to check on Skory. We were supposed meet at seven and go to the hospital. I knocked on his door and there was no answer. I waited a minute and tried again. Blackford came out of his room, and I asked if he'd seen the major. He hadn't, so I opened the door."

"Hold on. It wasn't locked?"

"No."

"How late did you stay with Cosgrove after I left?" I asked, slowing my pace as the guest quarters came into view. I wanted to get the facts straight in my mind before I saw the body. No matter how many times you visit a crime scene, it's always a shock. But more so if the victim is no stranger to you. It's the face. Instead of seeing the face of a corpse, you see the face of a friend or acquaintance. You can harden yourself viewing a murdered stiff whose name you never knew, but it doesn't work so well with a guy you talked to last night. It's distracting. Totally human and understandable, but it makes it difficult to focus on the evidence.

"Five minutes tops," Big Mike said. "I think he was embarrassed at losing his temper. He told me you were right about what you said, by the way."

"What was his mood when you left?" I said, stopping before the steps to the guest quarters. Blackford stood by Cosgrove's door, arms folded.

"Tired. Sad, maybe. I can't really say. It was late, so I went off to bed."

"Did you see Sergeant Jenkins?"

"The guard? Yeah, out on the porch," Big Mike said. "But we didn't speak other than to say hello. I went right to my room. And no, I didn't hear anything out of the ordinary all night."

"Okay, let's go on in." Big Mike was a heavy sleeper, enough so that a tussle in the next room wouldn't register if he were out cold.

"This is a terrible business, Boyle," Colonel Blackford said. "I can't believe Charles is dead." Blackford shook his head, his disbelief playing out in his slack-jawed look and unfocused eyes.

"Has anyone come by, Colonel?" I asked, wondering how long we'd have until the place was crowded and any evidence trampled into nothing.

"No one," he said.

"And you haven't gone in? Sir."

"No. Your sergeant told me you were both policemen before the war and you needed the area undisturbed, so I stayed out here. I will keep any bystanders at bay, but I imagine Major Snow should be notified. Promptly."

"Right after we've had a look around, sir," I said. "Once Snow's on the scene it gets official, and we'll lose control. I need to be able to search the area around the guest quarters before anyone shows up."

"Of course, Boyle. Do your job. Find out who killed Charles," he said and turned away, stiff upper lip and all.

I opened the door, not worrying about fingerprints on the latch. It was probably covered in them. I stood in the doorway looking over the room, taking it in while at the same time not focusing on Cosgrove. That was one of the things Dad had insisted on when he first let me come along to crime scenes as a patrolman. His way of teaching me the ropes was to bring me along for crowd control and door-to-door questioning. I didn't always like it, especially if it came at the end of my shift, but I never complained. At least not to him. I wouldn't have dared.

His idea was to take in the room, or the alley, or wherever you found the body. Absorb the details, all of them, so you could more easily see what was out of place. It took me a while to understand what he was getting at, but once I did, I stuck with his technique.

The room was much as I'd left it, except for Cosgrove's jacket tossed over the back of a chair. The rug bunched up beneath his feet.

And the bayonet stuck in his chest.

A Lee-Enfield socket bayonet, I noted as I kept my eyes moving, cataloging the objects in the room. Big Mike had said a knife, but this British bayonet was more like a sharpened spike.

"Big Mike, get over to the Home Guard canteen," I said. "Find out who was on guard after Jenkins, and if anyone's missing their bayonet." He left with a look of relief on his face. Big Mike was a tough guy, but he and Cosgrove had gotten friendly, and it took a *really* tough guy to hang around a pal's murdered corpse.

I stepped around Cosgrove's feet. He was on the couch, slumped to one side, his legs splayed out, heels dug into the thin rug. I checked the fireplace, but no sign of anything being burned or disposed of. I got on my hands and knees and peered under the couch, finding nothing other than dust. Same thing under the chairs.

I went into the bedroom. It was cramped quarters: a dresser, night-stand, and bed took up most of the space. An overnight bag lay on the floor, displaying rumpled underclothes and rolled-up socks. Two shirts hung in a closet. Cosgrove was traveling light. A single window was open a few inches. That could have been Cosgrove letting in fresh air. Or did the killer use the window to escape? It wasn't an entry point, since that would have alerted the major. But perhaps the killer needed a quick exit with the sentry on duty out front.

A small bathroom provided no clues other than that the plumbing was ancient.

How had the killer gotten in? Had there been a gap between Jenkins on duty and his relief? Or had one of them left the place unguarded?

Cosgrove was still dressed, so it couldn't have been too late at night. I needed to speak with Jenkins and find out how long he'd been on the porch, and if he'd seen anything.

Back in the sitting room, I took a closer look at Cosgrove. His face betrayed nothing. No frozen shock of surprise, no wide-eyed terror in his death throes. Which meant he'd died quickly. Immediately, based on where the bayonet had been thrust into his heart.

It was an odd murder weapon. The steel spike had no handle, nothing to grasp when wielding it as a knife. It had a socket that could be affixed to the end of the rifle barrel. Its one advantage, when not protruding from the business end of a Lee-Enfield rifle, was that it could be easily hidden. And there were a lot of them around. Every member of the Home Guard armed with a rifle had one.

I knelt and studied the angle of the blade to the body. It hadn't gone straight in. It was angled at maybe sixty degrees, meaning that the killer had thrust upward with significant force. It was the only way, really. With no sharp edge, the point of the spike had to be driven in, hard. The bayonet could have been hidden in a coat pocket or stuck in a belt. Either way, it told me that Cosgrove had known his attacker, or, at a minimum, had felt no threat from him, letting him get close enough to unleash a killing blow.

Or her? There were women here who'd been trained to kill, silently and up close. I leaned in and looked at where the bayonet had pierced Cosgrove, between the ribs and into the heart. There was blood, but the body wasn't soaked with it. The heart had ceased pumping the stuff in no time flat. This was a killer who had a practiced aim and a steady hand, and knew what they were doing. Which did nothing to narrow the field of suspects.

"Billy," Big Mike said, out of breath as he stood in the doorway. "Snow is on his way. He saw me in the canteen asking about the bayonet. I had to tell him."

"No problem, he was bound to find out," I said.

Then I saw it.

Cosgrove's hand, already stiffening, clutched a piece of paper. I'd been so focused on the bayonet that I hadn't taken it in. I withdrew the crumpled paper from his fingers, holding it by the edges in case we could dust it for fingerprints. It was manila-colored, heavy stock. A blank postcard.

Blank on one side. The other side had a blue stamp filled with Hitler's profile. There was a typewritten message in German, but no address had been filled in. As if a German postcard with Adolf postage wasn't surprise enough, there was a stylized drawing of what I took to be a horse. A red horse enclosed in a red circle. It looked like it had been put on the card with a rubber stamp.

"What the hell is that?" Big Mike said, looking over my shoulder. "It looks sort of familiar."

"That's Adolf Hitler, big guy," I said.

"Yeah, I hearda him," Big Mike said. Jokes were a cop's best armor against the realities of a crime scene, so I knew he'd recovered his wits somewhat. "I mean the horse. It's carved into a hillside near here. The Uffington White Horse, they call it. I saw it from the train once. Doesn't look exactly like that, but close."

"Well, this is a red horse, on a Kraut postcard, in a dead man's hand. I don't think it's a local tourist brochure," I said.

"Can you read it?"

"Hell no," I said, gesturing in the direction of his service coat. "But Kaz can. Open your flap." I dropped it in the roomy pocket of his jacket. I didn't need to tell him to be careful about prints, but I did make a zipper motion across my lips a second before Snow came in.

"Dear God," Snow said from the doorway. "Who did this?"

"Someone he trusted," I said, stepping back from the body. "Major, we need this area secured before people start sightseeing. I need to check the perimeter." Snow stood still, frozen, unable to take his gaze off Cosgrove's body. "Major?"

"Yes, yes, sorry," Snow said, coming to his senses and running a hand across his eyes, as if that might alter the scene before him. He'd been Cosgrove's friend as well, but I needed him to get over the shock and on with the job.

"A few guards on the path would be good," Big Mike said, guiding him out of the room. "A couple in each direction, okay?" Snow agreed, nodding slowly. Big Mike had a calming effect, especially when he loomed over you and patted your shoulder with one of those big hands.

"Okay, what'd you find at the canteen?" I asked, once Snow was on his way.

"There's gear lying all over the place. Turns out some of the guys dump their web belts and ammo pouches there before going on duty," he said. "They figure the Krauts aren't going to storm the place, so the rounds they have in their rifles are more than enough."

"What about bayonets?"

"There's a bayonet holder on each belt. Most held a bayonet. But a couple of guys I talked to said they don't carry the bayonet on duty, since they're afraid of some nutcase grabbing it."

"Did you see any bayonets lying around loose?"

"Yeah. One was being used as a paperweight and another was hanging from a nail in the wall, probably so one of the men could pick it up when he went off duty."

"Sounds like anyone could have wandered in there and snatched one," I said.

"It wouldn't be hard," Big Mike agreed. Then he leaned in to whisper, "Hey, Billy, isn't Colonel Blackford with the German Section at SOE? Maybe he could translate that card."

"Yeah, I'd forgotten that," I said. "But he was right next door. He's still a suspect until we rule him out. Best to wait and talk to Kaz."

"Right. What else do we need to do here?"

"I'm going to check around the building. Then we'll get Cosgrove's body moved. One of the doctors here should be able to do coroner's duty," I said. "I wish we could dust for fingerprints."

"They probably won't let the local constable in," Big Mike said. "Maybe Snow could call in Scotland Yard."

"I'll talk to him. Wait on the porch while I make a circuit of the place. Then have a chat with Blackford," I said. "Was Jenkins at the canteen?"

"No. He's expected in later. Same with the guy who relieved him last night. Private Martin Fulton."

"Yeah, I remember him. Young kid. We'll need to get them both in," I said, feeling every inch the homicide detective. Except that officially I was still a guest of His Majesty's Government at a high-security insane asylum, at least until Snow cut the paperwork.

I left Big Mike guarding the door and told Blackford we didn't need a colonel standing watch, but that I'd need to talk to him shortly. He said he had to meet with his recovering colleague, then get back to London. I reassured him I only required a few minutes of his time and wondered how in hell I could get him to remain against his wishes.

I stepped off the porch as he went into his room. I walked a few paces and estimated the distance to the Home Guard canteen. Two minutes at a brisk walk would do it. About the same distance to the main building. A little longer, perhaps, depending on what entrance you used. The farthest door, off the south wing, might have been ten minutes or so.

All of which told me that the entire population of Saint Albans was within a ten-minute walk of the crime scene.

Great detective work on my part.

I took a slow stroll around the guest quarters. In front, the steps led to a narrow crushed-stone pathway that meandered to the canteen in one direction and the center of the main building in the other. A few dirt paths, well-trodden shortcuts branching off and fading into green grass, ran to other outbuildings. No chance of a footprint or clue showing up in the hard-packed ground.

Around back it was different. The ground sloped away from the foundation, soft earth and rotting leaves left from the rainwater runoff. I walked the length of the building, checking the thick black soil.

There it was, right beneath Cosgrove's bedroom window. The sharp impression of a heel hitting the dirt. With the incline, the drop from his window must've been six feet. I stooped to get a closer view and made out sweeping marks made by a hand covering up the footprints. But in the dark, the killer had missed a spot, leaving the clear, curved imprint of one shoe heel. Not large enough to determine size, or even sex for that matter. But it told me that the guard had been on the porch, necessitating an acrobatic exit.

What was odd was that the killer had tried to shut the window behind him. He'd climbed out, hung there, and pulled the window down with one hand, leaving a gap of a few inches.

Why?

Why did he care about closing the window behind him?

Why did she care? I asked myself, trying that notion on.

I came up empty on that question and continued my search. I scanned the ground for traces of evidence, and in a few yards I spotted a fleck of beige paint, then another two chips, almost invisible on the loamy soil. Halfway from the window to the path. I tried to put myself in the mind of the killer, having just jumped down from the window and covered my tracks.

Moving back to the window, I saw where the paint had begun to peel. I set my feet near where the heel mark was, turned, and took a couple of steps, which brought me right to the beige chips.

I wiped my hands, as the killer must have, shedding the flaking paint chips.

I made a shaking motion with my hand. Yes, that made sense. He'd wiped the windowsill for prints with his handkerchief and picked up those paint chips. His handkerchief was still in his hand when he shook them free.

I went back to the window, wondering how he'd been able to hang there, close the window, and wipe the sill, all before letting go. Then I noticed the scuff marks on the wall. Two faint lines where he'd placed his feet, pushing back with one arm while using the other on the window. He hadn't hung straight down. He'd planted his feet firmly against the building with his body at an angle. Simple enough.

The killer was cold, calm, collected. A surprise knife thrust to the heart while looking Cosgrove right in the eyes. Out the window, closing it as best he could to sow confusion. Shaking out his handkerchief and strolling off into the night. Nothing pointed to panic or a sudden burst of anger. If there was madness at work here, it was the calculating kind.

I hustled up to the porch and told Big Mike to go around back and check out the rear window area for himself. I wanted someone else to confirm what I'd observed. If this were a homicide squad investigation, we'd have cameras and cops doing a wide sweep of the area. Instead, all we had were our two pairs of eyeballs.

Which made me think, as I sat down on the porch steps, that Saint Albans was the perfect location for a murder. Top secret. No local law enforcement allowed in. The kind of place where scandals are routinely hushed up. A large cast of unstable characters as part of the pool of suspects. And with me, one of the aforementioned, doing my best imitation of a real investigation. If I found anything the head honchos didn't like, they could blame it on my mental state. And if I did uncover a killer, it could be covered right back up. I'd be given a pat on the back and told *mum's the word, lad*, while Snow or his boss took the credit.

"Saw the boot heel, clear as day," Big Mike said, on his return. "Can't make any ID from it though. But I'll be on the lookout for anyone brushing paint flakes off their tunic."

"There's flaking paint all over this place, either the old stuff or the quick coat they threw on when they reopened the place. You notice anything else?"

"Yeah, the window. Either someone lowered it on their way out, which looks impossible, or there was another person inside."

"A witness hiding in Cosgrove's bedroom? Or did the killer close it?"

"No idea. Hell, the killer could have been in there when we were. Maybe he snuck in before the guard was posted and was waiting to ambush Cosgrove but skedaddled when we showed up. Or waited until we left and walked in on Cosgrove, taking him by surprise," Big Mike said. "It could have been anyone who spotted the major during the day. Cosgrove said he was familiar with some of the agents here."

"You're right, the killer could have been waiting, then took off when we came in," I said, telling him about my theory of the handkerchief. "Big Mike, go back to the canteen. Find out when Jenkins and Fulton are due back. If it's not within the hour, go get them. Roust them out of bed if you need to. We have to know who saw what on that porch."

"Billy, I don't have any clout around here," he said, mirroring my own worries. "I was chatting with the guys in there before, which was fine. But I don't think they'd take kindly to my giving orders about their non-com."

"Yeah, I know," I said. "We're short on official status. I'll ask Snow to bring them in."

"That'd be best," Big Mike said, then gave me a sharp look. "But hey, you didn't mention the tree."

"What tree?"

Big Mike beckoned me to follow him, past his quarters and around the far side of the building. He squatted and pointed at two cigarette butts, ground out in the grass a couple of yards from a beech tree.

"Sniff," he said, pointing to the shaded area by the trunk. I did. The faint, sour odor of urine arose from the soil at the base of the tree.

"Good work," I said. "Jenkins or Fulton spent some time over here, taking a piss and smoke break."

"I get the call of nature," Big Mike said. "But that's quick. Whoever it was hung around long enough to finish two smokes. You can't see the front entrance from here."

"Or maybe two people smoked them together," I said, looking at the side of the building. The porch wasn't visible. "That would account for the location."

"They couldn't be observed," Big Mike said, as he picked up the cigarette papers and tried to flatten them out. No dice. They were too shredded to identify the brand. "Either way, it means the killer had access to Cosgrove while the guard was down here."

"Okay, we need to talk to those Home Guards," I said. "Let's see what Snow's up to."

As we came around front, we spotted Snow setting out guards, two at each side of the guest quarters, a decent distance away on the path. Close enough to watch, far enough not to get in the way.

"Major Snow," I said, standing at a fair imitation of attention as he approached. "You can have the body moved now. I assume the hospital has a morgue?"

"Yes. I've already called for Dr. Hughes. He's a medical examiner and can do the autopsy and paperwork," he said.

"How are you planning on handling the investigation, sir?" I asked.

"What do you mean, Boyle? I shall conduct it. It comes under my jurisdiction as head of security," he said, putting his hands on his hips and jutting out his chin. "Charles Cosgrove was my friend, and I'll damn well find out who killed him. Starting with those Home Guard louts."

"What do you mean, Major?"

"I've contacted Army Headquarters and requested a regular army unit," he said. "It's evident these Home Guards are not up to the task. How could they be when an important visitor is murdered while they stand sentry outside his door?"

"There's a lot we don't yet know, Major. I'd like to question Sergeant Jenkins and Private Fulton. Could you have them brought in from the village?"

"Listen, Boyle," he said, taking me by the arm and walking me away from Blackford's door. "I know I asked for your help with poor Holland. That was one thing. But I can't authorize your involvement in a murder investigation. You're still a patient, for God's sake. They'd accuse me of letting the inmates run the asylum."

"Then cut me loose," I said. "I'll be back tomorrow with full authorization to investigate. Colonel Harding at SHAEF has connections with SOE. I can help you, Major."

"It's not that easy," he said, glancing back and forth between Big Mike and me. "I was planning on talking with Charles this morning about the paperwork to let you go. He's—I mean he was—high enough in the Foreign Office hierarchy to sign off on it. But he's gone, so all I can do is follow procedure."

"Which is what?" I asked.

"The Discharge Board must be convened. Dr. Robinson, Dr. Hughes, one other physician on a rotating basis, and myself. The medical men review each case and I make the final decision as regards to security. And the decision must be unanimous."

"Okay, so call a meeting. Robinson's on board for sure," I said.

"As soon as I can," he said through tight lips. I knew the look. It meant things were complicated, more complicated than I could possibly understand. "Right now, I want Hughes to perform the autopsy. And I need to make sure the replacement troops get here quickly. Keep a low profile, Boyle, until I take care of things. Understood?"

"Got it, Major," I said, knowing it was useless to argue. I wasn't exactly in a position of power, what with my medical status and my high-ranking champion dead on the couch. "I'm going to say goodbye to Colonel Blackford. He was pretty shaken up. Then I'll go get some coffee and stay out of your hair."

That mollified him. He told me to be quick about it and went off to organize stretcher bearers.

"You really going to do that, Billy?" Big Mike asked.

"Get coffee? Damn straight I am." I knocked on Blackford's door. "How about we meet at Kaz's room, after they pick up the body?"

Big Mike nodded and hunkered down in the wicker chair. Major Snow was determined to run the investigation, but he didn't know much about how it was done. You don't leave the body unattended, and you don't let a guy who was right next door to the murder scene walk away.

Blackford opened the door. He gestured for me to come in, and we arranged ourselves in the sitting room, which was a duplicate of Cosgrove's. Except for the fact that the resident was still alive.

"Anything to report?" Blackford asked, his voice weary with grief.

"Colonel, I'm not actually investigating this," I said. "I'm still a guest here, to put it in the best possible light."

"You look sharp enough to me," he said. "And I know Charles held you in high regard. Somewhat reluctantly, I'll admit, but that was his style." A brief smile appeared, then vanished.

"You two knew each other a long time," I said. I wanted to know more about Charles Cosgrove, and sometimes all it took was a grief-stricken friend to fill in the missing pieces.

"Since 1916," Blackford said. "We were both lieutenants in the London Regiment, serving in the 17th Battalion. We became acquainted at the Battle of the Somme, during the attack on High Wood. That was a ridge overlooking our positions, which had to be taken at whatever cost. They sent our entire brigade up that hill. The losses were terrible. At the end, Charles and I were among the few officers left. I had a bullet through my leg, and I counted myself among the lucky ones. When we were relieved, Charles stayed until all the wounded were taken off that bloody hill. He marched down to the aid station, checked on his men, and only then did he collapse from exhaustion."

"I wish I'd known him as a younger man, Colonel," I said, wondering if someday I'd be seen as a blustery old man, the deeds of my youth ignored or forgotten by the yet unborn.

"Well, Charles always had a musty side to him. Came from a conservative family. His father was a vicar, not one given to light amusements, shall we say. Charles was a bit older than I, and I always thought of him as a man of the last century. A proper Englishman."

"Do you have any idea who would want to do him harm?"

"Charles could be brusque, as I'm sure you know," Blackford said. "He never suffered fools gladly, and I'm certain there are officers who wished they had clashed with a man of lesser intellect. There was a lot of contention between the wars when our service was reduced. Competition for promotions and positions, never mind the political arena."

"Politics? How so? I thought the British Army steered clear of politics."

"I'm talking about rearmament. The need to rein in Hitler and the Nazis. Not every officer saw them as the enemy, you know. Charles was vocal about the shortsighted budget cuts to the military. All branches, not only the army."

"But who would kill over that?" I asked. "Especially now."

"Most especially now, young man," Blackford said. "Any officer who wishes to rise in rank could not bear to have his pro-fascist past come back to haunt him. We had our share of those. You've heard of Mosely and his Blackshirts, I assume?"

"Sir Oswald Mosley and the British Union of Fascists, right?"

"Exactly. His party was pro-Nazi and had a visceral hatred of the Jews. The government threw the blighter in jail at the start of the war but let him out on house arrest last year. Should have been shot, but there you have it. He had his supporters in the military, have no doubt. Charles had a role in contacting certain officers back in 1938, warning them to stay away from Mosley and his bunch. A fair warning, really, to save their reputations, but some did not take kindly to it. One was a cousin to the king's physician, a fascist supporter himself."

"Do you think it's likely that one of those men waited six years to take his revenge, and within a high-security facility to boot?" I asked.

"No, not really," Blackford said. "I am only thinking of those who would most wish Charles ill. Outside of any number of Germans, that is. I am sorry, Boyle, but there is nothing else I can think of."

"You and he worked directly together last year, if I recall. Major

Cosgrove mentioned a selection board and some project with your SOE German Section."

"Yes, well, the selection board business is fairly routine stuff," he said. "Evaluating potential agents after they've finished training. Selecting the best and matching them to planned missions or sending them on to further training to await assignment."

"Or sending them here. Like Griffin."

"Occasionally someone falls apart at the last moment or proves themselves incapable. When that happens, and if they possess classified information, we must place them in a secure environment. Those with medical issues come here. For the others, we have a suitable location elsewhere."

"Is there anyone here who was washed out by Major Cosgrove?" I asked.

"Not that I am aware of," he said. "Cosgrove, Snow, and I have served on these boards. Unless we were directly part of the agent's training, they would have no way of knowing who had a part in any decision. We do know how to keep secrets, Boyle. That is our business."

"Certainly, Colonel. I'm just trying to find anything that resembles a motive," I said, rising. "Thanks for your time. Will you be here much longer?"

"No. As I said, I have to meet one of my men," he said. "Lieutenant Paul Densmore. Case of exhaustion, they say, from overwork. Once I complete reviewing his files, I shall leave this place as quickly as possible and hope to never come back."

"I know the feeling, Colonel," I said, heading to the door. "One more question. Do you know the Uffington White Horse?"

"Of course I do," he said with an amused laugh. "Ancient cliff marking, not too far from here. Are you going sightseeing, Boyle?"

"If I ever get out of here myself, I may. But does a red horse drawn in that style sound familiar?"

"You said one more question, Boyle. That was two. Now I must get ready, please excuse me." He stood, unfolding his body into a ramrod-straight stance and drilling me with his still, dark eyes.

I left. He hadn't liked that question. Not one damn bit.

CHAPTER TWENTY-THREE

THEY WERE TAKING Cosgrove's body away as I left Blackford's room. Big Mike stood to attention as they passed by, and I followed suit. It was a demeaning way to die after everything Charles Cosgrove had been through. Two world wars, heart troubles, then finally getting back in the fight. And it all ended here, stabbed by someone he trusted, a fellow countryman or at least an American ally. And over what? It made no sense.

I watched the orderlies carry the shrouded stretcher down the path. No, it made sense to someone. There was reason and logic at work here.

"Ready to go see Kaz?" Big Mike said.

"No, you go," I said, as the stretcher-bearers disappeared behind a building. "I need that coffee. And to talk to a few people."

"You okay, Billy?" he asked.

"Yeah. I realized that I should start thinking about the inmates here as a positive, not a negative. It's a big pool of suspects, sure, but it's also a potential pool of witnesses. And besides, I really do need some joe."

"You think any of them saw something?"

"Who knows? Heard or saw something. I happen to know at least one of the mutes is faking it, for the most part at least. It's easy to underestimate the observational skills of someone you think is out to lunch."

"Okay. I'll tell Kaz what happened and ask him to translate the postcard," Big Mike said.

"I'll get over there as soon as I can. Once you're done, why don't you head to London. Get Kaz that envelope of cash."

"You think he still needs to go that route?" Big Mike said. "What with Cosgrove setting everything up with Harken already?"

"Absolutely. It's a guarantee that Hughes won't throw a monkey wrench into the works. He's still the head physician here. And when you come back, don't bring a jeep. Take a staff car. Something with a roomy trunk."

"Lined with a few blankets, maybe?" he said, leaning in and grinning.

"Now you're talking. You can bust me outta here if Snow doesn't come through. Talk to Colonel Harding if you can, see if he can spring me," I said.

"I don't know if he's back from France, but I have to report to him about Skory. I'll check on Skory after I see Kaz and then head out. If Sam ain't back at SHAEF, I'll get in touch with him by radio. Watch your back, Billy."

Big Mike moved off at a quick pace, much quicker than you'd expect from a guy his size. He had a big man's grace, a fluid movement of muscle and bone that was always surprising. It's always been Kaz or Big Mike watching my back, and each in their own way was the best at it. But as of now, I was on my own. And that meant constant vigilance.

Which called for coffee. I walked to the north wing dining hall, keeping an eye peeled for patients, Griffin especially. I had a sense he might have honed his surveillance skills sufficiently to observe more than anyone knew. And Faith as well. Her mute routine made her invisible, like a servant in a wealthy household.

I grabbed a cup of coffee and sat at the end of a long table, watching the few patients who wandered in and out. Most had probably already breakfasted and were going about whatever people did between electric therapy and appointments with their psychiatrist.

As soon as the caffeine jolt hit my brain, I began to worry about something else. Cosgrove had been working on the release of one hundred concentration camp inmates. What would happen to that now? If the Swedish government was behind the effort, it would likely proceed.

But would Diana's name still be on the list? Maybe Colonel Harding was involved or could get in touch with a contact at the Foreign Office. And if so, did I stand a chance in hell of getting Angelika's name on it as well? I had to be sure Diana got out and do anything I could to have Angelika join her.

But I couldn't do anything about Sweden right now, so I drank my joe and thought about things. About Holland, since that's where all this started. There was a tenuous connection between Holland, Blackford, and Cosgrove. The selection board. But was that enough to support my theory of Holland's death as a lure? Would Cosgrove have come if it hadn't been for Skory?

When I'd gone through Holland's file, I skipped over the selection board report. It hadn't seemed important, since I assumed his mission and subsequent treatment here held whatever information might have been significant. That's where I'd hoped to find clues, not by leafing through pages of mundane selection board minutes. Maybe I needed to take a closer look.

Murder, death, and fear for Diana notwithstanding, I began to feel hungry. I helped myself to powdered eggs and fried Spam, refilled my cup, and sat back down as Miller entered the room. It was a subdued Miller. The maniacal energy he'd displayed before was gone, which wasn't a bad thing. But the washed-out expression left in its place wasn't much of an improvement.

"Miller," I said, waving for him to join me once he'd gotten his chow.

"You were there," he said, calmly enough, as he set down his plate and utensils and sat across from me.

"I was. You remember?"

"It's coming back," he said, spearing a clump of scrambled eggs. "But I don't want to talk about it." He looked at me, his head slightly cocked, as if he were trying to work out why I seemed . . . what? Like myself, I decided. I didn't have the heart to tell him I'd been rescued at the last moment. We ate in silence. His demeanor was an improvement, I decided, since I didn't have to listen to his violent blather.

"Well look, it's the new and improved Miller," Iris said from behind me. She and Faith sat, clutching their cups of tea. "We like Miller better this way. Don't you, Boyle?"

Miller continued working through his eggs, saying nothing, showing no emotion.

"Somewhere in-between would be nice," I said. Knowing what he had been through made it hard to joke at his expense.

"I agree," Iris said. "This Miller is awfully boring. The old Miller was simply awful."

"I'm sorry," Miller said, setting down his fork. He looked like he didn't know what to do with the rest of his food, his eyes darting about, as if he couldn't figure out where he was.

"Oh," Iris said, her hand covering her lips as she took in Miller's state. "No, I'm sorry, dear. So very sorry."

Faith sat with her hands wrapped around her cup, drawing what warmth she could from it. It wasn't cold in the dining hall, but she was so thin she must have felt every breath of air. I looked at her, but her eyes were focused on some faraway image.

"You don't want the doctors to think you need the electric shock therapy," I said. "Believe me."

"You too?" Iris asked.

"Yes, but thank God, only a small dose. I'd hate for anyone to go through even that, especially if they didn't need it. You know, like someone faking a mental condition."

"He's right," Miller murmured, eating his eggs again.

"Thank you," Faith said, her voice a strained whisper, her eyes fixed on Miller's impassive face. Iris grasped her hand and gave it a squeeze.

"I can't wait to get out of this dreadful place," Iris said. "Is it true what they're saying? About a body in the guest quarters?"

"Major Charles Cosgrove," I said. "Stabbed to death." I wasn't surprised that they knew. Word travels fast in a hothouse environment like Saint Albans where there's little to do but eat, wait, and gossip.

"Civilian clothes? The one with the tall colonel?" Iris asked.

"Yeah. Colonel Blackford," I said. "You saw them?"

"Yesterday morning, wasn't it?" Iris said. Faith nodded her agreement. "They came looking for Lieutenant Densmore. He's a special guest, up on the third floor."

"How special?" I asked.

"He's not an agent and apparently here of his own accord," she said. "He suffered a nervous breakdown, and they brought him in for a rest. Robinson gave him the sleep cure and they wait on him hand and foot in a comfortable room, or so I hear. He doesn't like to talk to people. But not like Faith. I mean, he doesn't like to be talked *to*."

"How do you know all this?" I asked.

"Oh, don't say anything, Boyle, but Clarissa in the clerical office is a dear. And Densmore is simply smashing, a real looker. Isn't he, Faith?"

Faith smiled. Smashing, indeed.

"He was nice," Miller said, finished with his eggs.

"Who?" I asked.

"The civilian. I asked him to help get me out of here. Yesterday, before the . . . you know. He was nice."

"Yeah, he was a good guy," I said, surprised Cosgrove had managed to be nice to the old, brash Miller. "When was this?"

"Morning, I think," he said. "I'm still a little confused."

"He was with Colonel Blackford?"

"No," Miller said. He took his plate and left.

"Dear God, what did they do to the man?" Iris said. "I mean, he was unbalanced, but now he's nearly a child."

"It's supposed to help," I said. "Dr. Robinson is big on it. I prefer the sleep routine, myself."

"I think I shall have a talk with Dr. Robinson," Faith said. "Before he gets any helpful ideas. Thank you, Boyle."

"No problem. Tell me, have either of you seen Griffin around?" I said.

"No one sees Griffin," Iris said. "He sees you."

"What do you know about him?" I said.

"Nothing. He's close-lipped. He seems to be practicing surveillance techniques. Easy enough to do here, where no one pays any attention to odd behavior," Iris said.

"Have you heard of anyone going out after curfew?" I said.

"Where to? The local pub?" Iris laughed and Faith smiled. "Whatever for, Boyle?"

"A rendezvous with one of the guards? Or a doctor, perhaps?"

"Right," Iris said, sipping the last of her tea. "The first thing I thought about when I got here was a clandestine encounter with a paunchy old man or a pimply faced boy. Please."

"Griffin would be the one to do it, though," Faith said, clutching her sweater and pulling it tight around her. "Reconnoitering the enemy camp or some such nonsense. Writing things in that notebook of his."

"Where's his room?" I asked.

"No idea," Iris said. "The men's section is off limits."

"Why is Densmore stuck on the third floor? That's where they have the electric shock machine and the padded cells," I said.

"Those are along the side corridor on the third floor. The front corridor is much nicer. Offices and rooms for special guests like Densmore. A world of difference, I hear," Iris said.

"You hear a lot," I said.

"We are trained in intelligence gathering, Boyle. Now, shall we take a walk, Faith, and see if we can spot poor Griffin skulking in the bushes?"

"Tell him I want a word. About a new assignment," I said.

"He'll be so excited," Iris said, gathering up their cups and heading out, Faith trailing in her wake.

I cleared my plate and poured another cup of coffee. I stood at the window and took in the view outside. The day had turned blustery, the clouds leaden, and leaves swirled upward. Maybe the rain would send Griffin indoors. It was a slim chance that his notebook would contain anything useful, but I only had so much to work with.

I took a sip as Miller went by, listlessly walking the path, his unbuttoned field jacket billowing out at his sides like a green sail. I couldn't help smiling at his description of Cosgrove as nice. I could say many positive things about the man, but that one wouldn't have occurred to me. Miller was a troubled soul, and although Cosgrove wasn't one to suffer fools gladly, as Blackford said, he probably would spare a kind word or two for a patient.

Blackford and Cosgrove had visited Densmore. Then Cosgrove left, probably to see to Skory. After that, he came looking for me.

Densmore was Blackford's reason for coming to Saint Albans.

I still thought there was a hidden connection between Holland and Cosgrove. But the red horse postcard had been deliberately left in Cosgrove's hand. Blackford had refused to acknowledge it. Since Densmore and Blackford both worked in SOE's German Section, Densmore might be able to tell me more about it. Or, at least confirm it meant nothing and Blackford had been giving me the bum's rush.

I left my coffee and headed upstairs. The third floor was off-limits, except for those with the right keys. I tried to think up a story to convince the guard to let me in. An urgent message for Densmore, maybe. But the guard's station was deserted, a folded newspaper displaying a nearly finished crossword puzzle. Five across was still blank: an eight-letter word for a biblical betrayer. Iscariot. I picked up a pencil and filled it in. Who didn't know that? Maybe someone who didn't have to sit through Sister Mary Margaret's Bible study classes.

There was no guard on the third-floor landing either, only a solid door with a narrow, thick glass window leading to the main corridor where Densmore had his room. On the other side of the vestibule was the door leading to the cells and treatment rooms. I steered clear of that one.

The door to the corridor was open. Barely. It rested against the doorjamb, ready to be locked tight at the slightest bit of pressure. I pushed it open and stepped into the hallway. I eased the door closed, leaving it in the same position I'd found it. If anyone came along and pushed it shut, I'd be trapped.

I stepped into the hallway. This one sported a bright coat of paint and polished floors, a far cry from the decaying corridor where I'd been imprisoned and electrified. The door opened in the middle of a long hall. I took a right with a purposeful stride, the kind that said I belonged here, even though I was dressed in the plain fatigues of a patient. I passed an open door and caught a quick glance of a switchboard and a couple of desks with several telephones. That was the place that caused me all the trouble the other night. A woman at the switchboard placed a cord into a jack as another woman answered a call at the desk.

I was by them before they noticed me. To my left, tall windows let in what light there was on this cloudy day, blackout curtains pulled back and tied off. It was a different world up here. Clean and airy. I passed another door, thankfully shut, muffled voices sounding from within.

The next door was partially open. Inside four men sat at desks pushed together in the middle of the room. Electrical lines were strung from the ceiling. They sat hunched over wire recording machines, headphones on their ears, and pens scratching paper. Their ties were askew, and their shirtsleeves rolled up. They looked like they'd been at it awhile, whatever *it* was. Listening devices? Hidden microphones? Was this whole joint bugged?

I'd have to give that some thought once I got the hell out of here.

On the next door a small metal bracket held a blank card. Maybe one of the VIP rooms, currently empty? Then the jackpot. Densmore's name was on the next card. Luck was on my side. I raised my hand to knock, then thought better of it. The echo would rattle around the corridor, and I couldn't afford anyone taking notice.

I put my hand on the latch, figuring it wouldn't be locked. Even very important personages aren't allowed to lock themselves in at Saint Albans. I opened the door, whispering Densmore's name.

He sat in a comfortable armchair facing the window. By the angle of his neck, I knew he wouldn't be answering me. I felt for a pulse anyway and was rewarded with a touch of clammy skin. I drew away my hand.

It was trembling. I took a step back, stumbling against the open door. The room was hazy for a second and began to tilt. I managed to shut the door and get to Densmore's bed. I sat with my head in my hands waiting for the world to steady itself.

I didn't know what was wrong. Why had the shakes returned? This sure as hell wasn't my first dead body. I took a deep breath, but it didn't seem to take. I felt dizzy and my heart was beating like Papa Jo Jones keeping time with Count Basie.

Maybe I needed more sleep.

Maybe I needed to get away from death. It damn well wasn't staying away from me.

I lifted my head and opened my eyes. From my angle, I could see what Densmore was facing. I blinked, thinking I might be hallucinating. It didn't go away; it was the image of a red horse traced in blood on the windowpane.

I stood slowly, fighting off the dizziness, not wanting to faint and fall over his corpse. I held onto the corner of his chair, and noticed his arm hanging over the side. A dish containing the remains of his breakfast held a pool of congealing blood.

I sat back down again.

There wasn't a lot of blood. Trails of redness traced rivulets from his wrist. I managed to rise again and made it to the window. It was blood for certain. It was the same stylized drawing—a long, curved line for the tail, back, and neck. A single angled line for the head, a couple of lines for the legs, all enclosed in a red circle.

The cuts to his wrist were made after he was killed. Otherwise there'd be arterial sprays of the stuff all over the room. The killer would be dripping wet with it too. Blood will ooze out of the body with the help of gravity, which is what the murderer had done here, harvesting enough of the red stuff to paint us a picture.

Nothing felt right. I shouldn't be reacting like this, weak at the knees in the presence of a corpse. However, I was in a restricted area, and if anyone walked in here right now, I'd have a damn hard time explaining things. Things like how I didn't break Densmore's neck. All I had going for me was that there was no blood on my hands.

I looked at my hands anyway and was shocked to see a trace of darkened red. It was from the sheets. The killer had wiped his fingers clean on them. I gave mine the Lady Macbeth treatment right down to the fingernails.

I got up again, listening to the blood rushing in my ears and feeling the sweat drip in the small of my back. I steadied myself and began to search the room as quietly as I could. Once again, there was no sign of a struggle. Whoever did this wasn't seen as a threat.

It still could have been a woman, I thought as I leaned against the wall by the window. Densmore had some height to him but seated that wouldn't have mattered. Anyone could have leaned over and given his neck a twist with the commando move all SOE and OSS agents had been trained to use. It wasn't easy, but then again Densmore wasn't exactly an armed German on sentry duty.

Densmore's murder was the second killing linked to the SOE German Section. Cosgrove had worked with Blackford, and presumably Densmore as well. Cosgrove, Blackford, and Snow all had links to Holland one way or the other. Which meant the last two men were in danger. I needed to do something.

I'd removed the red horse postcard from the first murder scene. The fact that the symbol appeared here again showed that the killer wanted to link it to his victims. Maybe he'd do something stupid if I robbed him of that opportunity.

I took a napkin from the table where Densmore had breakfasted. I dipped it into a glass of water and scrubbed at the windowpane. The blood was coagulated but not fully dried. It cleaned up easily, especially after I found a handkerchief and did a final wipe down. I left the stained fabric near the bloody breakfast dish.

I checked the drop from the window. Too far and too visible. There was nothing to do but report the murder like any good citizen.

Okay. Time to go. I checked myself for telltale bloodstains and worked to calm my breathing. I still felt jittery, my breaths coming in rapid gasps. I placed my hand on the latch. It shook like autumn's last leaf.

The crack of a rifle shattered the air, the unmistakable sound echoing off the stone buildings. I let go of the handle. Footsteps thundered in the hallway and I stepped back, certain they were headed for me.

They kept going. I darted to the window. Below, two figures raced across the grass, making for one of the north wing entrances. Another shot split the air and I jumped. I couldn't see anything, but it was close.

A scream from the hallway drew me back to the door. I heard voices, questioning and worried, male and female. Someone shouted *this way* and I decided my best chance was to mix in with the confused pack as they evacuated the floor. I opened the door as two Home Guards emerged from the stairwell at the end of the corridor, calling for people to follow them to the basement. I stepped out, closing the door and mingling with some female staff and the shirtsleeved men who had been wearing headphones in the next office.

There was a rush to the stairs. One of the Home Guards stayed behind, while the other led the group down. Everyone was babbling a mile a minute and paying me no mind. I could have been dressed in a pink tuxedo and not a soul would have taken their eyes off the steps beneath their feet.

At the second-floor landing, I split off and made for my room, which is where I planned on saying I was the whole time if anyone asked. At my window I watched orderlies and patients running from the north wing while a single Home Guard took cover behind a tree and covered their escape. I couldn't see where he was aiming, but it seemed to be in the direction of the guest quarters.

Damn. Colonel Blackford was still there. But shooting at him didn't fit the pattern. The last two killings were quiet. Using what sounded like a Lee-Enfield rifle was anything but.

I headed out, not wanting to take any chances. Blackford knew more than he was saying, and if he ended up eating a bullet, I'd never find out what it was. I took the back way, easing the door open and watching for a threat. All I saw was Major Snow, running with his limping gait toward the soldier behind the tree, revolver in hand. He motioned for me to get back inside. So, of course, I ignored him.

I ran to the nearest tree, taking cover, and risking a glance in the direction of the shots. The first thing I saw was Sergeant Jenkins, standing in the walkway, motioning with one arm for the men behind him to halt. The other hand, hanging loosely at his side, held a pistol that he kept pointed at the ground. Dr. Robinson ran out from the north wing, joining him.

I couldn't see much else with the trees and buildings in the way, but neither Snow nor Jenkins was acting like the shooter presented a threat. Which was strange after several rounds had been fired off. Still, the guest quarters were in the general direction they were both facing, and I had to wonder about Blackford's safety.

I left the cover of the tree and ambled in Jenkins's direction. No threatening moves, just a fellow out for a midday stroll. At least that's what I hoped the guy with the rifle thought. As I drew closer to Jenkins, I caught his eye. He nodded and didn't tell me to stop, so I kept on. I noticed that directly behind him a Home Guard stood without his helmet or rifle, blood streaming from a scrape on his temple.

Near the path, I finally had a clear view. Midway between the guest quarters and the Home Guard canteen, two figures stood facing each other.

Sinclair and Blackford.

Sinclair had the rifle. The Lee-Enfield held ten rounds in the chamber, and I'd heard three shots. There was still a lot of damage to be done. But Sinclair wasn't pointing the rifle at anyone, and he and Blackford seemed to be busy arguing with each other. Sinclair had the weapon gripped close to his chest; the barrel pointed toward the sky.

"Hello, Sinclair," I said, stopping about ten feet away. Close enough to talk, but not so close he'd think I was trying to grab the rifle. "What's with the fireworks?"

"You tell him to leave me alone!" Sinclair shouted, thrusting the rifle in Blackford's direction, then pulling it back close to his chest. "I am done helping his sort. Done!"

"Colonel Blackford?" I said, looking to him for clarification.

"We were having a calm discussion, sitting on the porch, then all of a sudden Sinclair bolted off," Blackford said. "Didn't know he could move that quickly. He bowled over the young Home Guard who was coming around the corner from the canteen. Sent him crashing to the ground and fell on top of him. Next thing I knew he was holding that rifle and shooting it off."

"To keep you at bay!" Sinclair said, his rage spewing between gritted teeth. "No more, do you hear? You promised to get me out of here, but that hasn't happened, has it?"

"I thought you liked it here, Sinclair," I said, moving slightly to place myself between them.

"I say that, yes. But I want to go home," he said. "He said I could, if I helped him."

"Now Angus, be careful what you say. This is all classified, remember," Blackford said.

"Murder? Is that classified?" Sinclair said, his voice a hissing whisper. "Tampering with parachutes? Who does that get killed, eh? And now you want me to design a new transmitter? It's impossible!"

"Sinclair, you know what I think we should do?" I asked, wondering what the hell he was talking about. "I think we should go over and apologize to the young man you knocked over. He's bleeding, and I think it would be the nice thing to do, don't you? Then we'll go get a cup of tea and work this out. Okay?"

"You can't . . ." Blackford said, but I cut him off with a wave of my hand. Which wasn't shaking, I noticed with some small part of my brain.

"I'm terribly sorry," Sinclair said. "Sorry I caused so much trouble."

"Don't worry about it," I said. "You didn't shoot at anybody, did you?"

"Good gracious, no. It felt good, I must say. Awfully loud, though."

"It puts the exclamation point on an argument, doesn't it?" I said, patting him on the shoulder. "Why don't we give this back to the young man so he won't get in trouble, all right?"

"Of course," Sinclair said. We walked toward Jenkins, who had the sense to holster his pistol and tell his men to stand down. He grabbed the bleeding soldier, who had a handkerchief pressed to his head, and dragged him forward.

"Take yer rifle, sonny," Jenkins growled. "Then fetch yer helmet and stand to like a soldier."

"My sincere apologies," Sinclair said, offering the rifle as if it were a sword being surrendered. Snow approached the small group, holstering his revolver, and shaking his head. Robinson trailed behind him, keeping his distance.

"Angus, perhaps we should speak in private," Blackford said, laying a hand on Sinclair's arm. Angus shook it off.

"No! I told you the Great Panjandrum would not work, and neither will this squirt transmitter," Sinclair said, his hands in the air and his voice rising in pitch. "It's foolishness, but you won't listen. Boyle will, I'm sure. Come, let's have our tea." Snow and I exchanged looks, and I followed Sinclair. Snow began to speak with Jenkins, not seeming too pleased about events.

"Angus," Blackford said, running to keep up with him as he huffed off toward the dining hall. "You simply can't keep repeating these things. They'll keep you here forever."

"Panjandrum! Squirt!" Sinclair hollered, cupping his hands around his mouth. He uttered a few other words that were incomprehensible but was quickly drowned out by shouts from the main building. Shouts for Major Snow.

"What the devil is happening now?" Blackford demanded.

"Who knows?" I said, although I did. "Were you talking with Sinclair long, sir? I mean before he became upset."

"Fifteen minutes or so, why?"

"Just wondering," I said, watching Sinclair huff and puff his way to the north wing entrance. "Has this happened before?"

"His reaction? Well, you know he's unstable, but brilliant. He can't control himself, really," Blackford said.

"No, I mean has he refused work for you before? While stuck in here?" I asked.

"I can't say, Boyle. Security, you know." At that moment, Clarissa dashed out of the building, looked around, and waved once she spotted Blackford.

"Colonel," she said, her eyes wide. "Please come. It's Lieutenant Densmore. Someone's killed him."

"Oh no," Blackford said, stopping so suddenly I thought he might fall.

"Colonel?" I said. "Are you all right?"

"Boyle, please calm Angus down, but don't encourage him. They'll think he's mad if he keeps spouting secrets. It's for his own good. Oh, this is horrible news. I can't believe it."

"I'll try," I said, but Blackford was already off, muttering about how there had to be some mistake. Funny how people try to talk themselves out of believing bad news.

In the dining hall, I got Sinclair seated. I fetched him tea and got coffee for myself. I could hear voices echoing in the hallway and the tread of boots on stairs. The discovery of Densmore's body had stirred up a hornet's nest, and I wanted it to subside long before anyone took notice of me.

We were at the end of a table near a window. I let Sinclair settle down, watching as he added milk and sugar to his tea and stirred it hypnotically. He looked tired, with heavy bags under his eyes. His graying hair was disheveled, his forehead wrinkled, and he hadn't shaved in a couple of days.

"Angus," I said, getting his attention. "You shouldn't be saying those things. You know that, don't you?"

"Right now, yes. But in the heat of the moment, they all tumble out. Secrets. It is as if I am so full of them they can no longer be contained. I ought to be kept here, I know that. But I miss my wife."

It was a simple, heartfelt statement, and I had no idea how to respond. Plenty of people missed loved ones these days, but that wasn't what made Angus Sinclair dangerous. It was the secrets he knew. Robinson began to stare openly at Sinclair, which gave me a bad feeling.

"Listen, Angus," I said. "If Dr. Robinson speaks with you, try your damnedest not to say anything that's classified. Say you're sorry, you lost your temper, and it was all an accident."

"It was," he said. "An accident."

"Yes, but an accident involving a firearm and top-secret information. So do your best, okay?"

"I will," he said. "I hope Blackie doesn't get in trouble."

"He won't. Colonels seldom do, unless a general needs a fall guy," I said, taking note of the use of the same nickname Cosgrove used for Blackford. "You've known him long?"

"We did some work together. Wheezer and dodger stuff. Decent fellow, but a bit dense. There's no way to send coded messages in compressed bursts. I told him the squirt transmitter was a fairy tale! Can't be done."

"Angus," I said, shaking my head.

"Oh dear. Please forget I said that. Should have mentioned the Great Panjandrum instead. Utter failure, no need to keep that a secret. Wouldn't have been, if they'd listened to me."

"Angus, please."

"Two ten-foot wheels, powered by cordite rockets that rolled them forward, with an explosive payload lodged between them. For breaching barriers on the beach. Trouble was, it never went in a straight line. In one of the tests it almost rolled over the generals and admirals who'd come to watch the trials. You should have seen them run!"

"Okay," I said, "as long as we're spilling secrets. What was that about tampering with parachutes?"

"Tricky stuff, that," Sinclair said, sipping his milky tea. "The idea is to rig the parachute so it doesn't open."

"Sounds easy," I said, wondering why Blackford would want to do that.

"But there was a wrinkle," Sinclair said, wagging his finger and leaning in to whisper. "It couldn't look like it was tampered with. When the Germans found it, don't you see? It had to look like a real malfunction, not sabotage."

"Sinclair, Boyle, mind if I join you?" Robinson sat without waiting for an answer. Sinclair looked oblivious, but this wasn't your normal coffee break chat. "How are you, Angus?"

"Fine, fine," he said, catching my glance. "And I do apologize. It will not happen again."

"Somebody could have been hurt, Angus," Robinson said.

"A bird, perhaps," Sinclair answered. "Although I am sorry that I knocked that boy over. It was an accident, you know."

"I do, Angus, I do," Robinson said.

"What's all the commotion, Doc?" I asked, with as much innocence as I could muster.

"Not now, Boyle. I think Sinclair needs a rest. What do you think, Angus? Are you tired?"

"Yes I am, Dr. Robinson. Very."

"Wait a minute, Doc," I said. "There's no need to punish him.

Blackford shouldn't have pushed him. He shouldn't be working in here, should he?"

"No, and I will speak to the colonel about that," Robinson said. "Don't worry. Angus has had the sleep cure before. He'll be fine."

"The sleep cure. That's it?"

"Nothing but," Robinson said. "Are you ready, Angus?"

Angus was. Robinson snapped his fingers toward an orderly who was waiting in the hallway. He took Sinclair by the arm and led him away as Robinson promised to follow right behind.

"Paul Densmore has been murdered," Robinson said, keeping his voice low.

"That's Blackford's guy, right? In for a nervous breakdown?"

"I'd classify it as mental and physical exhaustion. A complete breakdown is something else. Whatever you want to call it, he was close to being released. What the hell is going on here?" Robinson said, rubbing his eyes.

"How was he killed?" I asked.

"His neck was broken," Robinson said. "Two brutal murders, Boyle. We've never seen anything like this."

"Don't forget Holland," I said. "I'm sure he was murdered too. Tell me, did you see the body?"

"I did. Snow called for a doctor, and I was the nearest one. Not that there was anything to be done. Dr. Hughes is going to be busy with autopsies, that's for sure. Why did you ask?"

"I'm curious," I said. "Did you see anything unusual? Signs of a struggle, anything like that?"

"Densmore had a cut on one arm, but it hardly bled. Other than that, nothing."

"A quick kill," I said. If Robinson had been surprised not to see any sign of the red horse, he did a good job of hiding it. "Any idea how long he'd been dead?"

"No, you'll have to ask Hughes about that. Now, I've got to attend to Sinclair," Robinson said as he stood. "Don't worry, no electric shock therapy for him. He'll be fine, and the sooner he's asleep, the better. That way Snow can't get at him."

"Think Snow would be tough on him?"

"Use your head, Boyle. Snow's in charge of security, and he has two or three murders to account for. He'll be looking for a fall guy, you watch. He was an SOE field agent in Italy, but here he's just another bureaucrat answerable to yet another bureaucrat. If he doesn't fix this, he's out. Disgraced."

Which made him dangerous. A scapegoat was a handy answer, and one that might even work for him. Unless the killer struck again.

CHAPTER TWENTY-FOUR

"NOT NOW, BOYLE," Snow said when I intercepted him and Blackford on the way into his office. The major was favoring his bum leg as he steered Blackford through his doorway, wincing as he turned to face me. Blackford wore a stunned look, his eyes wide with shock after seeing Densmore's body.

"Major, Colonel Blackford needs protection," I said, as Snow ushered the colonel into his office and began to shut the door.

"Don't tell me how to do my job, Boyle," he said, slamming the door an inch from my nose. I thought it was funny he didn't ask me where I was this morning, since I was involved in all this from the get-go. I would have been one of the first suspects I questioned, but I guess Snow was busy enough trying to clamp a lid down on this mess.

Or maybe my time would come. I headed over to see Kaz, wondering what an SOE interrogation might be like. If Snow brought in some heavies from SOE headquarters, things might get dicey. As I approached the hospital wing, I stopped and pulled my right hand out of my pocket.

Steady as a rock.

I'd forgotten about the shakes when the gunfire started, or they'd forgotten about me. I didn't like not knowing when they'd start up again, but dead bodies seemed to be a giveaway. Hard to ignore them in the middle of a war, even if that war was being waged by a person or persons unknown within the perimeter of Saint Albans.

I put aside my own worries and took the stairs up to Kaz's room. It was empty. The bed was stripped and the floor freshly mopped. I went hollow inside. The room swirled, and I had to steady myself, resting my hand on the doorframe.

I felt the tremble.

No, I told myself. There's no dead body. It's only an empty room. Go find Kaz.

Five minutes later I did. In what passed for the VIP suite on the top floor. A corner room with views of the walkway and a victory garden thick with cabbages and the leafy greens of potato plants.

Kaz sat in an armchair by the window. Off in a corner, an American major stood talking with two army nurses, both lieutenants. The major was tall and square-jawed, with thick red hair and an imposing presence. He folded his arms, stroking his chin as he listened to the women, each seeming to give her opinion about something he was considering.

"Billy," Kaz finally said, noticing my hovering presence. "Come in, tell me what has happened. I heard shots fired, but no one will tell me anything."

"I don't want to interrupt," I said, pulling a chair close to him. "You sure?"

"Yes," Kaz said, keeping his voice low. "These three have been at it for ten minutes. Deciding on my future, I imagine. The major is Dr. Dwight Harken, and his two nurses, Lieutenant van Brackle and Lieutenant Shirley."

"Did Big Mike tell you about Cosgrove?"

"Yes. About his death, but also how he was responsible for Dr. Harken coming to Saint Albans. I certainly owe him for that. Help me repay that debt by discovering who killed him."

"I hope I can," I said, wondering if Kaz would be so gracious if he knew Cosgrove had chosen to leave Angelika in Ravensbrück. I gave him a quick rundown on Densmore, just as the medical convention in the corner broke up.

Kaz made the introductions. Shirley van Brackle, her hair blazingly blond, stood next to Addie Shirley, with her shock of brunette hair. Otherwise they were of similar build and age, both scrub nurses that Harken said he relied on for every important operation. I gave up my seat and grabbed another chair from the hallway.

"We call them Blond Shirley and Dark Shirley," Harken said, sitting on the edge of the bed. "Helps to eliminate confusion." The Shirleys smiled. So far, so good. "Now, as to your request, Baron." Ah. Kaz had played the baron card. It worked well with maître d's, so now we'd see how it went over with surgeons.

"Dr. Hughes told me this surgery has never been attempted," Kaz said, seemingly steeling himself against rejection.

"Well, it has been performed once," Dr. Harken said. "By a British surgeon, Henry Souttar. He had a patient whose mitral valve disease was like yours. Dr. Souttar went in through the left atrium and repaired the damage. The patient survived and lived several more years before dying of other causes."

"What's the problem, then?" I asked, then apologized for butting in. This wasn't my affair.

"Good question, Captain Boyle," Dark Shirley said. "Dr. Souttar's colleagues were unhappy that he broke the cardinal rule of medicine and operated on the heart. They refused to allow any further surgeries."

"You have to understand that the medical community is inherently conservative. Most doctors still live by Billroth's dictum from the last century," Harken said. "He stated that a 'surgeon who decides to suture a heart wound deserves to lose the esteem of his colleagues.'"

"Aristotle claimed that the heart was the only organ that could not withstand injury," Blond Shirley said. "Which is understandable, coming from ancient Greece. But we have to deal with modern-day physicians who think we're practicing witchcraft."

"Excuse me," Kaz said, raising one finger. "This is all fascinating, but are you going to operate on my heart or not?"

"There is a significant risk," Harken said.

"The Nazis have failed to kill me. And not for lack of trying," Kaz said. "I must trust my heart to survive this challenge as well."

"Are you sure you should take the risk, Doctor?" Dark Shirley asked.

"Do you have misgivings, Lieutenant?" Kaz asked.

"Not about the operation, no," she said. "It is risky, but so is living with mitral stenosis. I'm talking about the issue of performing an unauthorized operation. If Dr. Harken gets into trouble over this, it could affect our work at the 160th General Hospital."

"I won't," Harken said. "I have that covered. Dr. Powell has agreed to operate. I will observe and assist."

"The same doctor who operated on Major Cosgrove," I said to Kaz. "With Dr. Harken."

"Exactly," Harken said. "As I remember, Cosgrove was insistent, even though he ran a greater risk than you do, Baron. You're in good physical shape other than your stenosis. But still, any heart surgery carries with it a risk factor. Are you certain you wish to proceed?"

"I have already told you about my family and the recent news that my sister was still alive. I swear to you, Dr. Harken, that nothing is more important to me than finding her. And I must have my health for that to happen. If I am reduced to a sickly civilian, I have no reason to live. And Angelika will have no one to care for her. So do your best. If you succeed, I will forever be in your debt. If not, I will have lost nothing but a meaningless existence."

Harken looked at the two Shirleys. Blond Shirley nodded an emphatic yes. Dark Shirley sighed and gave her assent as well. Harken rubbed his jawline and studied Kaz.

"Fine. We'll do it," he said.

"When?" Kaz asked, his gaze fixed on Harken. I was glad the doctor hadn't asked how Cosgrove was doing these days.

"Tomorrow morning," Harken said. "Powell is taking the train tonight, and we'll start early. I had asked Dr. Hughes to join us, but he isn't a believer in surgery involving the heart."

"He was fairly rude," Blond Shirley said. "I'm surprised he authorized this at all."

"I am sure he had a thousand good reasons," Kaz said. "What I would like to understand is how difficult an operation this is, and how long it will take to recover."

"Barring unforeseen complications, which is a physician's way of saying that the unexpected can always occur, the surgery should be relatively straightforward. We make an incision and spread the rib cage apart," Harken said. "I will then make an opening into the left atrium of the heart and insert my finger—a fine surgical tool—to correct the damaged valve. I basically work away at the scar tissue around the flaps to open it up."

"And then I am fine?" Kaz asked.

"There is likely to be some mitral valve regurgitation, which is blood flowing backward into the heart. A mild case of that is negligible compared to mitral stenosis, so it's nothing to be worried about. A severe case would require further treatment."

"I sense that is one of the unforeseen complications," Kaz said. "But I shall be concerned about that when and if the time comes. How long will I need to recover?"

Before Harken could answer, a knock sounded at the door. A US Army sergeant leaned into the room.

"Sorry to interrupt, Doc," he said. "All your gear is squared away. You need anything else?"

"Yeah, I need you, Marty," Harken said. "Sergeant Marty Stuart, formerly of the 1st Infantry Division," Harken said, introducing us. "Marty was wounded at Omaha Beach. He came to us after a field hospital had stabilized him, but he was riddled with shrapnel."

"Doc Harken fixed me up," Marty said. "Took a while, but he got it all out."

"Including the last tricky piece lodged in his heart," Harken said. "He'd had six surgeries already. I told him he could chance that piece never moving. Or we could go in after it, no guarantees."

"I told the doc to go for it," Marty said. "I didn't want to spend the rest of my life worrying about the damn thing."

"It's a difficult procedure," Dark Shirley said. "You're looking through an incision into the heart chamber for a piece of sharp metal that bobs in the patient's blood with each beat of the heart. When you have the culprit in the right spot, the pressure from inside the heart will shoot it out, like a champagne cork."

"Then you have to suture the wound before the patient bleeds out," Blond Shirley said. "Time is not our friend."

"They got the shrapnel out?" I asked Marty.

"Damn right they did. For me and near to one hundred other guys by now," he said.

"How long before you were on your feet, Marty?" Harken asked.

"Next day. Doctor's orders," he said with a chuckle. I began to think this was the standard routine with these guys. "Hey, I wasn't doing the Saint Louis shag, but I was getting around the hospital ward all right. When I was released, Doc Harken said he needed a driver, so I signed on to keep him out of trouble."

"Major Cosgrove said something about exercise," I said, remembering his description of Harken's regime.

"Movement is good for the mind and body," Harken said. "You'll be out of bed as soon as possible. Once the stitches are out, in about a week, you can pay us a visit at the 160th. We'll give you the once-over. Ask for Marty, everyone knows him."

"Remember," Dark Shirley said. "This is off the books. Don't talk to anyone but Marty, okay?"

"I understand," Kaz said. "Thank you all."

"Thank us when it's over," Harken said. "Now, let's see if we can find a decent place to eat in town, Marty."

"No can do," Marty said. "The place is locked up tight. We're here until you finish up tomorrow."

"Who says?" Harken wanted to know.

"The Home Guards say it's a British officer named Snow. Got a bee in his bonnet."

"There have been some incidents," I said, sugarcoating it as best I could. "Major Snow takes his job seriously, and, to be fair, this isn't your typical hospital. Saint Albans has more than its fair share of top secret types."

"Wonderful," Dark Shirley said. "British hospital food, the worst of both worlds."

The small surgery team began to file out of the room, giving Kaz cheery assurances. Harken waited until the three of them were in the hall and extended his hand to Kaz.

"I will do my absolute best, I promise," he said. "If it is within my power, I'll have you up and walking in no time. But it will be Dr. Hughes's call on a return to active duty."

"I am not worried about Dr. Hughes," Kaz said, grasping his hand. "I place my faith in you and your people. Tell me something, though."

"What?"

"Tell me what it feels like to hold a human heart in your hands."

"It's strong. Muscular. But since it's hollow, it's also surprisingly soft and light," Harken said, as he leaned down and placed his right hand on Kaz's chest. "It lies here, inches from my touch, beneath the sternum, which comes from the Greek word *sternon*, which means a soldier's breastplate. The warrior's shield."

He smiled, withdrew his hand, and quietly took his leave.

We sat in silence for a moment. I didn't know what to say, so I looked outside at the swirling branches, their leaves borne skyward by strong winds that buffeted the tall windows. I thought about the first time I'd set eyes on Kaz, hunched over his desk reading reports. I thought about his agonies after Daphne had died, the suicidal risks he'd taken, until finally he'd come around to the notion that life might be worth living.

I thought about finding him in Paris, near death.

"Are you sure about this, Kaz?" I asked, my eyes on the upswept branches.

"I am certain there is no other course," he said. I pulled my chair closer and sat facing him. "I was always ill as a youth. I have no desire to spend the rest of my life with that sort of weakness. You have given me a taste for life, Billy, as strange as that sounds amid this madness and carnage."

"We've seen some things," I said, the memories flitting across my mind. "Done some things." I almost smiled. Some of those things were good memories. Others were best forgotten, or at least not celebrated. "But what about Angelika?"

"I have thought much about her. If I do not have this operation, there will be nothing I can do but wait. Wait for the chance that she survives, wait for her to find her way home, although no such thing exists for her on the Continent. Wait for her to search me out, which would be extraordinarily difficult. Almost impossible. Can you imagine all the refugees and stateless people this war will leave once it finally ends? It will be chaos."

"You have to take this chance, then," I said.

"Yes. If I die from the operation, it would be the same as not having it. Angelika would be on her own. But if it succeeds, I will be back in uniform with at least some chance of finding her. Do you understand, Billy?"

"I do, Kaz. I do."

What was I supposed to say? That Charles Cosgrove had possessed the power to put Angelika's name on a list, but wouldn't do it? That Diana might come out safely, but Angelika would be left in Ravensbrück? That his chances at surviving the operation were better than Angelika's in that concentration camp?

"I'll find her," I said. "If you can't. I promise you." I laid my hand on his, and he clasped it tightly.

"You are a good friend," he said. I struggled to meet his gaze. I didn't like the secret I was keeping from him, but I had no choice. The truth would crush him.

"Hey, have you heard the latest?" I asked, leaning back in my chair and changing the subject. "I didn't want to spook Dr. Harken."

"Everyone heard the gunshots," Kaz said. "An orderly said it was target practice, which was not very convincing."

"Lieutenant Paul Densmore was found dead in his room. He was in the VIP section, third floor of the north wing," I said. I wanted to fill Kaz in on what I saw there, but I remembered the room with the recording devices. I had no idea how many hidden microphones there were.

"Who is Densmore?" Kaz asked.

"Colonel Blackford's assistant," I said, as I reached over to the nightstand for pencil and paper. "Densmore had been suffering from nervous exhaustion but was about to be released. Blackford was going to meet with him this morning before he left, but instead he got to talking with Angus Sinclair."

"The wheezer and dodger chap," Kaz said.

"Yeah. Apparently Blackford had some technical questions for him, and Sinclair flew off the handle. He took off, bowled over one of the Home Guards by accident, and picked up his rifle. He enjoyed himself firing a few shots into the air before I got it away from him. Right after that they found Densmore's body." I handed Kaz the note I'd scribbled.

I snuck in and found Densmore. Red horse drawn in blood on window. Got out fast. Saw room with listening devices.

"Densmore and Cosgrove, both connected to Colonel Blackford of the German Section," Kaz said, his eyebrows raised as he read the note. "Murdered."

"One by a knife thrust, the other by a twist of the neck," I said. "Quick and efficient."

"The way SOE trains agents to kill," Kaz said, ripping the note in half and giving one to me. "But it also occurs to me a physician would know where to pierce the heart and how to break a neck. Not an easy thing, either of them."

We both tore our paper into tiny bits and dumped them in a cup, the crumpled pieces soaking up the dregs of Kaz's tea.

"Why here, and why now?" I said.

"Densmore and Cosgrove were both here at the same time," Kaz said. "Perhaps that was important to the killer. Or the killer is a patient and couldn't reach them anywhere else. You said Densmore was about to be released."

"Yeah," I said, thinking it through. I leaned closer, whispering to Kaz. "There's one place I'm sure they bug. Robinson's office. He has people spilling their guts in there."

"Except," Kaz said, raising an eyebrow.

"Oh yeah. Neither Cosgrove nor Densmore were patients of Robinson. Well, Cosgrove wasn't for sure. Maybe Robinson did talk with Densmore. I'll find out."

"And Holland, the first victim, did not speak. It would have been difficult for him to say anything, much less utter something so earth-shattering that it led to three deaths," Kaz said.

"One thing that bothers me is Blackford enlisting Sinclair's help. I mean, the guy has half a dozen screws loose. Aren't there plenty of professors still working for the Directorate of Miscellaneous Weapon Development?"

"What did he want him to work on?"

I whispered to Kaz what Blackford had been shopping for. A foolproof way to fake a parachute malfunction and ensure a high-speed landing in Nazi Germany. The design for something called a squirt transmitter to send compressed bursts of coded messages.

"The first item seems clearly to be an execution," Kaz said, keeping his voice low. "The latter would be extremely useful. Sending encrypted messages via Morse code is terribly time-consuming. The Germans can listen in and track down the source if the operator stays on the air long enough. Perhaps Sinclair was the lead boffin on such a project. If so, it stands to reason Blackford would consult with him, even here. Perhaps you should ask more of Sinclair."

"Can't. Robinson took him away for a sleep cure. He's out cold by now."

"Convenient," Kaz said. "Isn't it?"

"Maybe. But Sinclair was worked up. He could've gotten into a lot of hot water for grabbing that rifle and firing off a few rounds, even if it was in the air. Robinson made it sound like he was doing him a favor."

"Perhaps," Kaz said. "By the way, it was good of you not to mention Cosgrove's death to Harken. I think it would be disappointing to the good doctor to hear his surgical work had been rendered superfluous by a spike bayonet."

"That's what I thought. But mostly I didn't want any of them worried about a homicidal maniac on the loose," I said.

"Which there is."

"Details. Hey, did Big Mike show you the postcard?" I said, keeping my voice low.

"Yes. It contained a warning," Kaz said, leaning closer. "From an organization called *das Rote Pferd*. The Red Horse. It seems to be meant for a Nazi Party official, suggesting he hang himself before the German resistance or the Russians get their hands on him."

"The Red Horse is a German resistance group?"

"That would be the logical conclusion," Kaz said. "The card appeared to be ready to mail. The stamp looked genuine, but SOE could easily have forged sheets of them."

"Mailed from where?" I wondered.

"It would need to be from within Germany. Censors would check foreign mail and spot the postcard in a second," Kaz said. "This affair involves the SOE's German Section, so ask Colonel Blackford."

"Not quite yet," I said. "I need to think this through. I assume Big Mike has the card with him in London. Is he coming back soon?"

"Right after Walter opens his safe. Dr. Hughes has been gracious so far, arranging this room for me. But he has dropped heavy hints about changing his mind if a gratuity is not forthcoming."

"I thought you might not need to go that route with Cosgrove putting things in motion, but with him gone, you probably do," I said.

"Yes. Bribes do have a way of binding people together. Do you have any suspicions about Hughes?" Kaz asked.

"Yeah, I'm suspicious he'll want more money," I whispered. "As for the rest, he's the coroner here. So I guess I have to trust him, for the moment. I'll check in the morning and see what he came up with."

"Why not now?" Kaz asked.

"I'll keep you company," I said. "You hungry?"

"No solid food for me. Are you hungry?"

"No."

"Yes, you are, Billy. I know you."

Kaz was right. I was hungry. I scrounged a sandwich and brought it back. We sat together as the light faded, daylight mingling with dusk, until the night sky drove the day to ground under the distant horizon. We talked of many things. Small things, important things. Daphne. Diana. Angelika. His princess friend in Rome. That mysterious woman on Tulagi.

I told Kaz about growing up in South Boston, playing stickball in the streets, getting into the kind of trouble a cop's son craves. Just bad enough to prove he's not a Goody Two-shoes, but not so bad that he can't sit down for dinner.

We talked about plans for after the war. These were more imaginary, since neither of us could come up with a clear vision of what things would be like. Kaz talked about where he and Angelika might settle. I suggested Boston. He preferred Rome.

An orderly brought him some soup. Nothing but clear broth the night before surgery, along with a pill to help him sleep. Kaz got into bed, and I took the comfortable chair, keeping up a friendly chatter that had nothing to do with murderers. Kaz dozed, and I got up to stretch. I pressed my face to the window, the glass cool against my cheek. I wondered if Kaz would be here for the sunset tomorrow, or had he already launched a journey to that far horizon?

"When I was a boy, I used to marvel at snowflakes," he said, his voice raspy and distant.

"Yeah," I said, returning to my seat. "I liked catching them on my tongue."

"I would remove my gloves and let them land in the palm of my hand," Kaz whispered, his voice catching. "Each one was so beautiful. Unique."

"No two alike, they say."

"Like lives, Billy. Each one a marvel and a mystery. And so fleeting. A snowflake allows only the briefest glimpse of itself before melting in the warmth of a hand. Then it becomes part of you. I never understood that until now."

"Me neither," I said, placing the palm of my hand on his. "Me neither."

Kaz slept, his breathing shallow, small gasps escaping like the faintest of words, whispering secrets of what was in store for us, and for Diana and Angelika. I couldn't hear the words, but each syllable became a part of me, fragments of indecipherable phrases charting our destinies, as intermingled as the air we breathed.

CHAPTER TWENTY-FIVE

I AWOKE TO the clatter of a gurney and hushed voices. Marty was helping Kaz out of bed under the watchful eye of Blond Shirley, who took Kaz's pulse once he was laid flat. Kaz managed a half smile, but I could tell he was groggy. His eyelids fluttered, then stayed shut.

"We'll take good care of him," Blond Shirley said. "It will be a while. Come back around noon."

"Don't worry," Marty said. "Doc Harken's the best." He wheeled Kaz out, leaving me in an empty room. I didn't want to think about the next few hours. I didn't want to think about Kaz never coming back to this room. I went to the window, lifting my eyes to the heavens and sending a prayer to Saint Camillus, the patron saint of physicians and nurses. Then to the archangel Raphael, known for his healing powers. Never hurts to ask the angels as well as saints. If sinners could lend a hand, I'd enlist them too.

As if the devil had heard my prayer, I immediately ran into Dr. Hughes in the hallway. I asked if he would be joining Harken and Dr. Powell in the operating theater.

"No," he said, with a sharp shake of his head. "They can experiment if they wish, but I'll have no part of cutting open the heart. The baron is extremely foolish to have requested this, if you ask me."

"His choice," I said. Not to mention his cash. "Have you completed the autopsies, Doctor?"

"Yes, I have," he said, taking me by the elbow and steering me back into Kaz's room. "Are you still looking into these killings?"

"I am," I said, truthfully enough. With or without Snow's permission.

"Major Cosgrove was killed with an expert thrust," he said. "Nearly instantaneous. The cardiogenic shock from this heart wound would have knocked the major out immediately. Loss of blood pressure resulted in death within seconds."

"It would have taken a good deal of strength, wouldn't it?"

"I said expert, Boyle. The thrust went in at just the right location. It was also an excellent choice of weapon. The shape of the spike made it perfect for an entry that avoided the ribs. A flat blade can be deflected easily. Not so with a spike."

"Could a woman have done it?"

"Perhaps. The angle of the wound suggests it was an upward thrust, so anyone with the element of surprise and a degree of strength in their arm could have accomplished it," Hughes said. He eyed me with a new curiosity. "Why do you ask?"

"Trying to narrow down the potential suspects," I said, as I watched heavy clouds tumble low along the horizon. "What about Densmore?"

"You may not know this, Boyle, but breaking a man's neck is not easy," Hughes said, glancing at the open door and lowering his voice. "It is easy to do a great deal of damage, but a clean killing break? That requires knowledge. Or an extraordinary amount of luck."

"Medical knowledge?" I asked, as fat raindrops began to splatter against the glass.

"No," Hughes protested, working at avoiding my eyes. "Well, perhaps."

"A physician would know the best route to the heart, right? And the location of the right vertebrae?"

"Yes, certainly," Hughes said, nodding his head. "The C2, commonly called the hangman's vertebra, for obvious reasons. And before you ask, a woman could do this as well, especially if Densmore was seated. It would have negated his height advantage."

"If?" I asked.

"I cannot speculate on the location of his murder," Hughes said. "He could have been killed while standing, then dragged to the chair. I am not a detective, Boyle, but I do see the advantage. Anyone opening the door might think him asleep in that armchair."

"That's true, Dr. Hughes," I said. "Did you notice anything else about the room? Anything out of the ordinary?"

"I'm not at liberty to say. Please see Major Snow if you have any further questions, Boyle," Hughes said, heading for the door as the wind whipped up and the sky darkened, turning the room dim and gray.

"What about my release?" I said. "Snow said he had to call a meeting about it." A rumble of thunder rolled across the sky.

"He hasn't," Hughes said, looking out the window, distracted. "Patience."

Thunder hammered the air, followed by a sharp *crack* of lightning. Bright white light flashed and vanished, replaced by deep grumbles of thunder and another lightning strike turning the sky electric.

The lights went out.

"Where's the operating room?" I said to Hughes, wondering about Kaz being prepped for surgery. Hughes directed me to the front of the south wing. I raced through the halls and scampered down the stairs, emerging onto the main floor as the lights flickered briefly and then went out, leaving the whole floor in inky darkness. There were shouts and questions all around me, but nobody seemed too worried. Of course, none of them were getting their chest split open.

I saw lights at the end of the hallway and heard the muted hum of a generator coming from deep within the building. The frosted glass in the operating room door was luminescent. As I approached the operating theater, I could hear voices from inside, calm and deliberate.

I stuffed my shaking hand in my pocket and stumbled off in search of coffee. Then Griffin and his notebook.

I found them both in the north wing dining hall, bright enough from the large floor-to-ceiling windows. Griffin in the open was a rare sight, but here he was, working through a plate of Spam and powdered eggs. I was hungry enough that it looked good, but I didn't want him to bolt on me, so I poured myself a quick cup of joe from the urn and sat down across from him.

"How've you been, Griffin?" I asked, letting the still-hot java seep into my bones. "Haven't seen you around."

"Alreet," he said, shoveling a load of pinkish meat into his mouth.

"Where are you from?" I asked, wanting to get him talking.

"Up Northumberland way," he said. "Why?"

"Just curious about your accent. I'm from Boston, myself."

"That why yor accent is all radgie?"

"Radgie?"

"Mixed up. You sound funny."

"So I've been told," I said.

"Come on, mate, I don't mean nowt by it. Only havin' some fun, enjoyin' the sound of home," Griffin said, giving a little snigger. "I can speak BBC English or sound like a toff as well, Boyle, have no fear. I'm told my French is also quite good. How about you?"

"I'm strictly *Bawston*," I said, exaggerating for effect. He smiled, for a moment.

"You're not an agent, then," Griffin said, his voice suddenly serious. "You'd never make it through a German checkpoint."

"Not like SOE or OSS," I said. "No. How about you?"

"I need more training, they tell me. The war will be over before I finish, at this rate," he said, dropping his fork onto his plate as the lights came back on. "Lekky's back."

"I can tell you're the observant type," I said, speaking more loudly to be heard over the murmur of voices as the lights flickered, but held. "You watch people."

"Reconnaissance and surveillance. Very important. You ought to know that," Griffin said, eyeing me as he smirked, a cackle of laughter escaping his lips.

"You must have picked up something about the strange things happening here. First Holland goes off the tower, then these two murders." I drank my coffee, eyeing him over the upturned rim.

"What about you, Boyle?" Griffin said, pushing away his plate and leaning closer. "I've seen you snooping around after curfew. You must have friends in high places, eh? Do the high and mighty let you roam about every night?"

"What are you talking about?" I said, playing dumb. Maybe he'd spotted me sneaking in and out of my room the other night, or maybe he was fishing.

"Come on, I saw you out and aboot the last two nights," Griffin said, wagging a finger in my face as he snarled at me and fell back into his north country accent. "Easy to spot a profile in the dark, especially with you wearin' that Yank field jacket and a wool cap."

"Two nights ago?" When Cosgrove was murdered.

"Don't play the fool, Boyle," he said, leaning forward across the table. "Though it suits 'ee."

"What time did you see me two nights ago? It could have been someone else," I said, folding my arms across my chest and smiling a challenge his way. I knew it was the kind of thing he couldn't resist.

"I'll tell you to the minute," Griffin said, taking his notebook from his pocket and flipping pages. "Five past midnight, exactly. I caught sight of you along the interior wall of the south wing, keeping to the shadows. Maybe it was you who killed that major. Was it?"

"That's it? A figure in the shadows, at night? Not much of an identification, Griffin."

"Best I could do, bein' under lock and key," he said. "Your build, your uniform. Logical conclusion, I'd say. And the night before last, it was you for sure. Walkin' 'round like you owned the place. Good move, that. I saw two Home Guards pass within yards and not give you a second look."

"Feel free to borrow my technique. You are observant, I'll give you that," I said, uncrossing my arms and placing my hands flat on the table. Steady as a rock. "Did you see anything unusual around the time Densmore was killed?"

"What time was that?" Griffin shot back at me. I shrugged. "Never saw much of him, not directly, anyway. Passed him in the corridor one time and he kept his eyes to the floor. Not much for conversing, that one."

"What do you mean, not directly?"

"His room has a nice big window. I've seen him standing there, looking out. Several times. He was crying. Not a gentle weep, either, but havin' himself a good gusher," Griffin said, standing and pushing his chair in. "Now I'm done with the debrief, Boyle. I've got things to do. Useful things, unlike you and your endless questions."

Griffin gave that creepy laugh again and shoved off. I had to admit he had a point. I was damned useless, sitting here while Kaz had his heart sliced open, and Diana went through unimaginable hell in a Nazi concentration camp.

He was also right about my questions. They were all I had. Even as I watched Griffin leave the dining hall, I thought of more. The way I saw things, Densmore was the main reason for Blackford coming to Saint Albans. But had he come before? How often? And was it to speak with both Densmore and Sinclair?

Had Griffin really spotted an American out the night Cosgrove was killed?

If Densmore had been suffering from overwork and had gone through the sleep cure, what was still bothering him? What did he see as he looked out his window?

Finally, what had he done that still brought him to tears? And who had he done it do?

CHAPTER TWENTY-SIX

I STILL HAD a couple of hours to kill before I checked on Kaz. I was tired enough to sleep, but I didn't dare close my eyes. I had to be there when he woke up.

He had to wake up.

I went out to walk the familiar path around the buildings and tried not to think about a world without Kaz in it. It was a soggy and windy day, the gray scudding clouds heavy with the threat of rain. I shoved my hands in my pockets and wondered who had taken a stroll two nights ago at midnight. If the guard posted at the guest quarters had been taking a smoke break under the tree, it would have been easy to enter Cosgrove's room. But as soon as the guard returned, our killer was stuck in there. The rear-window escape was the perfect solution.

I passed the clock tower where this all started. I hoped Holland was at peace, wherever he was. I tried to see that scene again in my mind, replaying the flash of movement and the color of the uniforms. It was too far away, and it happened too quickly. I wasn't expecting Holland to go over the edge, so I hadn't focused on what was going on up there. Not that I'd been able to focus on much of anything at the time.

Was it a fellow Yank in the tower with Holland? Was it a Yank who snuck over to the guest quarters and killed Cosgrove?

I picked up my pace as I approached the south wing. I sent up another prayer and tried not to look at the windows or think about Kaz on that table.

I shook off the surgical visions and hurried along. As I turned the corner, I decided there was no way to know if the person Griffin had seen had been an American. The hospital had to have stores of US Army uniforms. It would be easy for anyone to swipe a jacket and wool cap. Disguise complete.

There were real Yanks here, Robinson and Miller among them. I'd spotted a couple of other uniforms back when walking was my full-time occupation, but I hadn't seen those guys lately. The Brits had a few years on us when it came to operations in occupied Europe, and it showed in their population of patients suffering from both physical and mental wounds.

Those wounds were where these murders originated, I was sure of it. Something had happened behind enemy lines. A betrayal. Death. A promise broken and lives lost. Someone had lost something so dear that they needed to take their revenge on these three people.

Or maybe two, I had to admit as I rounded the rear of the main building. Holland's death was different. There had been no red horse on his body. Maybe it was suicide, maybe it wasn't connected. Or if there was a connection, it was only seen by the killer.

I picked up my pace, the wind howling at my back. I had to get away from the south wing where Kaz would be either getting stitched up or wheeled down to the morgue. Holland, Cosgrove, and Densmore, all dead. Angelika and Diana prisoners of the Nazis. V2 rockets falling on Paris. And me, still locked up in this nuthouse.

I began to run, feeling the cold splat of rain on my face and the terror rising in my gut. For all I knew, Kaz and Diana were already dead. A slip of the scalpel and a bullet from a Nazi guard. I stumbled, catching my toe on a loose stone and falling forward, arms flailing as I tried, and failed, to keep my balance. I went down on my shoulder, rolling off the path and onto the soft grass.

Lightning cracked, vivid whiteness shattering the sky. Thunder rumbled and rolled over me, and I crawled to the base of a tree as rain pelted the earth. Taking what little shelter the leaves offered, I lay on the sodden ground, grabbing a tuft of grass in my hand to steady my growing tremor.

The storm felt like hell. I considered the possibility that it was hell, and I was paying for all the lives I'd taken in this war. Some people certainly were healed and released at Saint Albans, but I seemed to be permanently moored here as those I loved drifted farther and farther away. How could I possibly help Diana?

Another bolt of lightning shot to earth, striking a tree on the edge of the forest. It exploded in a flash of fire, showering the lawn with branches and bark trailing red-hot embers onto the lawn. I scuttled backward, even though the burning tree was fifty yards away.

I wiped the rain from my eyes and watched the small fires burn out. Smoke mingled with falling rain and drifted on the wind. I got up and raised my face to the heavens.

You want to explain that one?

The Bible was full of signs and portents. Back in the old days, people were better at understanding them. All I knew was that it could have been the tree I was hiding under that got hit as easily as that old oak, now smoldering in the rain.

So, what's the message?

More lightning lit the sky behind me, and I got it. Keep moving. Always keep moving. Do something, even if you're still in a prison.

Back on the path, I headed for the canteen. I felt good. Nothing like a near miss by a blast of lightning to put things in perspective. There was still a lot to do, beginning with more questions for Sergeant Jenkins before I checked in on Kaz.

As I approached the entrance to the canteen, two men exited, buttoning up their rain capes. I entered, shaking off the wet onto the stone floor.

"We'll have to sign you up, Boyle, if you like spending time here so much," Jenkins said from his seat by the fire. "What is it now?"

"A minute or so, Sarge, if you can spare it," I said. His tone was friendly enough, if a touch impatient. I could feel the tension in the room as five other men huddled around the coal fire waiting for his response.

"I can spare it, and some of the warmth as well. Come, sit. You're soaked through," Jenkins said, waving a hand for his men to make room.

"I didn't have a chance to speak with you after that incident with Sinclair," I said. "Seemed like Major Snow was on a tirade."

"That he was. Said he wanted to get rid of the lot of us," Jenkins said. He didn't seem too upset at the prospect. Then he grinned. "The good major told me he'd been turned down by the army, and all he was getting were five military police, for two days. Said he planned on conducting a search with them. A thorough search."

"It's a big place," I said. "You ever been up on the top floor of the main building?"

"No. Off-limits to the likes of us. None but those with top security clearances allowed. They bring in people now and then, keep them there for a few days, then ship 'em out. No idea what they do up there."

Listening to recordings, I'd bet. Snow would need help eavesdropping, if only to catch up now and then.

"The night Major Cosgrove was killed, Private Fulton relieved you, right?" I watched the tiny wisps of steam rise from my trousers as the fire warmed the soaked fabric.

"That's right," Jenkins said. "He showed up about an hour after you left. Why? You're not suspicious of him, are you? He's a decent lad."

"No, but I wondered if he stayed at his post the whole time, and when he went off duty," I said.

"Of course he didn't desert his post," Jenkins said, sitting up straight and making a good show of being insulted. Without looking me in the eye, he said he'd ordered Fulton to stay until 0530, when the first light of dawn started to show itself.

"I didn't say desert, Sarge. I just want to know if he had to leave. Call of nature, or to talk to a pal."

Jenkins sighed. "He'd been to the pub. It's likely he had to relieve himself at some point. I wouldn't expect him to piss on the porch, so it would make sense that he left for a minute or so."

"Does he smoke?"

"He does. Picked up the habit once he joined us. Why?"

"I found a couple of crushed cigarette butts by a tree at the side of the guest quarters. The soil was still damp and carried a faint odor of urine. Is there a chance he met someone and shared a smoke?"

"Who?" Jenkins asked. "We were short on men, that's why I had him hauled out of the pub. I figured it was easy duty, sitting instead of standing for once. But I don't allow smoking while on duty, even if it's in a comfortable porch chair. Fulton knows that and probably took the opportunity to sneak a smoke. Do you think that's when the killer struck?"

"It's certainly possible," I said. "Or, the killer could have hidden inside before we went in. You didn't see anyone about, did you?"

"No. Major Snow found me in the canteen and told me to find someone to stand guard at the guest quarters. There was but one man with me, and he'd come off a double shift. Snow told me not to worry and to do the duty myself until midnight, then to check on you."

"That's right, I forgot he said he'd post a guard on my room as well," I said.

"Well, you were sleeping like a lamb, so I took myself off home. Shame that we're so short of men. But there's little reason these days for the boys to take the time away from work and family now that Jerry's not about to come knocking," Jenkins said. "Anyway, Fulton was willing enough once I got word to him, and he came as quick as he could."

"Okay. You're sure you saw no one lurking around while you were on the porch?"

"Positive. Other than you and that big sergeant," Jenkins said.

"Someone told me they saw a Yank out after curfew," I said. "Or at least someone wearing an American field jacket and wool cap."

"When I say I saw no one, I mean no one, Yank or not," Jenkins said. "Who told you? One of your fellow inmates?"

"Griffin," I said. "He may be off the deep end, but he's got a watchful eye."

"He's a strange one," Jenkins said. "I would put some stock in what he says, but I don't trust him. He's convinced this is a training camp. Could be dangerous once the truth of it sinks in."

"What about Miller?" I asked.

"Big talker. The kind of brash fellow who gives Yanks a bad name. Mad as a hatter. I'd think him capable of violence if he didn't talk about it all the time. But what do I know?" Jenkins gave a slight shrug and moved closer to the fire, rubbing his hands together.

"Robinson?"

"The head doctor? Bit of a stretch, Boyle," Jenkins said.

"He's a Yank," I said. "Not that many here. If Griffin is right, there was an American on the grounds the night Cosgrove was killed. But I've never seen Robinson out of his service uniform with that tailored Ike jacket."

"Oh, I've seen him a few times, early mornings, running around the place. He wore fatigues and a field jacket when there was a chill in the air. Wool cap, too," Jenkins said. "But even I managed to grab one of those caps. Nice and warm they are."

"That's right, Robinson told me he ran track in college. Looks like he's staying in shape," I said.

"Does any of this help?" Jenkins said.

"Everything helps," I said, standing and warming my hands at the fire. I thanked him and made my way outside. It was almost time to check on Kaz.

Everything did help, I told myself as I headed to my room. It helped to be doing something other than waiting. It gave me the illusion of having some control over my life. Or if not mine, at least over the killer's life if I could uncover who was responsible. But as for clues, it had been thin helpings. The killer could have been in Cosgrove's room or entered it unnoticed while Fulton was pissing on a tree.

The rain had stopped. The air was still after the heavy winds, the dank smell rising heavily from the ground. I went inside, took a hot shower, and put on a fresh set of fatigues.

I was ready. At least that's what I told myself.

CHAPTER TWENTY-SEVEN

As I LEFT my room, I heard the tromp of heavy boots coming up the stairs. The orderly at the end of the corridor looked up in surprise and backed up against the wall when two British Army Redcaps burst out of the stairwell and began to shout at the top of their lungs.

"Everyone out, now!"

"Out of your rooms!"

"You, against the wall!" one of them said, pointing to me. Since it was midday, most people were already out of their rooms, but one other patient stumbled out, looking confused. He and I were both pinned against the wall and quickly, but expertly, searched.

"Move along," the Redcap told us, giving me a hard shove. These guys were British military police, known as Redcaps for the red fabric covers worn over their service caps. I didn't argue and headed for the stairwell, wondering what sort of contraband their search would turn up, and if any of it would connect to the murders.

I doubted it. Glad to have something else to think about, I took my time walking to the south wing. Secret agents were trained to hide incriminating materials, so I doubt any clues were going to be found under a mattress. But there were plenty of other people here, staff included, who might not be as adept. I wondered what Snow expected to find, or if he was simply going through the motions to look like a no-nonsense head of security.

Good luck to him. And good luck to me if the news from Dr. Harken was bad. I'd already wished Kaz all the luck in the world, and now it was time to find out if he'd made it through. I paused at the south wing entrance, took a deep breath, and opened the door.

The main floor was quiet. A few patients in blue bathrobes ambled along the corridor, while a cluster of orderlies and nurses huddled on the far side of the nurses' station. Their whispers were harsh and worried, their faces creased with anger. As I walked by, I caught a few phrases before they took note of me.

Who do they think they are? Made a mess of my room!

The Redcaps had paid them a visit. They'd found something. People were always hiding stuff. Cash, drugs, jewelry they'd nicked from a coworker, love letters. All the secrets buried away in belongings and pillowcases would be pawed over by Snow's searchers. But they'd offer nothing but distraction.

I hoofed it upstairs, my heart pounding with dread as I neared Kaz's room.

It was empty.

It was half past twelve by the clock downstairs, thirty minutes later than when they'd told me to come back. I went out into the hall and waited for the sound of a gurney. I paced up and down, my imagination getting the better of me. I thought about checking the operating room, but I didn't know what the hell I'd do if I found that empty too.

To pass the time, I headed up to the top floor where they had Skory secured. There was still a guard at the door, and when I asked if Lieutenant Feliks Kanski was with Skory, he hesitated for a second before telling me to scram.

"Listen, you don't have to say Feliks is in there," I said. "But if he is, tell him his pal Kaz is coming out of surgery and should be downstairs any minute." I hoped.

"I can't comment on personnel. Now get a move on," he said. In sort of a nice way. I got the message that knowing Feliks's name had given me a touch of credibility, even with my obvious status as a nutcase.

As I exited the staircase, I spotted the two Shirleys at the end of the corridor, one on either side of a gurney pushed by Marty, with Harken at his side. They were still in their operating gowns, decorated with splashes and sprays of blood. I noticed another guy with them, also in an operating gown. Dr. Powell, it had to be.

"Is he okay?" I said, running to meet them as Marty wheeled the gurney into Kaz's room. All I could see of Kaz was his face, pale, drained of all color. He didn't look good, and the rest of them looked worn and worried.

"The surgery was successful," Harken said, his eyes fixed on Kaz.

"But?" I could sense the tension in the small room.

"His blood pressure dropped as we were closing," Dark Shirley said. "An alarming drop. We gave him a transfusion and he stabilized, finally."

"He'll recover, then," I said, trying to make my question sound like a statement.

"If nothing happens within the next few hours, he should be fine," Harken said. "We'll keep a close watch. Dr. Hughes was to have two nurses standing by."

"I'll organize that," Marty said, darting out of the room. Harken introduced me to Powell, and, with the help of the Shirleys, they transferred Kaz to his bed, carefully lifting him in his sheets. It looked like it took no effort at all. I knew Kaz had lost weight, but right now he looked like a bundle of sticks.

Harken listened to Kaz's heart while the nurses tended to him. Powell kept his fingers on Kaz's pulse and finally nodded as Harken glanced up at him.

"He lost a lot of blood," Powell said. "But he should weather the storm."

"Tell me about his heart," I said. "You fixed him up, right?"

"The mitral valve repair went perfectly," Powell said. "Once the patient wakes up, he'll start feeling better soon. The anesthesia will cause nausea, but once that wears off, he will notice a marked improvement, even with the pain of the incision."

"That right, Doc?" I said to Harken. I didn't mean any disrespect to Dr. Powell, but this was Harken's show. He was the heart specialist.

"Yes. I'll feel better about the prognosis in a few hours. We need to be sure he doesn't experience another drop in his blood pressure. Then it's just a matter of recovery time."

"You won't believe this, Doc," Marty said, bursting into the room. "Dr. Hughes said he didn't schedule the nurses because he didn't expect the patient to survive. He's sending them up now."

"Oh, I believe it, Marty," Harken said. "Do I ever."

The Shirleys stayed to brief the nurses while I went with Harken and Powell to a dayroom down the hall for medical staff. They discarded their gowns, and we sat near a window, rays of sunlight flooding the room as the sky outside cleared. A thermos of coffee and a tray of sandwiches had been laid out for them. At least Hughes thought the doctors and nurses would live through the operation.

"Congratulations," I said. "You did it. Hasn't been done since that guy in the twenties, right?"

"That's correct, young man," Powell said, pouring himself a cup of joe. "It was Henry Souttar in 1925. His colleagues saw so little value in it, they refused to allow him to perform the surgery again. Dr. Harken was even forbidden from removing foreign objects in the area of the heart in North Africa. One can only guess at the lives he could have saved."

"There is mention of suturing open chest wounds in *The Iliad*," Harken said. "Three thousand years later, the medical profession hasn't progressed far beyond the chest wall. I was lucky to have superiors here in England who saw that the war demanded a higher level of surgery." He grabbed a sandwich, studied it to determine its ingredients, but soon gave up and took a mouthful.

"But we have to move carefully," Powell said. "The American army hasn't given permission for this mitral valve surgery. It's not necessary to repair damage from the battlefield."

"Which is why it had to be off the books," Harken said, setting down his sandwich.

"My hospital is also not ready to accept any handling or cutting of the heart," Powell said. "For now, we simply have to be content with knowing it can be done. Your friend is lucky, but we are also in his debt, as are patients who will benefit in the future."

"So we keep this on the q.t.," I said.

"Absolutely," Harken said. "The time will come, soon. But as Souttar said, it never pays to be ahead of one's time. Especially in medicine. There are too many physicians, like your Dr. Hughes, who are blinded by their long-held beliefs."

"Sure," I said. I was about to say he wasn't *my* Dr. Hughes, but in a way he was. I had him in my hip pocket, since I knew about the bribe. Once he took it from Big Mike, he'd be nice and snug in that pocket.

I thanked them again and left them to their coffee, taking Harken up on the offer of a mystery-meat sandwich on the go. I went back to the room and found Feliks by Kaz's bedside. One of the Saint Albans nurses was taking Kaz's blood pressure, while the other looked on with a clipboard in hand.

"What happened?" Feliks asked. I held up a hand to silence him, waiting for the nurse to finish. She nodded and said it was holding steady. I paused a second to silently thank Saint Camillus. You had to follow through with the saints, as far as I was concerned. Calling on them when you were desperate was bad form, and they might not listen the next time if you hadn't given them their due.

"Come on," I said, pulling Feliks out of the room. It must have been a shock for him to walk in on Kaz in that condition. "Have you been away? I haven't seen you around."

"Yes. There was a meeting in London I had to attend. I am sorry to hear of Major Cosgrove's death. He was a good friend to us. But what happened to Piotr?" I could see the strain and confusion on Feliks's face. He had his own set of burdens in this war.

"There was some sort of problem with his heart," I said, keeping things vague. "They had to operate. The doctor said he came through it fine. They brought him back a few minutes ago. He'll be okay." He had to be.

"Thank God," Feliks said with a heavy sigh, thankfully not pressing me for medical details.

"How is Skory?" I asked, lowering my voice. The Polish scientist was one part of the puzzle that could lead to Diana's release, and I needed to stay in the know as far as that was concerned. I felt guilty for a moment, knowing Feliks was in love with Angelika, but I couldn't do anything about that.

"Recovering quite well," he said. "That was the subject of the meeting. The Foreign Office sent someone to take Cosgrove's place. Your Colonel Harding and *Duży* Mike were there as well."

"Doozy Mike?"

"No, *Duży* Mike," he said, slowing down the Polish pronunciation for me. "It is what we call Big Mike, your sergeant. He is a large man, even for an American."

"You're telling me Colonel Harding and *Duży* Mike are involved with Skory?"

"Yes. That is why *Duży* Mike and I arrived here together. Don't you remember?"

"Right, sure," I said. I had recalled their arrival, but this was the first time I'd heard that Harding was part of this project. If Sam was at a meeting with Cosgrove's replacement from the Foreign Office, he'd be involved with the trial release of prisoners. Maybe he could figure out a way to include Angelika. And ensure Diana had a top spot on the list. "Sorry, it's been a little crazy here."

Feliks didn't laugh.

"By the way, Billy, Colonel Harding has secured your release. He and *Duży* Mike will be here later this afternoon. Good news, yes?"

"Yes," I said. "Very good news." Feliks left, promising to stop and see Kaz later. I looked in on Kaz one more time. No change for the worse, or better. I took myself outside, thinking through what my release would mean. A soft bed, decent chow, and freedom. A chance to follow up with Harding on the Ravensbrück releases.

I looked up at the blue sky. Not a cloud to be seen; the rainstorm had blown away on the wind. I walked along the front pathway, staring at the rows of windows in the massive main building. Somewhere in there, or close by, was the person who murdered Charles Cosgrove. If I left, the only person investigating the killings would be Major Snow and his heavy-handed Redcaps.

One more night. That's what I needed. Another clandestine visit to the files. This time I'd pay more attention to the selection board notes in Holland's dossier. I'd have to convince Snow to let me stay so I could visit Kaz in the morning. Once he had my release in hand, it would make sense for him to give me a spot in the guest quarters instead of keeping me under lock and key. No more hanging sheets out the window.

As I passed the clock tower, I looked up to the third floor where Densmore's room had been. I wondered if staff worked through the night in the room with the recording devices. Transcribing conversations, maybe? No, that would just be a lot of complaints about the food and the doctors, and the general gossip of any large institution. Most likely, they must review the tapes and note anything suspicious.

I knew there were staff in the switchboard room. What I didn't know was whether the door to that floor being unlocked had been a fluke or if it was routinely left open. Even if it was open during the day, chances were, it was locked at night.

Still, it was tempting. There might be evidence of conversations that would be revealing, especially if the guest quarters had been bugged. I wasn't supposed to know about the eavesdropping, so I couldn't ask Snow. But he had to have thought about it and gone over the records.

Right?

I decided to check Cosgrove's room, if it was open. I circled around the main building and took the path to the guest quarters. Two women with cleaning supplies were on the porch, entering Blackford's digs. They told me he'd gone, and I should make myself scarce, patients not being allowed inside. I backed off, coming up on the porch from the other direction, treading lightly so they wouldn't hear.

I opened the door to Cosgrove's room. It smelled of carbolic and bleach. The bloodstained couch had been removed and the place scrubbed clean. If possible, it made the room even sadder and more forlorn. The windows were open to air the place out, the curtains wafting in and out like dying breaths.

I searched the room for a listening device and any telltale wires.

The place was void of decorative touches or any other spot to hide a bug. I stood on a chair and unscrewed the light fixture in the ceiling, getting nothing but dust and dead flies for my troubles.

No, wait. I spotted a small hole near the electrical wires. Maybe a microphone had been hidden in the light. Or maybe it was simply from the original fixture, long since replaced. Besides, the SOE spying on their own people was a stretch, even for that bunch.

Voices sounded from the next room. Laughter and a sharp retort. The cleaning women were having a back-and-forth. I couldn't understand them, not until I put my ear up against the thin wall. Then I heard the tail end of a story about a husband coming home from the pub and a problem with his suspenders. They laughed again.

What had we talked about in here that night? Sweden. Top secret stuff about Sweden and the Ravensbrück prisoners. Had Blackford overheard? And what if he did? He was SOE and knew how to keep his mouth shut. And as head of the German Section, he might well have known about the plan.

I got out of there before the cleaning ladies took a broom to me and headed to Doc Robinson's office.

I thought about telling Robinson there was a chance his place was bugged, but I wasn't sure how to go about it. He appeared to be a decent guy doing his best, and it didn't seem fair to him or his patients to have SOE listening in as they spilled their guts. But maybe that was the whole point. Maybe he knew and was looking for evidence of agents who talked too much or too freely.

Hell, that was a lot of maybes. *Maybe* I should drop in and ask for a session. It wouldn't hurt to scan the room for any stray wires.

I knocked on his door. No answer. As I began to walk away, a couple of Redcaps exited Major Snow's office down the hall. When I passed by, Snow looked up and called me in.

"I've been told your release has been authorized, Boyle. At the highest level," Snow said. "Congratulations. I'm sorry I couldn't get it sorted myself, but there hasn't been a minute for routine paperwork."

"Thanks, Major. Any luck with the search?" I looked at a stack of magazines and papers, and a small container on a table by his desk.

"I may have put too much stock in the idea of a search, I must admit," Snow said, rising from his seat and standing by the table. "Not to mention the investigative prowess of our military police. They seem to think pornographic pictures and unidentified white powders are important clues to two murders. All it means is I must listen to the outrage of staff who have had their belongings gone through. If these are drugs, it is serious, of course." He sighed.

"But not how you want to spend your time and energy," I said.

"Exactly. I told the Redcaps to bring me anything unusual. They must lead dreary lives if this mound of debris counts as unusual to them." He sifted through girlie magazines, French postcards, a couple of Italian art journals, and sheets of nude drawings done in pencil. Each item had a note attached with the name and location of the owner.

"Nice artwork," I said.

"Medical people have an eye for anatomy," Snow said. "And short tempers." He dropped the drawings and a small square of paper fluttered to the floor.

It was a red horse. The same stylized figure of a horse that had been on the postcard and drawn in Densmore's blood. I had to stop myself from blurting out I'd seen it in Cosgrove's hand. I didn't know what Snow's reaction would be to learning I'd tampered with evidence.

"What's that? It looks like the Uffington White Horse. Saw it once from the train," I said, remembering what Big Mike had told me about it. I noted the fact that it was nothing but a simple drawing, done in red ink, not a stamped postcard like the one found on Cosgrove.

"Well, it's obviously red, not white," Snow said. "But other than that, you're right. Does it mean anything to you?"

"No. Whose is it?"

"Dr. Robinson's. It was in one of those Italian magazines. He goes in for Italian paintings, evidently, and picked those up at a used book shop. He claimed he had no idea that the card was inside when they questioned him."

"The Redcaps were suspicious because the magazines were Italian, I guess." I took the card from him and gave it a quick study. Nothing else on it, just the primitive drawing. I handed it back. Snow tossed it on the pile of papers, giving no hint of recognition. I wondered what the hell Robinson was doing with it. Or who planted it among his possessions.

"If they were in German, they'd probably have shot him on the spot," Snow said, with a scornful laugh. "Too bad you're leaving us, Boyle. I could use your help."

"I may want to stay an extra night, if you don't mind, Major. My pal was operated on today. I'd like to see him in the morning when he's awake," I said.

"I understand your superior, Colonel Harding, will be here within the hour. As soon as I have the paperwork in hand, you're a free man. I'll put you up in the guest quarters, and you can visit your Polish friend. Everything went well?"

"Apparently," I said. "He had a scare when his blood pressure dropped, but they said he should be fine."

"Glad to hear it," Snow said. "Dr. Hughes wasn't so sure of the outcome."

"He seems to be a prickly guy," I said. "How'd he react to the search?"

"He was actually cooperative," Snow said. "He volunteered to have his rooms searched first, to show that everyone was getting the same treatment. Good of him."

Yeah, I thought as I left Snow to his mound of contraband. He wanted the search team long gone when his envelope of cash arrived later today.

CHAPTER TWENTY-EIGHT

I SPOTTED ROBINSON in the foyer on his way in. I felt less inclined to warn him about the possibility of his office being bugged. I needed time to think about the red horse drawing found in his room, as well as the Italian art journals. I doubted there were many Italian spy rings left in operation, but picking up books and magazines at a used-book shop would be the perfect way to handle drops and messages.

"How are you doing, Boyle?" Robinson asked as we met in the hallway. "I haven't seen you in a while. I have time to talk this afternoon if you want."

"Thanks, Doc," I said. "But looks like I've been sprung. Honchos in London cut through the red tape. I should be gone by morning."

"Well, good luck to you. And I hope for the best for your friend," he said in a quiet, heartfelt voice. "Take care of yourself. Get some rest if you can."

"A long hot bath and a fine meal are tops on my list, Doc," I said. "You have your quarters searched yet? People seem hopping mad."

"Yeah. It wasn't a big deal. They made a mess, but that's to be expected. I'm used to cleaning up messes the war leaves behind," he said. It was the most personal thing he'd ever said to me.

"Hey, I wasn't that messed up, Doc," I said, forcing a laugh.

"Boyle, you're a smart guy. Smarter than you let on. You know damn well you were in seriously bad shape," Robinson said, his voice angrier than I'd ever heard. "And you're aware a lot of people here are worse off than you. That doesn't even include the ones who may never be released."

"Sorry, Doc. You're right."

"Didn't mean to blow my stack," he said. "You'd think a psychiatrist would have better self-control. Anyway, best of luck to you."

"Thanks," I said. "When I got my walking papers in Snow's office, I saw your Italian art magazines the MPs confiscated. Hope you get them back." I watched his eyes for any sign of surprise. Nothing. He took it calmly.

"They were only a few pence at a used-book shop, no big deal," Robinson said. "The MPs had to be grasping at straws to think they were evidence of anything. I don't care about the art journals. But I do hope I can get to the Continent when the shooting's over and visit a few museums in France and Italy."

"I'm not much of an art lover myself," I said. "But I do want to see the Uffington White Horse. You heard of that, Doc?"

"Sure. It's beautiful. Over three thousand years old, they say. It's a short trip, worth a train ride from London. Enjoy yourself, Boyle. You deserve some relaxation."

We shook hands and he went on his way, leaving me wondering exactly how much self-control he had. He hadn't said a thing about the red horse found in his magazines and betrayed nothing at the mention of the look-alike White Horse. Either he was one cool customer, or he didn't know why it was important.

I got to the south wing as a US Army staff car pulled up. Colonel Harding jumped out of the rear while the wheels were still rolling and strode over to me.

"It's good to see you up and looking well, Billy," he said, clapping me on my shoulder and grinning. "Really good."

"Uh, yes sir," I said, raising my hand in salute and trying to hide my amazement. First, Sam Harding had never once in the more than two years I'd known him called me Billy. It was always Boyle or something else less than flattering. And grins were at best a once-a-month phenomenon. "Glad you're here, Colonel."

"It's the least I could do, Captain. I've got your release papers right here," he said, tapping the pocket of his trench coat. "Signed by General Colin Gubbins, head of SOE himself. That should satisfy the local pencil pushers."

I had to admit, it was nice to be called captain. It made me feel more like myself.

"Billy, how's Kaz?" Big Mike said, unfolding himself from the driver's seat.

"It went well. The operation, that is. They had some trouble with his blood pressure, but they said he should be okay. I'm hoping he's awake by now," I said. "Do you have that package?"

"What package?" Harding asked, as Big Mike gave a discreet nod.

"It's a long story, Colonel," I said. "Nothing to worry about."

"Jesus, Boyle, some things don't change. Forget I asked. Take us to Lieutenant Kazimierz."

That was the Sam Harding I was used to. Ornery, ramrod straight, professional army all the way.

Kaz was awake, propped up on pillows, and still looking pale. But his eyes were lively, and he managed a smile and a wave as we entered his room. Dr. Harken was listening to his heart with a stethoscope as Dark Shirley took notes.

"You're doing fine, Baron," Harken said, shooting a glance at Harding. He looked concerned, and I introduced them quickly, not wanting Harken to think the brass was running him down for an unauthorized operation.

"Hello, Colonel," Kaz said, his voice thin and strained.

"His throat is sore from the breathing tube," Dark Shirley said. "Otherwise he endured the anesthesia well."

"He's going to be okay?" Colonel Harding asked.

"His heart sounds perfectly normal," Harken said.

"What was the problem?" Harding asked him.

"Colonel, that's part of the long story. Probably best we don't go into details," I said.

"I came here at the request of Charles Cosgrove," Harken said. "He was a patient of mine and thought I could help. You knew Charles?"

"Yes. A damn honorable man and a fine soldier," Harding said, momentarily distracted from asking too many questions.

"All right, Baron, let's get you up and walking," Harken said. He and Dark Shirley helped Kaz sit up and swing his legs off the bed.

"Wait," Kaz whispered, and looked to Big Mike. "You have the package from Walter?"

"Yeah," Big Mike said.

"Good," Kaz said. "I would like to thank Dr. Hughes for everything he's done. Could you ask him to stop by?" Big Mike gave him a thumbs-up and vanished.

"Should he be walking so soon?" Harding asked, as they got Kaz standing.

"Colonel, I wouldn't dream of interfering in your military plans, so please, if you don't mind, don't question my medical decisions," Harken said, holding on to Kaz's elbow and guiding him out of the room.

"I like that guy," Harding said. "Tell me, who is Dr. Hughes, and what does he have to do with all this?"

"As little as possible," I said. "But he has agreed to sign off on Kaz being fit for duty."

"Hmm," Harding said. I could see the wheels turning. "It does sound like a long story. A story for another day. Right now, tell me what you've learned about Cosgrove's murder."

We sat in the corridor on a narrow bench and watched Kaz being slowly walked up and down the hall. I quietly filled Harding in on Densmore's murder and the red horse image on the windowpane.

"Did Big Mike show you the postcard?" I asked.

"Yes. It looks like some sort of black propaganda project aimed at Nazi Party officials," he said. "Before we drove up, we dropped in at Scotland Yard and asked Inspector Scutt to do us a favor and check it for fingerprints." Horace Scutt was a detective with the Metropolitan Police, well beyond retirement but still in harness to fill in while the younger men went off to war. We'd worked with him on a case several months ago, and he knew what he was doing.

"That'll take a few days to process," I said. "And a lot longer to check against their files."

"Scotland Yard has access to fingerprint records of all SOE personnel. Part of the security check they run. I told him to start there, given the card was found within a secure SOE facility."

"That'll help," I said. "There's something else. Have you ever heard of a squirt transmitter? Or a means to tamper with a parachute so it will malfunction without looking like it was tampered with?"

"Negative on both counts," Harding said. "Why?"

"Colonel John Blackford came here with Cosgrove. Blackford's director of the SOE German Section, and he was pressing a fellow named Angus Sinclair about designing a transmitter that would store and send out compressed bursts of messages, if I understood correctly."

"That would be helpful in avoiding German radio direction finding," Harding said. "But I've never heard of it. What's the idea with the parachutes?"

"I don't know. He wanted a way to rig them so it would look like an accident if anyone investigated. Sinclair is some kind of wizard professor who had a nervous breakdown. I got the sense he'd done work for Blackford before. He's one of the wheezers and dodgers."

"Ah. Churchill's madhouse inventors," Harding said. "Does this have anything to do with the murders?"

"Well, both victims were involved with the German Section. Holland, the guy who was pushed from the tower, must have had some connection as well. I just don't know what it is yet. But I do have a plan," I said. "Once you deliver my release papers to Major Snow, he's agreed to let me stay in the guest quarters tonight. So I can check on Kaz in the morning."

"Hello," Kaz croaked as he approached us, walking solo with Harken and Dark Shirley close on either side.

"You're looking good, Kaz," I said. He did have a bit of color back.

"My chest is sore, and I am tired, but I do feel better. Like I can breathe again," Kaz said. "But now I must rest. Are you staying long, Colonel?"

"I have some business with Lieutenant Kanski," he said. "I'll see you later." Kaz smiled and allowed himself to be steered into bed.

"It doesn't seem to me that you need to check on him in the morning," Harding said. "What's going on?"

"Do you want to know, Colonel?" I said, my voice hushed as an orderly passed us by.

"No, never mind," Harding said with a heavy sigh. He bowed his head, rubbing his temples. I'd never seen him like this. He seemed defeated. "I owe you an apology, Boyle."

"For what?"

"For all this. For the baron, for Miss Seaton, and the trouble you got into with the Kraut drugs. I should have planned better, gotten you out sooner, I don't know. I'm sorry," he said, looking me straight in the eye.

"Colonel, Kaz would have had a heart attack sooner or later. Having it sooner meant he got to be treated by an expert, maybe cured for life. That's good, isn't it? As for me, I'm fine now, and it was my own fault for overdoing it. Kaz and I both knew what we were getting ourselves into." That last bit wasn't exactly true. No one could have foreseen the situation in Paris, rife with sudden violence and betrayals.

"I feel responsible for Miss Seaton," he said, his voice barely audible. It seemed to pain him to say the words.

"Cosgrove told me about the release," I said. "One hundred prisoners, to be turned over to the Swedish Red Cross. Diana's name is still on that list, isn't it?"

Harding stood and walked to the end of the corridor where a tall window looked out over the front pathway.

"Sorry," I said, following him and huddling against the glass, away from the flow of people in the hall.

"Yes. She is," Harding said. "Feliks told me about Angelika. I'm sorry, Boyle, there's nothing I can do. It's not a string I can pull."

"Kaz can't know about this. At least not until he's fully recovered," I said.

"I agree. There's no reason for him to know it was even a possibility," Harding said. We both were silent for a moment, staring out the window and making believe we didn't feel like bums.

"There's something else going on here," I whispered. "If you're ready to deliver my release to Major Snow, I'll tell you about it on the way over."

Harding agreed. We stopped in at Kaz's room. He was in bed and being fed spoonfuls of soup from a steaming bowl by one of the Saint Albans nurses. He did look better than he had before the surgery. Surprising, after having his chest cut open.

Big Mike returned and told Kaz Dr. Hughes was on his way. When the nurse finished up and left, Big Mike slipped Kaz a thick envelope. Harding pretended he didn't notice and told Kaz we'd be back soon. I took Harding along the pathway to the rear of the main building, giving us time and space to talk.

"I think they've bugged some of the rooms," I told him. "There's a restricted area on the third floor of the north wing. I saw wire recorders and men with headphones, three or four of them. They were so busy taking notes they didn't notice me."

"They let you into a restricted area?" Harding asked as we approached the guest quarters.

"No. I snuck in to speak to Densmore. He was a bit of a recluse. But I found him dead, so I got out fast, after I erased the red horse drawn in his own blood on the window."

"Okay, I understand why you took the postcard. Having it finger-printed was a good idea. But why get rid of the picture on Densmore's window?" Harding asked as he looked up at the dark, imposing building to our right.

"The red horse is important to the killer. He wanted people to know Cosgrove and Densmore were guilty of something connected to it. By removing it, I thought he might make a mistake when he showed it again." I filled Harding in on Robinson and the drawing found in his Italian magazine.

"Do you think your psychiatrist is the killer?" he asked.

"He does have freedom of movement. And one of the patients said he saw an American on the grounds after curfew. But I think it's more likely something was said to him in a session and overheard by SOE."

"Snow and his security team," Harding said, sticking his hands into his pockets.

"Yes, they would have been the first to see any mention of sensitive information. But I'd guess anything suspicious is passed on to SOE headquarters in London. Is there any way you can look into how they operate, Colonel?"

"I had to call in a lot of markers for Gubbins to sign your release order," he said. "Getting a secretive bunch like SOE to open up about their own internal security is hopeless. Worse than hopeless, since it would reveal what we know, and we'd get nothing in return."

"I guess," I said, pointing out the guest quarters where Cosgrove had stayed, and where I hoped to be tonight. "Do you think Blackford would receive reports if someone here talked too much about the German Section?"

"If the person was a real security risk, sure," Harding said. "Section heads have top-level clearances. But if you're looking at Blackford as a suspect, I'd worry about any agent he was sending into Germany."

"You mean the parachute rigging?"

"Yes. I can understand him pressing Sinclair on the design of a radio transmitter that would compress messages. That would save lives and play hell with the German radio detection units. But the parachute tampering sounds like a method to dispose of one person."

"But why go to all the trouble of making it look like a malfunction if the agent fell into Kraut territory? Maybe he was thinking about sabotaging parachutes for the Luftwaffe, especially if they were made by slave labor."

"I doubt it," Harding said. "Pilots and paratroopers don't take anything for granted when it comes to their parachutes. Someone would notice. No, I think he's after a way to dispose of a single person. Might be worth looking into."

"I'd been considering Blackford as a potential victim," I said, stopping in my tracks. "He and Cosgrove, along with Snow, were so chummy I didn't consider him as the killer. I was more worried about protecting him."

"It would fit," Harding said, surveying the grounds and outbuildings. "He gets a report and heads here. Two people connected to the

German Section die. He leaves. If I were a German Section agent about to board a Lysander, I'd be worried."

"I wonder if we can get a list of their agents and see if any have a connection to Holland," I said.

"Impossible," Harding said. He was right. SOE would never divulge those names. "But why are you curious about Holland? He was French Section."

"Holland has to play a part in this. And I know I saw someone throw him from that clock tower, which was before Blackford arrived," I said.

"Boyle, you were imagining things when you were first brought here. Lots of things. You have to accept the possibility you were mistaken. From what Big Mike said, you just settled down recently. *After* Holland's death."

"Okay, okay," I said as we resumed our walk. "I wonder if Vera Atkins might have any insight to offer?"

"She's a smart lady," Harding said. "If there was any scuttlebutt, she'd be sure to pick it up. As for sharing it with you, doubtful." Vera Atkins was the head of intelligence for the SOE French Section. I'd met her before, and I was sure she'd at least hear me out.

"I might give it a shot when I get to London," I said. As we walked, I spotted Griffin dart from a building to the cover of a thick tree trunk. We were apparently his surveillance targets for today.

"You've mentioned Robinson and Blackford. Any other suspects?" Harding asked.

"Too damn many, Colonel. That's the problem with this place, it's chock-full of people trained to kill. Not to mention the corrupt Dr. Hughes," I said, moving on quickly before Harding could put two and two together. "Then there's Dr. Fielding, who wanted to practice some kind of electric shock therapy on me. Major Basil Snow, who operated an SOE network behind the lines in Italy. He was wounded and has a pronounced limp. I don't think he's crazy about this job. But fieldwork is out of the question, so it's probably the best he can hope for. He's in over his head."

"And he can't call in the local police or even Scotland Yard," Harding said.

"Right. Which is why he asked me to poke around."

"Okay, who else?"

"An American OSS agent named Miller. Talks a lot about his violent tendencies, but it's all talk. They scrambled his brain with the electric treatment, so he's not much help. Then there's the fellow stalking us, Griffin."

"Behind that tree," Harding said, crooking his thumb behind us. "What's his story?"

"Washed out of a mission at the last minute," I explained. "He's convinced himself this is a specialized training facility. He's honing his skills."

"Which would include assassination," Harding said. "Who else are you looking at?"

I told him about Iris and Faith, and Faith's connection with Holland. Even Sergeant Jenkins, who I'd thought was a commando back when I was sleepless and confused.

"Faith might be taking her revenge," Harding said. "In some way we don't understand."

There were many things I didn't understand about this place. But there was one thing I did know for sure as we passed beneath the clock tower. Harding held my ticket out of here.

CHAPTER TWENTY-NINE

WE FOUND SNOW at his desk. He looked weary as I did the introductions, and Harding handed over the release order.

"There's certainly no arguing with this, Colonel Harding," Snow said, his eyebrows raised in surprise. "Captain Boyle, you are free to go. If you still wish, you may stay in the guest quarters tonight, next to Colonel Harding and his sergeant." He opened a file with my name on it and stuffed the order inside. I was surprised at how thick the folder was.

"I'd like a receipt for that order, Major," Harding said. "In case the captain has to prove he's been released. I wouldn't want an orderly or guard to get in trouble for detaining him."

"Good point, Colonel. As you can imagine, we don't get many people eager to extend their stay," Snow said. "Well, none at all until today." He wrote out a statement on Saint Albans letterhead, signed and stamped it. It looked official. Maybe I'd have it framed. It was nice to have written proof I wasn't a lunatic.

"Anything new on the search, Major?" I asked, glancing at the pile of contraband on his table, the red horse sketch still at the top.

"Nothing helpful, I'm afraid," he said, waving a hand over the accumulated contraband. "Have you come across anything?"

"Other than wondering about Colonel Blackford, no," I said.

"Well, he's safe enough. I spoke with him by telephone not an hour ago," Snow said. "He was eager for any news. He worked closely with Densmore, and, as you know, he and Cosgrove were close. We all were." He tapped his pen and looked away from my eyes. Stiff upper lip at all times.

"If he's in London, he should be safe," I said. "All the potential killers are still here."

"Or will be, until you leave, Boyle," Snow said. "Not that I suspect you, but as a policeman I'm sure you'd understand a wide net must be cast."

"Well then, what about Blackford? You haven't suspected him at all? Two people close to good old Blackie are killed and he leaves for London. Isn't your net wide enough for him?" I asked, acting as if I hadn't just thought about Blackford myself.

"Ridiculous! I would never let friendship get in the way of my duty," Snow said, throwing the pen down on his desk. Then he gave out a sigh and leaned back in his chair. "But perhaps you have a point. This has all been a shock, and I may have let my assumptions get the better of me. Don't they say most people are murdered by someone close to them? Or is that only in detective stories?"

"It's true enough," I said. "Especially if murder is the primary focus of the killer, not robbery or some other lesser crime. People who are on intimate terms with each other have more cause for friction. Arguments, disagreements, that sort of thing. My Uncle Dan is a homicide detective, and he always told me, 'Familiarity breeds attempt.'"

"Perhaps I should question Blackie," Snow said, drumming his fingers on the desk. "I'll ask the sergeant in charge of the military police to come along and make it official. I don't want anyone to think I'm playing favorites. Unless you wish to volunteer your services, Captain."

"He doesn't," Harding said. "I have plenty of work waiting for him, and it's time he moved on. Good luck, Major Snow."

"Sorry, Major, but you have the right idea," I said. "Talk to Blackford if only to eliminate him as a suspect. While you're at it, you might want to ask why he was after Sinclair to design a parachute failure."

"What do you mean?" Snow asked, obviously taken by surprise.

"When Sinclair went off his rocker, Blackford had been asking for his help on a new transmitter design and a method to sabotage a parachute so it wouldn't look like it was tampered with," I said. "You were there, right?"

"Yes, but all I heard Sinclair going on about was the transmitter. Are you sure?"

"Absolutely. Sinclair told me about it in the dining hall afterward. Right before Dr. Robinson took him away for a long nap." Of course, I realized. Snow hadn't been in the dining hall.

"I did not know that," Snow said, his brow furrowed. "A despicable notion, if Blackford indeed intended it for one of his own. I shall pursue this, Captain Boyle. Thank you for bringing it to my attention."

"Thanks, Colonel," I said, once the office door shut behind us. "I sure as hell didn't want to be part of Snow's investigation. He's right to be worried about playing favorites, but I think mainly he wants to put on a good show and save his job. Although he did seem genuinely upset about the parachute tampering."

"It doesn't impress me as much of a job," Harding said, looking up and down the looming corridor. "Security officer in an asylum must be a letdown after being in the field with SOE."

"Someone said it was temporary, while he recuperated from his leg wound. Maybe he's expecting a promotion and wants to impress his bosses."

"Or is he covering up his own involvement?" Harding asked as we stopped in the foyer outside Clarissa's office.

"It's possible. He knew Cosgrove from way back, but not Densmore as far as I can tell. But I'm sure Holland is the link to the killer. I'd like to know more about how he connects to everyone," I said, my voice lowered to a whisper.

"Whatever you do, be careful. Listen, I have to get back to Skory," Harding said, glancing at his wristwatch. "But first, come with me."

We walked to the staff car parked by the south wing. He opened the trunk and took out a small valise. I opened it and was rewarded with the sight of neatly folded clothes, including one of my olive drab wool shirts, complete with captain's bars and SHAEF shoulder patch.

"Big Mike thought you might want some decent clothes," Harding said. "He asked Walter at the Dorchester to pack a bag for you."

"Thanks," I said, running my hand over the fine fabric. It felt wonderfully strange, from another time and place. "It's hard to believe I'll be back there soon."

"Tomorrow," Harding said. "Provided you don't get in any trouble tonight. Skory is recovered enough to travel, and we're taking him to the Rubens Hotel in London first thing in the morning. We'll drop you at the Dorchester after that."

"I'll be ready," I said, and gave Harding a proper salute. He snapped one back and hurried inside the south wing. I usually didn't put much effort into saluting, but something about those shiny captain's bars and the deep chocolate-brown wool shirt brought out the army in me.

Doesn't happen all that often.

I went inside, toting my suitcase and feeling upbeat. Except for the killer on the loose, I was coming up aces. Kaz was in good shape, Harding was in on the prisoner exchange caper, and I would be lounging in a first-class hotel this time tomorrow.

Maybe tonight I'd find something helpful in the files. Then I had to work on getting Angelika on the prisoner release list. As I approached Kaz's room, I banished those thoughts from my mind. I couldn't look him in the eye and think about Angelika being left behind.

I stood aside while Dr. Hughes exited Kaz's room. As he walked down the hall, I saw him pat the pocket of his white lab coat. An unconscious gesture, making sure the envelope was snug and safe.

"Hughes looked happy," I said to Kaz. He was alone in the room, sitting up in bed and wearing his silk robe. "How are you doing?"

"Tired and sore, but well," he said, in a voice still scratchy and strained. "Thankful."

"Everything okay with Hughes?"

"I will be released within the week and cleared for a return to active service," Kaz said. "The two Shirleys have already had me up for another stroll. Dr. Harken is doing remarkable work. Hughes was grudging in his assessment of my operation but had to admit it was successful."

"I'm surprised at how much better you look so soon after the operation," I said.

"Harken said it is due to the heart muscle doing its job properly. At long last, I must say. Now, tell me why you come bearing a valise. Are you leaving?"

"Big Mike brought this back, courtesy of our pal Walter. My own duds. I've got my walking papers, so I can leave this joint in style. I'll be at the Dorchester tomorrow, and I'll come back for you when you're ready," I said, grasping his hand.

"Why wait until tomorrow?"

"To see you in the morning," I said. Then I leaned in closer and whispered. "I'm going into the file room tonight. I want a deeper look at Holland's file."

"Be careful," Kaz said. "I will feel much better when we are both rid of this place."

"You and me both, buddy," I said. We sat together quietly, looking out the window at the fading sunlight. Kaz was alive, and I wasn't off my rocker. We were still partners. The war had treated us roughly and played with the lives of people we loved.

But we were still in the fight.

THE GUEST QUARTERS had names on three doors. Me, Harding, and Big Mike. The fourth, Cosgrove's room, was thankfully empty. I hung up the uniform Walter had packed for me and sorted through the fancy toiletries he'd sent. Saint Albans had never seen such luxury. I washed up and stretched out on the couch for a catnap. I hadn't changed into my uniform yet. If things went south tonight, I didn't want a SHAEF shoulder patch front and center. The worn and faded fatigues I wore were perfect for a midnight skulk.

There was no sign of Harding and Big Mike at suppertime, so I ate alone in the dining hall, counting myself lucky that this would be my last brush with mutton stew. Miller was there but kept to himself. I wondered if he'd been cured, or his brain was permanently fried. Iris and Faith drifted in as I was finishing up. They both had plates of unidentifiable fish surrounded by boiled potatoes and carrots.

"We hear you're leaving us, Boyle," Iris said as they sat across from me.

"Word travels fast," I said.

"Gossip is even faster," Faith said.

"Speaking in public already? Nice recovery," I said. "But why do you say gossip?"

"Release order signed by Gubbins?" Iris said. "That's like a communiqué from God himself. You do have friends in high places, Boyle. Why are you still here?"

I gave them the rundown on Kaz and explained I was bunking in the guest quarters. I recalled they were friendly with Clarissa, and she may well have filed away my release paperwork. I asked if they'd drop in on Kaz tomorrow and check on him. They agreed, more enthusiastically when I reminded them he was a baron.

"About time we got a higher class of inmate around here," Iris said.

"I wish you both luck," I said. "I hope you get out soon."

"I'm ready enough," Faith said, picking at her fish. "I'm dying for a decent meal."

"I volunteered for the sleep cure, if only to pass the time," Iris said. "It's so boring here."

"They took Griffin away an hour ago," Faith said, lowering her voice. "For the long nap. Clarissa said they had to wait until he returned to his room. They couldn't find him anywhere."

"That's a testament to his skills," I said. "I hope the treatment helps."

"Goodness knows I'll be glad to be free of him for a while," Iris said. "He's harmless, but it is disconcerting to have him dart from one bush to another when you least expect it."

I said goodnight and walked upstairs to my former quarters. I showed the guard my note from Snow, but he'd already heard as well. I told him I wanted to grab a few things from my room and went in that direction. Not that I wanted a keepsake, but I did grab my wool cap, a shirt, and the Dopp kit I'd been issued.

Then I went down the hall and checked over my shoulder. The

guard wasn't watching. I slipped into Griffin's room. I went through his clothes and looked in the bedsheets. There weren't too many hiding places, so it took less than a minute.

His notebook wasn't here.

Did he take it with him? Or had he tumbled to the setup and stashed it somewhere safe? He was paranoid about secrets, and I didn't see him handing it over easily. I left the room, retracing the steps Griffin would have taken on his way in. First stop was the communal washroom. A row of sinks, the porcelain discolored, the faucets pitted and rusting. Bare pipes underneath. Showers with cracked tiles and dripping fixtures. The toilet stalls had no doors, the ancient plumbing on full display. Nowhere to hide a notebook, unless he had a waterproof container. Possible, but retrieving it from a toilet water tank would have been time-consuming and difficult without privacy.

My eye was drawn to a cabinet bolted to the wall, probably used to store cleaning materials and toilet paper. I tried the handle, but it was locked tight. As I did, the cabinet wiggled a bit, so I checked the side. There was a gap where one of the bolts had worked loose from the wall.

There it was, wedged in the gap near the top of the cabinet. A quick and easy hiding place. I grasped a corner of the notepad and pulled it loose. Sticking it in my wool cap, I carried it out in a pile with the other stuff from my room.

I didn't risk a look until I was back in the guest quarters. I sat on the couch and began to leaf through the pages, hoping to find a clue, perhaps something Griffin had seen without realizing its importance.

But I couldn't make head or tail of it. The whole damn thing was written in some sort of code, a combination of letters and numbers that made no sense. The question was, had they made sense to Griffin?

There was only one thing left to do. I hotfooted it back to Kaz. He was a fan of code breaking. He could do the *Times* crossword in pen. Me, I couldn't understand half the clues.

"Kaz?" I said as I knocked gently on the door to his room. He was asleep, and Dark Shirley was seated in a chair by his bed looking half-awake herself. She put a finger to her lips, but it was too late. Kaz stirred, opening his eyes slowly.

"Billy," he said, his voice groggy but without the harsh rasp he'd had earlier.

"Sorry," I said, acknowledging Dark Shirley's frown.

"Your friend needs his rest," she said.

"Just a couple of minutes, I promise. I have to leave in the morning, and I wanted to say goodbye."

"You have as long as it takes me to powder my nose, and that's it," she said, glancing at Kaz who smiled graciously. His look turned quizzical as soon as she was out the door.

"What is it?" he asked.

"This," I said, taking the notebook from my jacket pocket and handing it over. "It's Griffin's. He's off for the sleep treatment so I nabbed it. I thought he might have noted the movements of the killer."

Kaz fumbled for his eyeglasses on the nightstand. I handed them to him, and he opened the notebook. He began to leaf through the pages, his brow wrinkled as he studied the strings of letters and numbers. I could see his eyelids flicker behind his glasses. He looked ready to fall asleep, and I felt bad about bothering him so late.

"It is a combination of code and cipher," he said, closing the notebook.

"A code is where each word is replaced with a code word or symbol, right?"

"Yes. That is where the numbers come into play, most likely. For instance, Saint Albans could be represented by the number 191, which I noticed in several places. *S* being the nineteenth letter and *A* the first. It is most useful for words that are often repeated. Mixing a code with a cipher complicates breaking both."

"And a cipher is where each letter is replaced with a different letter," I said, recalling that Kaz had explained all this to me once before when he broke a code. Or cipher, I guess.

"Exactly. It could be as simple as a substitution cipher, where each letter is replaced by another a fixed number of positions down the alphabet. If this is more of a personal diary, it may not be difficult to decipher. But if it requires a matching text, then it will be somewhat harder."

"Like the page of a certain book," I said.

"A book that we do not possess," Kaz said. "I am sorry, Billy, but I cannot concentrate at the moment. They gave me something to help me sleep, and I am about to surrender to it." He laid the notebook on the nightstand and removed his glasses, setting them on top of it.

"Take your time, pal," I said, my hand on his shoulder. He was already asleep, his breathing steady and rhythmic.

I hoped everyone would sleep as soundly as Kaz did tonight.

CHAPTER THIRTY

AFTER MIDNIGHT, I eased open the door and stepped out onto the guest quarters porch. I stood still, listening for the sound of anyone patrolling nearby. Except for the faint snores coming from Big Mike's room, the night was silent. No light shone in Harding's quarters. They'd both come in a couple of hours ago while I lay awake with the lights out. Now it was time to move.

I walked slowly, sticking to the shadows and keeping an eye on the guards' canteen. It was a lot easier not climbing down a bedsheet ladder and worrying about someone spotting it. I was a free man, and no one had told me to abide by a curfew. That was my story if I was stopped.

I came to the corner at the front of the main building and knelt, scanning the walkway in each direction. I heard the scuff of shoes on gravel from my left and shrunk back into the shadow cast by the partial moon behind drifting clouds. Two guards appeared in the dim light, their rifles slung and murmuring voices low. I waited until they disappeared, then waited some more.

It was a quiet night at the insane asylum.

I headed for the clerical office window, praying that no one had locked it since my last visit. I craned my neck to check on the upper floors. There were a few lights on, but none directly above me. I got a foothold on the sill and hoisted myself up. If anyone happened by, I'd find myself back in the padded cell, signed release from Gubbins or not.

I pushed on the window frame. It creaked and groaned, the old wood swollen from the wet weather. But it moved. I forced it up enough to give me room to slip inside. I winced at the noise as I shut it, but no guards came running. That's the advantage to an old, dilapidated building. People get used to the sounds of it settling.

I took careful steps to Clarissa's desk, using the moonlight filtering in through the windows. I found her letter opener and popped the desk-drawer lock. Simple.

I felt around inside the drawer for the keys.

Nothing but paper clips, rubber bands, and pencils. No keys strung together with ribbon.

Damn. She must've found a more secure spot after losing track of them, courtesy of yours truly. But where? I squinted, trying to see more clearly in the dark and spot another locked drawer or cabinet. The other desk? Maybe, but Clarissa seemed to be in charge. I doubted she'd hand over responsibility to someone else.

Her other desk drawers weren't locked, so that ruled them out. I checked the drawer I'd opened again, pulling the office debris to the front. I stuck my hand all the way back and felt a piece of silky ribbon brush my fingertips. Shoving my hand in farther, I grasped the keys, pulling the ribbon off a small nail at the end of the drawer. Clarissa must have hung them there to keep them out of sight. Relieved, I grasped the key set tightly in my right hand.

Which did not shake one damn bit. My luck had turned. All I had to do was remember to put the damned keys back.

Now came the tough part. I didn't have the blackout lantern, but I had taken the stub of a candle from my quarters. I couldn't light it yet and risk anyone seeing the flame. Instead I went to the *G-L* filing cabinet, found the *H*s, and rummaged around until I found Holland's file, his last name and initial clear enough to see.

I crawled under Clarissa's desk, lit the candle, and prayed the light wouldn't give me away. I went to the selection board report. I glanced at the photograph of Holland, then the one with him and his buddy Georg in Paris, 1938. Smiling and carefree, like much of Europe before the Nazis started grabbing real estate.

Why was this photo included in his file? Was Georg part of SOE? I hadn't thought much about him before, but perhaps he played a role in all this. This wasn't a scrapbook of Holland's life. It was an official SOE file.

I read on. There was discussion about Holland's character. Steady nerves. Ability to carry on under stressful conditions. A willingness to take risks and accomplish the mission, no matter the cost. The perfect SOE agent.

His fluency with French and German was noted. Reference was made to the perfect accent his German-Jewish mother had imparted to him as well as his high marks in language courses at the Sorbonne. His mother had been investigated by Scotland Yard. A sensible precaution, given her place of birth and her son's service with SOE.

I glanced at Robinson's assessment again and noticed another mention of Holland's mother. He'd asked Holland if he wanted to talk with her. No dice. He wouldn't even break his silence for his own mother.

Then I saw it. The first clear link between Holland and SOE's German Section. Holland had volunteered for any mission available into Nazi Germany. Admirable, the notation said. Request denied, the next line said.

This agent is too valuable.

Made sense, I guess. If working in occupied France was high-risk, an assignment within Nazi Germany itself had to be ten times as dangerous.

But wasn't that what SOE was all about? Missions that could get you killed?

Holland had brought up the name of his friend, Georg Markstein, touting him as a native German speaker who was also ready for a mission to the Reich. Markstein was a fellow SOE trainee, a German Jew born in Berlin whose family had fled to England as soon as Hitler came to power. Smart people. Markstein was now known as George and spoke English as perfectly as he did German, according to Holland's enthusiastic recommendation.

Refer Markstein to German Section. Candidate for Operation Periwig.

Apparently, George Markstein was not as valuable as Holland, but enough of an agent to be considered for a drop into Nazi Germany. Would he survive Operation Periwig, whatever that was?

Holland's selection board report concluded with a recommendation for further radio operator training and then deployment by SOE Section F into occupied France. I already knew what happened next. But I'd learned two things.

First, there was a definite link between Holland and the murders connected to the German Section of SOE.

Second, no one involved had mentioned it. Cosgrove had taken that knowledge to his grave, and Blackford had sloughed off Holland's connection to his Section as nothing but routine procedure. Yet here their signatures were, scratched boldly on the last pages of a report documenting Holland's eagerness for a mission with the German Section, and his volunteering of a fellow trainee for the same thing. Densmore had been there as well, his signature below his boss's.

What secret were Cosgrove and Blackford protecting?

What made Holland too valuable to risk sending him into Germany?

Why was Markstein better suited to the German Section?

And finally, was George Markstein a possible suspect?

I took the photograph of Holland and Markstein and stuck it in my pocket. I doubted anyone would be consulting the file of a dead agent, and even if they did, one missing photo might not be noticed. I didn't know where this link would lead, but I knew there was a good chance I'd need to show those faces around.

I returned Holland's file to the cabinet and looked through the *M* drawers. No Markstein. Whatever happened to him, he hadn't been through Saint Albans. First order of business when I got back to London would be to ask Blackford about Markstein, assuming no one killed Blackie before I got there.

I searched for Robinson's file. I didn't have any reason to suspect him, but, even though it had probably been a plant, the drawing had been found in his room. Add to that the fact that he was the first to hear everyone's deep, dark secrets, and maybe he should be higher on my list. It took me a while to locate, since staff files were in their own cabinet. I grabbed Robinson's, Snow's, and Hughes's files and crawled back under the desk.

Robinson's was thin. A medical report pronounced him physically fit and mentioned his athletic prowess. Which told me he'd have the strength to heave a guy from the clock tower, but little else. His army record was clean, but there was an interesting mention of his membership in an Italian American art society that had links to the Fascist League of North America, a pro-Mussolini group.

Possible sympathies for Italian fascism.

Was he an art lover who'd associated with the wrong people, or was that a cover for his political beliefs? Either way, I couldn't see how it mattered. Italy was on our side these days, and Mussolini got by on handouts from the Nazis. Hardly sympathetic.

I gave Dr. Hughes's file a quick once-over. Squeaky clean. He may have taken other bribes or stolen drugs for all I knew, but if he had, he'd kept it to himself.

Major Snow's file was hefty. He was professional army, so it went back a while. I reviewed his medical report, which had cleared him for a return to duty earlier this year, but with a recommendation for a period of light duty. Saint Albans may have fit the bill, but that had been before the bodies started piling up.

His SOE activities in Italy were impressive. Part of a three-man team, he coordinated weapons drops for Italian partisans and ambushed German convoys bringing troops and supplies to the front lines. Snow's main purpose was to unite the various guerilla factions and link them up with the Italian government. But there was bad blood all around, since most of the resistance groups were Communist, and Prime Minister Pietro Badoglio's royal government of King Victor Emmanuel III was anything but.

Snow's mission ended in tragedy. Just as he was about to broker a clandestine meeting between the leaders of a Communist partisan group and representatives from the monarchist government, his team was betrayed to the Nazis. No one knew which side had sabotaged the meeting, but Snow's SOE men were killed, and he was wounded, barely escaping capture after they were ambushed.

Snow's leg was riddled with shrapnel, and, according to doctors here and in Italy, he'd likely walk with a limp for the rest of his life. Bad luck, but at least he was still alive. I flipped through the rest of the pages until I came to memorandums from Dr. Robinson and Dr. Hughes. They'd both been ordered by SOE to approve Snow's return to duty.

Hughes was straightforward in his summary. Since the job didn't require Snow to run, he would be fine and see further improvements over time. That fit with what I'd thought about Snow moving on to another job with SOE. Not in the field, but a step up from babysitting worn-out agents.

Robinson's report on Snow was more detailed, beginning with personal data. Snow's parents had been killed in an automobile accident when he was young. With no living relatives, he'd been sent to an orphanage and joined the army as soon as he was of age. Robinson wrote that the army had been a replacement for Snow's family, giving him a sense of security and belonging that had never properly developed after losing both parents so early. Interesting, but Robinson had other, more current concerns. He counseled Snow to see him for additional sessions to work out the stress and depression brought about by the disaster in Italy. Snow had been close with his fellow SOE agents and had thought he could trust the Italian fighters and government representatives he had worked with. The betrayal hit him hard, the sense of loss accentuated by his identification with the military as family. According to Robinson, Snow had developed an unhealthy obsession with tracking down those responsible.

Not unreasonable, in my book. There was no mention of any further sessions. I figured Snow was aching to get back to real SOE work to find out who blew the whistle on their rendezvous. I felt a sympathy for him, thinking of Kaz and his intense desire to stay in the game for Angelika's sake.

I closed the file. My candle was burning low, and I couldn't think of anyone else's file to snoop through. I did think about mine, but after reading through all these, I decided I didn't want to know what was in it.

I returned the files, making sure everything was in its prope
I blew out the candle and put the keys back, using the letter o_1
to relock Clarissa's drawer.

Now for the hard part.

I eased the door open and stepped into the foyer. All quiet. I took
careful steps, listening for any sounds. I walked down the main hallway,
watching the windows for any sign of patrolling guards. The building
was silent, and every footfall seemed loud enough to wake Griffin out
of his deep sleep.

I finally came to a door that opened to a stairwell. This is where
the guards had come from when they'd evacuated the building while
Sinclair was popping off rounds. I wasn't surprised it was unlocked,
since the main doors were locked tight. The patients were all under
guard on the second floor, and I knew from my time there that these
stairs didn't connect to that floor.

The question was, would the third-floor door be locked?

I took the steps as lightly as I could, pausing on the landing to catch
my breath. I had no idea what or who I might find up here, but if there
was a chance to sneak into the listening post, it was worth a shot.

I took one last deep breath and steadied myself. I put my hand on
the latch, thankful for a steady grip. It opened, the rusty hinges creaking
in protest. I left the door ajar and stood back, listening. Nothing.

From inside the stairwell, I peeked out into the corridor and saw a
splash of light as a door opened at the other end. A figure walked away,
his footsteps echoing as he clattered down the far stairwell. The hall
was deathly silent. Was he the only one on duty? In the dim light from
the hallway windows, I could see the other doors were shut. I walked
past Densmore's room, then stood in front of the listening post. No
telltale light spilled out from the edges of the door; no murmurs or
sounds of recording devices came from inside.

Luck was with me. For now.

I opened the door and was greeted by darkness. I shut the door
behind me and let my eyes get used to the blackness. In a minute I
could see that the blackout curtains were drawn, and, as my vision
improved, I could make out the headphones and hardware on every

surface. Wires dangled from the ceiling like trailing vines. How many rooms were bugged?

I decided to risk lighting the candle. It wouldn't be spotted from outside, and the light was too faint to leak out under the door. I hoped.

I struck a match and lit the wick. There was a small stub left to the candle, and it gave off a faint flickering glow, barely enough to read by. And there was plenty to read. Stacks of typewritten sheets adorned each desk. It was a small room, made even smaller by the array of recording devices, headphones, and typewriters. I sat at a desk and tried to make head or tail out of the typed entries.

Each one was preceded by a code of some sort. MB, NW, SW, GQ, CN, and SP. Easy enough to figure; main building, north wing, south wing, guest quarters. CN and SP, I had no idea. Did CN stand for canteen? Maybe. The two-letter codes were followed by a number, probably denoting the location of the bug. I flipped through the papers until a name caught my eye.

MB32: Subject DENSMORE tells BLACKFORD he will soon be ready to return to work. BLACKFORD says more Periwig missions are imminent and needs him back soonest.

That was two days ago, and Densmore was dead not long after. Was that connected to Periwig and Markstein? Intrigued about the guest quarters' bugs, I flipped through the pages until I found a recent one, hoping for some clue as to Cosgrove's killer. The only transcription was from the day Blackford arrived.

GQ4: BLACKFORD met with subject SINCLAIR and asked if he felt well enough to return to work. SINCLAIR declined. Much unintelligible. Argument ensued about a transmitter and parachute malfunctions. SINCLAIR called BLACKFORD a murderer and departed.

That was the same dispute they'd had the day Sinclair grabbed the rifle. Blackford certainly had been persistent.

GQ4: COSGROVE enters. Tells BLACKFORD he has business with the Poles. BLACKFORD suggests a drink later with SNOW. COSGROVE agrees. Asks BLACKFORD about a red horse. Unintelligible. Laughter. COSGROVE departs.

They both knew about the red horse. As soon as we got a fingerprint report from Scotland Yard, I'd have to show that postcard to Blackford.

I moved to another desk and rifled through the paperwork. There might be full recordings somewhere, but it looked to me like they were mainly monitoring conversations and noting anything suspicious. A lot of it was innocuous. And boring. What did these guys ever do to deserve a detail like this?

NW7: Subject MILLER attempted to engage subject GRIFFIN in conversation. Began story about his mission. GRIFFIN promised to report him if he continued, then departed.

Most of it was along those lines, with plenty of names I didn't recognize. Any slip of security was noted. I went through more of the sheets, which were arranged at each desk in chronological order. Near the bottom of one stack, I found these.

MB5: Subject HOLLAND spoke in session with ROBINSON. Asked for a glass of water. Nothing else.

MB5: ROBINSON asked subject HOLLAND if he wanted to talk. Long period of silence. HOLLAND then asked about members of the Stationer circuit. How many survived. ROBINSON said he had no information. Urged HOLLAND to talk about his arrest. HOLLAND silent.

MB5: Subject HOLLAND asked ROBINSON to find out if a friend from SOE training was alive. GEORGE MARKSTEIN. HOLLAND had recommended him for German Section. ROBINSON said prohibited by security. HOLLAND silent.

That was it for Holland in Robinson's office. Faith had told me he'd begun to speak, and it seemed his entire focus was on finding out about his SOE team and his pal Markstein. It wasn't much to go on. But the fact that SOE had eavesdropped on Dr. Robinson was unsettling. I didn't much like the thought of a government bureaucrat typing up my innermost thoughts about Diana and Paris. Was Robinson aware? Was his role to encourage agents to spill their guts, to see who could keep their secrets bottled up, as Griffin had said?

There was one more stack to go through. As I carried the candle to the next desk, I realized there wasn't any storage to speak of in this room. Each stack I'd gone through so far went back no more than ten days. They must cart this stuff off to be filed away somewhere, maybe here or at SOE headquarters.

The candle flame was guttering, the wick about burned away. I went through the papers, stopping here and there when a name popped out at me, but nothing struck me as important. Until I came to a mention of Densmore in Robinson's office.

MB5: Subject DENSMORE in session with ROBINSON. Agitated. Stated subject HOLLAND had approached him. Recognized him from SOE Selection Board. Asked about MARKSTEIN. DENSMORE refused comment. Told ROBINSON he felt tremendous guilt over the red horse business. Said he sent men to their certain death. Wept.

One of the murdered men had expressed guilt about his role in a German Section operation. Densmore felt responsible for the death of Periwig agents. Densmore was already suffering from nervous exhaustion, so it wasn't surprising that he took it hard. But that was what SOE did, wasn't it? Sent men and women to certain death? Diana and her group were all dead or captured. The life expectancy of a wireless operator in occupied France was only six weeks. In Nazi Germany, it had to be even less.

This entry was significant, proof of a link between Holland and the others who'd been murdered. I folded the sheet and put it in my pocket, next to the photograph of Holland and Markstein. I still wasn't sure what it all added up to, but at least I had a couple of souvenirs from my last night at Saint Albans.

Footsteps sounded in the hallway. Voices echoed against the walls, headed this way.

I blew out the candle and froze, listening. Two men, talking, sounding like they were in a hurry, and coming this way.

There was nowhere to hide.

I ducked under the desk farthest from the door.

The door opened and the lights flashed on.

"Come on, get this stuff together," one of them said. "The courier is waiting. Snow'll have a fit if he finds out we weren't ready." I heard a briefcase snap open.

"Take it easy, mate. The driver is having a smoke," the other said as I heard them packing the papers. "Snow's dead asleep. He'll be none the wiser."

"You know how he is about these notes. Mighty particular. Hurry up. Hand me that last bunch, and we're done."

That bunch was on the desk I was hiding under. Luckily the other fellow reached across the desk with a grunt and grabbed it without stepping around.

"Let's go," I heard, and the case was latched shut, the lights flicked off, and the door slammed behind them. I finally exhaled.

I got up and blinked my eyes, adjusting to the dark after the bright lights. Then I spotted it. The candle I'd blown out was still on the desk, a small waxy stub that had no business being there. In their rush, they hadn't even noticed.

I snatched up the candle. I'd used up all the luck of the Irish I was entitled to for one night, so I made my way back to the guest quarters. GQ, that is.

CHAPTER THIRTY-ONE

WE PULLED OUT at 0700. Big Mike and me in a jeep, and
Colonel Harding and Feliks in the staff car with Skory, who'd managed to walk out of the hospital under his own power. His arm was
in a sling, and he sported a bandage over one eye, but he was in good
spirits. Hell, who wouldn't be after getting a one-way ticket out of
Nazi-controlled Poland?

I'd only had a minute with Kaz. He'd been drinking tea and studying
Griffin's notebook. He told me to leave him alone, which was his way
of letting me know he was feeling much better. I told him to leave a
message at the Dorchester if he came up with anything.

"*When* I come up with something," was all he'd said, sipping tea and
keeping his eyes riveted on the numbers.

It was nice to have Kaz back.

"How's it feel?" Big Mike said as the gate to Saint Albans closed
behind us. I looked back as he shifted gears and sped away from the
asylum. The last thing I saw was the clock tower.

"Strange," I said. "I don't like leaving Kaz there, but he's in good
hands."

"The Shirleys say he's doin' great," Big Mike said. "Don't you worry
about him. Just make sure your head stays screwed on straight."

"Amen to that," I said, holding out my right hand. Steady as a rock.

"Okay, so spill. What'd you find out last night?" he asked.

"I found out how Holland fits in," I said. "At least how he's connected to the German Section. Blackford, Densmore, and Cosgrove were all on Holland's SOE selection board. Seems like Holland volunteered for a mission into Germany, which is probably why Blackford and Densmore were on the board. But they decided he was too valuable to risk, although I don't think they ever told him that."

"Pretty tenuous connection," Big Mike said as we took a turn. He glanced back to make sure Harding's vehicle was keeping pace, and eased up on the accelerator. We were driving through forested land on a narrow road, trees blocking out the light of the rising sun.

"Here's the real connection," I said, holding up the photograph of Holland and Markstein. "George Markstein and Holland were pals in college. Both spoke perfect German, and both joined SOE at the same time. Holland had asked the selection board if they could be assigned to the German Section together. For some unknown reason, they decided to take Markstein, but not him."

"Is the guy still alive? He might be a suspect," Big Mike said.

"Don't know. If he was dropped into Germany, all bets are off. But if he's still in England, I sure do want to talk to him."

"What are you going to do? Tell Colonel Blackford the name George Markstein just popped into your mind? He ain't gonna tell you a damn thing," Big Mike said.

"Well, I've got a couple of things going for me," I said, enjoying the feel of fresh air against my face. The woods began to thin out as the road dipped and brought us through cultivated fields. "I'm going to start with Vera Atkins. You remember her?"

"Yeah. Head of intelligence for the SOE French Section. She knew Diana," Big Mike said, then caught himself. "I mean, she *knows* Diana." Vera had been involved in the planning for Diana's missions into occupied France.

"Right. I don't think she knows about the upcoming deal with Himmler and the Swedish Red Cross. She might help if I bring her the news that Diana may be released," I said. "Maybe she can find out where Markstein is."

"Maybe," Big Mike said, slowing as we passed a farmer leading a donkey hauling a cart full of potatoes. The countryside unfolded itself as we left the woods, its gently rolling hills filled with ripening crops and dotted with small farmhouses. The air felt pure and clean in a way it never had at Saint Albans. "But those SOE types are tight-lipped. What's the other thing you mentioned? I hope it's better than that."

"I go direct to Blackford and tell him Markstein can lead me to whoever is killing people associated with the German Section," I said. "Any information he gives me can help save his own life."

"Persuasive," Big Mike said. "You know, it's strange Cosgrove never owned up to knowing Holland wanted in with Blackford's outfit. Neither of them. Must be something damned important they're hiding."

"There's a truth here that explains everything," I said, lifting my face to the sun and letting the warmth and the wind wash over me. "A truth we've yet to find."

I went on to detail Robinson's association with a pro-fascist Italian society, and the background to Snow's betrayal and wounding in Italy.

"Any connection there?" Big Mike asked.

"Not unless an Italian American art society, Communist partisans, and the Badoglio government are all in cahoots," I said. "Snow is chomping at the bit to get back at whoever ambushed him and threw a monkey wrench into plans to better organize partisan support."

"Coulda been the Krauts, the Commies, or some stuffed-shirt monarchist," Big Mike said. "I hope he's got something to go on."

"Can't blame the guy," I said. "His pals were killed, he'll have a gimpy gait for the rest of his life, and he couldn't fulfill his mission."

"It would eat at me, I gotta say. So, anything else?"

"Two mentions of something called Operation Periwig. Once in reference to Markstein, and once in a conversation between Densmore and Blackford," I said, and told Big Mike about my foray into the listening post.

"Periwig, eh? What's that mean, anyway?"

"No idea. I should've asked Kaz," I said. "Blackford wanted Densmore back because of it, though. He'd also pestered Sinclair about a transmitter and ways to make a parachute look like it malfunctioned."

"Sounds like he wanted to dispose of someone and make it look like an accident," Big Mike said.

"Sinclair did call him a murderer," I said.

"Set Europe ablaze," Big Mike said. "That's what Churchill ordered them to do when he set up SOE. I'd call that highly organized murder. Maybe Sinclair's confused."

"That's putting it mildly," I said. "I also found out that Holland had started to talk. He'd been mute, but recently he'd spoken to Faith and Dr. Robinson. All he managed with Robinson was to ask about his SOE team and his friend Markstein. When Robinson couldn't help, he clammed back up."

"Wait, they bugged the psychiatrist's office? That's low," Big Mike said.

"Yep. I wonder if Robinson knows. I half thought about telling him," I said. We passed through a small village, and houses and shops started to fill the roadside. Farming country slipped away, and we approached the outskirts of London. I pulled out the sheet I'd pinched from the listening post and read it to Big Mike.

"Be careful who you show that to," he said. "That's classified information."

"Yeah, I'll be careful. But this tells us Densmore was feeling remorse about Periwig and the red horse organization. Then he turned up murdered," I said.

"Right after he confessed that to Dr. Robinson, who has a soft spot for Mussolini," Big Mike said.

"I wish I knew what Periwig was all about," I said, thinking about the obvious point Big Mike had just made. Maybe I was right last night, and Robinson needed to be higher on my list of suspects. "As for the red horse, that appears to be a German anti-Nazi group. Makes sense that the German Section would be involved with them."

"But then why would Densmore feel bad about it?" Big Mike said. "Anyone in SOE ought to have a thick hide when it comes to agents. I can't see Vera Atkins falling apart over the chances her people take in France."

"You're right. There's something else at work here. Something we don't understand. Yet."

We drove on, passing through Edgware and leaving the last of the green fields behind. The area became thick with more shops, houses, and apartment buildings. I recognized the road that would take us right to Hyde Park and the Dorchester Hotel.

It had been a long time. I was eager to track down George Markstein, but I planned on a long bath and a solid meal first. I began to daydream about what I'd order. Even with rationing, the kitchens at the Dorchester could work wonders.

We stopped at an intersection. I turned to check on Harding, giving a quick wave as the staff car pulled up behind us.

The world exploded.

Suddenly, violently, the road before us erupted in a massive flash, mushrooming fire, smoke, and debris high into the air. The concussive blast hit us like a tidal wave of hot fury. I threw my hands up, shielding my eyes from the smoking cinders that rained down on us. I had no idea what was happening. I craned my neck to scan the skies for bombers and listened for the sputtering sound of a V1 rocket about to fall. There was nothing but blue sky marred by ghastly smoke rising from the shattered street.

Big Mike was ahead of me, brushing debris from his shoulders as he dashed to the staff car, asking if everyone was okay.

"We're fine," Harding said, stepping out of the sedan. "What happened?"

Sirens began to wail, heralding the fire trucks racing to the scene. Harding told his driver and Feliks to stay with Skory, and we walked across the intersection. A bobby, a look of total bewilderment on his face, was escorting several dazed and bloody civilians away from the scene.

Windows were shattered on the buildings nearest us. People filed out, many of them bleeding from shards of broken glass sent flying by the explosion. Neighbors ran out of undamaged buildings to help them, everyone wearing expressions of stunned incredulity.

More sirens announced the arrival of ambulances. Shrieks and cries sounded as shock was replaced by pain, numbness giving way to gasping horror.

A woman's leg laid in the road, wisps of smoke curling up from flesh, the shoe still sporting a dainty green bow. We gave the limb a wide berth and made our way through the glass and wood shards scattered in the street.

The sight ahead was pure devastation. A jumble of bricks and shattered timbers surrounded a crater ten feet deep. Flames crackled from the interior of the pile as smoke swirled into the sky, riding the heated air and sending aloft a beacon to mark the disaster.

"What was it?" Big Mike asked. I didn't know if he meant the explosion or what had once stood here.

I touched his arm and pointed, words failing to find a foothold. All that was left standing was a single wall on the left side of the structure. The roof and three floors had been blown away, but, for some reason, that wall stayed upright. Fireplaces along the chimney marked three living rooms. A second-floor bathtub was suspended crazily, dangling from its pipes. One picture still hung in a place of pride, scorched and blackened. It was like looking at a dollhouse that had been vandalized by a vindictive child.

A man shuffled toward us, his clothing covered in soot, and brick dust coating his hair. He appeared uninjured, but his eyes were wide with shock.

"What happened?" Big Mike asked him. "Did you see anything?"

"A silver flash in the sky," he said, then looked up. "I saw it out of the corner of my eye. By the time I looked it was gone. Then everything exploded." He walked away, weaving through the rubble until he disappeared into the growing crowd of onlookers, police, and firemen.

"*Rakieta*," a voice said from behind us. It was Skory, with Feliks holding on to his good arm. He spoke Polish to Feliks, urgently.

"This was the V2 rocket, he tells me. No sound, no warning. Large explosion," Feliks said.

"That guy told us he spotted a sliver flash in the sky," I said. Feliks translated. Skory nodded his head and spoke a few words.

"Definitely the V2. It has begun," Feliks said.

"Let's get out of here," Harding said. "We have work to do."

It took almost an hour to extricate ourselves from the traffic jam created by the emergency vehicles and closed-off roads. I spent most of that time thinking about Diana and the V2 facility at Ravensbrück. I hoped to God she wasn't working there, since that might mean the Krauts would refuse to release her. If this strike was any indication of the power of the V2 rocket, I could see them doing anything to protect its secrets. I hadn't thought much about the implications of this new weapon, but that woman's leg had had a sobering effect.

"No need to bring me to the Dorchester," I said. "After you deliver Skory to the Rubens Hotel, I'll walk to Scotland Yard and look up Inspector Scutt. I'd like to know how he's doing with the fingerprints." I didn't mention the fact that I wasn't in the mood for a hot bath. It didn't seem right. Nothing did.

"You sure?" Big Mike asked. "You don't need a rest or anything?"

I held out my hand. "Steady as a rock. I'll be fine. But I need to do something. I think I'd go crazy waiting around."

"Okay. But head to the Dorchester when you're done. I'll check in with you soon as I can," Big Mike said. "Then we can track down Vera and Blackford, see if they're in at Baker Street."

"All right. I can hoof it to Scotland Yard in about fifteen minutes, a little longer back to the Dorchester. I ought to be there by noon," I said, turning to watch the plume of smoke marking the V2's devastation.

We motored by the Wellington Arch, then passed Buckingham Palace on our way to the hotel. The Polish government-in-exile had set themselves up in a swanky neighborhood, right across from Buckingham Palace Gardens. I couldn't begrudge them a bit of luxury, especially since they needed to impress the Brits as a legitimate government. Someone was going to be making a lot of decisions about Poland once the war was over, and, now that the Soviets were edging closer to the Polish border, the free Poles were going to need all the support they could muster.

We pulled over in front of the posh Rubens Hotel, one of the fancier joints in a city full of them. Curved windows set in finished red brick stonework flanked the large entrance, where doormen sprang into action, only to be elbowed aside by uniformed men all wearing the red shoulder flash with POLAND emblazoned across it.

"That's quite a reception committee," I said to Harding as we stood aside for the Poles to escort Skory in, Feliks at his side. There were several high-ranking officers, both Polish and British, along with civilians in their standard somber civil service suits. They'd been waiting for Skory.

"There's a lot riding on the information Skory brought out," Harding said, as one of the civilians headed our way, a noticeable limp not slowing him down. Dark-haired, with an aristocratic nose and a languidly long but grim face, he shook hands with Harding. The colonel introduced me to Duncan Sandys, a Minister of Works in Churchill's cabinet and chair of a committee charged with creating defenses against German rocket attacks.

"Thank God he's alive," Sandys said. "I hope he's got something for us. Our people are poring over the parts he brought out, but no joy as of yet."

"We nearly drove into a V2 hit," Harding said. "South of Edgware, an hour or so ago."

"Mum's the word, Colonel," Sandys said. "The official explanation is that it was a gas-main explosion. We can't have panic."

"We spoke to one man who said he saw a silver flash in the sky right before the impact," I said. "If he saw it, others probably did as well."

"Yes, yes. But we still need a cover story for as long as it will hold. And I heard the damn thing myself. Knew it was a rocket from the sonic boom. Two loud cracks, unmistakable, at least for anyone with a bit of scientific knowledge."

"We didn't hear anything like that," Harding said.

"You wouldn't have. The sonic waves follow an object traveling faster than sound, like the wake of a ship. It flew over here on its downward descent, and the boom followed it," Sandys explained.

"Word will get out soon," I said.

"Yes. Which is why we need to talk with our Polish friend. He may know more about this rocket than anyone outside of Nazi Germany.

He's been assessing bits and pieces of crashed rockets for months. With this last haul, we may finally learn something that will help," Sandys said, his brow knitted in worry. He didn't sound exactly confident.

"And if that doesn't work, what then?" I asked.

"Then considerable bombing forces will have to be reassigned from their strategic missions to destroy every V2 facility we can identify," Sandys said. "We can intercept and shoot down the V1 rockets. Unless we can come up with a method to stop the V2s, we may have to reallocate bomber resources. Which would be a bit of a victory for the Hun in and of itself."

And a death sentence for Diana, Angelika, and countless other slave laborers.

"Get some rest, Boyle," Harding said, his hand on my shoulder. "Big Mike can drop you at the Dorchester."

"I'll walk," I said. "Do me good."

"Okay. Take it easy," Harding said, following Sandys into the hotel. He was trying to be considerate, but I liked the other Harding. The one who was perpetually angry and impatient. I didn't like being treated like an invalid. Or maybe I simply wanted everything back the way it was before Paris. Well, I was partway there. Kaz was making his recovery and would soon be back on duty. I wasn't shaky, incarcerated, or crazy. Okay, I could work with that. Next things were to catch a killer and get Diana out of Ravensbrück. With Angelika.

I had no idea how I'd accomplish that last bit.

CHAPTER THIRTY-TWO

Before I set off, I asked Big Mike to talk to Harding about finding out who was taking Cosgrove's place at the Foreign Office. Under the guise of ensuring we got every piece of intelligence we could about the V2 rocket production, I wanted to be a hundred percent certain Diana's name was on the list of inmates to be released. And to convince the new man to add Angelika, since she was picked up for her small hands, which meant she was also an underground operative the Krauts had unknowingly placed within the Siemens V2 factory.

It made sense to me, but it was still a long shot.

Big Mike said Sandys might be worth approaching. He chaired the Bodyline Scientific Committee, and it was their job to come up with a defense against the rockets. Sandys had something else going for him. He was Winston Churchill's son-in-law.

I liked the sound of that, since he could be approached from several angles.

I made my way down Birdcage Walk, a pleasant tree-lined street with Saint James's Park on one side and white stone government buildings on the other. It felt good to walk freely, dressed in my neatly tailored Ike jacket, though it was baggier than the last time I'd worn it. The battlefields of France and a spell in an asylum had taken their toll.

I took Horse Guards Road and passed the guarded entrance to Winston Churchill's underground lair. Soldiers were unloading fresh sandbags to replace the old sagging and leaking burlap bags. Someone was wasting no time. After all, a gas-main explosion could happen anywhere.

Across Parliament Street, I drew close to the Thames Embankment and the swirling waters of the river, where I craned my neck to take in the turreted, white-and-red brick headquarters of the London Metropolitan Police, aka Scotland Yard. At the duty desk I asked for Detective Inspector Horace Scutt. A uniformed constable brought me upstairs to the Criminal Investigations Department. When I walked into the room, I felt right at home. Cops at work. Desks pushed together, filing cabinets along one wall, and a large city map hung on the other. Heavy black telephones jangled, and a low buzz of conversation, sharp frustration leavened with rough laughter, carried across the room.

I saw Scutt in his windowed office at the far end of the room, telephone to his ear as he busily scribbled notes. His shock of white hair and mustache were easy enough to spot. Horace Scutt should have been retired by now, but the manpower shortage had kept him in harness. There'd be time to tend the roses once the shooting stopped.

I studied him through the glass. He looked thinner than a year ago, the last time I'd seen him. And perhaps more tired. He glanced up and motioned me to come in as he continued to nod in response to whatever the person on the other end of the line was saying.

"Yes, Chief Superintendent, we will," Scutt repeated, with the look of a man who had to listen to his boss go on far too long. "Certainly. Very good, sir." He cradled the receiver as a tired sigh escaped his lips.

"How are you, Inspector Scutt?"

"My ear is sore, and it's Chief Inspector these days. I see we've both come up in the world, Captain Boyle. You were a lieutenant last I saw you. You look a bit worse for wear, if you don't mind me saying so. Are you well, lad?"

"I'm recovering from a vacation in France. But I'm well enough and getting better," I said, surprised that I looked different enough for Scutt to notice. Then again, he was a cop, and noticing details was his stock-in-trade. "Congratulations on your promotion, Chief Inspector."

"Can't say I enjoy much of it. More paperwork and too much time behind this desk. And makes it easy for the chief superintendent to find me and pass down bad news. Truth be told, I'd rather be chasing villains in the streets. Only problem is, I'd never catch most of them these days, so here I am. Now, I expect you're here about the postcard your sergeant left with us."

"I am. Any luck with fingerprints?"

"We were able to lift several good prints, but matching them will take some time," Scutt said.

"Big Mike said you had a fingerprint file for SOE personnel," I said. "How long will it take to go through that?"

"Longer than I'd like. Our people must analyze ridge endings and ridge dots, then code them according to established patterns. Whorls, loops, arches and all that. It's not easy, nor quick. Plus our filing system is backlogged. We're short-staffed and this is hardly a priority. We have government security checks from the past four months to organize and file. That's not only SOE but anyone with a security clearance. We shall do our best, Captain Boyle, but it will take time."

"I understand. And I know this is not an official request, so I appreciate whatever you can do," I said. I was impatient, but there was nothing to be gained from pushing Scutt.

"Always glad to cooperate with our allies," Scutt said with a smile that vanished in a second. "But tell me, is this going to come down on my head? We're dealing with people who like their secrets kept under lock and key. I don't want the Special Branch blokes from upstairs to take me out of here in irons. It would be embarrassing."

"I can't promise a few feathers won't be ruffled. But I was asked to investigate a suspicious death at an SOE facility by the security officer there," I said.

"You don't have a written order, I imagine?" Scutt asked.

"No sir. I'll understand if you want to reconsider," I said.

"No need, Captain. I just don't like surprises. Unfortunately, we are more short-handed than usual. That call from the chief superintendent was about putting a detail together to assist with a nasty gas-main explosion out on Watford Road. A number of casualties, I'm afraid."

"South of Edgware?" I asked.

"Yes. You know the area, then?" Scutt's eyes narrowed, and I could tell he wasn't engaging in idle chitchat.

"We were driving on that road this morning. We were stopped at an intersection when a building in the next block exploded. It wasn't pretty," I said. "Funny, but I didn't smell gas."

"Odd, since the chief superintendent was quite clear on the subject. Faulty gas main. Did you see anything to suggest otherwise?" Scutt drummed his fingers on the wooden desktop.

"Listen, Chief Inspector, I'm not going to spout off about this, but you and I both know it wasn't a gas leak. I spoke to a gent who said he saw a silver flash in the sky a second before the explosion."

"The V1 rockets make a distinctive sound with which we are sadly familiar. No one reported anything like that," Scutt said.

"The V2 rockets are supersonic," I said. "Faster than sound, so no noise. I'm sure the chief superintendent covered that."

"Captain Boyle, trouble follows in your wake, doesn't it?"

"I tend to think I follow after it, but I take your point, sir. I can't reveal anything else, but it's safe to say this V2 business is connected to my investigation." To a small extent, but it was still the truth. Kind of.

"Very well," Scutt said, with a quick nod. "I trust you'll keep this to yourself. Apparently, a cabinet committee came up with the gas-main story in preparation for expected rocket attacks. Scotland Yard has been briefed. The idea is to prevent panic, but I think people will see through the lie fairly quickly."

"Duncan Sandys, right?"

"You *are* well-informed for a chap who's recently returned from sunny France," Scutt said. "You must have friends in high places indeed. Yes, Sandys briefed the powers that be here, but other than putting forward the cover story, he had little to offer. What about you, Captain Boyle? Any idea what we should expect?"

"No, sorry, I don't. I wish I could help," I said, feeling foolish for suggesting I might know more than I did.

"It's difficult, you know," Scutt said, leaning back in his chair, his eyes focused on something far beyond me. "For years we were bombed. We watched dogfights in the sky over our city. We slept in underground shelters. And we took it, for the most part, like good English men and women with faith in our leaders and our fighting men. We endured horrible losses and waited for the day when we could bring the fight to the Germans in Europe."

"That day has come," I said. "Paris is free, and the Nazis are scrambling to get home. I've seen it myself."

"Yes, and let me tell you, there were prayers of thanks and celebrations far and wide when we learned of the invasion. For a moment it was as if we could see the end of this blasted war. The bloody Luftwaffe was gone from our skies, and it felt like we could breathe once more. Do you understand, Boyle?"

"Yes sir, I think I do." But I probably didn't. Back in 1940, when London was bombed and burning every night, I was safe back home in Boston, still a civilian. Death and destruction were things you heard about on the radio, an ocean away.

"It was a week after D-Day that the V1 attacks began. Those damn buzz bombs, hundreds of them. You'd hear them coming, that *put-put-put* sound coming from their pulse-jet engines. Then it would cut out, and you knew it would hit in twelve seconds, exactly. Two streets over, perhaps, or right down on your head. Thousands of casualties, and everyone wondering, Is this what we endured for? To watch our city burn and our loved ones die? For these inhuman machines to slaughter us just when we imagined victory was in sight?"

"I didn't know, Chief Inspector. I'd been away," I said. The only real news I'd had was from a German Army magazine touting Hitler's new terror weapon. "I had no idea it affected people this way."

"Well at least many of the V1 launch sites have been overrun or bombed out," Scutt said. "There are certainly fewer strikes these days. Which will make a renewed offensive by these V2 rockets all the worse. Once again people are beginning to feel safe, and I fear a real panic may set in. You've seen the result of one strike. Imagine dozens throughout London. Sandys told us that while the V2 warhead is slightly larger—twenty-two hundred pounds of Amatol compared to less than nineteen hundred in the V1—its speed upon impact buries it deep, so the explosion is far, far worse."

"Gas mains it is, then," I said. "As long as the story holds. Are there any plans to evacuate children, like during the Blitz?"

"There's not much stomach for evacuations, leastways not around here," Scutt said, shutting his eyes for a moment as if to banish a bad memory. "You remember Roy Flack?"

"Sure. Detective sergeant. We worked together last year," I said, sensing this would not end well.

"In late June, he and his wife decided to send their children away. Twin girls, nearly six years old," Scutt said, glancing into the office where detectives were getting on their coats, some of them looking his way. "Their nursery school had arranged lodging for thirty children. Temporary quarters in a quiet village in the Kent countryside, with teachers and staff to care for them. Flack was relieved to get them out of the city. Two days after they arrived, a V1 dropped on the village. Hit the school square on. Twenty-two children died, including Flack's girls. No other rocket ever came close to that village. A malfunction, perhaps. God only knows."

"Jesus," I said. "I can't even imagine. How do you go on?"

"Eleanor Flack didn't. Killed herself two weeks later. Now get on with your investigation. I have to get to the blast site and help spread the story about gas mains while we search for any parts of the bloody machine still intact," Scutt said. "Check with me tomorrow. Here. You may have the postcard back, we're done with it." He handed me an envelope.

"Thanks. Leave a message for me at the Dorchester Hotel in case something comes up before tomorrow," I said as we left the office together. "I appreciate your help, Chief Inspector."

"We must help each other these days, Captain. There is little alternative," Scutt said, joining the group of men awaiting his orders. One of them looked familiar, but I wasn't sure. He turned away to speak to another detective. As I was taking the stairs down, I realized it had been DS Flack. It'd been only ten months since I'd seen him, but he was nearly unrecognizable.

I stopped and turned to be sure it was him. He was gaunt, his face sunken, eyes drooping from the burden of dark bags hanging beneath them. The collar of his shirt was loose around his neck. His shoulders were hunched, the weight of death too crushing to bear. He was a trace of his former self, a wraith shadowed by guilt and grief.

I had to look away.

CHAPTER THIRTY-THREE

Big Ben sounded the hour, the deep resonant tones solid and reassuring. I left Westminster behind and retraced my steps along Birdcage Walk to Hyde Park Corner. Nearly home. I hadn't been here for a couple of months, and my accommodations during that time away had ranged from a dusty foxhole in Normandy to the sagging mattress and iron bedstead at Saint Albans.

I was looking forward to the Dorchester.

The grand hotel sat opposite Hyde Park. When I'd first arrived in '42, the front had been heavily sandbagged. When I was here for a brief stay in June, they'd all been removed. Today, new sandbags were being unloaded by the main entrance. I wondered which high-ranking guest had tipped off the hotel staff.

I sidestepped the work crew and entered the lobby. Reception was to my left in a small area dwarfed by a black and white marble hallway. White flowers decorated the hallway, blending with the color of the marble and highlighted by soft white lights. It was a different world.

"Captain Boyle, it is a pleasure to see you," Walter said from behind the front desk. The same spot he'd occupied the first day I arrived in England. "Is Baron Kazimierz with you?"

"It's good to see you, Walter. Believe me," I said. "Kaz should be along in a few days."

"I trust he is well," Walter said. "It has been a while since we've seen either of you." Kaz was legendary at the Dorchester. A favored guest, since everyone knew the story of his family's last visit in the suite he still occupied, and what had happened in Poland after that. He'd made the hotel his home, unable to leave the scene of their last moments as a family. I was Kaz's friend, so the staff extended their graciousness to me, but I knew who was first in their thoughts.

"He's doing very well," I said. "Say, what's with the sandbags?"

"I have no idea. They went up again when the V1s started. When that threat seemed to have passed, we had them taken away. Now management feels the need to put them back. But with the Blitz and the V1s gone, what is the point?" Walter looked genuinely puzzled, so I figured word hadn't leaked out yet.

I agreed that it didn't make much sense, thanked him for the bag he'd packed for me, got my key, and went upstairs.

The room was quiet. I sat on the couch for a moment but couldn't settle. I checked Kaz's bedroom. Everything was neat and clean, not a speck of dust to be seen. My room was the same. I stared at the bed, the soft mattress and fluffy pillows looking strange and foreign. Everything looked perfect, nothing was right. No Kaz, no Diana, the fate of Angelika unknown, V2s about to rain down on London.

I couldn't sit still. I took my jacket off and tossed it on the bed. I reached up to the top shelf of my closet and took down a box. I put on the shoulder holster and loaded my .38 Police Special revolver. It fit snugly against my side, heavy and reassuring. If I was going to track down a killer, I didn't want to give him a chance to break my neck or stick a shiv between my ribs. I put my jacket back on and checked the reflection in the mirror. I'd lost enough weight for the loose clothing to hide the bulge of the pistol.

I left the room behind. It was too much. Too thick with memories, comfort, and loneliness. I told Walter I was expecting Big Mike and headed for the restaurant, grabbing a table by the door so I'd be able to spot him. I didn't feel hungry but knew I had to eat. I went for the chef's special, Haddock Monte Carlo, fish with spinach and a poached egg. It was good, but not as fancy as the name sounded. They liked to dress up the rationed amounts of meat served in each dish with a high-class moniker.

Big Mike appeared as I polished off the last of the grub.

"Welcome home," he said as the waiter removed my plate. "You want to rest up for a while?"

"Hell no. Order some food if you want, then let's get to SOE headquarters," I said.

"Okay, but I'm supposed to tell you Sam said I should make sure you don't do anything too strenuous. He's worried about you, Billy."

"Great. Message received. You don't want any lunch?"

"Naw," Big Mike said. "The Poles put out a spread. Getting Skory was cause for celebration." Big Mike didn't turn down food often. It must have been a helluva meal.

"Any news?"

"Another V2 hit in Essex. Put a big hole in a field, no one was hurt," Big Mike whispered. "Another struck Paris, several people killed. That's it as far as we know."

"Let's hope that's all for today. Anything else?"

"Yeah. Sam got in touch with Cosgrove's replacement at the Foreign Office. Douglas Tiltman. He's worked with the British Red Cross on prisoner exchanges with the Krauts. Sick and disabled POWs, that sort of thing. He knows Count Bernadotte of the Swedish Red Cross, so he's a good choice."

"We'll see," I said. "When can we talk to him?"

"Sixteen hundred," Big Mike said. "At Norfolk House." It wasn't far. The large building on Saint James's Square housed the main headquarters for SHAEF, and it was where Harding hung his hat when he was in town. I had a desk there too, but I hadn't seen it in months.

"Okay, we should have enough time to pop in and talk to Vera," I said, doubting SOE had many spur-of-the-moment visitors.

I filled Big Mike in on my talk with Chief Inspector Scutt as we made the short drive to Baker Street. The main SOE headquarters was at number sixty-four. Not close enough to the more well-known 221B Baker Street to draw attention, of course.

"You sure Vera Atkins works here?" Big Mike asked as he looked for a place to park the jeep. "SOE's got offices all over town."

"If she's not there, we'll ask where the French Section is located," I said as he maneuvered the jeep into a spot near our destination. "Their other offices are all in the Marylebone area."

"Yeah, SOE probably hands out maps to anyone who comes knocking at their door," Big Mike said. "You better get that gift of gab revved up, Billy. We're gonna need it."

The ground floor of the SOE building, also known as Michael House, was taken up by a tailor shop. Above it stood four floors of nondescript windows, all curtained and giving no evidence of what business was conducted there. The steady flow of uniformed officers tromping up and down the stairs may have provided a clue, but I was sure the locals knew to keep walking and avoid eye contact.

On the first floor, we waited behind officers showing passes to a sergeant seated at a desk. He studied each pass carefully, entering the name and time into a logbook. Only then did he hand the pass back and release each man with a sharp nod. Behind him stood an armed corporal, his hands behind his back, and his eyes on each person approaching the desk.

"Passes?" the sergeant said, his open hand extended.

"We're from SHAEF, and I'd like to speak to Vera Atkins," I said.

"Who?"

"Flight Officer Vera Atkins," I said. "Intelligence officer for SOE's French Section."

"Sorry, Captain, never heard of her. Now if you don't have a pass, please go back to General Eisenhower and give him my regards," he said. "Next."

Another officer presented his pass as we waited. The armed corporal edged closer to us.

"Listen, we've worked with Vera, she knows us. Can you at least get a message to her?" I asked.

"Captain, please do not make me pick up this telephone and call for guards to escort you off the premises," the sergeant said, resting one hand on the telephone as his buddy reached for his holstered pistol.

"Come on, Billy," Big Mike said. "This ain't gonna work. Let's see about getting a pass."

"How about I leave a note with you," I said to the sergeant, ignoring Big Mike's hand on my shoulder. "In case you suddenly remember Vera Atkins when you see her come in, you could give it to her."

"Step aside, Captain, if you will," the sergeant said, as a man in civilian clothes squeezed between us.

"Hello, Stanley," the fellow said. He wore a wrinkled black suit, dark hair edging over a worn collar, and his tie askew. He produced a pass and a smile.

"Go on through, Mr. Marks," Stanley said.

"Wait a minute," I said, the name ringing a bell. "Leo Marks?" Diana had mentioned him when our paths had crossed in a French château on the eve of D-Day. Her SOE team had been holed up there, and she was the radio operator. Leo Marks was her SOE code master.

"I asked you nicely, Captain," Stanley said, picking up the telephone.

"How do you know?" Leo Marks asked, his dark eyes darting back and forth between Big Mike and me, taking in our SHAEF shoulder patches and perhaps the size of Big Mike's shoulders. He sounded a touch worried.

"Juliet Bonvie," I whispered, giving Diana's code name during that operation. "I was in France with her, at the château in Dreux. She told me about the poem code. *The life that I have is all that I have. And the life that I have is yours.*"

"What's her real name?" Marks asked, holding up one hand to Stanley, who set down the telephone.

"Diana Seaton," I said. "She needs your help."

"I can vouch for these two, Stanley," Marks said. The poem had been written by Marks for use in coding. Diana had told me that before he came to SOE they'd used famous poems for encrypting messages. Marks had seen the danger in that, since the enemy could deduce the entire poem if they recognized any part of it. So he wrote his own. Unbreakable.

When we were logged in, Marks led us to his office at the rear of the building. We were followed by Stanley's partner. Marks told us it was standard practice to guard anyone who was let in without a pass. The sentry would remain at the door and escort us out when we were done.

"Explain yourself," Marks said as he shut the door and sat at his desk. "Quickly and convincingly, or you'll both be thrown into the street. Might take a while for your sergeant here, but we have our own behemoths lurking about." He snipped the end of a cigar and fired it up as I did the introductions.

I gave Marks the lowdown on Uncle Ike's Office of Special Investigations, without going into the family history. "I've known Diana since I arrived in 1942. I worked with her in France, most recently Paris."

"And where is she now?" Marks said, leaning back in his chair and affecting disinterest as he puffed away.

"Ravensbrück," I said. He already knew. And if I knew, it proved my bona fides.

"Alright," he said. "I believe you. Why are you here, and how can I help?"

"I can't say much, but there's a chance we can get Diana out. As far as I know, the Germans don't know she's SOE," I said.

"That's our assumption as well. To them, she's Malou, part of a Parisian resistance group," Marks said. "How are you planning on getting her out? Is this an OSS operation?"

"It's not OSS. But there is a plan in the works, that's all I can tell you," I said. Far as I knew, Bill Donovan and the Office of Strategic Services weren't involved.

"Are you wasting my time, Captain Boyle? It's evident you do know Diana Seaton, but I am at a loss to understand what you want of me," Marks said. "I don't have much time. I have a priority coding job to do."

"Do you know Charles Cosgrove?" Big Mike asked, doing a better job of getting to the point.

"Yes. Invalided out of the service for medical reasons a while ago. Now back in the game with the Foreign Office. He looked years younger last I saw him. Why?"

"He's been murdered," I said. Marks sat straight up. That got his attention.

"What about Paul Densmore?" Big Mike asked.

"Of course. Lieutenant Densmore is with the German Section. He's away on leave," Marks said, a look of dawning shock on his face.

"Murdered. Likely by the same person who killed Cosgrove," I said. "They were both killed at Saint Albans. You know the place?"

"Never had the pleasure, but I know it's a sanitorium for agents and others who need a place to rest and recover. Like poor Densmore," Marks said. "The connection to Diana Seaton?"

"Major Cosgrove was working on a plan that would get Diana out," I said. "I want to catch the killer and make sure the plan goes off without a hitch. Cosgrove was a good man. A friend. I owe him that. I want justice and I want Diana back."

"So do we," Marks said, tapping the ash from his cigar as he set it in an ashtray.

"Did you know Thomas Holland?" Big Mike asked, hitting him with another victim, this one even closer to home.

"Dear God. After all he's been through, don't tell me he's been killed at Saint Albans as well," Marks said.

"He was the first," I said. "You knew he was there?"

"Not precisely. I did know he'd come back in a catatonic state, so it stands to reason. I'd briefed him on codes before both his missions. Quite dedicated, and a courageous fellow, from what I hear. But I don't know the details, you'll have to talk to Vera about that."

"Where is she?" I asked.

"Listen," Marks said, puffing his cigar back into life. "I'm short on time. I'll contact Vera and let you know if she wants to talk. I think I'm treading close to a violation of the Official Secrets Act, and I have no wish to spend the next twenty years or so in one of His Majesty's dungeons. Where can I reach you?"

"Norfolk House or the Dorchester Hotel," Big Mike said, writing out our names and the SHAEF exchange where a message could be left. "Can you make it soon?"

"Of course, I'm sure our agent won't mind jumping without his codebooks," Marks said, blowing smoke in our direction and pointing to the door. "The corporal will escort you out. I'd recommend no sudden moves," he said, his pen poised over a blank sheet of paper.

"Just one quick question," I said as I neared the door. "Who is George Markstein and where can we find him?"

"I'd advise you not to ask that question outside of this room," Marks said. "Ever."

Leo Marks was a young guy, almost baby faced, his visage framed by his dark curls. But at that moment, with his cigar clenched between his teeth, he looked like a gangster measuring me up for a Chicago overcoat.

"That hit a nerve," Big Mike said, as our escort left us on the sidewalk. "Think it spooked him?"

"It tells us we're on the right track," I said. "But I hope it didn't push him over the edge."

The last thing we needed was to be cut off from Vera Atkins. She had the clout we needed to get some questions answered. Marks, I wasn't so sure about. He might be a genius with codes, but that didn't mean he could give orders within SOE. Except maybe to have us arrested.

"He seemed concerned enough about Diana," Big Mike said as we got into the jeep. "That's gotta mean something. Now let's see what this Tiltman guy has to say."

In fifteen minutes, we'd parked the jeep in a line of other military vehicles and were bounding up the steps at SHAEF HQ in Saint James's Square. Upstairs, we made for the conference room next to Harding's office. Harding was in the hallway shaking hands with a dapper gent in a three-piece suit, the classic image of a posh Foreign Service officer.

Harding introduced us. Tiltman had the face of an aristocrat, unblemished by sun or weather, smooth skin set taut over cheekbones, and hair graying at the temples just enough to impart a sense of maturity. As we shook hands, I felt the softness of privilege. I offered my condolences over the death of Major Cosgrove.

"A fine man," Tiltman said. "I understand you lent a hand with the investigation, Captain."

"Not very successfully," I said. Tiltman wished me luck catching the killer, while Harding ushered the three of us into the room.

I almost fell over.

Vera Atkins sat at the far end of the table leafing through a file.

"I believe you know Flight Officer Vera Atkins, Captain Boyle?" Harding said. Vera rose and nodded an acknowledgement, her blue Women's Auxiliary Air Force uniform lending a touch of color to the assembled gray pinstripes and khaki.

"I've had the pleasure," I said, shooting a quick wink to Big Mike, who enveloped her hand in one of his and shook it like he was priming a pump.

"It's been a while, Captain," Vera said as we all took our seats. "I'm glad to see you're well. I trust Saint Albans was restful?"

"I've never slept better," I said. I didn't know enough about Tiltman to start asking questions about Markstein in front of him, so I zipped it and settled down to see what Vera was doing here and learn what she knew.

"I have been reviewing the files Major Cosgrove left behind," Tiltman said. "It is all extraordinary, I must say. Still, Count Bernadotte and the Swedish Red Cross believe Himmler's offer is genuine."

"Does your source within the Swedish government concur?" I asked. There was a hesitancy in Tiltman's voice that I didn't like. I wanted to be sure he was fully on board with this scheme.

"What source?" Tiltman said, raising an eyebrow. Harding frowned, and I plowed ahead.

"When he was at Saint Albans, Cosgrove told us he had a source," I said.

"Right before he was killed," Big Mike added for emphasis.

"We've all worked with Major Cosgrove in the past," Harding said, laying his palms flat on the table, as if claiming control over the meeting. "We respected him and naturally kept everything he said confidential. Correct, gentlemen?"

"Yes, on both counts," I said, while Big Mike nodded in agreement. "The major told us that this Swedish contact was how he got Diana Seaton's name on the list of inmates to be released."

"Malou Lyon," Vera said. "To be precise. That is the name on the forged identity card we gave her. And that is how the Germans know her."

"And most importantly, how the Swedes know her," Harding said. "Because of Major Cosgrove's contact within the Swedish government, the Swedish Red Cross has agreed to place her name on the list of one hundred prisoners to be repatriated in this trial run. She may be able to provide us with important information about the German rocket program."

"Yes, I know," Tiltman said. "But we must be careful not to press the Swedes too hard. If they think this is more of an intelligence effort as opposed to a humanitarian one, they could close the project down entirely. I wonder if this agent's importance may be overstated, which is why I asked Flight Officer Atkins to be here."

"Malou Lyon is unique," Vera said, tapping one finger on the tabletop. "She is our only agent to be captured without the Germans knowing she is SOE. That has saved her life so far. But she could be betrayed at any time, and that would be the end of her. So do press the Swedes upon this point, Mr. Tiltman. You are a diplomat. I assume that means you know the exact amount of pressure required and how to apply it."

"You are aware of the rocket attack today?" Harding said.

"Yes. Two strikes here and one in Paris. The V2 supersonic rocket," Tiltman said.

"We believe Miss Seaton may be employed in the Siemens factory outside the camp," Harding said. "They produce components for the rocket there. Cosgrove thought she'd be able to report valuable information."

"But surely if the Germans have her working on V2 components, they'd never let her go," Tiltman said. "And by putting her on the list, we may be revealing she is an intelligence asset after all."

"To the Germans, she's simply working on unidentifiable machine parts. She may not know what they are for, but once we have her back and put her knowledge together with our other sources, it may help us find a way to combat these things," Harding said, without mentioning Skory and his planeload of salvaged parts.

"I'm not aware of other sources, nor do I wish to be," Tiltman said, then fixed his eyes on Vera. "Do you believe Diana Seaton is capable of intelligence gathering, even as a slave laborer? The conditions must be horrible."

"If she breathes, yes. Malou will do her job," Vera said.

"Very well, but I can make no promises," Tiltman said. "Count Bernadotte is almost ready to present the list to Himmler's representative. Obviously, we must maintain the highest level of secrecy if we don't want a disaster for all concerned."

"The one hundred prisoners, you mean?" Big Mike asked.

"Of course," Tiltman answered much too quickly. He couldn't hide the fact that it was a diplomatic disaster he was most worried about. "But it would also be a disaster for the Swedes if it looked like they were being used as a tool of British intelligence. It could harm postwar relations in Scandinavia."

"One war at a time," I said, seeing where this was going. Careers could be harmed as well. "There's one more name I'd like to ask you to add. Angelika Kazimierz."

"Who is this person?" Tiltman asked. Vera looked confused, and Harding looked ready to boil over.

"An intelligence operative, but not for SOE," I said. "She's with the Polish Home Army and was picked up in a sweep. The Germans rounded up young women, all city girls with thin, delicate fingers. Perfect for assembling small machine parts. She's in Ravensbrück as well."

"Absolutely not," Tiltman said, rising from his seat. "One name may be possible. Two could endanger the entire project. When would it stop? Colonel Harding, I will be in touch. Good day to you all."

"You had no authorization to make that request, Captain," Harding said through gritted teeth as soon as Tiltman cleared the door. "From this point forward, keep your trap shut or I'll send you back to Saint Albans for another long nap." Harding stormed out of the room, probably to mollify Tiltman.

"I assume Angelika is some relation of Lieutenant Kazimierz," Vera said, assembling her papers as she stood to leave.

"His sister," I said. "His only living relative. She's as likely to be working in that V2 factory as Diana. It would be important to get her out."

"No doubt," Vera said. "But to be blunt, my priority is getting one of my girls out. Don't get in the way of that, Captain."

"I don't think Tiltman even gave it a moment's thought," I said. "By the way, I wanted to ask you about a guy I met in Saint Albans, an agent by the name of Thomas Holland. Know him?"

"I do. He was one of our agents," Vera said. "A brave man. I was sad to hear he'd committed suicide."

"He was murdered," I said.

"Along with Charles Cosgrove and Paul Densmore," Big Mike added.

"I had no idea. I mean about murder. I'd heard Charles had died, but I assumed it was his heart," Vera said. She sat down, a look of confusion spreading across her face. "Paul Densmore too?"

"Yes. Colonel Blackford didn't say anything about it?"

"No. When I saw him earlier today, he didn't mention it. Who is responsible?"

"That's what we want to know. Does the name George Markstein mean anything to you? He originally went by Georg. A German Jew," I said.

"No," Vera said. But a sudden flash in her eyes told me otherwise.

"He was friends with Holland. From before the war. They did their SOE training together," I said, taking out the photograph of the two smiling young men and sliding it across the table to her.

"I said no," Vera repeated, pushing the photograph back in my direction without much of a look at it.

"Somebody killed Holland and tried to make it look like an accident or suicide," I said. "Then stabbed Cosgrove and broke Densmore's neck. Holland had wanted to volunteer for duty with the German Section, but he had been turned down. But they took Markstein. He's the only link," I said.

"Charles Cosgrove never was part of the German Section," Vera said. "That doesn't make sense."

"He served on the selection committee that rejected Holland and took Markstein. That was enough to get him killed," I said. I pocketed the photograph since she was working so hard not to look at it. I held up the postcard instead. "Recognize this?"

"Where did you get that?" Vera said. Her face flushed red.

"It was left on Cosgrove's body," I said. "A message of some sort. The image of this same red horse was painted in Densmore's blood on his bedroom window. What's going on, Vera? What does the red horse mean?"

"Asking such questions will endanger Diana. You should know that, Captain," she said, getting up and walking to the door. "As well as yourselves. Be careful. Or as your Colonel Harding so elegantly put it, keep your trap shut."

"We know about Operation Periwig," I said, trying to sound like I knew more than the name. It stopped her cold.

"You are a reckless man, Captain Boyle," Vera said. "No one outside of SOE should know that name, much less bandy it about. Perhaps Scotland Yard needs to pay you a call. I'm fairly certain you've violated our Official Secrets Act, if not your own Espionage Act. I doubt even your famous uncle would intervene if the British government complained about your interference."

"I'm reckless? You're ignoring a murder spree aimed at SOE's German Section, and you call me reckless? Give me a break," I said, as I felt Big Mike clap a hand on my shoulder and, not for the first time today, pull me back.

"Be careful," she said. "Consider that a friendly warning. The next time it won't be friendly, and it will be much worse than a warning."

"It's Blackford who should be careful," I said. "He's the next logical victim."

"Well, you'll be the first suspect, I imagine. Unless they've let anyone else out of Saint Albans today. Goodbye."

"Always nice to make new friends," Big Mike said as Vera stalked out and slammed the door shut.

"Let's get out of here before Harding comes back," I said. "I need a drink."

CHAPTER THIRTY-FOUR

WE GOT TO the bar at the Dorchester before the off-duty crowd started to filter in, ordered our Burton Ales, and sat back to consider our next move.

I wasn't sure we had one.

"We can hope Inspector Scutt comes up with a fingerprint match," Big Mike said, with little enthusiasm.

"That could take days, or even weeks," I said. "He could show up to arrest us before he's done if Vera wakes up cranky tomorrow morning. Maybe Kaz can make some sense out of Griffin's notebook. Before they put us in the Tower of London."

"Vera was right about Ike, you know. He wouldn't side with his favorite nephew if it endangered Allied unity," Big Mike said, taking a healthy swig of ale. The Brits would frame it as an American junior officer interfering with SOE secret operations. No way Uncle Ike could take sides.

"Yeah. Feels like we're boxed in," I said. "You'd think Cosgrove's friends, if Vera Atkins and this Tiltman guy were his pals, would want justice for him. But nobody cares."

"We do," Big Mike said, polishing off his pint and signaling for the barman to pull another. "We'll get him, Billy. Even if it takes a while."

"Excuse me, Captain," Walter said, suddenly materializing at my side. "This was delivered moments ago." He handed me an envelope.

"Walter, there's no name on this," I said, looking at the blank creamy white paper.

"Yes. The gentleman said it was to be delivered to you posthaste," Walter said.

"What gentleman?" I said to Walter's retreating back. I shrugged and tore open the envelope.

Pick me up at the Marble Arch. 9:00 P.M. sharp. Bring this note. 12.13.

"What?" Big Mike said. "Pick who up?"

"I dunno," I said, studying the paper. "Maybe it's the killer setting a trap. Or maybe Vera wants to apologize."

"But what's with the twelve, thirteen?" Big Mike said. "A signature?"

"I don't get it," I admitted, finishing the last of my ale as I turned the heavy paper stock over. I caught a faint smoky odor. I put it up to my nose and sniffed. Then I counted on my fingers.

"It's a code," I said. "A simple code, but that's the point. It tells us who sent it."

"Leo Marks?" Big Mike asked, his brow wrinkled as he scanned the note. "Oh yeah! It's his initials."

"The twelfth and thirteenth letters of the alphabet," I said. "I think Leo wants to talk, but he's not leaving any evidence."

"Smart guy. He doesn't want Vera to put him in the slammer. He's discreet. You should take notes, Billy," Big Mike said. "Now let's get something to eat."

Big Mike was full of good ideas. Especially that last one.

We polished off a meal of chicken with potatoes and asparagus, and, not long after, Big Mike was piloting the staff car up Park Lane, with Hyde Park on the left and the Marble Arch dead ahead. Big Mike braked as we took a left, the white marble of the arch gleaming in the evening darkness. The late summer sun had set, but there was enough lingering light to make out Leo Marks, with his trench coat collar turned up and his hat brim snapped down.

"Hop in," Big Mike said. "Where're we going?"

"Do you have the note?" Leo asked as he clambered into the rear seat, setting a briefcase beside him. I handed over the note and watched him methodically tear it into tiny pieces. "Turn around, head south across the river."

"What's with the cloak-and-dagger stuff?" I asked.

"I liked Charles Cosgrove," Leo said. "He was a decent fellow. Served king and country well and came back for more. Gave himself a second lease on life. I didn't like that being cut short. He deserved more. He deserved to see victory."

"No argument from us," Big Mike said, heading back the way we'd come, toward Westminster Bridge.

"You're going to help us," I said. "How?"

"I am not going to tell you anything. I am not going to reveal any secrets. This trip never happened. Do you understand me?" Leo said, leaning forward and keeping his voice low, as if he might be overheard.

"No," I said.

"Good. Now turn left up ahead onto London Road."

"Where's that lead to?" Big Mike asked.

"Never mind," Leo said, swiveling his head and checking the traffic behind us. Big Mike looked at me and shrugged. Why not go for a ride? It wasn't like we had anything else to do.

We drove east for half an hour, motoring along the south bank of the Thames as full darkness blanketed the countryside. The sprawl of the city gave way to villages, and, at each turning, Leo gave a direction and not a damn thing more.

"In twenty minutes, we'll be at the Gravesend RAF base," he said. "Don't say a word. I'll handle the guard at the gate."

"Gravesend? Sounds cheery," I said. "What happens there?"

"You keep quiet. Don't draw attention to yourselves. Watch and listen. Nothing more,"

Leo said. We drove on, the road illuminated only by the thin slit of light from our headlamps and the faint, soft glow coming from houses and shops under the new dimout regulations. It was more nighttime light than I'd seen in years.

Road signs were still down and navigating in the dimout wasn't much easier than in the blackout. Leo pointed out a few lefts and rights, and soon enough we found ourselves at the gate to RAF

Gravesend. Sentries stood on either side of the car, weapons at the ready. Leo rolled down his window and presented papers to a sergeant who gave him a friendly nod in return. He didn't seem to be a stranger here.

"They're with me," Leo said, pointing to something in the paper-work. The sergeant eyed us and handed the papers back, signaling for the gate to be lifted. We went through, passing giant hangars, squat brick buildings, and rows of prefabricated Nissen huts. Royal Air Force personnel stood outside one hut; the red-and-white Polish banner was visible on a flagpole.

"The Polish 306 Squadron," Leo remarked. "Your friend Baron Kazimierz would have enjoyed this visit. How is he, by the way? I heard the surgery went well."

"You tell us. You seem to know a lot more than we do," I said.

"Resting comfortably as of two hours ago, I'm told. There, that last hangar," he said, tapping Big Mike on the shoulder and pointing to the right.

"Mustangs," Big Mike said, passing a row of P-51 fighters with the RAF roundel. "American fighters in the Royal Air Force with Polish pilots. Now that's Allied unity. Hey Leo, why not show some unity and spill. What's going on here?"

"That," Leo said, pointing to a large dark form looming ahead of us. A Short Stirling four-engine bomber, painted black, a hallmark of the Special Duties Squadron, SOE's air transport service.

We parked in front of the hangar where we saw another matte black bomber, this one a four-engine Whitley. Both the Stirling and the Whitley had been retired from regular bombing duties, but the aircraft were kept active as transports, giving SOE a reach beyond the range of the single-engine Lysander.

Leo led us to a Nissen hut off to the side of the hangar, hidden from the rest of the airfield. Smoke curled from a steel pipe chimney, and we heard the murmur of voices from within as we approached the door. We entered. Half a dozen RAF officers in flight suits were gath-ered around a large wall map at the end of the room, checking routes laid out with red twine on the map boards. One path went over the

North Sea and into northern Germany, where the drop zone was marked outside of Kiel. The other cut across France to a drop zone in Bavaria. Navigators with clipboards took notes, studying the map, and tracing routes with their fingers as calmly as if planning a Sunday drive.

I heard Polish being spoken as well as English. I knew Poles had dropped supplies to their comrades during the Warsaw Uprising and wondered if these men had flown over the besieged capital knowing how doomed the Polish Home Army rebellion was.

"Josh, good to see you," Leo said, shaking the hand of a British Army lieutenant. "Is Schiller all set?"

"He's ready," Josh said, nodding in the direction of three men dressed in civilian clothes who were gathered around a table piled with sandwiches, cups of tea in their hands. "Who are your friends?"

"Observers," Leo said, forgoing introductions. He turned to a young fellow in a Royal Navy uniform. "Peter, your chaps all right?"

"They're fine. Ready anytime you are," answered Peter.

Leo turned to whisper to us. "Stay close and keep quiet."

"Listen, Leo, I know the drill. I've flown in a Lysander, so I know about Joes," I said. The SOE flight crews called their passengers Joes, a common name that held no emotion or connection. Joes were cargo.

"They're not Joes. They're Bonzos," he hissed. "Now shut up."

Bonzos? I glanced at Big Mike, who looked as puzzled as I felt.

Josh and Peter led their charges to a table. They were what SOE called conducting officers, guides for agents during their final preparations for a mission. Josh stood on one side with his man, Schiller, while Peter took the other side with his two agents. Leo was the SOE code master, and all eyes were on him as he sat at the head of the table and opened his briefcase. Big Mike wandered over to the food, watching the aircrew as he grabbed a ham sandwich. I sat in a chair along the wall and focused on the men at the table.

First, Leo went over codes with Schiller. He gave him a sheet with German phrases, each with a four-number group adjacent to it. He translated for Josh, explaining that 2819 stood for *I have been unable to make contact*, and 2800 meant *so-and-so can organize a resistance group*.

There were more precoded phrases. Schiller interrupted a few times with questions. His English was good, but his German accent was unmistakable. As Leo reviewed the codebook with Schiller, Peter and the other two agents whispered among themselves, nodding their approval. Their whispers were in German.

There was enthusiasm over Leo's codes, which would shorten Morse transmissions. He distributed onetime pads—coded sheets intended for a single use. The sender and receiver both had the same sheet, and the agent was to destroy his after each use. Unbreakable, Leo said. Then he turned to the other two agents. They were going in together on the Whitley headed to Bavaria. Their codes were different but used the same format as Schiller's.

Leo was a coding wizard. He probably liked puzzles and could give Kaz some competition at getting the *Times* crossword puzzle done.

He liked games.

This was a game! A challenge for Big Mike and me to figure out what Leo didn't want to say out loud. He had scruples and wisely took the Official Secrets Act seriously. But that didn't mean he couldn't deliver a message indirectly.

If we were smart enough to decode it.

So, what did I know?

This was obviously an SOE German Section operation. Two drop zones inside Germany. German-speaking agents. Both Peter and Josh, speaking in German, broke in on occasion, likely to explain something as clearly as possible to their agents.

Leo explained that the coding materials would be kept with the suitcase radios, which would be dropped along with the agents. He stressed the importance of destroying the codebooks if capture was imminent.

Leo gave Schiller a coded list of names and addresses in the Kiel area. Contacts in the German resistance, he said. Some of them Nazi Party leaders who had given up all hope of a Nazi victory. He reviewed the key to the cipher code, then gave a similar encoded list to the other two agents. Theirs contained ten resistance contacts in Munich.

Peter and Josh went over the codes with Leo and the agents, making sure everyone understood their respective cipher keys. As the discussion began to focus on which resistance members were to be contacted first, I began to think about my SOE mission.

On the night of June 5, the eve of the D-Day invasion, Kaz and I had gone through our own briefing with Vera Atkins prior to being flown into occupied France in a Lysander aircraft. It had been a short hop compared to the trip these men were making. We'd landed in a grassy field in northern France, no need to jump into the night and trust our lives to a parachute.

What had been different?

It had been less crowded, for one thing. It was just us and Vera, and a third agent who was dropping by parachute. Along with a delivery of weapons canisters.

We had another Lysander flight after that mission was completed. But instead of returning to England, we were sent to the Swiss border. Except the Lysander didn't make it. Struck by German fire, we crash-landed short of our objective. We survived the crash, but our pilot hadn't.

I shook off the memories of the burning aircraft.

I watched the three agents listening to their last-minute instructions.

I glanced at the aircrew, now smoking cigarettes, checking wristwatches, and talking among themselves as they waited for the briefing to end.

I studied the map, the bright red strings leading to the drop zones and charting the return flights home.

The image of German tracers seeking our low-altitude Lysander refused to go away, playing itself out at the back of my mind.

Something wasn't right.

I heard a truck brake outside. Doors slammed, and RAF enlisted men carried in piles of clothing, suitcases, and two parachutes. Everything was set out on the table.

"One more parachute?" Peter asked.

"Be here in a moment, sir," one of the airmen replied and took his leave with the others.

"Right," Josh said, separating out the bundle of clothes. "Time to change, chaps." The SOE was expert at outfitting agents in clothing appropriate to the country and the false identity of the wearers. Still, I was surprised by the Wehrmacht uniform provided for Schiller. It was startling to see, even though it was a disguise.

"Oberfeldwebel Dieter Ratz," Leo said, checking the phony identity papers. That was close to a staff sergeant in the US Army. "Bit of a promotion, eh Schiller?"

Schiller grinned as he donned the Wehrmacht-issue underwear and uniform. The other agents were dressed as workmen in worn corduroy trousers, wool shirts, jackets, and caps. They were each handed a parachute. The aircrew left to board their aircraft and start the final check before takeoff.

Josh checked the suitcase with Schiller. Looking much like a brown traveler's suitcase, it contained the standard SOE radio. The codebooks and other papers were stashed inside. Once they determined everything was in order, Schiller put on dark coveralls, a jumpsuit designed to protect his clothing during the drop.

A car door slammed outside, and an RAF flight lieutenant carried in the last parachute. The lieutenant helped Schiller into it and checked the harnesses several times. Once satisfied, he clapped him on the shoulder and wished him luck.

The other agents and Schiller shook hands. Leo did the same, then Josh led Schiller outside where the sound of the Whitley's powerful engines turning over reverberated against the metal building.

Peter repeated the process with his two agents. A final check of clothing and the radio. Leo added a stack of postcards to the coding sheets. They matched the one I had in my pocket. The red horse was going to Germany.

The jumpsuits went on, then the parachutes. Peter walked his agents to the waiting aircraft. As they passed us, one of the two men approached me, his hand extended, a look of determination mingled with dread playing across his face. I took it and wished him the best of luck.

They left, and we heard a mighty roar of engines as Schiller's aircraft taxied down the runway, beginning its long journey to northern Germany.

We were alone in the Nissen hut with Leo. I didn't much like him right then.

"They're all dead men," I said.

"Schiller is, for certain," Leo said, slumping in his chair, his face buried in his hands.

"What?" Big Mike asked.

"The parachute," I said. "Remember Blackford was after Sinclair to design a parachute malfunction? One that looked like the chute hadn't been sabotaged?"

"How did you get that from one parachute delivered late?" Leo asked, his curiosity overcoming his previous self-imposed silence.

"He boarded first, but his parachute came last. Delivered by an officer who made sure it went straight to him. One of yours, I assume?"

"Let's say he's not on the books at this establishment," Leo said. "And before you condemn us, it should be known that Schiller was—or, I should say, at least for the next two hours, is—a double agent. We know this from the POW camp where he was recruited. He's an ardent Nazi who bragged to his friends that he could trick us into believing him. Well, we're a tricky bunch ourselves. As he will find out in his final moments. The chute is rigged to fail."

"That can't be a good way to die, tugging at a ripcord that won't work," Big Mike said.

"Yes. I agree. This is the closest I've come to killing a German soldier. I can't say it feels pleasant at all," Leo said, a sigh escaping his lips. "But it had to be done."

The second aircraft revved its engines, the growling sound echoing against the steel walls.

"Same with those two?" I asked, tossing my jaw in the direction of the tarmac.

"I'll tell you in the car," Leo said. "I'd like to leave this place."

As he opened the door, I looked back at the map with its telltale strings pointing to the cruelest of destinations. The agents' discarded clothing lay bunched on the floor, as if they'd turned to ghosts and vanished into the night.

Close enough, I thought as we stepped outside.

The Short Stirling taxied to the runway, its prop wash blasting our faces, leaving the scent of exhaust and betrayal lingering long after the aircraft lifted off into the night sky.

CHAPTER THIRTY-FIVE

"HOW CERTAIN ARE you about Schiller?" Big Mike asked as the gate went down behind us at RAF Gravesend. He had a cold edge to his voice, and his white-knuckled grip on the steering wheel threatened to snap it. He looked in the rear mirror, piercing the code master with a sharp stare.

"I've been told it has been confirmed. Bugged quarters in the POW camp, as well as informers," Leo said.

"The other two?" I asked.

"I've revealed too much already," Leo said. "I told you to observe, and you have. Draw your own conclusions. If that helps with your investigation, all to the better. If not, well then I'll simply thank you for the ride."

"Bullshit," Big Mike said, braking hard and pulling over to the side of the road. We were on the outskirts of town. The only thing visible was a farmer's fence and a grassy field stretching into the dark. Big Mike turned to face Leo, who seemed to shrink into the back seat. "You're going to come clean, pal, or I'll throw you into the ditch right now. By the time you find your way back to London, we'll have made a call to Inspector Scutt at Scotland Yard about some cigar-smoking punk blabbing government secrets."

"Chief Inspector Scutt. I forgot to tell you, he's been promoted," I told Big Mike.

"Even better. A chief inspector carries more weight. Now spill,

Marks," Big Mike said, one beefy arm on the seat rest, close enough to grab Leo. "You can't just clam up and wash your hands of this charade. Tell us what's going on."

"It is a charade," Leo said. "A pretense, a sham, a tragic farce, all rolled up in one operation. Periwig. But let's not linger out here. Drive on, and I'll explain. But you may regret insisting."

"What's the matter, you scared of the dark?" Big Mike asked as he hit the accelerator a little harder than required, sending Leo sliding back in his seat.

"More than ever," he said, craning his neck to look up at the stars.

"Okay, I understand Schiller," I said. "Assuming what you said is true, he got what was coming. The Krauts will find his body and the canister with his equipment, including the phony code books."

"Yes. Although they're real enough. We hope they'll buy *Herr* Schiller as an SOE agent with a bad parachute and use the radio to make contact as if he were still alive. Any information they send will be false, which is valuable when we know that's the case."

"And his contacts in the German resistance?"

"As phony as Schiller's papers," Leo said. "With any luck, the Gestapo will arrest some stalwart Nazis and give them a taste of what goes on behind their prison walls."

"Okay, I'm with you so far. What's the story with the other two?" I said.

"Christoph and Lukas. German POWs who volunteered. Anti-Nazis."

"Double agents, like Schiller?" Big Mike asked.

"No. They are genuinely committed to ending Hitler's rule in their country. We've found that volunteers fall into three categories. Diehard Nazis like Schiller, who want only to serve the Reich. Anti-Nazis, such as Christoph and Lukas, who believe in ending the regime and the war as soon as possible. Then men who simply want to return to their families. They're terrified of the Russians and the Allied bombing. Sad, that last lot."

"So, Christoph and Lukas have good parachutes?" Big Mike asked. "And real contacts?"

"Yes," Leo said, stretching out the word. I turned to look at him. "And no."

Then it dawned on me. The reason for the name they gave these agents. "Remember," I said to Big Mike. "They don't call them Joes. They call them Bonzos."

"Jesus," Big Mike said. "It's all a setup."

"As you said, a charade," Leo told us. "The purpose of Operation Periwig is to create the illusion of a widespread German resistance movement. To sow chaos among the ranks of Nazi officials and to make everyday Germans mistrust each other."

"The Red Horse is the phony resistance group," I said. "That's why you didn't give any postcards to Schiller."

"Exactly. If the Germans found those on a recently parachuted agent, they would see the Red Horse as a fraud. Christoph and Lukas are under orders to hide them or mail them promptly. Still a bit of a risk in case they're apprehended early, but one worth taking," Leo said. "As determined by German Section, to be clear."

"I doubt it was Blackford's German Section alone. This has to be approved at a higher level," I said. "Gubbins himself, I bet."

"These are not questions one asks at Baker Street," Leo said. "My task is to provide codes. No one has asked me to chime in on the morality of this scheme. Or any other. I'm a code master, not God himself."

"What tipped you off?" Big Mike asked me. "The parachute?"

"It wasn't the first thing. I kept thinking about my Lysander trip with Kaz. Our second flight crashed. If that happens to either bomber, the crews and the agents aboard will have seen everything about the other mission. The drop zone down to the clothes the agents were wearing, as well as their physical description and equipment."

"It'd be a gift to the Krauts if they talked," Big Mike said.

"Right. Our briefing was given by Vera, no one else around. We didn't see the pilot until we got into the Lysander. He didn't know a damn thing about us," I said. "There was zero security at Gravesend."

"Precisely," Leo said. "It's standard procedure with Periwig."

"Just so I understand," Big Mike said. "You're sending these guys you call Bonzos on a suicide mission. You're hoping they get caught so the Gestapo will buy the phony evidence of a German resistance group."

"In SOE's defense, there have been sabotage missions as well. Two fellows dropped near Karlsruhe blew up a section of rail and escaped back across our lines in August," Leo said. "But your description is not that far from the mark, Sergeant. I understand your anger. It doesn't seem fair, does it?"

"We're not even in the vicinity of fair," I said.

"No, I suppose not," Leo said, pausing to give directions at an intersection. "Personally, I hope those two lads are not caught. But I must admit, the dissemination of false information by captured Bonzos is SOE's objective."

"You only use POWs?" I asked.

"Only German-born volunteers," Leo said. "Mainly POWs, since there's an ample supply, but it's not a hard and fast rule."

"No English SOE agents are Bonzos?" I asked.

"No. SOE is a cold-blooded outfit, but that would take ice water in one's veins," Leo said. "The unspoken rule is that Germans are fair game, but Englishmen are Joes, not Bonzos."

Big Mike and I exchanged a look. Thomas Holland had cheated death at the hands of the German Section by virtue of his English birth. But he'd offered up an unwitting sacrifice in the form of his German-born friend, George Markstein.

"George Markstein was a Bonzo," I said.

Leo's confession was wreathed in silence.

CHAPTER THIRTY-SIX

WE WERE ALL quiet for the next few miles. I thought about the poor bastards who'd volunteered simply to get back to their families. What went through their minds when they contacted someone, thinking it was a member of the Red Horse resistance group, only to be turned over to the Gestapo? If the Gestapo ever learned the Bonzo's true identity, it would mean a concentration camp for their family. At best.

The Nazis practiced what they called *Sippenhaft*. It was a law that held an entire family liable for one member's crimes against the state. Between the Russians to the east, bombers overhead, and their own secret police on the ground, these families were bound to suffer one way or another.

As we drew closer to Westminster Bridge, I had to work at staying awake. It had been a helluva long day. I should have been glad to have a piece of the puzzle fall into place, but there were still too many questions.

Who was close enough to George Markstein to take revenge for what had happened to him? I thought about the cast of characters back at Saint Albans and went through the list. When I got to Angus Sinclair, I suddenly understood another part of this mystery.

"The squirt transmitter," I said, snapping my fingers. "Now I get it."

"What?" Leo asked from the rear.

"You haven't heard of it?" I asked, with more than a hint of suspicion in my voice.

"No. Schiller and the others had the normal SOE radio, the Type 3 Mark II. Standard issue right down to the brown leather suitcase."

"Blackford was after Sinclair to design a device that would send out bursts of compressed Morse code," I said. "He called it a squirt transmitter. Sinclair told him it was impossible."

"Of course," Leo said, waking up to the idea. "If the illusion of a widespread resistance network is to be believed, there has to be an explanation for the lack of radio traffic from within Germany. The rumor of a new communications device explains it neatly."

"Blackford probably wanted a few ideas from Sinclair that he could use to brief agents about a new machine," I said. "A few technical phrases good enough to offer a hint to the Krauts."

"Yes. The story could also be that there weren't enough of them yet, which is why tonight's missions were sent out with the old models," Leo said, getting into the spirit of the deception. "Ingenious notion."

"The whole thing is ingenious," Big Mike said. "Doesn't mean I have to like it."

"Nor I, Sergeant. I'm not going to shed any tears over *Herr* Schiller, but he's an anomaly, the first double agent I've encountered. It's the other Bonzos who have been cruelly used. They placed their trust in us and thought we were battling a common enemy. SOE betrayed them. I played a part in that, but I cannot claim a great deal of enthusiasm for it."

"Listen, I get it, you're in a tough position," Big Mike said, with a quick look back at Leo. "All this didn't sit well with me, and I took it out on you. You didn't have to bring us along in the first place."

"We all have to find ways to keep our sanity and soul intact, Sergeant," Leo said. "Remember this is all top secret. Breathe a word of it, and they'll put you somewhere that will make Saint Albans look like holiday accommodations. And I'll swear I never told you a thing."

"Fair enough," Big Mike said, slowing as we took a turn near the river. "I just wish this got us closer to the killer."

"We need to know more about George Markstein," I said. "Along with the people close to him. Stands to reason anyone who cared about him would be upset if they knew how he was used."

"Upset enough for murder?" Big Mike asked.

"Life is cheap these days," Leo said. "We've learned to kill in numbers great and small, for causes glorious and ignoble. Blood revenge is not as unthinkable as it might have been five years ago."

As we crossed the Thames, I thought about that. Leo was right. Years of large-scale violence had produced an ethical numbness when it came to human life. The brass thought in casualties by the bushel and in trade-offs of a hundred deaths in the morning to save a thousand next week. Take that hill, cross that river, assault that village, and then the next, and the next, stretching out into a limitless horizon of viciousness. War was brutalizing in how commonplace it made suffering, violent death, and betrayal.

And treachery perpetrated by your own side was the darkest and deadliest of all betrayals. It robbed you of not only life, but trust.

Blood revenge. Now there was a motive.

We dropped Leo off on Charing Cross Road, near a bookstore at number eighty-four. Marks & Co. was an antiquarian bookshop owned by his parents.

"I suppose I owe it all to my father," Leo said when he pointed out the establishment. "When I was eight years old, I came across a first edition of *The Gold Bug* by Edgar Allan Poe. The story contained a message in code. It entranced me, and I began my career in code breaking that day. Never thought it would lead to all this."

"Seven fourteen," Big Mike said, as Leo opened the door.

"And a good night to you, Sergeant," he answered, a smile lingering on his face as he waved goodbye and faded into the darkness.

"Impressive," I said, remembering how Leo had signed his note.

"I did have to count on my fingers," Big Mike said. "But I thought he'd appreciate it."

CHAPTER THIRTY-SEVEN

I HAD NO idea where I was. I had no idea what was making a racket right by my ear. And I was so tired I didn't care.

Telephone. It was the telephone by my bed. At the Dorchester.

I fumbled with the receiver, trying to sound coherent as I blinked the sleep out of my eyes and focused on the clock. Six-damn-thirty in the morning.

It was a message from Chief Inspector Scutt, delivered by someone whose job it was to be up this early. There was news on the fingerprints, and could I be at Scotland Yard within the hour.

I hung up, my mind still groggy, barely remembering collapsing on the bed late last night, glad I'd managed at least to get my shoes, jacket, and shoulder holster off. The room still felt strange, as if I were trespassing or maybe running away from some greater responsibility. Diana was still in Ravensbrück. As was Angelika. Kaz was in the hospital, and rockets were falling on London. The person who murdered Charles Cosgrove was at large.

I shook off the cobwebs. After a hot shower and room service coffee, the room didn't seem so alien any longer. Just lonely.

I left a message at the front desk for Big Mike, who'd be checking in with me at eight, and hoofed it over to Scotland Yard. The desk sergeant sent me straight to Scutt's office.

"There's been another V2 attack," Scutt said by way of greeting, motioning for me to sit by his desk. "One hit a farm in Maidstone. Eyewitness reports say it appeared to be disintegrating as it fell. Damaged a barn and frightened the livestock, nothing more, thank God. Shut the door, will you."

"Maybe they're not ready," I said as I grasped the doorknob. Or were slave laborers sabotaging the damn things? Delicate hands and thin fingers can make the tiniest of mistakes.

"We can only hope Adolf pushed them to begin the campaign before they had all the technical stuff worked out," Scutt said. "Whatever the reason, I'm glad they are not raining down on my city in the same number as those damned V1s."

Scutt waited until the door was secured, checking the morning shift through his window as they filtered in. Once he was satisfied nobody was looking in on us, he opened a file and turned it around for me to see.

"Don't touch the file, if you don't mind," he said. "This fingerprint business can work both ways. We found three sets of useful prints. I think this first fellow can be cleared as a suspect."

"Morton Bisset," I said, checking the photograph of a man with thinning hair and full lips. "Don't recognize him."

"Forget you saw him. Captain Bisset runs the SOE forgery and printing department. I doubt he ran the printing press, but it would have been his job to check and be sure every detail was perfect."

"Okay, who's next?"

"This fellow," Scutt said, closing Bisset's file and opening another. A photograph of George Markstein stared up at me. "Means something, doesn't it? I can tell by the look on your face."

"It does, Chief Inspector. Markstein is directly connected to two of the murder victims. The card you took the fingerprints from was found in the hand of Charles Cosgrove of the Foreign Office. Markstein was a close friend of Thomas Holland, who was also killed at Saint Albans. They trained together as SOE agents."

"Well, I hope this helps," Scutt said. "Nothing on the third set of prints yet. No surprise there, we were lucky to get these so soon."

"What else is in the file?" I asked, itching to turn the pages myself.

"Research into his family, friends, and coworkers. He was originally Georg Markstein but changed it to George when his mother got out of Germany. Born in Heidelberg of Jewish parents. Father died when he was young but left a trucking business to Markstein's mother. She was able to send him to university in Paris. Smart lad, it looks like."

"That's where he met Thomas Holland," I said, showing Scutt the photograph. "Anything about a possible familial connection between Holland and Markstein?"

"The name Holland doesn't appear," Scutt said, leafing through the pages. "The mother's maiden name was Weisskopf. She's still alive, listed as next of kin. No other relatives mentioned. She and the boy got out of Germany in the mid-thirties. She sold the business for a pittance and came to England with the help of a fellow who used to do business with her husband. He gave her a job, and she's still with him over in Swindon."

"No suspicions of her being a plant?"

"None," Scutt said. "This Swindon bloke did import business with her husband. He's Jewish himself and fought in the last war. He confirmed she's legitimate and that, although her husband fought for the Kaiser, he was a good man. They'd never met but had come to know each other through correspondence."

"That sounds solid," I said, reading the statements that had been gathered from Mrs. Markstein's coworkers. They were glowing.

There was a knock at the door. Scutt moved to cover up the files and relaxed when he saw who it was. A woman police constable, or WPC, as the Brits called their lady coppers. He motioned her in.

"This is WPC Halford," Scutt said. "She's been at work all through the night on your fingerprints. Halford, ignore this Yank. He's not here."

"Certainly, sir," she said, showing no evidence of having squinted at hundreds of fingerprints through the graveyard shift. "I did find a match for the last print."

"Excellent work," Scutt said, taking the file from her. "Now go get some kip and forget you ever did it."

"Oh dear," Scutt said, opening the file. "If this fellow is a suspect, you are in dangerous waters, my friend." He laid it down in front of me.

Major Basil Snow.

"Another resident of Saint Albans, I see, although not a patient," Scutt said. "Head of security. Was he involved in the investigation?"

"He never saw the postcard, if that's what you mean," I said, puzzling through the implications. Why Snow? What was the connection, the motive? "At least not after the murder."

"An exemplary officer," Scutt said, leafing through Snow's service history and commendations. "Too young for the Great War, he joined up in the twenties. Slow progress in a lean peacetime army, but he was promoted when war broke out. Fought in France, evacuated from Dunkirk. Volunteered for SOE shortly after. 'Desirous of action,' it says here."

"So, what was he doing with a Red Horse postcard?" I said, more to myself than to Scutt.

"I'll not even ask what a red horse signifies," Scutt says. "But our Major Snow put his hand to that card, no doubt."

"Anything else of interest in his file?" I asked. "Mention of Markstein, perhaps?"

"Seems not," Scutt said, flipping through the pages. "Nasty business in Italy. There's a brief report on his wounding. Some Eyetie tipped off the Germans to a partisan meeting Snow had brokered. A disaster, from what this says."

"Yes, he told me about it. The betrayal hit him hard."

"Well, SOE thinks highly of him," Scutt said, his eyes scanning another page. "He was posted to Saint Albans temporarily, light duty while he recovered."

"Family?" I asked, hoping for a link to Markstein, Cosgrove, Holland, or Densmore. So many victims, so little to go on.

Scutt pulled out a sheet of personal information. Parents deceased, no next of kin listed. His mother had died of tuberculosis in 1925, his father dying ten years later after too many years in the Northumberland coal mines. Snow had attended one year at a technical college in

Newcastle, then joined the army. His fitness reports were all excellent, and he'd scored high marks in all aspects of SOE training.

"He has a future ahead of him," Scutt said. "Professional army, combat record, skilled agent. SOE obviously is grooming him."

"A future, maybe," I said, looking at his life summed up in terse bureaucratic form. "But not much of a past." No relatives. Religion was marked CE. Church of England, which told me nothing about the man.

"That's the story of a lifelong serviceman," Scutt said. "All too often it means a life left behind." He gathered up the papers and began to close the file.

"Wait a minute," I said. The glimpse of something familiar had flown by as he stacked the sheets. "The page with his personal information, what was his mother's maiden name?"

"Here," Scutt said, pulling it out. "Weisskopf. Well, I'll be damned."

"Same as Markstein's mother," I said, as we both took in the implication. "Was that ever followed up?"

"No, but there would be no call to. The woman died nearly twenty years ago. Hardly cause to suspect her as a German agent," Scutt said.

"Then why is Snow hiding his connection to Markstein?" I asked. "And what about this Church of England entry if his mother is Jewish?"

"Not remarkable in itself," Scutt said. "Folk are free to decide their own religion. But still, it does raise a question or two."

"If these two Weisskopf women are related, sisters perhaps, then George Markstein is Basil Snow's cousin," I said, letting that relationship, and the fact that Snow had hidden it, sink in.

"And what does that tell you?" Scutt asked.

"The motive. Blood revenge," I said, as WPC Halford knocked again at the door.

"Sorry to bother you, Chief Inspector, but there's an urgent telephone call," she said.

"Who is it then?" Scutt growled.

"Well, it's a woman, and she'll only give her first name. And she wants to speak with a Captain Boyle, an American," Halford said. "I told her there were no Yanks about."

"Well done," Scutt said, then looked to me. "Who knows you're here, Boyle?"

"I left a message at the hotel for my sergeant, but that's it. Wait, who is this woman?"

"Name of Clarissa, Chief Inspector," Halford said, scrupulously obeying his instruction to ignore my presence.

"St. Albans," I whispered, fear gnawing at my gut as I prayed it wasn't bad news about Kaz.

"Put her through," Scutt ordered. I picked up as soon as it rang.

"Clarissa?"

"Is this Captain Boyle?"

"Yes. Is Kaz okay? Lieutenant Kazimierz, I mean."

"The baron is fine, he asked me to call you. He said it was urgent," Clarissa said. I heard voices in the background.

"Who's that with you?"

"Iris and Faith. Things are all a muddle here, Captain. I didn't know what to do."

"You did the right thing to call," I said. I'd thought the three of them were chummy. From the whispered conversation on the other end of the line, I could tell I was right. And that something was wrong.

"He's broken the code. The baron, I mean. He said to tell you Griffin saw Major Snow enter Dr. Robinson's quarters shortly before he had them searched. In and out, quickly, according to Griffin's notebook. He said it was important," Clarissa said. "I called your hotel and they gave me this number."

"It is important, thank you," I said. That's when he hid the drawing of the red horse in Robinson's Italian magazine, knowing it would be searched by his military police. "But what's wrong? What are Iris and Faith doing in your office? Isn't that frowned upon?" I tried to make light of the muddle Clarissa found herself in, making a long-distance call to Scotland Yard.

"They brought me to visit the baron yesterday and came first thing today with the news about the code. But it's all so strange," she said.

"What is?"

"Well, I went to see where Major Snow was. We all decided I should contact you, but I didn't want him walking in while I was putting the call through. He's gone, Captain. Without a word. Apparently, he left more than an hour ago."

"With one of the MPs?" I asked, remembering he'd talked about taking the non-com with him to interview Colonel Blackford.

"No. That's who I asked. He left alone. No one knows where he went."

"I do, Clarissa. Find Sergeant Jenkins. Tell him Major Snow is armed and dangerous. He should be detained if he returns. Tell him to be careful."

"Oh dear," she said. "Are you certain?"

"I am. And give Dr. Robinson a message for me. Tell him his office is bugged. SOE has been listening to all his patients."

"I can't believe it. Really?"

"Have you ever been up on the third floor?" I asked her, glancing at Scutt who was listening intently.

"No, it's not allowed," Clarissa said, her voice a whisper, as if they were listening right now. Maybe they were.

"Now you know why. Tell him, please."

She promised she would. It wasn't much, but I figured I owed Doc Robinson for all his help now that I knew he wasn't a spy or a murderer.

I did know one thing for certain. Basil Snow was coming to London to kill Blackford. To take his final blood revenge.

CHAPTER THIRTY-EIGHT

"I DON'T SUPPOSE you have a telephone number for the Special Operations Executive?" I asked Scutt as I glanced at my watch. Eight o'clock. If Big Mike was running on time, he'd be picking up my message at the Dorchester about now.

"No one telephones SOE," Scutt said. "Who do you need to talk to?"

"I'd better not say. You've done enough already, Chief Inspector," I said, as I weighed my options. The fewer people involved, the better. And the better for Horace Scutt's pension if his help remained unofficial. "I know SOE has a lot of offices in the Baker Street area. Do you have any idea if the German Section is housed at the main office, number sixty-four?"

"That I can help you with. All the country sections are a few doors down at Norseby House, eighty-three Baker Street. I know because once we had to send a courier there for personnel files. Good luck, Boyle. With that bunch, you'll need it."

I didn't disagree.

I only had to wait a couple of minutes outside Scotland Yard before Big Mike pulled up in the staff car.

"Baker Street," I said, giving him the number. "You armed?"

"Good morning to you too," Big Mike said, maneuvering into traffic as I shut the passenger door. He pointed to the glove box. "Who we gonna shoot?"

I gave him the lowdown about the connection between Markstein and Snow, Kaz breaking Griffin's code, and Clarissa's report about Snow traveling to London.

"He could already be at Blackford's office," I said, opening the glove box and pulling out Big Mike's .45 automatic. "Hurry up."

He hurried, as much as London traffic would allow, barely avoiding a collision with a black cab as we zoomed through Piccadilly Circus. Minutes later we spilled out of the double-parked car and made for the entrance. We found ourselves in a marble-floored lobby with a desk manned by two guards, both of whom jumped to their feet at the sight of Big Mike buckling his web belt with the holstered automatic.

One went for the telephone, the other for his revolver.

"Halt!"

"We have an important message for Colonel Blackford," I said, skidding to a stop and raising my hands. I knew that in our rush we must have looked like a threat.

"Has Major Snow from Saint Albans been here?" Big Mike asked, adjusting his belt and tugging at his Parsons jacket, sounding completely reasonable.

"Who are you Yanks?" the sergeant asked, his hand resting on the butt of his revolver. The other, a corporal, spoke into the telephone, one hand cupped over the receiver.

"We're from SHAEF," I said, producing my identification in case our flaming sword shoulder patches didn't impress sufficiently.

"They let anyone barge into General Eisenhower's headquarters, do they?" he said, unimpressed with either the paperwork or the embroidery.

"Just tell us if Snow's been here," I said, as I heard the thudding of boots in the stairwell coming up from the basement. I guess that's where they kept their behemoths at number eighty-three.

"Never heard of the man," the sergeant said, as the other fellow set down the telephone. Three more soldiers spilled out from a door at their rear: two privates with Sten guns followed by a lieutenant with his Webley revolver drawn.

"Hold on, guys, no sense chipping the marble floor," Big Mike said, flashing the grin that had made him so many friends. These three evidently had all the friends they needed.

"Hands up," the lieutenant snapped, as his men went to our sides.

"No," I said. "Call Colonel Blackford. It's important. He'll talk to us."

"We can't confirm anyone by that name is in this building," said the lieutenant. Now I knew we had him. He'd already given up on enforcing the order for us to reach for the sky.

"You don't have to confirm anything, just get on that phone and tell Blackford his life is in danger. And God help you, not to mention Blackford, if Major Basil Snow is with him. Hurry!"

The lieutenant wavered, glancing at his men, probably wondering how harshly they were judging him.

"Listen, Lieutenant," Big Mike said, in the softest tone he could muster. "We know the German Section has offices here. The French Section too. Call Vera Atkins, she knows us. We saw her yesterday."

"Corporal, has anyone by the name of Snow been logged in this morning?" the lieutenant asked, moving his finger off the trigger.

"No sir," the corporal answered, running his finger down a list of entries.

The other guard picked up the telephone and had a whispered conversation.

"Are you Captain Boyle?" the sergeant asked. I nodded.

"Flight Officer Atkins will be with you in a moment," he said, the slightest of shrugs aimed at the lieutenant.

That calmed things down enough for one of the Sten gunners to be sent away as we moved to the rear of the lobby, making the place look less like a bank holdup gone bad. In seconds, Vera appeared from the lift.

"How did you know it was me?" I asked.

"Armed Americans, one of them as large as two grenadiers, enter a secret SOE facility. Who else, Captain Boyle? Who else?" Vera said, a sharp laugh escaping her lips. But her narrowed eyes carried another message. "What do you want?"

"I have good reason to believe Major Basil Snow is coming here to murder Colonel Blackford. Snow left Saint Albans this morning and should be here anytime," I said.

"You have evidence of this accusation?" Vera asked. The lieutenant took a step in the other direction and whispered to one of his gunmen, who took up a position facing the entrance. He evidently took the threat of a murderer's visit seriously.

"Evidence exists, but it will never see a courtroom, I'm sure of that. But I know Snow is a killer."

"That's what he was trained to do, Captain Boyle."

"Yeah, well, he's a bit mixed up as to who the enemy is. Right now, it's the SOE German Section, and he's after Blackford," I said.

"Where is the colonel?" Vera said to the non-com.

"He left thirty minutes ago, ma'am," he said, his finger working through another column of entries. "Signed out a vehicle and headed for Radlett, a village on Watling Street. Having a meetup at the Cat and Fiddle. Pub, it sounds like."

"Where's Radlett?" I asked.

"To the northeast, out past Edgware. You take Watling Street from there and you can't miss the place," the sergeant added helpfully. We were all friends now.

"That has to be Snow," I said. "He's luring him away. Let's go."

"We have our own security people, Captain," Vera said, her hand on my arm. "They are effective and discreet."

"Then get them on the road, but we're leaving now," I said. "And to hell with discretion."

We dashed to the car, getting out of there before Vera could decide to have us detained. SOE thrived on secrecy, and she may have preferred a dead Blackford to a public confrontation.

Big Mike gunned it toward Edgware as soon as we'd cleared the worst of the city traffic. We had to slow down at the site of the V2 strike where heavy trucks were hauling away debris.

"Pubs don't open until eleven thirty, right?" I said, checking my watch. "That's two hours from now."

"Doesn't mean anything," Big Mike said. "Lots of pubs keep their back door open for regulars. They'd get fined for selling drinks, but that doesn't mean you can't pull up a chair. Or it could be as simple as Blackford throwing his weight around."

"I'm not buying it," I said. "This is way too early for any publican to be at work."

"Think Snow's going to grab him outside?" Big Mike said.

"That, or simply plug him in his car. The pub could be nothing more than a recognizable meeting point. Blackford parks and Snow puts a round in his head. Or takes him somewhere to do the deed. Away from witnesses."

"And there's no reason for Blackford to suspect Snow," Big Mike said. "We sure didn't."

"Don't remind me," I said as we drove on. Before long we rolled into Radlett, a quiet village of white-timbered buildings alongside flintstone shops and ivy-covered cottages. A quaint spot for murder. Right past the village center, the Cat and Fiddle Pub sat by the roadside, its white stucco bright in the morning sun.

We parked behind a jeep. The bumper bore a black square with an ID number. Black was the color for medical units. I checked the hood. Still warm. Big Mike tried the pub door, then went around back. Nothing. The place was locked up tight.

"They could be anywhere," Big Mike said, looking up and down the street.

I looked around too, hoping for a clue, some hint of where Snow had taken his next victim. I caught a flutter out of the corner of my eye and saw a magpie fly out of a tree, the long-tailed black-and-white bird circling around, gaining height, then settling in on the topmost branch.

Of course.

"I know where they're going. Come on."

We were in open country and Big Mike floored it. There was only one place that made sense. The clock tower, where this all started. Snow's first murder. There was a symmetry to it, a logic that fit. His last victim would go out in highly visible style. He didn't need to hide anymore.

"It's his home turf," I said to Big Mike. "He feels comfortable there. In charge. He knows people and can tell them the truth, the story behind his vengeance."

"And then he kills himself," Big Mike said, slowing for a steep curve.

"There's nothing left for him," I said. "He and George must have had a strong bond. And we know how he detested the notion of betrayal. It ate at him after Italy. So when he learned about SOE's betrayal of George and the other volunteers, it was too much."

"He figured it out from the bugs," Big Mike said, putting the final piece together.

"Yeah. We know Holland had started to speak, but it could have been Densmore just as easily," I said. "He was feeling guilty about something."

"We're about a mile out," Big Mike said a while later. "What's our plan?"

"He doesn't know I've talked to Clarissa," I said. "If Jenkins is ready for him, maybe we won't need one."

"Billy, Snow is a trained agent. Jenkins is Home Guard. And he's bound to have some hesitation, taking the word of a former patient against his commanding officer. Snow will have the upper hand, if only by his rank," Big Mike said.

He was right. It would have been better not to say anything. Damn.

We sped to the gate at Saint Albans. Two Home Guards and one of the regular army MPs approached the car. The gate stayed down.

"Open up," I barked. "Where's Major Snow?"

"Afraid we can't let you in, Captain," the MP said. "We have a situation. You'll have to turn around."

"Captain Boyle? Sir?" It was the Home Guard kid who Sinclair had bowled over. Private Fulton. "He's shot Sarge!"

"Hush up, lad!" the MP growled.

"How bad?" I asked, ignoring the Redcap.

"In the leg. Dr. Hughes came right away. Said Sarge'll be okay. But what's going on, Captain? The major didn't look in his right mind!" Fulton said.

"He's not, Private. Did he have another officer with him? Colonel Blackford?"

"He did. He took Blackford into the tower and locked the door. Let him in, willya?" Fulton said to the MP.

"Do it," I said. "I'll take responsibility."

The gate went up in a flash.

The Union Jack atop the clock tower flapped in the brisk wind, as it had the day Holland went over. Some of the same people were there. Robinson and Hughes stood craning their necks, shouting at Snow to give himself up. An MP and a couple of guards stood in front of them, rifles aimed at the tower.

A shot cracked, echoing harshly against the stonework. The bullet zinged against the gravel walkway, sending stone shards into a dance.

"No weapons!" Snow shouted. "Rifles on the ground!"

He pushed Blackford forward, both leaning crazily over the parapet. He put his revolver to Blackford's head.

"Lay them down," I said. The three soldiers didn't need any prompting. "Who's in the building?" I whispered to Robinson.

"One MP and some of the patients," he said. "What's going on?"

"No time to explain," I said, motioning for Big Mike to go inside. I cupped my hands and hollered to Snow, "Major! I'd like to come up and talk. I know all about it."

"You don't know anything!" Snow yelled, pointing his pistol at me. I didn't flinch. Even at this distance, I could see his hand shaking. The Webley was a decent revolver, but any farther than fifty yards out, it was hard to hit the target. Hardly a comfort.

"I know about your cousin George," I shouted. "I know why you did it. Don't you want people to understand?"

"Get people out here, I'll tell them all," Snow said. "Hurry, or old Blackie goes over." With that, he gave Blackford a sharp rap on the side of his face with his pistol. A rivulet of red ran down the colonel's face.

"He's going to kill him anyway," I said to the small group of onlookers. "But let him talk, it'll buy us time."

"Sorry, Boyle, but I won't let my patients out here. Seeing this could set them back. This place is supposed to be a refuge, not some macabre theater," Robinson said.

"Some of us are strong enough, Doctor," Iris said, stepping out from the front door, Faith at her side. "Why don't you get all the guards, staff, and orderlies out here? A few of the south wing patients too. It may be enough of a crowd for a speech."

"All right," Robinson said. He told Snow he needed time to gather people. He got five minutes.

"We have five minutes to pick that lock," I told Faith.

"Simple," she said. "Especially if I don't have to worry about being discovered." We went inside and through the foyer, heading for the clock-tower door. Clarissa was leaving her office and joined us.

"The keys are gone," she said to Big Mike, who must have sent her to look. "The major has a set, but he must have taken the spare as well."

"Give me a minute," Faith said, withdrawing a thin strip of metal from within the folds of her dress. She worked the lock, cursed like a sailor, and worked it some more. Then, a click. She grabbed the latch and it opened.

"Keep Snow talking out there," I said, drawing my .38. "Big Mike, if he even looks like he's going to shoot into the crowd, you let loose. Make him keep his head down, okay?"

"Got it. Hey, maybe I should go up. You're better at talking than I am. You could keep him occupied."

"You're too big a target, pal. Let's get this over with."

Big Mike left to join the crowd outside. Faith shut the door carefully behind me, minimizing the sound from the creaking hinges. As soon as it was closed, I felt cut off from the world. Alone, with a homicidal maniac. Two, if you counted Blackford and his death sentences.

I had maybe one full minute left on Snow's deadline. I slipped off my shoes and took the stairs silently, listening for him to start ranting. I was halfway up when I heard my name.

"Boyle! Where the devil are you? Show yourself!"

He was looking for me in the crowd. It would be hard for him to keep an eye on the door behind him as he searched for me down below. He called out again, and I raced up the remaining stairs. I got to the top, took a deep breath, and opened the door.

Snow had Blackford by the collar, shoving his face onto the rough stonework as he gazed down.

"Boyle, damn you! Come out!" Shouts and cries came up from below as he cursed.

I moved forward. He turned.

I ducked as he squeezed off a shot, then darted right, using the wooden framework of the flagpole as cover. Another shot, and a round thunked into a beam by my head. Snow had spun Blackford around, putting him between us as a shield. I rushed him, grabbing his gun hand and forcing it up as he fired again. The three of us were in a bizarre embrace as Snow reached out and grabbed me by the wrist, immobilizing my weapon while keeping a bleeding and stunned Blackford between us.

We careened against the wooden beams, then back to the crenellated stonework, Snow and I trying to bash the other's hand or head hard enough to gain an advantage. Snow was grunting, Blackford moaning, and I yelled in indecipherable rage.

Snow twisted us halfway around, sending Blackford's head against the hard stone with a crack. Blackford dropped, dead weight falling against Snow who stumbled backward, losing his grip on my wrist, flailing with his one free arm as he tried to keep his balance.

Before I could bring my pistol to bear—whether to shoot or threaten, I couldn't say—he stumbled, the weight of his upper body tipping over the edge of the parapet. I still had him by his gun hand, but he wrenched it away, freeing himself as the pistol went flying and he vainly reached after it. His body wavered with the growing force of gravity, and I wondered if this is what it had been like with Holland. A struggle and an unintended outcome.

It would have been easy, just another second, just a breath of wind to send him down to the hard ground.

Gasping for breath, I grabbed his legs and pulled him toward me. I shoved Snow against the wall and twisted one arm behind his back. Snow's face was contorted with agony, but it wasn't from pain in his arm. He was crushed at still being alive.

CHAPTER THIRTY-NINE

FEET POUNDED ON the stairs. Big Mike came through first, automatic at the ready. Then Doc Robinson and a couple of nurses. Big Mike patted Snow down as Robinson checked Blackford.

"He took a hit on the head," I managed. "Passed out." Like I wanted to right about now.

"You should have let him go over," Faith said, spitting out the words. "But I am glad you're unhurt."

"Thank you," I said. "Blackford owes you his life."

"I wonder what it's worth," she said, and then turning away, laughing.

"Not much, the bastard," Snow said, as Big Mike kept him in a firm grasp.

"You're welcome," I said, looking over the edge at the drop I'd saved Snow from, not that he'd been in the mood to thank me. "Let's get downstairs. I think I've developed a fear of heights."

Big Mike had a firm grip on Snow, as Robinson led us into his office. Hughes had shown up in the tower to take Blackford away and assess his concussion. I'd asked Faith and Iris to tell Kaz what had happened. Big Mike pushed Snow into a chair, then stood guard behind him.

Robinson and I were in our usual seats. That felt strange.

"You know about Operation Periwig?" Snow asked. "The Red Horse?"

"All of it. I know Holland and George were friends, possibly went into SOE together. Holland volunteered for the German Section but they turned him down," I said.

"Too British," Snow said. "But he sent George in his place."

"Holland didn't know," I said.

"I didn't mean to kill him," Snow said. "I found him up in the tower the day after I learned about Periwig."

"From the recordings," Robinson said. "So much for medical ethics."

"Ethics? Don't make me laugh. Anyway, I lost my temper, told him what I'd heard. He didn't believe me. Next thing I knew, we'd exchanged blows and he went over."

"He wasn't mute?" I asked.

"He was coming out of it. I can't say we had a coherent conversation, but he got his point across. He said he'd report me for the recordings," Snow said. Which meant the murder had been deliberate. On some level, at least.

"How did you get the postcard?" I asked.

"George gave it to me. He shouldn't have, but I saw him on leave before his mission. He was so proud. He said he'd palmed it and wanted me to have it as a souvenir. Since I'd inspired him, he said." Snow's face broke. Tears bled from his eyes.

"But why keep the Weisskopf family connection secret?" I asked.

"I wanted to be a soldier. A career professional. How far do you think I would have gotten in the twenties if people knew I was half German? My mother came over before the war. She was the oldest child of a large family. George's mother was the youngest, and she came later. Being known as a half Hun and a half Jew to boot would've ruined my chances. The British Army is quite hidebound. Plenty of the pure-blood English would have given me bad marks for one or both. Anti-German sentiment was running high after the last war, whereas anti-Semitism is always lurking behind the stiff upper lip."

"That's why you listed no next of kin?" I said.

"Indeed. By the time this war rolled around, I knew I wanted to move up in the intelligence services. If SOE found out I had family in Germany, I would have been suspect."

"Why?" Robinson said, his fingers steepled as if he were in session.

"I could be turned if caught, my family's survival used against me, forcing me to act as a double agent. Not that I expect many Jews in Germany are left alive. But if any relatives are, I could have been offered their lives."

"In exchange for your services," Robinson said, nodding his understanding.

I began to understand something too. A notion was beginning to form, indistinct and likely dangerous, growing out of Snow's comment about an offer. But I had one more question for him before I moved on.

"Charles Cosgrove was your friend. Why did you kill him?"

"He ceased being a friend as soon as I learned he'd betrayed George. I saw it in Holland's file. Charles conveyed him to Blackford, who sent him on to his death," Snow said, his voice turning to a snarl. "When I showed him the postcard—"

"That's enough," I said. "I don't want to hear any more of your excuses. Unless you have a good one for trying to frame Dr. Robinson."

"What?" Robinson said. The steeple came apart.

"A diversion, that's all it was," Snow said. "An attempt to sow confusion."

"He planted a red horse drawing in your quarters. I'll explain later. Right now I could use a favor, and it's got to be quick," I said. I told him what I needed. After the revelation of the secret recordings and Snow trying to cast suspicion on him, it wasn't a hard sell.

I left Robinson and Big Mike to take care of Snow and headed over to the south wing to see Kaz. When I got there, I found Kaz dressed and sitting in a chair by his bed. Clarissa, Faith, and Iris were clustered around him. His color looked good, as did his languid smile. Kaz always did attract the ladies.

"Billy," he said, standing and waving off three offers of assistance. "Thank God you are unhurt."

Then he hugged me. A strong hug. I held him gently, afraid something might break, but I hugged him back. "Thank God you're alive,"

I whispered. I heard him gasp and took him by the shoulders, looking for what was wrong.

"It is these damned stitches," Kaz said. "I will have my physician in Harley Street take them out after we go home." Home. That had a nice sound.

"You're being released?" I said.

"I am leaving," Kaz announced. "With the head of security uncovered as a murderer, there is some confusion as to authority. So, I shall take advantage of the situation and be done with this place. If they want me, they know where to find me. Right, Clarissa?"

"Why, I don't even know who 'they' are at the moment," she said. "Dr. Hughes should be in charge, but he told me to refer any questions to Dr. Robinson."

"Hughes pronounced me fit. I see no reason to remain, other than for the lovely company. But I must find some decent clothes and have a good meal," Kaz said, as he stretched out his arms, showing off the baggy British Army tunic and the worn wool shirt. "Ladies, I shall miss you. Please call on us if you find your way to London. Billy, are you ready?"

I was more than ready. But first, I asked Clarissa for help in getting an outside line and making a telephone call. I walked Kaz to the car, marveling at his pace and his stamina. I got him settled in and went to meet Clarissa in her office.

By the time I hung up the telephone, I believed my plan might work.

Or, I'd end up in Leavenworth.

CHAPTER FORTY

THEY RAISED THE gate without question. No pass or identity papers required. A friendly wave from Private Fulton was all it took for the MP to let us pass. Strange what happens when order is upended, and people start thinking for themselves. It would be nice while it lasted, but soon enough SOE would send in a hard man to take over. Saint Albans would never be the same.

I didn't tell Kaz or Big Mike what I was up to. There was no reason to get them involved in case things went south, so I acted as if everything had been said and done. On the way to London, I filled Kaz in on what we'd discovered about Periwig and Snow's relation to George Markstein. I sat in the back with him, Big Mike at the wheel.

"It sounds as if he may have blamed himself, if only unconsciously," Kaz said. "George was following in his footsteps, after all. If Snow couldn't admit to his own complicity, he may have found it easier to blame others and take out his rage on them."

"Or maybe he's nuts," Big Mike said.

"Or that," Kaz said, with an easy laugh I hadn't heard in a while. "What will happen to Snow now? Where is he, anyway?"

"He's secure," I said, and changed the subject.

At the Dorchester, the sandbag wall was finished. Kaz stepped out of the staff car, eyed the doorman, and said, "Good afternoon, Richard. Redecorating?"

"Welcome back, Baron," Richard said, holding the door open for Kaz. "It's on account of those flying gas mains. Not to worry, sir."

I explained the remark to Kaz as we entered the lobby. It hadn't taken Londoners long to see through the cover story. As soon as Walter spotted Kaz, he snapped his fingers at an unseen staffer and rushed forward. Kaz was home. By the time we got to the lift, Kaz had an entourage of well-wishers and was busy assuring them that he was just fine.

Upstairs, we found flowers on the table and a bottle of champagne on ice. Now I knew what that snap had been for.

"I have to see Harding," I told Kaz and Big Mike. "You guys crack that champagne, and I'll join you in a while."

"You want me to come along?" Big Mike said.

"No, you keep an eye on Kaz. Make sure he doesn't have too much booze his first night back," I said, giving Big Mike a wink to let him know I was kidding about the booze but not about watching over Kaz.

"I shall work on an order for room service, a dinner for the ages," Kaz said, flopping down on the couch as Big Mike popped the cork. "When will you return?"

"Coupla hours, maybe a little more."

Or never. It could go either way.

COLONEL HARDING GREETED me with a curt nod when I entered the conference room at Norfolk House. This was one of the grander rooms, with walnut paneling, heavy curtains over tall windows, a large map of Europe along one wall, and a highly polished ten-foot table at the end. It looked like the kind of room where secrets from past wars still hung heavy in the air.

Or maybe the people assembled here had carried in the whiff of secrecy with them. Vera Atkins, her glare alternating between fury and curiosity. Douglas Tiltman of the Foreign Office, affecting a look of boredom as he scribbled on a notepad. Duncan Sandys, chair of the government committee charged with defending against the German missile threat, with his nose buried in a file. It didn't hurt that he was married to Churchill's daughter. A little pull in the right quarters could go a long way. Or save my bacon if things went south.

Lastly, Major-General Sir Colin Gubbins, commanding officer of the Special Operations Executive. I hadn't met Gubbins before. He sat erect and motionless; his neatly clipped mustache was turned up slightly at the ends. A face as long as it was sharp turned in my direction.

"Captain Boyle, tell us what the hell we are doing here," Gubbins said in a rough Highland accent. "And be quick about it, man."

"If you'll excuse me for a few minutes, the captain will brief you," Harding said, leaving the table. I'd asked for fifteen minutes alone with this group. For his own good.

"Interesting," Sandys said, closing the file in front of him as he watched Harding leave, shutting the door firmly. "What do you have for us?"

"This," I said, taking the Red Horse postcard from my pocket and sliding it across the table to Gubbins. "Do you know what this is, General?"

"You should not be in possession of that," Gubbins said, looking me in the eye and avoiding a second glance at the card.

"But I am. Makes you wonder how it came to me, and how many other people know about it. Outside of your German Section, I mean. And outside of those who received it in Germany."

"Well-done forgery on the stamp, old boy," Tiltman said, reaching for the card and holding it up. "You've captured Adolf's essence."

"The purpose of this meeting again?" Gubbins said, his voice like iron.

"I have something for all of you," I said. "First, for Vera, a guarantee that one of your F Section agents will be released from Ravensbrück. Mr. Sandys, to you I offer the debriefing of two slave laborers from that same camp who have worked at the nearby Siemens factory."

"Where they make parts for the V2," Sandys said. "Keep talking, Captain."

"Mr. Tiltman, you will do good works with the Swedish Red Cross, but also for your nation, if you ensure these two names are on your list of one hundred prisoners to be released. *Both* names," I said, as I took a slip of paper and gave it to him.

"Malou Lyon and Angelika Kazimierz," he read. "I am familiar with the first, but not the second. And neither sounds Scandinavian, Captain Boyle. As I told you, this project is run under their auspices. One might work, but not two. Never."

"What project, damn it!" Gubbins said, the first hint of confusion shadowing his face.

"A trial run, so to speak," Tiltman said. "Himmler has authorized the release of one hundred concentration camp inmates. More to follow if Hitler doesn't find out and have him shot. Mostly Swedes and other Scandinavian prisoners."

"Those names are important, Mr. Tiltman," I said, as I watched Vera. I could tell by her expression that she was on board. Getting one of her girls back was a top priority. "Both have access to vital information. I won't settle for 'one might work.' I want you to make sure both are released."

"Yes, I understand what is at stake, particularly with the latest rocket attacks. Am I to understand my reward shall be in heaven, so to speak? Nothing more practical?" Tiltman said.

"How about a chance to avoid some bad publicity on the international stage?" I said, my eye on Gubbins.

"Always of interest to the Foreign Office, if a bit vague," Tiltman said. "But what about General Gubbins? What have you for him?"

"Basil Snow," I said.

"Who?" Gubbins said. I didn't think he was stalling. Snow wasn't high up in the SOE command, and Gubbins couldn't be expected to know every operative.

"Security officer at Saint Albans, General," Vera said. "Captain Boyle was at our office this morning, warning us that Major Snow was on his way to kill Colonel Blackford."

"Not an impressive security man," Gubbins said. "Dead bodies in piles from what I hear. But hard to believe one of our own is the killer."

"He's left three dead in his wake," I said. "All because of that postcard."

"Colonel Blackford left to meet Major Snow this morning. Both are now missing," Vera said. Gubbins picked up the postcard, turning it over in his hand.

"Exactly how did you come by this postcard, Boyle?" Gubbins said, studying it carefully for the first time.

"From Snow. It was given to him by a Bonzo. A relative," I said.

"Ah," Gubbins said, beginning to understand. "Is that who revealed the nature of Operation Periwig?"

"No. Snow learned that on his own. He'd planted bugs throughout Saint Albans and overheard a conversation, enough to piece together what was in store for your German anti-Nazi volunteers."

"This is a dangerous game, Captain Boyle, if I understand you correctly," Gubbins said, drumming his fingers on the table.

"We live in dangerous times, sir. You will have Snow in hand by the end of the day, and Blackford as well, in one piece. All I want is an assurance from everyone in this room that those two names will be on the prisoner release list."

"And if I say no?" Tiltman asked.

"Snow gets his time in the sun. He wants to speak to the newspapers. He wants the world to know about Operation Periwig," I said. "The whole truth."

"Careful," Gubbins said, his eyes narrowing as he gave me a grim look.

"It's you who should have been careful, General. Those were your men, brave men, whom you sent to a terrible death," I said. "I don't much care for Basil Snow, but at least he thought he was righting a wrong. Maybe the truth *should* come out. It's up to you."

"I take it this Periwig business is something SOE would prefer never to see the light of day?" Sandys said, looking to Tiltman who betrayed nothing.

"Yes," Gubbins said, his voice a low growl. "There would be repercussions if it got out."

"The Foreign Office is aware of this operation," Tiltman said. Gubbins looked at him in shocked surprise. "Even diplomats have their sources, General. I can tell you we have grave concerns, especially about how this would be perceived postwar. One day in the future, we shall need decent Germans on our side. Pity if you've sent the best of them to their deaths."

Gubbins said nothing.

"You can deliver Snow? That's a promise?" Sandys asked.

"Absolutely," I said. "Alive." Back at Saint Albans, I'd realized that nobody knew where we'd found Blackford and Snow. SOE would get around to searching there sooner or later, but for now, no one had any idea where Snow was. I'd set up a twenty-four-hour lock on communications with Clarissa and Robinson, who seemed to be the only two staff who'd kept their heads about them. Snow was in one of his own padded cells, out of sight and silenced.

Gubbins looked at the others.

"I could have you arrested," he said, turning his hardest stare on me.

"Go ahead. If I don't make a telephone call within the hour, Snow will be singing like a bird," I said. "After that, I don't care what happens to me. I'm sick of all these lies and betrayals. Either put those names on the list or deal with the consequences. I'm ready to do the same."

"I want my agent back," Vera said.

"I want a chance to talk to anyone who's been in the Siemens facility. I'd kill for it," Sandys said.

"I can handle the Swedes," Tiltman said, and puffed out his cheeks in a sigh. "Two names can be done."

"How do I know I can trust you?" Gubbins said to me, as he pocketed the postcard.

"You can," Vera said. "He's almost one of us."

"A conniving, dirty fighter, eh? Well then. If you can't trust a right bastard, who can you trust?" Gubbins said.

"I fully agree, General," I said. He shook my hand in a crushing grip before he stalked out.

"I have a favor to ask," I said to Tiltman. "Maybe Sandys can help." The three of us put our heads together, and the discussion ended with Duncan Sandys telling me to wait by the telephone.

"Do I want to know what this Periwig business was all about?" Vera asked as we filed out.

"What Periwig business?"

"Ah, you are, indeed, one of us, Captain Boyle. God help you."

CHAPTER FORTY-ONE

THE BOAC FLIGHT from northern Scotland to Stockholm, Sweden, took several hours, most of it spent watching for German fighters. It was a neutral Swedish airplane, manned by members of the Royal Norwegian Air Force. The Germans didn't know that, I hoped, but that didn't mean some trigger-happy Fritz wouldn't want to bag a lumbering, unarmed transport.

From Stockholm it was a small plane, then an automobile provided by the British embassy to the coastal port of Trelleborg, not far across the water from occupied Denmark.

I stepped out of the Volvo four-door and told the driver to keep the heat on. It was a windy day with cold sheets of rain and seawater blowing over the harbor wall. I buttoned my trench coat and pulled my trilby tight on my head. I was in civilian clothes, traveling on a phony passport, but there wasn't much to worry about. Sweden knew which way the war was going, and no one was going to raise a fuss about who was meeting the noon ferry from Lübeck.

I watched the squat two-stack ship approach the harbor; it wallowed in the whitecaps, taking on a calmer course as it passed the breakwater. I walked onto the jetty, saltwater pelting my face, searching the crowd along the starboard side, all of them eager to debark onto neutral soil.

The gangplank went down, and passengers flooded off the vessel, most of them women dressed in rags, faint remnants of what once might have been summer dresses or nightgowns. Some wore pieces of cloth wrapped around their feet for shoes. They were drenched, pale, and painfully thin. Many smiled, a delirious joy palpable as they looked at each other, embracing and exulting in this final step to freedom.

Red Cross workers came forward, speaking in Swedish and Norwegian, directing them to a warehouse where hot soup and clean clothes awaited. The women broke around me as if I were a rock in a fast-flowing stream. I searched the faces coming toward me, fear in my belly as I tried not to think the worst.

Where was Diana?

There were about a dozen women left, walking slowly, some of them limping.

I saw her. She looked like a ghost, dressed in the white evening dress she'd been wearing when the Gestapo arrested her. It was gray and filthy now, hanging off her gaunt body like a burial shroud. Her honey-colored hair was chopped short, stiff and dirty even in the driving rain.

She had her arm around a girl with blond hair sticking out from a rag tied around her head. Every step looked torturous, but, with Diana's help, she shuffled forward, away from the ferry, away from whatever horror had been inflicted on her.

Diana stopped in front of me, her head cocked to the side, and her eyes squinting as if trying to get a better focus, not believing what she saw.

"Billy. Billy. Help us," she gasped.

Diana fell into my arms, the girl tottering and almost collapsing. I got one arm around her, and, between us, Diana and I got her moving forward.

"Billy, is it really you?"

I nodded. I could not speak. Tears mingled with rain and sea spray, stinging and salty. I was afraid to say a word, afraid to break the spell, terrified this was a dream that would vanish, sending me back to walk the endless paths of Saint Albans.

"This . . . this is Angelika," Diana said. "How did this happen? How did we come here?"

"Later," I said. "Come on. We're almost there, Angelika."

She looked at me, her face contorted in pain. "You are Billy. My brother's friend?"

"I am, Angelika. I am."

She stumbled, and I lifted her up, Diana grasping her hand. We came to the Volvo and the driver opened the rear door. Warm air wafted out and Angelika shrieked.

With joy. Kaz reached out and we eased her inside. They embraced, rocking back and forth, the last of their family, wounded, hurting, but desperately, against awful odds, alive. Together.

I helped Diana inside the warehouse, knowing Kaz needed this time alone with Angelika, as I did with Diana. Red Cross workers came with a blanket and towels, draping Diana as we sat together, embracing. Our hands intertwined in every possible manner, as if searching for a way to remain together, always and forever.

"I knew I'd see you again," she said. "But I never thought it would be this soon."

"We got lucky," I said. "What happened to Angelika?"

"Medical experiments," she said. "The so-called doctors took some of the Polish girls and cut them. Deliberately infecting them, breaking bones, cutting nerves, and other horrible things. Then assessing different treatments." She shivered, even with the warm blanket around her. "They took her only about ten days ago. If she gets medical treatment immediately, she has a chance."

"She's safe," I said. "You're safe. There's so much to tell you."

A nurse brought Diana a cup of broth. She sipped it hungrily, burying her face in the steam that rose from it.

"I was there less than a month, Billy," she said, her eyes fixing me through the steam. "I don't know how those women have survived for so long. Poles, French, Danes, women from all over Europe. It was inhuman. Unspeakable."

"They never realized who you were?"

"I am Malou," Diana said, setting down the cup. "She saved my life.

I think a part of me will always be Malou," she said, one hand smoothing out the once-elegant gown. "They gave us the clothes we were arrested in for the voyage here. Isn't that ludicrous? German efficiency. They had every item stored away. Bloodied, worn, and dirty, it didn't matter. They saved it all. Even this."

She produced my empty red, white, and blue tube of Pervitin tablets I'd left for her to find when she was taken. It was a sign that I knew, that I'd witnessed her arrest, that she wasn't forgotten.

"I'm sorry I couldn't stop them," I said, grasping her hands as if in prayer. "I am so sorry, Diana."

"We will stop them, Billy. I have scores to settle," Diana said, raising the cup to her mouth and draining the last of the broth. "A month in that place was time enough to make enemies for life. And death." There was hurt in that voice, pain that I couldn't fathom. But there was spirit as well. I'd feared the worst, feared that Diana might come out of this as damaged as I was after Paris. It didn't seem so. I prayed that would hold. For both of us.

"First thing, let's get Angelika to a doctor. The embassy has it all arranged."

"Yes. And then, my dear Billy, take us home. All of us. To somewhere warm, green, and peaceful." Taking the cup from her hands, I embraced her, feeling the warmth of her breath on my cheek. My entire world was contained in the circle of our arms.

HISTORICAL NOTE

WHILE SAINT ALBANS Special Hospital is a fictional creation, the British Special Operations Executive did operate a facility dubbed "Number 6 Special Workshop School" at Inverlair Lodge, located in the remote Scottish Highlands. The purpose of this top-secret facility was to secure agents who had failed their training and possessed classified information, or who had been withdrawn from assignments in occupied Europe for various reasons and needed to be kept incommunicado.

The story of Inverlair Lodge fascinated an English writer named George Markstein. He was the cocreator of the classic television series *The Prisoner*, which imagined a much more elaborate retirement home for secret agents. Aficionados of *The Prisoner* might recall that Patrick McGoohan's character is given the rank of Number Six, perhaps recalling the designation of the SOE facility. Markstein was inspired by Inverlair Lodge in this creation, and subsequently wrote a novel titled *The Cooler*, set at the Number 6 Special Workshop School during the Second World War.

My character George Markstein was named in homage to the original and creative Markstein.

Operation Periwig was a program of the Special Operations Executive to simulate the existence of a large-scale anti-Nazi resistance movement within Germany. The idea was primarily to fool the Nazi security apparatus into hunting non-existent resistance groups, and, secondarily, to create the illusion of such groups in the hopes that some Germans would be moved to resist Nazi rule and shorten the war.

German prisoners of war were recruited for Operation Periwig but never informed that the resistance organizations, such as the Red Horse, were pure flights of imagination. These volunteers were parachuted into Germany in the hopes that they would either surrender or be captured and reveal the supposed existence of widespread resistance activities.

Fifty-three men were sent into Germany in 1944 and 1945. Some survived and a few even managed to complete their sabotage missions and evade capture until the end of the war. Some disappeared, while an unknown number were captured and executed.

The story of the double agent Schiller and the faulty parachute was reported by SOE Signals Officer and code-breaking genius Leo Marks in his fascinating autobiography *Between Silk and Cyanide*. Marks did brief Schiller before his last jump.

Dr. Dwight Harken was a groundbreaking pioneer in heart surgery. He was forced to leave the Mediterranean Theater of Operations after the chief medical officer there forbid all surgical procedures to remove foreign objects in the area of the heart. Harken was sent to the 160th General Hospital in Great Britain, where he was allowed to operate on the heart, removing shrapnel in over one hundred and forty cases without losing a patient. He did have to overcome the widely held belief that a patient could not survive manipulation of the heart muscle.

This belief was so strong that Dr. Henry Souttar, who in 1925 did the first successful surgery to repair mitral stenosis, faced the censure of his colleagues and was not allowed to repeat his success.

Following his success with heart surgery during the war, Dwight Harken performed another groundbreaking procedure when he operated on a stenotic mitral valve in 1947. I have used creative license to allow the good doctor to perform this operation on Baron Kazimierz three years prior to his first *recorded* operation, and I hope readers will not mind this authorial sleight of hand.

There was a large-scale prisoner release program undertaken by the

Swedish Red Cross and the Danish government which resulted in the freeing of over fifteen thousand inmates from the Nazi concentration camps. About half were Scandinavian. The initiative was supported by SS head Heinrich Himmler, who hoped the Swedish Red Cross would help in his bid for a separate peace treaty with the Western powers.

Most of the releases occurred in 1945, shortly before the end of the war. But in late 1944 there was a preliminary release of 103 inmates, which gave me the idea for the trial run envisioned in these pages.

The vast majority of released prisoners were transported on the white buses of the Red Cross. The vehicles were painted white with prominent red crosses to avoid misidentification with military vehicles. Over three hundred Swedish army troops and medical staff operated thirty-six buses and as many other vehicles in this humanitarian rescue, which was done in complete secrecy.

ACKNOWLEDGMENTS

I AM INDEBTED to first readers Liza Mandel and Michael Gordon, for their scrutiny of this manuscript. It is a gift to have careful readers who can look at the story with fresh eyes as it nears completion; they see the forest and the trees.

My wife, Deborah Mandel, works on editing and proofreading these stories with an amazing diligence, helping to keep the story true through every step of the writing process. She also puts up with the occasional neurotic writer behavior with grace and patience.

The staff of Soho Press is a wonderful bunch. They make this work enjoyable, and I look forward every year to a new adventure with all of them.

Finally, I gratefully acknowledge the readers who have been with Billy Boyle from the beginning, and those who have joined the brigade of fans along the way. Hearing from them is a great joy, and without such devoted readers this fifteenth novel would not have been possible.

Thank you.